SILENT CATS:
DEADLY DANCE

JD WALLACE

Silent Cats: Deadly Dance

A SHORT ON TIME BOOK

Fast-paced and fun novels for readers on the go!

For more information, visit the website:
shortontimebooks.com

To Cheryl - For the support and motivation all the way to the finish line.

CHAPTER 1

Netanya, Israel
August 2005

"She is here with the two young ones. I have eyes on them," the red *keffiyeh-clad man whispered, with a strong Sunni Arabic dialect into his mobile phone. Hidden behind his newspaper, he had been watching them from his seat in the corner of a white façade seaside café since their arrival. The café bustled with 'lunchers' on a late Wednesday afternoon and the heavy smell of coffee mixed with the aroma from an adjacent hedge of Madonna lilies filled the air.*

"Do you have the number to call?" the female voice on the other end inquired.

"Yes. Did Brother Nazim place it correctly this time?" He casually took a sip of his Turkish coffee.

"I watched him. Finally, we will avenge the deaths of our brothers. Twenty years we chased this Jew bitch. Praise Allah!"

"Allahu Akbar!" [God is great!] he replied quietly, but jubilantly, disconnecting the call.

The man continued to watch and listen to his prey.

* * *

The mother waved the café owner over. "Moti, we're ready to leave."

Alyn felt at ease in Moti Lichtenfeld's café. Moti, a squat man sporting a heavy beard approached with a limp, a permanent reminder of his Mossad days. The longtime family friend and son of the founder of *Krav Maga* placed the tab on the table.

"Thank you for coming, Alyn. Please tell your sister to come by next time she's in town. We miss her and ... dare I say ... her energy," he said in soft Hebrew, giving her a warm smile.

"I will." She pulled three fifty Skekel notes from her purse and placed them on the table to cover her tab.

Moti looked at Alyn's daughters, and said, "Good-bye girls. Next time I shall tell you about the bull your mother and I wrestled when we were kids." He winked at Alyn.

Alyn grinned at her friend and stood up. "Let's go, ladies."

Jade, the youngest, looked up with intense interest. Her inquisitive eyes sparkled at Moti, "Really? A bull?!"

Moti nodded and chuckled.

Electra watched her sister's antics with an *I-don't-believe-this* look while Jade continued bouncing around her mother. "Aww Mama, come on ... You wrestled a bull? Just a couple more minutes, pleeease."

Alyn shook her head, pulling her long, straight black hair up into a high ponytail. "Later Jade, now move."

"Yes Ma'am," Jade replied, extending her lower lip.

Alyn glanced around the café, then up and down the street. She smiled at the patrons who thought they recognized her as a famous local model. Electra, her oldest, a near replica of her statuesque mother, streaked up the sidewalk followed by the younger brown-haired, green-eyed Jade. It was a beautiful sunny day in the city as Alyn put on her Dolce & Gabbana sunglasses and continued to scan the area.

The lone Palestinian's dark eyes followed the mother and her daughters.

Jade jumped in the air and shouted, "SHOTGUN!"

"No way, you can't call shotgun, Dad isn't here," Electra said, looking to her mother for support. "We only do that with Dad."

"Jade. Let Electra ride shotgun this time. After all, we're heading to *your* favorite mall." Alyn raised her eyebrows at her fearless daughter.

"Yes Ma'am, but I get it on the way home."

The threesome approached the old, meticulously-cared-for red convertible Fiat Pininfarina Spider. It was the first car Alyn bought after being assigned to her Embassy post in Naples, Italy, and the car that transported her, and her then soon-to-be husband, all over the Mediterranean.

"Electra, take that bag and throw it in the backseat, please." Alyn motioned toward the car then stopped dead in her tracks. Something was off.

The Palestinian watched over the edge of his newspaper, a gleam of anticipation on his gaunt face, he was unconsciously holding his breath.

The girls plowed into the car.

"Hurry up Mom," Jade shouted, jumping over the trunk into the backseat.

"Stop touching my hair, Jade!" Electra yelled.

Alyn's highly-trained mind was racing through all the possible security options, when Electra called out, "Mom! Come on!"

Ultimately, she convinced herself everything was fine, gave the girls a loving smile, and entered the driver's side.

"Thanks Mom. I love you," Electra said, adjusting in her seat and shutting the door.

Alyn snapped in her seatbelt and turned the key.

There was a "click."

Her mind became a torrent of thoughts, emotions, dreams, and experiences. They spanned nearly twenty flawless years of being a wanted intelligence officer. Her brain raced through the memories: From her conscript day, to her first Mossad assignment, to the last Kidon assignment a month ago, to her wedding, to her first child, to her second child and finally to the facial expression of her husband when they met for the first time. It all went black. This was the moment it ended and two precious daughters with it. The man of her dreams being unheroically left behind.

Sorry girls. Sorry Marcus.

She dropped her head to her chest and closed her eyes without enough time to even shed one tear.

Then ... nothing. She lifted her head and turned to see Jade playing with her mobile phone in the backseat, repeating the same sound again, "click."

Alyn exhaled a deep breath and shook her head. *Whew. I am getting too old for this shit.*

Hearing the engine start, the Palestinian flipped open his phone, and pressed the auto-dialer number one button. He smiled and said, "Assalam O Alekum!" [Good-bye!]

The explosion blew the red Fiat into the air and rocked buildings across the whole block.

CHAPTER 2

Three bodies flew from the red fiat like cannon fodder. The facade of the restaurant next to the car crashed down on its patrons and two pedestrians. People stumbled out, coughing and crying as the smell of phosphorus, motor oil and almonds burned their noses.

Moti knew exactly what happened without seeing or hearing anything more. This was not an uncommon event in this part of the world. Pain shot down his spine as he rushed to the sidewalk. His patrons were in shock and stood motionless while others ran screaming down the street away from the explosion. Smoke and dust from the debris billowed and swirled. He looked up the street and gasped at what was left of the flaming red convertible and then turned his attention to the carnage directly in front of his café. There he saw Alyn, his childhood friend. Her crushed, burned and bloody body was sprawled across the hood of a white sedan. He reached her in seconds and looked into her soft understanding eyes. There was a flicker of awareness. She tried to reach out for him just as the light in her eyes and the life in her body disappeared. She was gone.

The Palestinian watched Moti hobble up the street one leg dragging behind the other. He still needed confirmation that all three females were dead and followed the gimping café owner.

"Oh, Electra." Moti spotted her black hair in the rubble of a restaurant three buildings up the street from his café. Her arms and torso were burned to the bone with blood cascading from the back of her head. He gently closed her eyes, something he had done too many times before. "We will meet again, young one," Moti said, then spoke a few words of the Jewish Mourner's Prayer, *El Malei Rachamim*. His attention next went to finding the youngest daughter.

Moti found Jade's crumpled bleeding body lying on the opposite side of the street from the flaming Fiat with a backdrop of the deep blue Mediterranean. He fell to his knees at her side. Her breathing was raspy but her green eyes still sparkled when she met his gaze.

"The bull?" she asked, with no fear or concern for her inevitable future.

Moti held her small hand. He could do nothing for her. Her clothes were burned onto the bones of her rib cage, blood from the gashes on the side of her head and neck oozed onto the street. He gently slid her head onto his lap and caressed her blood-soaked hair. She coughed up blood. He knew the ambulance would never arrive in time.

With tears streaming down his face he said, "Your Mom and I grew up next to this big farm. And there was this bull ..."

The young girl's body shuddered one last time and her eyes went vacant. Without struggle, without anger and without apprehension, her energy dissipated into the atmosphere. Moti let go a deep sigh knowing she had taken her place alongside the many millions of young girls who perish needlessly at the hands of men.

"Sweet child, you and your sister died without being given the opportunity to make this world a better place. I am so sorry ..." He bowed his head and closed his eyes in prayer, "... and will merge her soul with eternal life. Amen." Moti gently laid Jade down, closed her eyelids, and looked up. With Jade's blood dripping from his outstretched hands he cried to the heavens, "Why must *men* leave this tragic legacy of harming the innocent?"

The Palestinian watched the café owner with the dead child. He sneered, pleased with himself, then turned away and flipped open his phone. "It is done. Another Mossad-Kidon eugenics lineage has been eliminated. See you soon, my love." He snapped his phone closed, took a deep proud breath before walking to his car. In the next instant, he felt three odd stinging sensations in the middle of his back. His breathing became difficult, his heart pumped erratically and the energy in his legs vaporized. He grabbed his chest and thought his insides were on fire. He clumsily turned, fell to his knees, and looked up at the heavy set café owner standing over him.

Moti stood rigid with his Berretta 70 still trained on the man. "Didn't think I saw you following me, did you, you sick twisted Muslim bastard? I hope Marcus blows *your* entire pathetic family ..." Moti put one final bullet in the middle of the man's forehead and watched the Palestinian fall over and his eyes go blank, "... to hell."

The outgoing message she heard on his voicemail was distinctly her son-in-law. It was difficult to speak the words, "Daylily. Marcus. Daylily," Tirzah said. She hung up the phone and wept inconsolably.

CHAPTER 3

Flagstaff, Arizona, USA
August 2005

By eight o'clock in the morning, Marcus had pulled another ten hours of straight overnight driving. This last stretch included the mountainous Highway 70 and 191 from Denver to Flagstaff.

I told her we should have sold all this stuff and I wouldn't have to drive thirty hours from Chicago to San Diego. Oh no ... we may come back to America she says.

He felt he was making good time when he pulled his black Toyota pickup truck and twelve-foot U-Haul trailer into the Denny's parking lot. He turned off the engine, grabbed his mobile phone and got out; there was a message and played it.

Daylily—was all Marcus heard. His heart raced, his facial muscles tightened and his teeth started to grind. With his mind wandering uncontrollably; his thirst, his hunger and his fatigue all disappeared. This word, this normally beautiful word, meant pain and anguish. He could have gone his whole life without hearing it.

Protocol dictates that all intelligence officers be assigned an emergency code word by their handlers, and with a family of covert operatives, it was imperative that every family member have one. *Daylily*—a flower that represents the mother, was his wife's. If his mother-in-law had called then his wife was too injured to call.

At least she didn't give me the kids' code words, he thought as he dialed.

"Hallo." The Jewish grandmother's voice was labored.

"*Bubbe,* it's Marcus."

"*Aidim.* It is so horrible. I do not know how to say this." Her shaking was apparent through the phone.

"What happened? Is she alright?" Muscle fatigue overtook him as he leaned against the truck for support.

"They found her ... and the girls."

Marcus knew exactly who *they* were, but stopped.

And the girls? "What do you mean ... *the girls?*" Marcus realized what he was asking. It made him violently ill.

"Car bomb. In Netanya. All three. Gone. Please come now." She couldn't continue the conversation and hung up the phone. He understood.

My beautiful wife. My lovely girls. All dead.

Marcus climbed back into his truck and slammed the door. Time became a dimension that was of little consequence. He grabbed the steering wheel with both hands and thrust his head down hard then closed his eyes. He stayed there for a long moment and had to remember to breathe. When he opened his eyes, he spotted it. There on the floor mat was a large ketchup stain. His mind flashed to the time he caught Electra driving with a hotdog in her hand. The smell invaded his nostrils. His body shook as the tears flowed. His heart, his soul, his reason for living, ripped from his chest in the worst possible way. Was this cosmic payback? If so, it was more painful than any torture he ever committed or received.

Marcus thought about their last conversation when he dropped them off at O'Hare just two weeks before. They were excited and happy. What exactly were the words they spoke? Did he tell the girls he loved them? Did he hold Alyn long enough to leave her scent on him? More questions rushed through his mind – all unanswerable. Years of memories cascaded down on him, but he closed the door on the past. Now was not the time.

Marcus raised his head defiantly and glanced at the dashboard clock: 8:26 a.m. The sun was up and beating down hard already. His facial expression turned cold and callous; his sorrow deceptively surged into a volcanic lava flow of anger.

Marcus spit out the window and formulated a plan. He drove to the closest storage facility and walked into the office. A pimply nineteen-year-old boy with long brown hair looked up from his McMuffin and smiled. "How can I help you?"

Marcus pulled out a wad of cash. "How much for a ten-by-ten? I'll pay six months in advance."

The boy perked up. "Well, you're in luck today. We're running a special and ..."

"I don't care about any special. I just need a ten-by-ten – now! Just tell me how much and include the price of a lock," he said with an unwavering azure focus.

"Okay. Got it." The boy shuffled papers in Marcus' direction.

Marcus dug deep into his years of training. *Don't show what's going on inside. Just be done with it and be gone.*

Eleven minutes later, with gritted teeth, Marcus walked out of the office and drove to storage locker A46. He had just opened the garage-type door when his phone rang. It was his father-in-law's private number. He'd been expecting his call. "Sir."

"Marcus. I'm sending a plane. Where are you?"

The strain in Gideon David's voice was discernible, but his composure was rigid. He had already lost a son, and now Alyn and his two eldest granddaughters were gone as well.

"I'm in Flagstaff, Arizona."

"Hold on a minute."

Hebrew could be heard in the background.

Marcus had to wait but thirty seconds.

"That's the Pulliam Airport. I'll have a private jet on the ground in ten hours. Do you need anything else?"

"Thank you. Not right now. I've just got to ..."

"I know. We'll get you home."

Marcus stared at the phone before tucking it away in his pocket. It registered then – the reality and the absolute finality of it all. *Stay focused. Empty everything. Turn in the U-Haul. Sell the truck. Get to the airport. Go see my ...*

His body involuntarily spasmed with emotional pain – but he set it aside. Marcus opened his trailer and stared at the well-packed jumble of labeled boxes and keepsakes Alyn had insisted they put in storage for a while – until they got settled – or came back to the States.

No coming back now.

He grabbed the first box and walked it to the back of the storage room. "Kitchen" it said – in Alyn's handwriting. He forced himself to set it down and with ever-increasingly heavy legs plodded back to get another, then another. Jade's handwriting on her "Toys" box caught him by surprise. He snapped – his frustration building into anger then morphing into rage.

He stood at the back of the trailer and heaved box after box into the storage room. He heard glass break, but didn't care. A child's bright red 21-speed Peugeot bicycle was the last thing he lofted on top of the pile. He was soaked in sweat and having trouble catching his breath, but not from physical exertion.

He closed up the U-Haul but before he shut the storage room door, Marcus spotted a box with his handwriting on it: "Photos." He pulled it out, closed the door, locked it, and tossed the key onto the roof of the storage building.

From Carl's referral, Marcus found his way to Teddy's Used Cars. Marcus' pickup was worth at least twelve grand to a dealer, but he took seven. He would have taken nothing if he could have erased Electra's ketchup stain from his mind.

He climbed aboard the plane with only a medium-sized green cargo bag hanging off his shoulder and a cardboard box filled with photos under his arm. He immediately downed three shots of Gideon's *Macallan Imperiale* scotch from the handblown faceted crystal decanter. The smell of hand-stitched Corinthian leather filled the air inside the Gulfstream G550. He forced himself into a deep sleep, something he'd taught himself to do over the years, no matter how extreme the conditions or impossible the odds. One final thought carried him forward.

Wherever you are, no matter how high or thick the walls, no matter how many men or armaments are in my way ... I will find you ... and you will die.

CHAPTER 4

Sourasky Hospital, Tel Aviv, Israel
August 2005 – 22 hours later

Alone. Marcus stood at the door, loathe to enter *the room*. When he finally opened the door, his senses were sharply assaulted with the all too poignant smell of cold cleanliness. In reality it was the lack of life's fragrances. The powerful bone-shaking chill of white tile and stainless steel faced him. He was back where he had been many times before – in one of *those rooms*. This time the room seemed bigger, longer, and lonelier. He stared down the full distance of the rectangular space to the opposite end. It appeared to be a football field in length, but in truth was a barren expanse that was a lifetime walk to reality. At the far end stood a wall of doors – that opened *the boxes*.

This was cold storage.

He stared at the three silver tongue-like slider shelves pulled out in a fixed yawn – *The eternal gateway*, he thought. On each shelf was an inert figure – one adult female, one teenage female, and one near-teenage female. His heart sank and his legs nearly failed him. He paused. Marcus wasn't sure if he had the strength to traverse this corridor of death, but given the chance he would have willingly walked to his own death for them, walking now to honor them was his responsibility.

The Israeli medical examiner turned to the quiet, well-dressed man who had entered the room. *Oh God, it's him*, he thought. "Sir, please come with me to make the identification," the medical examiner said in a respectful monotone. "As you know, the torso and extremities were significantly traumatized on all three bodies, but their faces are at least recognizable. Please accept my personal ..."

The medical examiner's voice was inconsequential yet magnetically pulled Marcus farther into the room.

"... condolences."

Duty carried him the rest of the distance. He stared down at Alyn with her straight jet-black hair, dark rings around her eyes and vampiric pale skin. He looked longingly into her face wishing this was some horrific nightmare he could wake up from and all would be well. A tear dropped onto her cheek. He prayed she would suddenly sit up laughing; telling him this was all a practical joke. *That would be just like her.*

Marcus' body quivered reliving the argument they had before she left for Tel Aviv. *I told you not to go without me.* This was how it ended after sixteen years – gazing down at this corpse who had given life to their two beautiful compassionate daughters and who showed him how to be human despite his own genetics, family upbringing and military training. And who he was in awe of and had loved with every cell in his body from the first moment he laid eyes on her.

He stared at the bodies of the three most important women in his life, committing each to a last visible memory. The overwhelming urge to roar in indignation and pain was only moments away from bursting forth.

He closed his eyes.

Marcus stood rigid, a storm brewing within. His eyes filled with tears, his mind retreated to a safer place sixteen years earlier; memories and events, before Alyn became his wife ...

CHAPTER 5

Rome, Italy
December 1989

"Welcome to first class. May I get you a drink?" The bouncy blonde flight attendant directed her question to the portly man standing in the aisle wedging his Louis Vuitton bag in the overhead bin.

"Metaxa brandy," he snapped over his shoulder, "if your little airline can afford my family's *du vin*." His accent was affluent and condescending with a *Romeo y Julieta* cigar box proudly displayed in his *too-tightly-fitted* shirt breast pocket. It made him look more like a pathetic version of a cigar-advertising Ghostbusters' Stay-Puft Marshmallow man than a wealthy Greek tycoon.

"Certainly, Mister Metaxa, always available for you," she said, more like a cheerleader than a stewardess.

Bag secured, his bulky body blocked the aisle while surveying the other passengers in first class. His eyes rested too long on a pretty dark-haired girl of about nine. He deliberately ran his fingers through her hair then bent over to smell it.

"Hallo little girl, would you like to come sit on my lap?" he said.

The mother shot a disgusted look at him. "*Párte makriá, sas Lolíta!*" [Get away, you Lolita!]

Alyn heard the woman call Metaxa a *Lolita*. She recognized the common Greek slang term used to address pedophiles taken from a book she read at University, written by Vladimir Nabokov in 1955.

He turned and directed his attention to the woman reading a magazine seated in the window seat next to his aisle seat.

"Hallo. Adonis Metaxa," he said, offering his hand.

"Alyn." She neither looked up nor accepted his hand. *The guy owns a brandy distillery, likes little girls, and thinks he owns the world. Creep.*

Metaxa looked down, taking Alyn in like a chateaubriand with white wine and shallots. Despite his view of her being partially obstructed, he could see the contrast of her dark red lips, coal-black hair and silky skin wrapped within a loose halter top and form-fitting knee length skirt. Testosterone bubbled up in his ego. *Feisty, beautiful, and immaculate, I must have her.* His curiosity peaked. *How much will she cost me?*

Metaxa was not to be ignored. "Can I interest you to share with me some fine Greek brandy?" he said, as he sat down.

Still not looking at him, Alyn said, "Definitely not." *Oh harah. I'm being hit on by a fat old Greek who smells like anchovies, Kouros cologne, and Balli cigars.* Alyn didn't need to know anything more about who, or what, he was. *Let him try and come on to me. I will fix this pervert's schvantz.*

The plane lifted off and the Greek's self-aggrandizing banter continued, followed by his premeditated *accidental* touches across her breast and thigh during the plane's ascent.

Touch me one more time you misogynistic putrid festering slob. I dare you. You'll think twice before disrespecting any woman, or child, ever again.

A half hour into the flight they experienced some turbulence. The Greek donned a paternal mien and placed his rough, calloused paw on the inside of her thigh. "It's okay," he soothed.

Her muscles tightened. His hand scratched her skin inching higher underneath her skirt bringing with it a sharp memory from her childhood. It hit her with its dirty, disgusting tentacles, *"Ready,*

Alyn?" she heard her uncle's voice, *"Let's play pony."* He would say that each time she straddled him on his lap. His large scratchy fingers rubbed her while he slid her up and down. *"Giddy up, Alyn."* She was only six when it started, but she knew even then it was wrong.

Yes, Jews have pedophiles too, she thought returning to the present.

Alyn held her revulsion and contempt in check and made direct eye contact. He removed his hand and brought his fingers to his lips with a self-pleased, cruel smile. She met the gaze of the smelly egomaniac.

It's payback time.

"Hey, my *special* boy. You have me *sooo* turned on. Why don't you meet me back in the coach lavatory in about two minutes and we can take care of that growing problem you have."

She gave him a big, pearly-white smile batting her eyelashes. She ran her finger up the inside of his twenty-year-old polyester slacks. They were so tight, that when she did, she could see the small tip of his penis move inside his pants.

"Yes! Very good, my sweet thing," he said. Droplets of sweat accumulated on his upper lip. There was a smug gleam in his eye as Alyn got up.

She purposefully dropped her clutch in the aisle to bait him further, sliding her skirt up just enough and bending over letting him see her light blue satin panties.

Alyn entered the small restroom and the Greek arrived shortly thereafter.

"Welcome to our love nest, my special boy. Looking forward to joining the mile-high club?" Alyn mimicked the tone and speech pattern of the flight attendant combined with bad porn dialogue while perching herself up on the wash basin.

"I want you to rub all over me your woman juice," he gravelly whispered, pushing her skirt to her waist and leaning in to forcefully shove his tongue in her mouth.

"Whoa there my special boy, how about we let the big guy out for a walk?" She grabbed his pants and unzipped him.

Metaxa's excitement was quickly replaced with apprehension. Whether it was from performing a sex act on a plane or how unwomanly strong she was, it was too late to figure it out. He was between her legs and his penis was already in her hand.

"Aww look, he's happy to see me." The smile on her face turned to a sneer. "Listen up you grotesque purulent pus bag. I know you rich freaks assume women of all ages are toys to play with, so let me give you something to think about next time you want to play this game." She reached for the twenty-three centimeter polycarbonate blade strapped to her back.

"You fucking bitch, I'll ..."

"You'll what?" Alyn squeezed harder to immobilize him. "Let me introduce you to my *leetle fren*," she said, speaking with a feminine Tony Montana accent, a la *Scarface*. In a quick fluid motion, she cut through the man's belt and continued slicing down his pants and briefs. This exposed his fluorescent moon tan, more hair than a bear, and a cloud of smell that would make a taxidermist cry.

"WOW! Ever heard of baby powder? How can any woman, much less your wife, tolerate this stench?"

His clothing fell to the floor in relief of their many years of thankless service. Metaxa opened his mouth to shout.

"I don't think so, naughty boy. Surely you're smarter than that." Alyn's eyes stopped him cold. She expertly twirled the knife a couple revolutions to solidify his attention. "Good. I wouldn't want to relieve you of your appendage before we had a chance to chat."

Metaxa closed his mouth and nodded, his eyes the size of saucers with a face like a cartoon figure about to be hit by a truck.

"Listen, you sick fuck. For starters, you're going to stop with the constant blabber and YOU WILL stop touching me."

He nodded.

"AND you will stop ogling and touching little girls or ..."

"I don't do that."

Alyn squeezed harder.

He tried to reason with her. "Ask for it they do, you know? Likeable, I am. What can I do?" he said, attempting a half smile.

Alyn held her temper, "Let me make myself crystal clear. If I ever hear of you molesting a child, I will come after you, I will find you, and when I do, I will take this knife and shove it so far up your ass, you will taste it. Am I clear?"

Metaxa looked like he was going to pee himself, but couldn't if he wanted to. In combination of a raging hard-on and Alyn's death grip, he was blessed and cursed at the same moment.

"Yes. Please. I'm-m-m sorry." The man nodded violently like a bobblehead in a wind storm.

"Wait five minutes before you come back to your seat. Stop crying ... it isn't manly." She gave him a Cheshire cat smile.

Pedophiles or misogynists, it doesn't matter to me. He's lucky he's still breathing.

In a flash Alyn had her blade sheathed, her skirt smoothed out, grabbed her clutch and was out the door. She left the man sitting on the toilet trying not to cry. He stared down at the two belt pieces, a huge rip in his pants and his destroyed briefs. The price for his rendezvous with this beautiful woman was paid.

Metaxa slithered up the aisle with his hand clamping together the huge rip in his pants. He returned to his seat still shaking from his violent encounter with his briefs distorting his jacket and the belt peeking out from his inside pocket. Alyn had her blindfold on, a blanket up around her neck and was fast asleep.

CHAPTER 6

Camp Peary, Virginia
December 1989

"You want me to, what? My department doesn't rubber stamp status changes from your department." The bespectacled psychologist, Joan Merriwhether, jumped out of the chair ass jiggling like Jell-O as the size twenty-four rayon pants strained under the pressure. She stared down across the desk at the Section Chief. "No way, Jack. He is unqualified – not under-qualified. Sinclair is ... unqual-i-fied ... sir." Joan put her hands on her hips and stood her ground with the echo of her sharp New York accent still reverberating in the metal walled office.

The emaciated New Englander, Jack Barnett, was steely calm. "Since you're new here, Joan, let me rephrase this for you. I need Marcus Sinclair moved up to GS-13, a Clandestine Service Operations Officer. The Ops Officer status is a must so he can go dark, or ..."

"Or? ... Or what?" Joan cut in, her tone incredulous, "Retire me, or owe me a favor? Just so I understand. You have an uneducated Army Ranger washout who you've trained for the last five years in the paramilitary program – against regs I might add and ..."

"Give it a rest, Joan." Jack leaned back in his chair his bony fingers weaved behind his head. "He's a legacy, trained in human intel-

ligence and martial arts since birth by his uncle using Agency subconscious techniques. And an uncle, who is a highly-respected Intelligence Star recipient, I might add. I recruited Marcus, at
eighteen years old, directly from the U.S. Army Ranger program,
he didn't wash out. You're twisting the story to fit your own
agenda."

Joan's eyes went wide. "My agenda? Nothing in his file says anything about an *uncle,* much less what his real name is. His psychological profile paints a picture of him growing up in a Norman
Rockwell portrait. From what I've gathered over the last two years,
he's a genius with zero empathy who can burn a lie detector. He's
given me so many dissembled stories, I can't tell if he's a psychopath, a sociopath, or both. Where he needs to be is in a mental
institution, not in the field."

"Just stop." Jack held up a hand. "You and I both know the
higher the IQ, the lower the empathy. His emotions are reasonably
under control – that should be worth something. Traits found in
great interrogators. You should know. You trained him."

"I know I trained him – for interrogation – not solo black bag
missions." Joan shook her head. "You sandbagged me, Jack."

"No sandbagging, just not the whole story, there's a difference.
Thanks to you and your team he can read facial expressions better
than anyone I've ever seen, and he can fake empathy quite well. He
could have been an A-list actor ... instead he'll be our best *hunter.*"
Jack shrugged, "Hell, for the last two years he's been pretty much
on his own, anyway."

"I want to know the truth, Jack, for professional reasons. Or ...
no sign-off." Joan crossed her arms defiantly leaning against a filing
cabinet and nearly tipping it over.

"You can't handle the truth ..." he replied in his best Jack Nichol-
son impression, followed by a shrewd grin. "Hmff." *Professional reasons, my butt.* "I have Delta and SEAL Team 6 guys from Ivy league
schools who can't think their way out of a paper bag. This kid, in a
mere three weeks, chased down a Panamanian dictator, successfully
tortured a Panamanian general, blew up a town, saved a U.S. Ma-

rine officer, and never broke cover. And what his assignment is ... is none of your damn concern. Now, let's get him signed off so I can reassign him – A-SAP. We can discuss trading favors later."

"I want to see him first. Then we can discuss *my* favor," Joan said, getting in the last word.

CHAPTER 7

Alyn woke up when the plane touched down in Athens, removing her sleeping mask she glanced over at the Greek. He was sitting up straight, facing forward, bags under his eyes, coat lying over his lap with the ice rattling in the lowball glass in his hand.

She grinned to herself with a sense of accomplishment.

Nothing was said when they deplaned. She held back a giggle at the sight of this reformed misogynistic pedophile trying to manage his coat and carry-on bag with one hand and keep his torn pants up with the other.

When Alyn reached the baggage area she saw her old friend, Nyssa Kostopoulos. They were in the same intelligence school class. Nyssa came from a ten generation Greek-Jewish family often referred to as *Romaniotes*. She was an honor graduate of Queens College, Oxford University, with one of two majors in game theory mathematics and was one of Mossad's go-to officers for strategic operational planning.

"Alyn, how are you? Hey ... Hello? Where are you?" Nyssa waved her hand in front of Alyn's face.

"Oh. Nyssa, I'm fine. I missed you so much." She gave her friend a big hug and kiss with one eye on the Greek, then chirped, "Hey, wait. Look at the guy holding his pants up over there."

Nyssa slowly turned to see a disheveled, broken man shuffle through the baggage claim area, desperately trying to hold his pants up with a fluorescent white butt crack showing.

"Oh Alyn, what have you done now? Still pulling pranks on bad men, I see." The crease between her eyebrows deepened.

"I taught him an overdue lesson. I'll tell you about it later."

"Oh—my—gawd, will you ever change?" Nyssa put her hand up to her mouth to keep from laughing out loud.

"I certainly hope not." Alyn flashed a sly grin.

They walked outside, waved down a taxi, and climbed in.

Alyn shot Nyssa a sideways glance and said in Hebrew, "Why are you working in Athens? I thought you were headed for Asia, Miss Asian Studies."

"I did. I was in Bangkok. It was fantastic, but my grandmother got sick and I had to take the Athens Security Officer post for now. I'll get back."

"Sorry to hear about your grandmother." Alyn rubbed her friend's shoulder.

The taxi ride was short and deposited them in front of the Embassy of Israel at the corner of Mouson and Leoforos Kifisias. It was a plain, almost square, three story structure surrounded by similar plain, almost square, three story apartment buildings. It had a six-foot, cement brick fence as a barrier, which was ... plain, almost square.

Nyssa and Alyn walked into the embassy tittering about the Greek. Alyn recognized many faces from the last time she visited.

"Hallo Gretchen. Good to see you," Alyn called out to one of the clerks. *I have had this cover as a Rome Security Officer for nearly two years and still only Nyssa knows the truth.*

The two professional women arrived at Nyssa's office deep in the embassy. Nyssa shut the door and pointed to a big, puffy old leather couch for Alyn to sit.

Nyssa picked up the coffee mug from her desk. "Here's the situation. I'm going to be your handler, not Jacob. There are three serious candidates for President of Greece who are very close in the polls ..."

"You're my handler?" Alyn broke in. "Excellent! Which one do I take out? Is this a senior level assignment?" Alyn's eyes gleamed in anticipation.

"Whoa." Nyssa shook her head then sat down at the other end of the couch and turned to face Alyn. "No. Sorry."

The twinkle in Alyn's eyes faded.

"You will take out the campaign manager of the candidate for the Independent party who is number two in the polls and implicate the campaign manager of the number one candidate from the *Nea Dimokratia* party."

"Aww, come on, a lowly campaign manager? Really?" Alyn pouted.

Nyssa ignored Alyn's remark. "This will give the candidate Israel supports from the *Panellinio Sosialistiko Kinima* party the number one position. Israel will finally gain a foothold in Greek politics that has eluded us for several decades. This also guarantees Mossad will let me return to Thailand as a Katsa Jumper. That's why I specifically asked for you." Nyssa flipped off her shoes putting her mug on the coffee table.

"A wet-works job with a frame, that's the best you could come up with?" Alyn was still sulking, her bottom lip turned up.

"Hey, look," Nyssa said briskly, "it may be a small hit as far as your ambition is concerned, but this is huge for Israel. This could be your last medium-level contract. This is bigger than you ... think about the big picture. Also, as a bonus, you will get to use all those cool gymnastics moves you have."

Alyn stared at Nyssa. *Gymnastics moves ... Serious? This is how she sees Parkour? One day, I will take her to the Parkour Centre in Rome and show her what freerunning and obstacle passing is really about.*

"There is another bonus. Both targets are psycho-playboys. A man-hater like you should love this job. You're still gay, right?" Nyssa rubbed her hands on her thighs, nervously.

Alyn blinked twice. "Is that how you see me – a man-hating lesbian?"

"Well. You were when *we* were together."

Alyn slid across the couch, placing her hand on Nyssa's thigh. "And it was the best relationship I ever had, but you know the door swings both ways with me. I just have a hard time living in a world where women are subjugated to men, where most men see women as insignificant playthings, designed solely for their pleasure. We are way more than *significant*."

"I'm sorry. I missed you so much. Very few people understand me like you." Nyssa kissed Alyn on the cheek and gave her a long hug.

Alyn jumped up. "Okay. Okay. Do you have what I need to stage the scene after the hit?"

"Done." Nyssa stood up and walked back over to her desk. "Here are the schedules of both men. Go get some rest. This is the key to a little motel down the street."

"A motel? Really?" She rolled her eyes and left. *Senior Kidon officers get five star hotels. I get a flea bag motel.*

CHAPTER 8

Williamsburg, Virginia
December 1989

The rain fell in cold sheets over the lush forest ten miles outside
of town. A rusted, black Toyota 4x4 pickup pulled up to the gate of
the *well-known*, secret military facility.

"Good morning sir, how can I help you?" An imposing figure
dressed in camouflage fatigues with no identifying marks bent
down to look at the driver.

"Hey Brian, it's just me," Marcus said. "I'd think you'd know my
truck by now, considering I own your ass in poker every time we
play." His laugh was infectious.

Without moving his head, Brian's eyes indicated the fence-
mounted camera. "You know we're on video, Marcus. Need to look
professional if I'm gonna get a slot in the next program." The loom-
ing figure did a visual search of everything in the cab and in the bed
of the truck, giving Marcus a final once over.

"You've got my vote," Marcus quipped. "Not that it means
much."

The security guard entered the shack and picked up the phone.
After a brief conversation, Brian returned. "Dr. Meriwether wants
to see you before you meet with the Chief." He waved the truck
through.

Marcus, attired in a worn tan Carhartt jacket, blue long sleeve Carhartt T-shirt with the pocket half torn, ripped Levi 501s and half untied black boots, got out of his truck and threw his jacket over his shoulder. He approached the two-story, green roofed structure, oddly designed like a Mesopotamian ziggurat with a dual obelisk entryway turning his attention to a tall, older, skeleton-of-a-man smoking an unfiltered Marlboro.

After field stripping the cigarette Jack turned his focus to Marcus. "Well, well, well. Look who has returned – *El Mercader de la Muerte.* How does it feel to be back in the States?"

Marcus held back a bitter laugh. "Are you kidding me with that shit, Chief? Do you get some kind of sadistic pleasure by keeping me locked up with those *lifeguards* down in Little Creek? Panama better be my last training gig. I now have *another* knife and gunshot wound – thank you very much. Man, you fuckin' suck."

"Stop crying, just one knife and one bullet? I could show you ..."

"Yeah, yeah," Marcus waved him off, "tell me another one of your Nam stories later, Skeletor. Besides, the shrink wants a piece of me first."

"My office after," he directed, shaking his head with a smirk.

Marcus Sinclair weaved his way through the building's many hallways until he reached a door labeled: "Joan Meriwether, PhD – Psychologist – Clandestine Services – Psychological Operations Group."

Marcus knocked.

A familiar woman's imperious voice replied, "Enter."

"Yes Ma'am. Reporting as requested, Ma'am," Marcus said, standing rigidly in front of the big woman's desk.

"The mics are off. We can speak freely." She waved for him to sit down.

"Cool beans. Is there anything I can do for you ... or more to the point ... *to you?*" he said, knowing her disgusting penchant for lust.

"Let's circle back around to that," she replied, raising an eyebrow. "First, Jack wants me to sign off on your interrogation training and your promotion."

"Okay. Am I done?" Marcus rose up a millisecond after his butt hit the seat.

"Not yet." She waved him back down. "I want to know the truth about your family. I need to do some ... umm ... situational prediction modeling." She nodded, more to herself than Marcus. "It's for my research, not for the Agency."

"You know I'll report this to Jack," he said defensively.

"Fine with me," she said, refusing to be intimidated.

Marcus rolled his eyes. "Okay. Here's the short version. At ten, my parents tell me they're actually my grandparents. I won't even get into the hornet's nest called my mother. At twelve, I'm not Catholic, I'm actually Jewish. At nineteen, during my father's, *er*, my *grandfather's* funeral, I'm told all these 'stories' and nobody is who I was told they were while growing up. Even my idiot Uncle John, who I thought was a bank teller, actually works for the Federal Reserve. Oh, and the father who I was told was my father back when I was ten, isn't. My *real fucking* biological father, number three if you're keeping count, is a cop and a Naval Intelligence Officer in San Diego. If I find him, you can bet I'll ask for DNA. Uncle Bill, who spent lots of time teachin' me stuff and I grew up believin' was a truck driver – he introduced me to Jack. The rest is history. I never returned."

Joan sat in her chair staring at Marcus and thought, *that answers that question ... he's both a psychopath and a sociopath suffering from lack of empathy due to genetics coupled with absence of caring from within the family unit. Interesting. Maybe he'll fit right in with Jack's division after all.*

She stood up, walked over to the couch motioning for him to do the same then placed her hand between his legs.

"Is this where you tell me you feel bad for me and tear off my clothes to 'help' me?" Marcus smiled perfunctorily. *Talk about being a tool. She's as fucked up as I am.*

"Don't worry, precious – none of this will be on any official paperwork," she said, her lips forming a crooked smile.

On the other hand, Marcus mused, *they're paying me to torture people and have sex with this sloth-o-potamus. Women are just sperm vessels anyway, I say let's throw some flour on her and shoot for the wet spot.*

The chubby shrink grinned ear to ear as she created a Carhartt clothes pile on the floor. "By the way, this will probably be our last session."

Marcus smiled inwardly. *Praise Jesus! Praise Moses! Praise ... OUCH, watch the teeth!*

CHAPTER 9

Athens, Greece
December 1989

The alarm in Alyn's watch buzzed. A mouse scurried across the floor as she rolled off the creaky bed.

I'm a Walmart assassin. What a career path.

Alyn pulled clothes from a cardboard box and organized her tools from another. Once ready, she slammed the motel room door and got in the car with her two escorts.

"We're heading to *Gazi*, Ma'am," the passenger said. "Both targets live within three blocks of each other."

The car pulled up to a building two blocks from the first target's location.

The Gazi District is an upper class neighborhood of Athens, similar to New York's theatre district, adorned by beautiful stone buildings with distinct neoclassical features. With a plethora of cozy restaurants, trendy cafes, small bars and Greek restaurants which add to the picturesque atmosphere of the entire district and is home to many of the top political figures of the country.

"Ma'am, it's three in the morning. Can you do both targets in time?" the passenger said, without turning around.

"I guess you'll just have to wait and see." She slipped out of the car and flashed them a wink and sideways grin.

Within seconds the escorts could hardly see her moving up the wall to the second floor corner apartment – entering the window effortlessly. She found the target working at his office desk.

Mister Airgun would you care to assist?

She hit the target in the leg.

"Oww," he yelled. His head bounced off the back of the chair landing on the keyboard, unconscious.

Alyn left scrape marks and fight bruises all over his body and leaned him back in the chair to strategically place blood droplets in wounds and clothing. On the shelf behind the desk she found a Greek Athame and tucked it away.

"Your life, as you knew it, is now over." She stepped back and observed the scene. "Not that your life was worth anything anyway."

I am good. Like the Greek police could figure this out – too much Baklava.

* * *

Thirty minutes later, Marcus showed up in the doorway of his boss's office. The black on white door plaque read: Jack Barnett – Section Chief – Special Activities Division – Special Operations Group.

Barnett shut the door without preamble or pleasantries. "Marcus. Listen to me clearly. I went out on a limb for you in respect to your Uncle Bill. You're the smartest guy in the division with the highest situational awareness rating I've ever seen. But ..."

"Why thank you, Chief." Marcus looked like he just swallowed a canary.

"I need to know if you can come off the porch and play with the big dogs? You have no Ivy League education and until these last two years with the *lifeguards*, as you put it, SEAL Team 4, you had no tier-two combat experience. My boss is trying to force me to keep you on the porch, pooch."

"That's such ... crap." He slapped the top of the filing cabinet by the door.

"I'm concerned. You're brilliant, brash, hot-headed, unempathetic and *still* very unsophisticated. Your knowledge and experience DO NOT match your intelligence ..." Jack said, with a tenor of concern.

Unsophisticated? What's wrong with that? The women around here seem to like it, Marcus thought.

"You need to be careful. Someone's going to trip you up." Jack stood nose to nose with Marcus using all six foot four and one hundred seventy four pounds to get Marcus to physically understand what he was saying. "Look Marcus, I was also recruited in a similar fashion and had a rough and tumble upward progression until I received my degree from Brown. So, I really do understand."

"Your boss is a cube. Screw him! You've had me taking shit for over five years ... five fuckin' years, Jack. I've never missed a target and aced every course. You send me to swim with SEALs for 18 months of bullshit, *operational readiness*, while you had me pulling off-book contracts. What thanks do I get? This Panamanian FUBAR catastrophe I just got back from!" he said, waving his hands at Jack in frustration.

"Hey. Panama wasn't that big of a FUBAR. You're alive, aren't you? All thanks to your good training. You should be thanking me," he replied, walking around his desk to sit in his chair.

"Great. You call it good training, fine Skeletor. I've done twice as much in half the time as any of those *Hedera-yahoos* – Ivy League, my ass. You owe me the black site interrogator job in Thailand. Have I not done every damn thing you asked of me?"

"Yes, despite that smartass mouth of yours."

"Better than being a dumbass ... I'm a work in progress." His voice trailed off as his temper waned taking a seat across the desk from Jack.

"Calm down. The Director was happy with what you did in Panama."

"So? Am I going to Thailand, or not?"

Like a dog with a bone, his years of testing and training; poking and prodding; and blood, sweat, and tears were coming to an end. He felt he had made it.

"No, you are not," Jack said, unequivocally.

CHAPTER 10

"Well," Marcus said, slouching in his chair, "that just fuckin' figures. 'Welcome to the Agency, see the world, but not your aspirations' ..." The proverbial bone fell from his mouth.

"Shut up and let me finish." Jack pointed a pen at Marcus. "Country comes before self."

"I'm not a Marine! You jarhead."

"Obviously, I know you're not going to be a *company man*. That's fine, but I have a classified operation which I doubt anyone can do. It would mean a lot to me if ..."

"You're pulling a bait and switch sprinkled with guilt," he cut in, tilting his head, "on me? The guy with no empathy, ironic wouldn't you say?"

"It's a company need. Get over it," Jack said, through pursed lips.

"What is it?"

"It's long and complicated is what it is. I'll keep it short. Ten years ago we were investigating board members of the Federal Reserve who were funding terrorism to further their corporate agenda in countries with assets that could be cheaply exploited." Jack opened a file labeled, 'CIA Director's Eyes Only'.

"Americans don't fund terrorism. Who are you kiddin'? A conspiracy theorist is not what I took you for, Jack," he said, the side of his mouth turned up.

"The CIA funds terrorism, or if you like *freedom fighters*, why not corporations? If I may continue ... the investigation took many twists and turns. Ultimately, we found a connection between the Fed and the Intelligence Support Activity (ISA). Over the last couple years several members of the investigation team died in freak accidents."

"The Fed? You're saying a government agency is using ... who? Another government agency to ... what? Are you off your friggin' rocker?" Marcus crossed his arms in disbelief and stared intensely at Jack.

"First. The Fed is not *federal*, nor is it a *reserve*. The Federal Reserve System is a group of banks who are, in turn, private corporations owned by several foreign corporations. Because the whole system is private, no one really knows who owns the Fed. These same foreign corporations have been buying and selling senators, congressmen and presidents for over a hundred years – most of the time, without their knowledge. America is one big corporation, run by both domestic and foreign corporations. It's a shell corp nightmare."

Marcus ignored the bank explanation. "Wait. You want me to infiltrate *The Activity*? Them ... a group so secret congress can't investigate them? That's not an assignment, that's a death sentence, Jack. They're funded by the DoD for Christ's sake. They're *untouch-a-ble*. When they retire people, it's as if they never existed." *Facing Goliath as David,* Marcus' mind swam. *This guy must think I'm made of magnesium – burn bright, die fast.*

"Look Marcus," Jack said, slapping the arms of his chair, "this is not for the weak of heart, or skills."

"Ya think?"

"That's why the Agency needs you. Despite what Americans think, there are places Congress cannot go. One is the banking system and the other ... the deep dark corners of the Department of Defense."

"Sure," Marcus said, with nervous sarcasm, "piece of cake."

"Let me summarize, Marcus. The owners of the U.S. Federal Reserve planted a mole inside the DoD's ISA. The only people who can investigate inside the Pentagon, are Pentagon employees – the fox guarding the hen house, so to speak. This means that foreign, and possibly domestic, corporations can use U.S. military resources against *any entity* in the world. To bring this closer to home imagine this, the militarization of all U.S. Law Enforcement Organizations (LEO). Let's say, hypothetically, by *selling* LEOs extra equipment the military ... *doesn't need*. Are you following me now?"

"I'm heartless, not stupid. Let me get this straight. You want me to infiltrate, and I apologize for belaboring the point, *The Activity?* An agency filled with wraiths, wrapped in ghosts, cloaked in shadows making Mossad look like toddlers at a daycare. And without getting my head detached from my body, find a mole selling information who's on some mysterious banker's payroll ... to do what, exactly, when I find this person?"

"Yes." Jack nodded approvingly, subtext implied.

"Oh ... now you're talkin'!" Marcus said, raising his hands in exhilaration. "Where am I going?" His initial fear was gone.

"Good attitude. First you're headed to a black site in Bogotá, then to Naples. One of my interrogators was killed down there and I don't have anyone available. You can practice your *interrogation skills* on a drug cartel detainee. Here's the package." Jack handed him a large yellow envelope.

"Sounds as straight as Lombard Street," he said, jumping up from his chair. "Keeping my same name?"

"Yes. Oh by the way, your Uncle Bill is down there."

You're such an asshole. Marcus slammed the door on his way out.

CHAPTER 11

"Okay. Thanks for the info." The passenger hung up the car phone. "The intel unit watching the second target says he just returned about an hour ago."

"Thanks guys. See you soon." Alyn closed the car door and dashed off to scale the wall to the dark third story loft.

'Gymnastics moves' Nyssa says. She has known me for all these years and she still doesn't know what Parkour is. Oy vey. Am I obsessing?

Alyn reached the third floor and pulled a small bottle of dark liquid from her bag. She squirted the fluid all along the side window guides of the old, wooden window then waited.

"Can you see her?" The passenger said, peering through high powered binoculars.

"No. Can you?" The driver was squinting.

"Nah, she like, blends in with the wall like a shadow. Damn, she *is* good."

Pssst. Alyn opened the window with hardly a sound. She dropped to the floor and stopped to listen. With the moonlight at her back she could make out most of the details of the living room.

"Get the thermal. She's in the loft," the driver said.

The passenger radioed, "Cinderella is at the ball."

The loft was much larger than most in the neighborhood. Shadows of modern sculptures, artwork and very expensive furnishings gave the feel that they danced around the room. She noticed the dusty, black rectangular Domino dining room set. Down the teak hardwood hallway, she heard the target snoring.

Good taste, but damn, he could wake the dead.

The bedroom door was open. A dim bedside lamp cast a shadow over the target lying on his back, mouth wide open, wearing blue silk pajamas covered in oranges yelling Greek obscenities.

She stared down at the target. *Yeah, those pajamas aren't obnoxious.*

Alyn took the ancient Greek Athame from her bag and plunged the ceremonial dagger into the target's chest up to the hilt. The dagger vibrated with each heartbeat. The man attempted to bolt upright to a sitting position. Alyn already anticipated his reaction and placed her right knee across his neck and chin. While her left hand twisted the knife mercilessly, her right hand covered his mouth, forcing his head deep into the pillow. With his arms and legs flailing, he struggled grabbing at Alyn with all his remaining strength. The form fitting black leather pants and knee-high boots provided no place to hold.

Now the wait, I could run a mile by the time this guy dies.

Alyn's strength was overpowering. The knife stopped vibrating as the blood on his chest slowed and jellied. She left the shiny Greek blade monumentalized in his ribcage and returned to her bag to pull out several small baggies and vials. The skin tissue from the prior target was still fresh and easy to delicately place under the nails of the dead man. She spread the skin tissue from the remaining baggies throughout the bedroom, living room and dining room as if it were a light sprinkling of snow.

Why did Nyssa really call me for this job? Does she want to pick up where we left off or is it something else?

She retraced her steps, feeling confident with her work she tossed the bedroom to make it look like there had been a fight. She wiped her dusty footprints from the hardwood floor, went out the way she came in, and closed the window behind her.

The driver started the car as the passenger radioed, "Cinderella has left the ball."

* * *

Nyssa was sitting at her desk in the embassy writing a report when Alyn found her.

"Are we good?" Nyssa looked up.

"The assignment is complete and your guys can handle the rest. I need a ride to the airport because I have a ball to get ready for," she said, with an air of faux arrogance.

"No problem. I'm guessing Cinderella *really is* going to the ball." Nyssa grinned. "Going to meet your Prince Charming, huh?"

"Yeah right, no glass slippers there and charming princes don't exist." She laughed shaking her long black hair loose leaving Nyssa staring longingly at her back.

CHAPTER 12

Marcus deplaned and hailed a taxi to the *La Quinta* hotel in Bellavista. He walked into the lounge, made sure no one was watching and pulled a playing card taped under a table.

The Joker, seriously? My uncle is such a dick.

He walked back outside and stood curbside subtly wiggling the card in his left hand between his middle and ring finger. Within minutes a car pulled up, the back door opened and Marcus got in. Both driver and the passenger were wearing blue button-downs, grey polyester slacks and black two-button suit jackets.

The passenger turned around. "Hello nephew, how are you doing this fine day?"

Marcus handed him the playing card. "I don't prank people anymore, but I can change that if you wish, Uncle Bill," he said, tightening his gaze.

"Training wheels are now off I'm guessing?" The jolly plump uncle turned back around.

Marcus tapped the driver on the shoulder. "Can we get some grub before we get started?"

* * *

The three men walked into Marco's Diner on Revolution Ave.

Bill gave the hostess a twenty and in Spanish said, "We're in a rush. Three carne asada burritos and keep everyone way." He reached over the counter, grabbed a bowl of chips and salsa and headed to the back. Marcus and the driver followed.

"Si senor," she said.

Bill drenched a chip with salsa. "We're closing in on Pablo Escobar, you know, the head of the Medellin Cartel. Ever heard of him?"

"Nope, sorry, I don't do drugs," Marcus said, exuding sarcasm.

The men stopped talking.

"Carne asada burritos," the waitress said. "Algo más?"

Bill gave her the 'okay' hand signal, waved her away then turned back to Pantera. "Funny. I'm guessing you don't watch the news, either."

The men spent the next ten minutes in silence. Marcus watched his uncle eat enough for two people. *My uncle's a fatty, my boss is a skeleton. You guys must have been the Laurel and Hardy of Vietnam.*

"The guy we have in custody will be good interrogation practice for you." Bill rammed the last of the large burrito into his craggily toothed mouth.

"From what I hear, you got your last interrogator killed. Maybe *you* should be retired," Marcus said, raising both eyebrows and finishing the last bite of his burrito.

"Always the smartass," Bill said, with a sigh.

Marcus didn't need to say anything. Bill knew what his response would be.

"Take me to him. Let's get this over with." Marcus finished his drink then slammed the empty glass down on the table. "You can stick the rest of those chips ..." He grinned as he got up.

* * *

It was a half-hour drive to an old, abandoned barn on the outskirts of a war-ravaged town called, *La Calera*. The area was desolate except for the black-clad American military operators surrounding the lonely barn.

Look at these lifeguards from SEAL Team 8. And that's some damn fine camouflage. He chuckled, looking at what his future would have been, if not for his uncle and Jack. Marcus fondly recalled his days camping in the hills of West Virginia as a kid, but unlike most special operations forces, he never wanted a career living in a jungle.

Bill pointed at the detainee as the three men walked into the barn. "And ... without further ado, I present to you, Pablo Escobar's number three man, Jose Carrillo. We'll need to know everything he knows. Prepare him to answer our questions."

Marcus smiled and nodded.

The barn was a two-story structure with most of the second floor destroyed by age and bullet holes. There were over half a dozen men in black fatigues, fully armed, strewn around the hay bale lined walls of the barn.

"*Vete a la mierda. Ustedes bastardos americanos. No te diré nada. Moriré como un mártir.*" The detainee yelled at the top of his lungs rocking the chair side to side.

Marcus looked the Colombian in the face. "Sorry brother, I don't speak Spanish," he said, giving mock sign-language gestures to further insult the detainee. "Anybody want to tell me what he said?"

A voice came from the darkness, "Nothing important."

"Excellent." Marcus pulled out a syringe and small bottle from his bag and withdrew about ten cubic centimeters of clear liquid. "Does chuckle-nuts speak English or would I be wasting my time trying to talk to him?"

"We can translate."

"Tell him I'm giving him a shit-load of adrenaline, this will jack his nervous-system up so high that a kiss on his dick will make him cry." Marcus shot a small stream of fluid from the syringe into the air.

One of the men walked up behind the detainee and translated.

"Then ... I'm going to take these acupuncture needles coated with my own poisonous concoction and insert them in a nerve plexuses in each shoulder which will turn off movement in his arms. Instead of making his limbs feel numb, they'll feel like they're on fire. I can do this for days, so he has a choice – die fast or slow. Either way ... he's going to die," he said, unrolling a pocketed piece of fabric holding a number of unusual looking instruments.

"Let's try to make it faster than *days*. I have a hair appointment." Bald Uncle Bill laughed and whistled Wagner's *Ride of the Valkyries*, from the movie *Apocalypse Now*.

Marcus looked over with a sneer then chuckled at his uncle swaying to his own music. *Gawd I hate you.* "Anyway, I'm going to start an IV just in case," he continued, inserting a catheter into the detainee's left antecubital fossa and plugging the tubing into a bag of D5W. "The additional fluid should make him urinate more. Just part of the entertainment, I won't charge you extra."

Humiliation helps the interrogation, that's what you said, right, Dr. Meriwether?

Marcus watched as the Colombian's pupils dilated, pores opened and sweat covered his body. He slapped the detainee on the back making him scream as if he were splashed with hot grease.

"You fuckin' Americans ... you'll get nothing from me!" he yelled, starting to shake as if coming down off a heroin addiction.

"He does speak English, so it seems," Marcus said, giving a sideways look to Bill; "Time for the show." He broke the skin with the needle about three finger widths above the clavicle.

The Colombian yelled so hard Marcus thought he heard a vocal cord snap.

"Cry baby," Marcus chortled, continuing to push the needle deeper, "I haven't even started."

Laugher broke out around the barn loosening the tension.

"Just got to make sure I don't hit the brachial artery. And BAM! Got it." He raised his arms in the air like a soccer referee.

The movement in the man's left arm stopped.

"Mi brazo izquierdo no se mueve!"

"He says his left arm won't move," a voice said.

"Good. Let's see, I'll give it a little wiggle to get the poison going." He turned to Bill. "Efferent nerves are off and afferent nerves are still on."

"Whatever. I don't need a play by play. Just get it done," Bill snapped.

The Colombian screamed and swung his head around trying to remove the needle. Blood flew out of his mouth like a low budget horror movie, spewing all over Marcus.

Bastard, that wasn't in the manual. Note to self: next time bring coveralls.

Marcus grabbed Saran Wrap from his bag and wrapped the Colombian's head to the center pinnacle of the chair. The man started suffocating. "Are you sure you don't want to talk," Marcus barked, clenching his jaw and bending over with a pointed index finger within an eyelash from the detainee's eye.

The Colombian's eyes' grew large, but he shook his head in defiance while the plastic covering his mouth thumped in and out.

CHAPTER 13

Marcus took two fingers and poked a hole through the plastic over the man's mouth. The man gasped for air as the plastic around his mouth flapped like a flag on a windy day.

"I can do this for as long as it takes," he said, taking a seat next to the detainee.

After an hour of solitaire, watching every vein in the man's body engorge, and tears pool under his eyes inside the Saran Wrap, Marcus inserted another needle into the detainee's other shoulder. An unusual shrill came from the broken vocal cord, plastic wrapped head.

"That sounded like some kind of bird." Marcus rubbed his neck and spoke to the ceiling. "When are we going to eat again? I'm starving. You gotta candy bar or something?"

Bill motioned and the other company man left.

Marcus knew his uncle was evaluating him, just like when he was an insolent teenager. He wouldn't say it out loud, but he respected his uncle and wanted to show him that he was ready and confident for his new career.

One of the operators threw Marcus a Snickers.

"Ah, yes. Snickers really satisfies." He glared at the Colombian as he took a bite, smiling with chocolate in his teeth.

Marcus felt nothing for the man before him – wrapped in Saran Wrap gasping for air, arms duct taped to the chair, with huge acupuncture needles sticking out of him. The Colombian's body flailed but his arms looked like cooked spaghetti as Marcus could see the big, clumsy gears in his head spin slowly.

He will realize what he is facing shortly. The cartel will fade away once he comes to grips with his own mortality.

Marcus understood mortality, academically. However, just like empathy, the concept of his own mortality eluded him.

Every few minutes Marcus gyrated the needles to check the Colombian's pain level. He would shriek in pain, but wouldn't go unconscious.

Go unconscious, goddamn you. That will shake your concept of mortality.

After hours of no results, the stress of Uncle Bill's quiet impatience forced Marcus to recall one of his first interrogation training sessions – the difference between *advanced* interrogation techniques and *enhanced* interrogation techniques. "Enhanced techniques rarely provide results. Advanced techniques always provide results," the instructor repeated; "This is one of many secrets the Agency will never let Congress find out."

I know Jack said interrogators' jobs were stressful, but damn. Looks like I need to get creative.

An idea jumped into Marcus' head, *Cerebral Spinal Fluid. Fuck yeah!*

"Guys, I need a large bore needle or a drill and a small drill bit," Marcus said, over his shoulder.

Everyone in the barn looked at each other trying to figure out what he was talking about.

"Bill, this will work. Trust me," he said, walking over and standing tall in front of his uncle.

Bill threw a set of keys to one of the operators. "There's a cordless drill in the SUV. Go get it."

The operator returned with a large gray plastic case with "Milwaukee" across the side.

The Colombian had a clear view of Marcus throwing open the case and pulling out a battery-powered, M12, three-eighths drill and a one-sixty-fourth inch, Thunderbolt Black Oxide drill bit.

Zzzzzz! Marcus said, to the drill, "I was trying to figure out a common, but really painful, malady a human can have – a headache, or more specifically – a migraine. I'm about to give this cretin the fast track to the mother of all migraines ... watch this boys." He revved up the drill again making sure he had the detainee's full attention.

The Colombian's head fell into his chest, chin splashing in the sweat-saturated T-shirt. Flying insects, attracted by the urine and feces, crawled all over him. His fight was leaving, his yelling less vigorous.

The stench was so stifling Marcus' eyes watered as he prepared.

The man's eyes followed Marcus' every move.

The operators looked on inquisitively.

Marcus walked behind the detainee and broke off a spine of the chair without weakening it. He tore the shirt away from the skin and caught a huge concentrated dose of special sulfur-infused methane gas.

Ugh. What did this guy last eat?

Marcus knocked away a couple large insects and placed his middle finger on a bump on the detainee's spine. His index finger found the next lower bump on the spine. Between the two fingers was the space between the third and fourth lumbar vertebrae. He centered the drill bit between his two fingers.

"Please don't wiggle. It will be much worse if you do."

The high-speed drill howled as it burrowed into the intercalated cartilaginous disc, blood and skin flew off the bit like sparks from an arc welder. The Colombian's body jolted as he felt a small pop. The subarachnoid space of the spinal cord was penetrated. His eyes went so wide they almost burst out of his skull and his head stretched against the plastic wrap with neck veins bulging.

Marcus could see the pain ripping through his body when his toes curled up like tiny pill bugs.

The detainee fell unconscious.

Gawd damn right, I AM the man. "Perfect," he said, standing up and looking at the closest operator. "When this fine specimen of will power wakes up, make sure he understands that I just poked a hole in his spine. Over the next several hours the fluid in his spine will drip, drip, drip out of his brain – slowly giving him a migraine headache that would cripple an elephant. Simply put, his brain will implode. It won't kill him and I can reverse it if he's willing to talk."

All the operators in the room looked at each other, smiled and nodded.

Tired of waiting, Marcus stabbed the Colombian with an Epipen. He woke up, started crying and praying out loud. There was renewed excitement in the barn. Within an hour he was screaming that his head was on fire and felt like it was going to explode. He fought to keep his eyes open while his body shook like a crack-addicted hula dancer's hips.

"Por favor ... matar ... mí. Voy a hablar, por favor, me acaba de matar," then in English, "Please kill me, I will talk, just please kill me."

Bill walked over and immediately asked the detainee questions. He answered quickly and efficiently for the next two hours – through his bloody screams.

Marcus waited for Bill to finish. "Well sir. Would you like some popcorn with the show? And if you don't need me for anything else, I'm outta here."

"One of the operators said you could reverse that hole in his back," Bill said, putting his hands on his hips.

"Normally yes, if I actually had a spinal tap kit, but I don't. I lied. Something I'm well-trained at, right uncle?"

Bill looked at Marcus and raised an eyebrow. "Yes. You were well-trained, and I'll make no excuses for what my brother did. May he rest in peace," he said, changing from uncle to section chief. "We'll clean up here. You did well. Very creative I must say. Hope our paths cross again."

"No offense, uncle. I know you tried to help way back when, but keep that *gawd-damn-freak-show* of a family away from me. If you do decide to tell them we spoke, tell my mother she can burn in hell. I'll see her, *at her* funeral," Marcus said, pointing into the air and squinting at his uncle.

"Sure. I understand." Bill gave Marcus a firm handshake. "Stay safe, nephew."

"Thank you sir, I'm now off to score some Italian tail."

CHAPTER 14

"So the whole assignment went flawlessly, you say?" The manicured gentlemen sat staring inquisitively across the desk at Alyn.

"Why, Michoel? Did you hear something different?" Alyn's eyes narrowed.

"I have Nyssa's report and the *Kathimerini* right here," he said, pausing for dramatic effect, "and it looks like you were right. Flawless. The Israeli supported candidate is now first in the polls with the other two candidates falling rapidly."

Alyn inhaled, re-inflating her lungs and confidence. "Did you think I would do otherwise?"

"That makes six for six on your assignments since being here. What can I say?" Michoel leaned back wrapping both hands around his coffee cup.

"You can say ... I'm done staying in flea-bag motels and hitting middle level worker bees." She cocked her head grinning with eyes wide.

"You go where you're needed. I don't have control over where you stay. It's easier to arrange *accidents* for assistants, than to retire high ranking officials. You know what a pain it is replacing them. That's how we got into this Greek situation in the first place. Has your training not taught you that?"

"Of course, I don't care about the target, it's the accommodations. Besides, father thinks I should be ..."

"*Ta'ase li tova.*" Michoel broke in, pointing at Alyn. "Your father loves you, but you ... you are not your brother."

"I know. He's just so sad when he looks at me. I don't know what to do." Alyn's shoulders slumped.

The intercom buzzed. "Miss David, you have a call on line 2."

"He will come around. Give him time." Michoel waved Alyn away.

Alyn left the large dank office, returned to her office down the hall and picked up her call on line 2.

"*Alyn David. Ayk any ykvl l'ezvr lk?*" [Alyn David. How can I help you?]

"*Achut.* Good Morning!"

"Alona," she exhaled. "Where are you?"

"We're in New York City for the big banker's ball. I'm standing on the balcony of the top floor suite in a boutique hotel called, *The Time.* It's adorable. We're going to kiss in Times Square at midnight ... how romantic is that?! *Figlio di una cagna,* it's cold. We left right after Chanukah, sorry we missed you. How was Athens?"

She gets a suite in New York City and I get a crap-ass motel room in Athens. "It was Athens, plain, almost square," she said, a tinge of jealousy in her voice. "I did my job, as I always do. Not that father would be interested. I sent him the paper, but he never returned my call." The envy was replaced with disappointment.

"*Achut.* Please stop obsessing. Adamm's death was not your fault. How many times do I have to say that? Father does not blame you. He is mourning. You cannot replace Adamm in father's eyes. Sons are more important than daughters in our culture ... *and the world.*" Alona's voice was firm yet supportive.

"I could've chosen a different path than Adamm."

"No, you couldn't. The eugenics program places us all on our path, it's the way Jews survive. You cannot change the way of our people. Our country's needs must come before our own. Besides, Adamm trained you. He was very proud of you."

"I miss him so much. I keep thinking ... if I had blown my cover I could've saved him." She chewed on the ends of her hair.

"Please. Please don't think that way. He didn't train you that way and you know a blown cover is a death sentence for members of your group. Not only would I have lost a brother, I would have lost a sister. A sister I love very dearly! Now, can we get back to me, please? I'm in New York, yeah! Where are you going for New Year's Eve?"

"I have to work the Ambassador's security detail at the US Embassy. Oh joy. I get to look forward to excess smoke, excess food, excess drink and over-indulged, ostentatious pus-bags grabbing my ass – just like last year. Oh so much fun." She made a gagging sound. *Wonder if I could be assigned a hit at a foreign embassy's ball. Now that would be fun.*

"So no Giancarlo as a date this year?"

"You're kidding, right? He's lucky I haven't dropped him down a well, or retired his *schvantz*, for what he did. Men. Nothing but ... *hatichat hara mizdayen batachat.*"

"No date at all?"

"No men. Nyssa is back in Athens."

"You are going to start that up again? Swinging to the other side are we? Make up your mind, you're making me dizzy."

"Don't know. It was good to see her though." Alyn looked off into space.

"Stop bringing me down and do me a favor. Grab some ugly dude, kiss him at midnight, do him in the ambassador's office and never see him again. A hot-beef-testosterone injection would do you some good. I know it's going to do me some good!" Alona let out a single burst of laugher.

"Wow. Something I would not have expected from you, big sister. Thank you for the visual. I'll never be able to remove that image from my mind. Talk soon. I love you."

"Love you, *Achut.*"

* * *

"Good morning First Sergeant. HM2 Marcus Sinclair reporting for duty." Marcus stood rigid in front of the First Sergeant's desk in the admin office of the 33rd Logistics Command, Navy Support Activity, Naples, Italy.

"Good Morning, Petty Officer, at ease. A Navy SEAL Corpsman slash interrogator, transferring from the States I see. First time assigned to an overseas duty station?"

"Yes, Top." Pantera mentally paged through the backstory of his cover.

"Looks like your paperwork's in order. Over there is your command paperwork and indoc sheet. Take it to Gunnery Sergeant O'Malley. You'll be assigned to second platoon as their medic and interrogator. Dismissed, Petty Officer."

"Thank you, Top." Marcus snapped to attention, took one step back, did an about-face and walked out of the office. He took a right turn and within minutes he was in the common room.

He smiled. *Well, that freakin' Army Pathfinder navigation course really paid-off.*

He turned around and made his way to the second platoon administration office.

"Good morning Platoon Sergeant, HM2 Sinclair reporting as directed by the First Sergeant." He stood at attention in front of the desk.

"Relax, Petty Officer. You can call me 'Grit', or 'Gunny' if you prefer. Do you know where you are?" Grit directed Marcus to a chair in front of his desk.

"Yes Gunny, the 33rd is a covert hunter-killer unit sponsored by the United Nations Security Council under the guise of the UN Special Operations Group."

"Very good, and you know what that means?" Grit gave a closed-lipped smile.

"Yes Gunny."

"Anything less than 110% out of you can get one of your buddies killed. Sometimes even that isn't enough. This unit loses five to ten guys each year. We're tasked with more covert actions then any unit on the planet. We never leave hostiles alive, we never leave buddies behind. Keep that in mind," Grit said, using his relaxed Tennessee drawl.

"Agreed." *Love the creed,* Marcus thought.

"From what I read you've been through several combat missions and have saved a number of team members under fire." He paged through Marcus' personnel record.

"It was a slow day." *I did? Maybe I should read my file.*

"Since you've never lived outside the States, know this – Americans are the minority here. You're not in Kansas anymore, Toto. Get your head wrapped around that and don't you forget it."

"Thanks for the info, Gunny." Marcus sat rigid in his chair playing the part of a good soldier. *What's with the damn dog analogies, Jack now Grit.*

"Righty-O, you'll be bunking with Bullseye and are assigned to the Med-shop and ISA. ISA functions as our G-2 here. Since you're an interrogator, you'll function as our intelligence officer as well as our field surgeon. You can weenie-weld with your bunkmate later and we'll assign your testing and evaluation officer next week."

Marcus stood up immediately after Grit.

Grit walked around the desk and shook Marcus' hand. "Welcome. Go stow your gear, grab some chow and get your dinner dress uniform in order. You, Bullseye, Baby-face, Cracker and I have been directed by the Commanding Officer to attend the US Embassy New Year's Eve Ball tomorrow night in Rome."

Suck my left ball. No way in hell. Sounds gay. "Uh, Gunny? Please don't think I'm trying to skirt out of a security detail, but I'm NOT a pomp and circumstance kinda guy. I wear Carhartts and boots ... rich pompous assholes deserve, well, you know."

"I agree with you. It's not a security detail. It's a simple, walk around. Military presence keeps the peace amongst those types."

You've got to be kidding me. Marcus rubbed his wrist behind his back.

"In addition, eat all you want. Stay away from the drink, and especially, stay away from the women. They're both ridiculously dangerous."

HUH?! Italian tail? NFC – no fat chicks?! With my Southern accent and charm ... like shooting fish in a barrel. I—am—sooo—there.

Grit could see his eyes light up. "Let me, *re—i—ter—ate.* Stay away from the women."

"Ah, yeah, sure Gunny. It'll suck, but country comes before self, right?"

"Good man. Adapt and overcome, OOORAH. Tomorrow. Sixteen hundred hours at the train platform. Dinner dress uniform. Move out."

"OOORAH Gunny," he hastily replied, trying to hide the jubilant smile percolating just under the surface.

CHAPTER 15

Music and laughter filled the damp night air at the United States Embassy New Year's Eve Ball where hundreds of embassy members, civilians and military advisory staff from many countries attended. The 17th-century *Palazzo Margherita* had been purchased by the United States in 1946 and renovated several times. The ornate and garish ballroom was typical in style, size, and complete with the austere pontification from previous eras.

The expression on Marcus' face said it all as his eyes darted around the room. *Holy shit, they're right, I'm not in Kansas anymore.*

Grit grinned as he saw, *the look,* so common to people when they enter for the first time.

"Shut your trap, Petty Officer," Grit quietly barked. "Your tongue is hanging out."

Bodies swayed and floated on the dance floor, varied uniforms and dress attire blended and turned like a kaleidoscope of whirling color as Marcus Sinclair and members of his unit from the US Navy base, entered the ballroom – reasonably unnoticed. It was not unusual for members of this elite unit to attend such events, often requested to function as covert security.

"Gentlemen, you know the drill. Keep conversations light. Keep moving. Keep the rookie in your sights at all times." The tall blonde, muscle-armored Marine told his team with full knowledge

Marcus would get into trouble. It was just a matter of when and with whom.

Marcus and his four highly-decorated buddies: two U.S. Marines, one member of the South African Special Forces and a fellow U.S. Navy SEAL Corpsman stood at the doorway to the grand ballroom in dinner dress uniforms observing the activities within the room.

Marcus looked sideways at Grit, and said, "Thanks, Gunny." *Now where are those hot Italian bitches.*

Heavy chain-smoking bureaucrats interacted with guests – meant to be an intimidating portentous dance unto itself about power and position, while others strutted and paraded themselves on display. A game within a game, many guests watched persons of interest as they themselves were being watched. Others simply enjoyed the free-flowing alcohol, caustic hors d'oeuvres, and the seductive exhibition of the gala.

* * *

One of the Israeli security officers spotted the UN contingent and radioed the rest of the security team. "The UN shadow team has arrived."

Alyn's ears perked up, curious about whom they brought with them this year – she only knew them by face. *There they stood,* she thought, *the Shadow Warriors.*

The Shadow Warriors, as Mossad called them, were the big game hunters of the covert world: mythical by reputation, mystical by skill set, and mysterious by nature.

"Je suis d'accord ambassadeur adjoint. La situation dans les Balkans est quelque chose qui doit être étudiée. Maintenant, si vous voulez bien me excuser." [I agree Deputy Ambassador. The situation in the Balkans is something that needs to be investigated. Now, if you will excuse me.]

She watched cautiously from across the room as she subtly ended her conversation and moved to a better vantage point.

* * *

Within an hour Marcus had a hot little Arabic beauty in a black dress picked out and was tracking her, waiting for the time to move in for the kill. Unbeknownst to him, he was a moth and she was the proverbial flame.

He felt uncomfortable in this powerful environment and quietly wished for a bucket of KFC, a beer and his tailgate, but couldn't help admire the baroque style architecture, the lavish mosaics, ornate fixtures, and the gaudiness of a culture long since gone. The smoke, perfumes and combined body heat from so many people left a cloying effect on Marcus. He continued to watch his quarry from afar.

* * *

"Buenas noches a su Excelencia. Me alegra ver que está teniendo un buen momento. Puedo tomar ese vaso vacío para usted." [Good evening your Excellency. Glad to see you are having a good time. I can take that empty glass for you.] Alyn watched each of the shadow warriors as they moved around the room. One in particular caught her eye as the others fell away. Not because he was good looking, he wasn't. There was something unique about his mannerisms. Not moving like he had any training in this environment, nonetheless gliding effortlessly within it. He seemed internally uncomfortable, but externally polished.

How natural he looks. Now where are you from, Navy boy?

Her instincts led her to believe he was imperceptibly following her – hunting her. She realized she was always in his sights without being obvious, even to the trained eye.

The American thinks he can hunt me, does he? Let's see about that.

CHAPTER 16

The girl in the black dress glanced at Marcus, trying to avoid her gaze he turned away. When he turned back, she was gone. With external calm he searched feverishly, but found nothing.

Damn, just my luck.

Across the room two shadow warriors watched this ritual-like dance transpire. One motioned to the other in acknowledgement, as they continued their vigil.

After several drinks and a plethora of unidentifiable food, Marcus sat scanning the room for his next target. The hunt was draining.

From behind him came a woman's voice. "*Maken a'eteqd a'eta alameyrekyewn tesl beshewlh.*" [I didn't think Americans gave up so easily.]

Alyn walked up behind Marcus in a freakishly stealthy move. Marcus stood up slowly and turned, compensating for the rush of adrenaline. He studied her for a second trying to muster the appropriate Arabic response. Grit and Bullseye moved within striking distance behind Alyn – just in case.

"*Lem nef'el delk. Wenhen da'ema alheswel 'ela feryesh ledyena. Anet baletakeyd hey jemyelh jeda.*" [We don't. We always get our prey. You certainly are very beautiful.] He was so shocked, the words tumbled out in a horrific Southern-accented, academic Arabic.

The slight upward turn of the corner of her mouth gave away how truly bad his pronunciation was, but she nodded accepting his gesture graciously.

He thinks I'm Arabic. What fun and what a relief, I was really itchin' to stab someone and that arrogant French prick who pinched my ass was going to be first on my list. "Thank you. Who are you and why are you following me?" she said in English, adopting the humble demeanor of a low-level embassy employee.

Her sharp yet delicate features and her alabaster skin framed by long obsidian hair in a Hime style gave an ethereal illusion that she was not of this world, more like an Egyptian goddess. She was very real and even more beautiful than he originally thought.

"I am ... *Pan-ter-ra*," he said, over pronouncing in the best *Maverick* impression stealing from the movie *Top Gun*, "and I'm just *pretending* to be a U.S. Navy Corpsman." He gave her a wink and a big smile. "As for followin' you, lil' lady, you musta be mistaken." He ended with an over emphasized Southern accent.

Navy boy is trying that country farm boy routine on me – in a creepy-good way. What am I thinking? "Pretending to be a U.S. Navy Corpsman, are you? So you're some kind of super spy? And ... *Pan-ter-ra?*" she said inquisitively, blinking her eyes shyly which could have caused hurricanes in Thailand.

"Yup, I'm a super-duper spy. Just come to dese tings and just walk 'round." He rubbed his nose. Pantera was giving her mixed signals just in case she could read faces equally as wellas himself.

"Sounds like fun. Where was your mother when they named you? You are from America, the South?" she continued with the Arabic accent, not sure what game he was playing.

She measured him toe to head: shiny corfams, dinner-dress uniform, one service stripe, two chevrons, caduceus, gold parachutist wings, pretty ribbons, and a large golden badge with an eagle, flint-lock, and trident. She arrived at his face, finally getting a good look at the clean-cut, iron-jawed, U.S. sailor. *Definitely not the pretty playboy I am used to, but handsome in a rugged sort of way.*

There was something about him. A hardness and determination that made her quiver, she shook her head. *Did someone drug me? Because if not, I have to ask myself, is this guy for real?* Her knees became wobbly shifting her mind into high gear, not something she was used to.

Pantera knew he was being assessed, but he couldn't get a clear read – by whom. *Who are you? You're giving off this secretary mannerism but your facial expressions indicate you're hiding something.*

She blinked and he caught a quick uncertainty in her demeanor.

Pantera smiled. *Aha. I'm seeing zebras where horses are. Forget it, time to score a hot little Arabic secretary.*

They stood inches apart and stared at one another. Pantera's eyes took in every detail of her model-esque face, manicured eyebrows, dark-lined red lips, and big blue eyes – his heart beat so fast it was nearly non-functional. Words tumbled around in his mind like boulders in a rockslide.

Run and run fast. She—is—out—of—your—league.

Five years of military training and shit-storm combat hadn't prepared him for how scared he felt at this moment. He wanted to be on the next plane out of Italy. Although garishly huge, the ballroom became suffocatingly small. He searched for the closest door when another horrid thought entered his mind, even more frightening than the first.

I can't make a fool out of myself. By man rules that would be a death sentence at my new unit. No unit, no mole. Damn.

He recovered and threw the ball back in her court, but accepted the fact that he was underprepared for this form of combat. "It's just my call sign. If I may ask, who are you and why are *you* ... following *me?*"

Rethinking the logic of her current cover, she said, "My name is Katryna, but my friends call me ... *Kat.* I work at the Israeli Embassy. And how dare you ask me if I was following *you* – a lady would never." She gave a small pout to avoid any deeper questions, but decided to push him further and try to catch him off guard.

"Would you like to dance?" she asked, recognizing the uncomfortable look from before.

Pantera readjusted again. "Sure, after you."

She took his hand leading him to the ballroom dance floor.

Pantera's grandmother entered his mind. *Yes grandma, waltzing is important. Sorry for all the shit I gave you about those lessons.*

They positioned themselves with the appropriate posture and frame.

"I'm not very good. Let me apologize now if I step on your toes," he said sheepishly.

She looked down at her feet then back into his eyes. *Navy boy is humble. How adorable.*

CHAPTER 17

Around the room stood four shadow warriors in three different locations watching the two cats dance. Grit and Cracker stood together.

"I told that knucklehead to stay away from these women," Grit snapped, creasing his brow.

"You know that just made him hornier. You should've bought him a piece of ass before coming to this thing. Not that it would've helped against *her feminine wiles.*" Cracker shot Grit a sideways look.

"At least I gave him the warning."

"Do you know who she is?" Cracker put his glass down on the table and readjusted for a better view.

"Of course, we ran into her last year. Name's ... *Kat, Israeli.* Did you catch the thigh piece?"

"Saw that earlier. Didn't Mossad discontinue those?"

"They did," Grit said, stonefaced.

"So she is second, maybe third generation, huh?"

"That's what I'm thinking. Look, did you see that move?" Grit's eyes flickered.

"With the card? Yeah. Her backup plan if she doesn't snag him tonight." Cracker's laser focus could have picked up Helen of Troy, also known as the queen of hearts, in a game of Three-card Monte.

"Two silent cats, this could be a deadly dance to remember." Grit held his wrist behind his back rocking just slightly up on his toes and back. "Like an E ticket ride at Disneyland."

"I wouldn't worry. We can keep him from going back to her place tonight for the ride of his life – then end up *accidentally* dead," Cracker said, using air quotes. "Definitely easier than filling out all that damn paperwork the UN requires."

"True. Keep your eye on him. I have to go see a man about a horse." Grit faded into the crowd.

* * *

It was approaching midnight as the two cats waltzed around the ballroom not unlike a scene from *Beauty and the Beast*, both oblivious to their environment.

"I could use a drink," she whispered in his ear.

"Me too." He held her hand formally, as they left the dance floor.

They both snatched a champagne flute from a floating server and headed to the outdoor balcony. The fireworks kicked off in time with the first gong of the big clock in the piazza. The sound and light reverberated throughout the embassy as the smell from the wall of Gardenias filled the air.

Here goes ... remember, go 90% ... let her come the other 10%. Pantera leaned in, staring into Kat's eyes stopping just before touching her lips.

The farm boy wants to kiss me. Oh, what the hell, what have I got to lose? At least he never tried to grab my ass. I've definitely done more with less. Kat closed her eyes and leaned up to accept the moist lips of the imposing figure's gesture.

The clock tower in the background continued to ring its mandatory twelve bells and the fireworks exploded over the water in the piazza, creating two light shows with equal intensity.

Pantera decided drowning with her was far better than death of embarrassment. Their lips met lightly and the kiss lasted long enough to give them both pause. Pantera wasn't breathing and the thought crossed his mind that he had just stuck his toe in the water to see if it was cold.

She is so hot! Hope she lives close by.

After a couple hours of talking on mundane topics Pantera's fear lessened when through the fog of visualizing himself drowning in her breasts, he caught a word escape her lips – *Parkour.*

"What? Parkour?" *She does Parkour?*

"Yes. Ever heard of it?" she said, wondering if he was still engaged in the conversation.

There it was. The moment when Pantera's drowning feeling, pit in his stomach and over-whelming desire to flee fully disappeared, now replaced by a sensation elsewhere.

"In a magazine," he replied, hiding his enthusiasm, "Do you know of a place to go? I'd like to try it."

Kat's earpiece beckoned. *"Alyn David. Heshegreyr 'ezeb at hay-erv'e. Hepret lebyethevn 'ekesheyv hegy' lemseqnh. Lhezver lebseys."* [The Ambassador has left the event. Security detail has now concluded. Return to base.]

She trained her dark blue eyes on his lighter blue eyes, and said, "I really have to go."

"Gosh lil' lady, I was hoping we could move this par-tee back to your place."

Look buddy, try pulling that shit on me and you WILL wake up on the wrong side of the bed with a glass slipper permanently stuck up your ass. Damn frat-boy with a hokey Southern charm. "Not tonight. Sorry." She smiled with a sense of disappointment behind her teeth at his frat-boy interest. "Maybe we will meet again."

Crap. No poontang. "Can I get your number?" he said, scrambling.

Her demeanor changed to cold and professional. "No."

"Well, um, Happy New Year ... *Kat.*" *Guess the kiss didn't go as well as I thought.* He stiffened up, took her hand and kissed it. *"Heta nelteqy merh akhera."* [Until we meet again.]

Fat chance you adorable dunderhead. Wait until Alona hears about this.

CHAPTER 18

The train ride back to the base was quiet. For over an hour five men sat on the ItaliaRail still reeling from the excitement of the embassy ball and the near death experience of their newest member.

Pantera thought about his first two days in Italy. He begrudgingly attended his first formal event, kissed the most beautiful woman he had ever seen, and got dumped by the same woman in the same night. If he died tomorrow, he would take these two days in Italy over two years in America.

Welcome to Italy! He smiled to himself as he stared out the window into the darkness.

Grit moved up behind Pantera as Cracker took a seat across the aisle. "We need to have a li'l chat," Grit said in his low Tennessee accent.

"I know Gunny, I know. I drank too much. I'm sorry." He bowed his head.

Grit smiled at Cracker. "If you think that was drinking too much, boy have you got some learning ahead of you. It wasn't the drinking. It was the woman."

"The woman? Are you kidding me? You said to stay away from *dangerous* women. That's what I did." Pantera ran his hands over his new high and tight haircut.

"You think *that* woman wasn't dangerous?" Grit rubbed his palms together.

"Oh hell no, she was just some cute Arabic chick who works in some cube at the Israeli Embassy."

"I have to ask. What do you know about embassies?" A grin walked across Cracker's face.

"Ah, nothing," Pantera said, with a shrug.

"Good. Learning is about to commence," Grit said, re-adjusting in his seat.

"Embassies are foreign soil. Right? Meaning the soil IS that country," Cracker started.

"Yeah." Pantera nodded.

"From a purely logical perspective, is it possible a non-Israeli would work in an Israeli Embassy? Let's try something equally logical and closer to home. Would the U.S. Government allow non-Americans to work in an American Embassy?" Grit marched the lesson forward.

"If you're asking, then I will say – 'no'."

"Good answer. She told you she was what?" Grit turned his ear toward Pantera but kept his eyes on him.

"She just said she works at the Israeli Embassy. I *assumed* she wasn't Israeli." Pantera didn't understand where Grit was going with the conversation.

"Now, we're in agreement. She is Israeli ... who also speaks Arabic." Cracker raised and lowered his head slowly in an attempt to get Pantera to follow.

"Yeah, so what, she's an Israeli secretary who speaks Arabic. Big deal."

"Here comes the fun part. Stay with me now. What you apparently didn't see was the .32 calibre Beretta 70 on the inside of her thigh." Grit gave a small visual gesture.

"I was trying to be a gentleman. You know, for country and all. So she's a *well-armed* secretary." Pantera was growing impatient.

Cracker jumped in. "Beretta 70s were discontinued as the preferred weapon issued to Mossad officers about a decade ago. She's not only Mossad. She's the daughter, or sister, of a Mossad agent. Weapons are a heritage thing with them. And another point, on the inside of her thigh, without walking like it's there, is an enormously difficult skill. Try it some time. A skill, I might add, she pulls off perfectly."

Pantera took in a breath. "You're telling me … this *Kat-woman* is possibly a well-trained, legacy, Mossad officer?"

"Yes." Grit nodded with a sigh. "And even more disturbing, in addition to being an extremely beautiful woman, she is probably much more than a simple security officer at the embassy. My friend, you had a near-death experience. Congratulations and welcome to Italy." Grit slapped Pantera on the back then bounced back against his seat.

"Ex—cel—lent! I danced with a hot Mossad agent," he said, bobbing in his seat and rotating his arms like a belly dancer as the other members watched. "How cool is that?!" His fear of the Mossad gripped him then the thought of *The Activity* took hold. *Aww shit, I danced with and kissed a Mossad agent.*

Cracker dropped his head into his hands and Grit crossed his arms, closed his eyes and shook his head.

Pantera realized his faux pas and changed his behavior. "Just kidding. I get it. I get it."

"Look in your pocket." Grit pointed to Pantera's jacket.

Pantera reached into his pocket and found a card. "Holy crap, who put that there?"

It was an Israeli Embassy business card, but with no name on it. On the back written in Arabic:

> It was a pleasure to meet you,
> Alyn Katryna David – 55587329.

* * *

Back at the barracks, Pantera stretched out on his bunk. A twinge of pain shot through his body. It was a good pain as conflicting thoughts rushed into his mind.

I'm gonna do that hot Israeli chick after all. Is she friend or foe? If foe, can I kill a hot chick? Whatta waste. Can I do her and then kill her? If friend, should I do her and ask her to help me?

Pantera's physical desire for Kat played ping-pong with the deep psychological hurdles of his assignment – while trying not to get too wrapped up in the superficialities of his cover. His last thought before sleep overcame him, *Mmmm ... Kat.*

CHAPTER 19

Kat sat quietly at her desk working studiously on the mind-numbing paperwork required to keep her cover intact. Her concentration wandered as a range of emotions entered her head replaying the conversations she had with the American. One minute he was a silly superficial frat-boy, the next, he would come up with some deeply coherent philosophical statement. She surprised even herself by giving him her number without being asked, wondering if he would indeed call her – then hoped he wouldn't.

Nyssa or Pantera? Nyssa is a known quality and is readily available. Maybe Nyssa will come to Rome? But this ... this attraction to Pantera ... what is this?

Kat raised her eyes at the sound of someone shuffling down the hall. She saw the back of a man walking down the corridor and bristled as recognition of someone from her past took hold.

Wait one minute. That looked just like a thinner version of ... nah ... it couldn't be him. It just couldn't be.

She refused to indulge in the past and continued her work. A few moments later, she was interrupted with the familiar soft-spoken voice of her boss, Michoel. He beckoned her over the intercom.

"*Alyn, yesh lek deqh?*" [Alyn, do you have a minute?]

"*Beth, lheyvet tesvedq b.*" [Sure, be right in.]

She walked into Michoel's office to find *him* sitting there. *Him*, also known as, Avner Hershfeld, currently a Senior Intelligence Analyst for Aman, Israeli Directorate of Military Intelligence (*Agaf ha-Modi'in*). He was Kat's handler on her second worst assignment – behind the assignment where she lost her brother, Adamm. Avner ran from his post, abandoned her during a hell-on-earth firefight, and left her for dead in a hostile country. He was lucky to be alive and if Kat had her way, not for very much longer.

Kat's heart echoed in her ears, her pupils dilated and the muscles in her jaw tightened. In an effort to produce a louder than usual "click", she unsheathed her polycarbonate blade. The sound reverberated in Michoel's dark hollowed office. She mouthed the exact words uttered the moment she realized Avner betrayed her.

Pain, more pain, then if you're lucky, maybe death – nobody will miss you.

Michoel made a quick sound and she stopped. Avner squealed running to the opposite side of the office. Kat looked at both men with rage and distain. This scar, born of betrayal, stung her very soul.

Through clenched teeth she pointed the blade at Avner while looking at Michoel, and said, "Why?! Why is this fuckin' *hatichat harah* [piece of shit] who isn't worth his skin on the black market ... here?"

Avner could do nothing but hang his head in shame.

"Miss David. Please. Put your partner away and sit down. Please." Michoel waved them both to chairs in front of his desk. "I think you will want to hear what he has to say."

"Coming from him, I'm pretty sure I won't," she said, sheathing her blade and pulling the empty chair to the side to face Avner as steam emanated from every pore in her body.

"Speak, *partzuf tahat*." [Ass-face.]

Avner knew this discussion was going to be difficult, but how difficult he could not have imagined. He came from a wealthy influential family giving him privileges not normally afforded to others. Given the position as Kat's handler without the necessary experience of being able to predict a target's actions, Avner failed to create an end strategy – a skill handlers in the field live and die by.

Kat was rescued, given a new handler, and the assignment was completed successfully. After the major catastrophe with Kat's assignment Avner was immediately removed from Mossad and transferred to a desk with Aman. He did consider himself lucky to be alive, until now.

I guess I could cut you a small break. Your incompetence got me this post. I will never tell you that though.

"Good Morning, Miss David." Avner avoided making eye contact with her.

She crossed her arms, still seething and said nothing.

"Six months ago, we had a … um … breach of sorts. The extent of this unfortunate breach is still not yet known. What we do know is … a file containing a list of female Mossad agents was accessed through the Aman system. In the last three months three Katsa females have been killed. The most recent, Raz Klein, a Katsa Jumper assigned to Thailand. We have no leads as to who breached our security, but we believe the two events are linked. This person has been code named: *Katsa Killer.*"

Raz? She replaced Nyssa in Bangkok. Whatthefuck? It could have been Nyssa.

Michoel asked, cocking his head, "Let me guess, the breach was made from within your department at Aman?"

With hands clenched in front of his crotch Avner responded in defense, "It wasn't connected to me!"

"*Lech timkor kerach!*" [Go sell ice!] Kat couldn't help yelling at Avner.

Michoel's gaze on Avner was cold. "That is yet to be determined. Do you know anything else?"

Avner shook his head. "No."

"Thank you Avner, I can take it from here," Michoel said, in a slow, calm voice as he adjusted his cuff links.

The emotionally demoralized man stood up and without looking at Kat, he nodded at Michoel and left the office.

"You could've been a bit more congenial." He raised an eyebrow at Kat.

"Congenial? Absolutely not. I will never forget what he did to me. I will skin his loafer-wearing ass one day."

"I don't like the coward either and I'm not sympathizing with the guy, but he has been blacklisted from Mossad and holds no security clearance at Aman. He's lucky to still be employed. I honestly thought they would have sent him to a Kibbutz. Forget him. Didn't you do an assignment with Raz?"

Kat rubbed her hands and slowly inhaled to get control over her adrenaline level and slow her pulse. The memories caused her pain. She remembered the fun they had during a short but intense time in Thailand not so long ago.

"Yes, we did a catch and render for the Americans. Caught the bastard in Tokyo and transferred him to the *Udon Thani* CIA black site. That was a wild time. Raz replaced Nyssa, you know. Wait one second here, Michoel. Are you telling me *my name* could be on that list too?" Kat's eyes went wide.

"We would be stupid to ignore that possibility." Michoel shrugged. "You were also a Katsa Jumper. I sent a message to Hannah Pasternack, asking for help."

"Hannah?" Her mouth remained open pulling her head back.

Michoel nodded. "Didn't you attend university at the same time?"

"Yes? We were language majors together. Why?"

"She is now the Southern European Lead of the Katsa Jumpers with a cover as a professor at your alma mater. Since she was an Asian Katsa Jumper also, we need to know if this has an Asian component, how extensive the breach was, and how it was breached. Go meet with her. I'm hoping the two of you can put some of the pieces of this puzzle together."

And I need to call Nyssa. I need her here ... to protect her.

CHAPTER 20

It was a week since the embassy ball and Pantera was focused on his indoc checklist –similar to what every military person does after arriving at a new command. Simultaneously, he had to make sure his cover was securely anchored as he made subtle inquiries about the ISA office. Pantera walked into Grit's office to get the paperwork to give to the Testing and Evaluation Officer (TEO).

"Have you called her yet?" Grit asked nonchalantly.

"No, hadn't thought about it." Pantera lied, caught off guard.

"Any reason why not?"

"You said she was dangerous and I should stay away, just takin' your advice." He sat down making eye contact with Grit as he thought about the last time he acted as himself instead of how his cover, a mid-level SEAL petty officer, would act. He won't make that mistake again.

"*Carpe diem*, my friend."

"What is that, some type of fish?"

"Seize the day, you Icarus. Don't be so damn intimidated. Are you a fuckin' pussy or what? Now that you know, it's much less dangerous. Knowledge is power, am I right? Besides, if you're going to fly next to the sun, you know." Grit looked up from behind his desk and surveyed the effects his words had on Pantera.

"I don't have wax wings, Gunny." He paused. "You're right, no way is some chick going to intimidate me." Pantera's spine stiffened. He was relieved Grit gave him the go-ahead with Kat. Breaking even an "implied" order in this military group could compromise him.

"You're not going to let the rumor mill control your actions, are you?"

"Rumor mill? What rumor?"

"That you picked up an Italian model, but she was way too hot for you," he said, laughing.

"Huh? That's not true," Pantera said, shaking his head.

"Life's full of lies. Baby-face started the rumor. I thought it was hilarious, all part of the hazing. Welcome to the unit. Now it's time for you to step up to the plate or get off the field."

"Now I know what baptism by fire means. You guys are *such* assholes!" Pantera laughed.

This situation propelled Pantera from the "Fuckin' New Guy" to the go-to-man for, not only medical advice, but long-distance relationship advice – conversations that bordered on comedy given his own "dating" history, if one could call it that.

"Yes we are. Let's be honest. To you she's just another piece of ass. Am I right?" Grit looked up at him from behind a stack of classified reports and slid his glasses farther down his nose.

"Yeah. Maybe. Honestly. I don't know." Pantera admitted.

"Look brother, we're extremely high-speed here. Life in this unit is intense, dangerous, and stressful. Finding someone to spend time with, even superficially, is better than a magazine, Vaseline, and a sock. She could be good spook training for you ... if you think you want to head in that direction. Didn't you say she does *Parkour?*"

Pantera nodded in the affirmative.

"Well, Mister Parkour Champion, I think this is a good place to start," Grit said, staring at his young charge. "Try KISS. Keep It Simple, Stupid. You'll probably get her answering machine anyway."

"Now you're recommending I call her?"

"Yes FG," Grit said, handing Pantera his paperwork. "Go over to building twelve. Ask for SFC Terry Fountain. He'll be your TEO for the rest of your indoc period."

Okay. I, the 'fuckin' genius', can KISS her answering machine. Right after the thought about KISSing an answering machine, Fountain's face entered his mind. *No way. Jack didn't put any Army time in personnel file. Let's just hope Fountain and Grit don't talk, about me. Christ!*

* * *

Pantera walked over to Building 12. It was a cold January day and the wind stung his face and hands as he approached the standard two-plane hangar bay taking in the sight of all the parachute equipment stored in the cavernous building. Planes came and went, creating strong breezes rocking the training dummies hanging from the rafters in badly rigged harnesses covered with vast amounts of ketchup. One dummy hung upside down with half a head. Pantera spotted the first Black Hat he could find and approached.

"Good morning. I'm looking for SFC Fountain?"

The man turned around and Pantera erupted in laughter. "Sergeant First Class Fountain." Pantera shook his head in disbelief. *Oh shit, it's him.* "What brings you to Italy?"

"I'm from Italy. Who are you?"

SFC Terence "Terry" Fountain, a stocky man of average height with dark Italian facial features was chewing tobacco and sporting a chronic smirk. He had been Pantera's Army Airborne school instructor, before he joined the Agency.

Fountain measured Pantera. An expression of acknowledgement came over him. "Marcus Sinclair? You're what, Navy now? Wait just one friggin' minute. I thought you came from Sand Hill at the 198th to Airborne school. Weren't you going to Ranger school? How long has it been, five … six years?"

"About that." Pantera hoped he would remember, but not with that much detail.

"Why are you in the Navy with the *lifeguards*?"

"Long story … how about the abbreviated version?" he said, hopping up to sit on the parachute-packing table.

Fountain nodded, spitting into his Coke can he leaned back against the other side of the same table.

"Grandfather died, transferred from Army to Navy. End of story. What about you?"

"Me? Not so exciting. After Airborne school, I transferred to an instructor position with the Military Free-Fall School at the Yuma Proving Grounds. About a year ago, finally got orders for Camp Darby up near Pisa. If you remember my wife, she's from Milan and I'm from Monopoli so nothing could have made her happier. I get to retire here. And when you get married someday, remember this ... happy wife, happy life."

"If you say so," Marcus said, but thought, *Hell. I'd settle for a nice piece of ass for now.*

"Guess you're here because I'm your TEO. Paperwork?"

"Right here." He handed Fountain his folder. "I was told three weeks. I'm ready."

"Good. Let's review week one. Monday: small calibre handgun range. Tuesday: small calibre handgun range with suppression equipment. Wednesday: large calibre handguns. Thursday: HUMINT. Friday: Naples civilian hospital."

"What kind of schedule is that? Human Intelligence and Hospital?" Pantera scrunched his face.

"Your first day of HUMINT is for reviewing policies and procedures of ISA and how they interact with your unit. The hospital is for keeping your medical skills sharp when not in the field. You're the only medic *and* interrogator so you have to split time. Sorta opposite ends of the spectrum I would say. You can harm and heal – now that's pretty extreme." Fountain nodded giving him a half grin.

Pantera nodded back. *I get to rummage around ISA without raising suspicion. Nice work, Jack.*

"You'll do your high-altitude, high-opening and high-altitude, low opening free fall quals in week two with me. We can discuss that later. Handgun training is over in building six. Enjoy."

Another man came in wearing the same uniform as Fountain, including the black baseball cap with the Military Free Fall Jumpmaster insignia above his rank. "Hey Terry, you have six going up with you today. Hope that's okay," he said, in a subservient tone.

"Frank, this is Sinclair. Petty Officer Sinclair." Fountain pointed from Pantera to Frank and back. "Sinclair, this is SFC Frank Caglione, or 'Cag' for short. Dual meaning. I'm sure you get it." He gave a sideways grin at Pantera then moved from the table to spit into his Coke can. "Hey Cag, remember one of my stories about a guy I had in jump school who purposely FUBAR'd his uniform at every morning inspection so he could go play in that muddy gig-pit? This is *that* guy." He tilted his head toward Pantera.

Pantera smiled cautiously. "You remember that? Damn dude."

Fountain grinned back at Pantera. "What can I say, you're memorable."

Yeah, that's not good, Pantera thought.

CHAPTER 21

Kat was back at her desk on the phone. "Hallo Gretchen, Alyn David from the Rome Embassy. Can you find Nyssa for me?" she said, in a firm Hebrew.

"Certainty, Miss David."

Nearly ten minutes past. Alyn fidgeted in her chair and stared out the window, thinking about how she could convince Nyssa to come to Rome.

Nyssa's voice came on. "Hi Alyn. How are you? What's up?"

"I would like you to come to Rome."

"You would?" she asked, suspicious of the request since Alyn's voice sounded strained. "Why are you asking?"

"It's been a long week. I miss you and I want to see you." *I miss her touch – a touch that satisfies me. Don't give her any hint of the Katsa Killer.*

"It'll have to be after the Presidential elections. I still have a lot of work to do here in Greece. I'll come to Rome in about two weeks."

Two weeks? That's too long. "Are you sure I can't change your mind. I could really use your *friendship*," Kat begged.

Kat couldn't even hint about the urgency of the situation, personally or professionally. She had to let Nyssa come on her own.

"Hey, I've got have a job to do here. Just like you, I love my job and take it just as seriously as you take yours," Nyssa replied with a flare of temper in her Greek-accented Hebrew.

"I did not mean to imply ... I am sorry. I will see you when you get here," Kat said, slowing her speech as she white-knuckled the phone.

The intercom buzzed. "Miss David. You have a call on line 2."

"Nyssa. I have to go. I am really looking forward to seeing you. I miss you."

"I miss you, too. See you soon."

Kat tapped line 2 and disconnected from Nyssa's call.

"This is Alyn David," Kat answered professionally.

"*Achut.* What are you doing?!"

"Alona? Where have you been? I have been trying to call you."

"We've been all over. I met his parents and then we traveled to Amsterdam and Copenhagen. It's been a whirlwind vacation." Alona responded with exuberance. "What about you?"

What about me? Do I tell her I'm vacillating over my feelings for two people? "Look, I cannot talk long, but I met ... a man at the ball." She bit her lip.

"No. Did you *do* him ... in the ambassador's office like I said?" Alona knew it was not out of the realm of possibilities.

Just spit it out, Kat. She's your sister. "Stop it. No, but I let him kiss me," she giggled. "Now I'm waiting to see if he is brave enough to call me."

"So you're thinking about sleeping with Nyssa and dating this guy?"

Damn. I knew it. "I haven't thought that far ahead."

"You never do. That's the problem," Alona said, her tone changed into the big sister voice of reason.

There was a knock at the door.

"Hold on Alona."

"Come in," Kat said, authoritatively.

The doorway opened halfway. "Courier. Envelope for Alyn David," the front office clerk said.

"Alona, I will call you back. Are you guys back in Switzerland?"

"Yes. Call me back. We have lots to talk about."

Kat hung up and signed for the letter. It was a postcard in a diplomatic security sealed envelope.

Bibliothèque de la Sorbonne

2 P.M. – Jeudi

HP

Kat quickly packed up her desk. She walked into Michoel's office, handed him the postcard and envelope, and without saying a word she was gone from the office and the embassy.

Michoel read the postcard, pulled out a lighter from his pocket, lit them both on fire, and let them burn in the metal trash can behind his desk, not wanting to walk to the burn barrel.

Stay safe. He hoped his thoughts would somehow enshroud her.

* * *

Pantera's schedule slowed enough for him to contemplate the decision he had to make: whether or not to call Kat. With the approval from Grit, he decided it was a risk worth taking. The physical component was the main goal, but the professional component would be an added bonus. On his way back to his room, he caught Baby-face in the hallway.

"Just wanted to thank you for starting the rumor about that chick at the ball," he said, poking a finger in Baby-face's chest.

"Anything I can do for a buddy." Baby-face smirked. "All part of the welcome package." He waved and continued down the hall.

Since he was off duty early, Pantera had time to join a basketball game at the gym, but couldn't hit the hoop with a guidance system. He intended to school a couple guys on the rock climbing wall then proceeded to fall off, twice. His SSS (shit, shower & shave), wasn't much better. He slipped in the shower, which gave him a contusion to his right periorbital space – black eye. To end this chain of calamities, he cut his chin while shaving. Pantera grabbed some chow thinking, *I'm a useless mess today. I'll make that hari-kari call after chow.*

Despite being verbally smacked around concerning his injuries during dinner with remarks like: "Two weeks, man, you haven't been here long enough to get injured," and, "Dude, a corpsman can't get hurt more often than his teammates", he continued undeterred letting his buddies have fun at his expense. He finished eating and returned to his room. It had been over a week since he met Kat. *Will she still remember me?*

With the fortitude of a lion and a nervous hand, Pantera grabbed the phone. *Time to KISS that answering machine.*

"Hallo?" A female voice answered.

He waited for the rest of the message causing a long pause.

"Hallo, *chi sta chiamando per favore?*" [Who is calling please?]

Agh. So much for KISSing the answering machine. "Uh ... Hi," he said, his mind teaming with disconnected thoughts. "This is Marcus Sinclair, is Kat there?"

"Yes. This is Kat. I don't know a Marcus Sinclair. Sorry. Goodbye."

"Wait!" Pantera practically yelled. "I'm sorry. I introduced myself as Pantera the other night at the embassy ball." He was fist thumping his leg with his other hand.

There was a pause on the other end of the phone.

Oh my, he actually called me. What stones for an American.

She had prepared herself for him not to call. Now that it had been over a week, she wanted him to sweat for taking so long to build the courage to call her.

"So," Kat said, with obvious irritation in her voice, "Your real name is Marcus Sinclair, is it?" *So I have your name, if that is your name, and a location. Make a wrong move Navy boy. I dare you.*

"Yes. It really is. And I'm sorry for not giving it to you at the ball, but you didn't give me much of a chance," Pantera stammered, hoping the guilt would soften her biting tone.

"That's okay. I will let you off the hook ... *this time*. What can I do for you, Mister Sinclair?"

Or is it what can I do TO you, kitty-kat? I think that was an invitation if I ever heard one. "You mentioned you're familiar with Parkour? Maybe you could show me some Parkour moves – *to start with* – and then ... go to dinner?" he said, remaining humble while sexual entendres banged around in his head.

Kat made no sexual invitation, only in Pantera's typical twenty-something mind.

"Parkour, then dinner, hmm." Nyssa's loving face jumped into Kat's head. "I'm not very good. Maybe you can teach me?"

Pantera spotted the coy act immediately. *Yeah right. Mossad Kat-girl can't Parkour. This girl's hilarious.* "I'm not very good either, ya know. Magazines and all. Let's just have some fun. Like a jungle gym – two cats in the jungle, right?"

I will give you 'two cats in a jungle' ... I have claws, just keep playing with me. "Okay Navy boy. Let's go play in the jungle then you can buy me dinner. Be prepared. I can eat as much as any man," Kat said, fighting the visage of the last man she dated. A sour taste dried her mouth.

Navy boy? What the hell. Oh little kitty, you need a spanking. "Why thank you Miss David. I look forward to seeing you," Pantera replied, in a formal manner.

They agreed on Saturday. She gave him the address of the Parkour Centre and he gave her the phone number to his room. The trap was set, but who was hunting whom.

CHAPTER 22

By the time Kat reached the entryway of the Sorbonne University Library it was 1:45 p.m. and she had already circled the buildings twice. The dark domed administration building, standing resolute over the quad for over seven hundred years, gave a sense of fear and warmth. Kat remembered the words of her proctor on orientation day, "You stand in the footsteps of Marie Curie, first female professor and Nobel Prize winner in both physics and chemistry; Dr. Ruth Westheimer; and Princess Caroline of Monaco." Her mind flooded with memories – four long years, many alcohol-induced fuzzy nights, and an earth-shattering, beyond-stressful first relationship for a young academic ingénue. Her first male relationship was so emotionally destructive it would have turned even the strongest woman homosexual. The academic workload was not too difficult coupled with the help of several professors who facilitated an angry young girl's plight through the murky waters of self-discovery, self-realization, and self-determination made those memories, by and large, enjoyable. She smiled to herself. It was like returning to an ugly, old, warm coat.

What a different world I live in now.

She turned the corner and walked through the library into the pristine white stone inner courtyard. Hannah was sitting on a bench – her nose buried in a book. Hannah Pasternak, a short, wider-than-normal woman with brown hair, brown eyes, and thick

Coke bottle glasses. She would never be mistaken for a spy, much less the Head of the Southern European Katsa Jumper group.

Kat sat down startling Hannah.

"Oh! Why do you always do that?!" Hannah regained her composure. "Master Kat-sa, how are you?" Hannah gave Kat a big welcoming hug and a two-cheek kiss.

"Wow. Still the same ol'Hannah. Geekiest of the geeks. A professor now, good for you. So, whatcha know?" Kat flipped the book up to read the title.

"You mean the security breach? Not much. Just female agents were accessed. It's very weird. No one knows which list of females, or how many. There are no suspects in the first two assassination cases. The third one, in Thailand, a dark-skinned woman, dressed in black, was seen leaving the scene."

"This is a first witness account of the suspect? And that's it?"

"Yeah. There are no other commonalities with the three officers. However, Raz was a Katsa assigned the kill order for one of the Libyan intelligence officers responsible for Flight 103 – the Lockerbie bombing. Something I'm sure you know, but in case you didn't, we struck back in retaliation for the loss of a senior Shin Bet officer who was the actual target on the flight. Your Dad issued both kill orders."

"Of course, I had the other kill order," Kat said, pushing Hannah's hair behind her ear.

"Stop, please." Hannah slapped Kat's hand. "You have to admit." Hannah adjusted her glasses. "It was fun watching the Americans think the bombing was about them. Egomaniacs ... the lot of them. There was this interesting other thing though." Hannah dove into the bag on her lap. "This one unique piece of information I couldn't ..."

A small flash of light near the clock beneath the dome of the administration building caught Kat's attention as the sound of a golf ball hitting a watermelon hit her ears. She looked back at Hannah.

"HANNAH!" she yelled, turning to see a small bead of blood creeping down the side of Hannah's face as her body slumped over.

Kat caught Hannah in mid fall then turned her to use as a shield. Two more shots hit Hannah in the back.

Mother-pus-bucket!

Kat pinpointed the exact location of the shooter. She dropped Hannah's limp body to the ground and jumped into the alcove as a bullet ricocheted off the bench.

A man walked out of the library directly in the line of fire. There was no time to get his attention. Struck in the neck he dropped to the ground grabbing his red bubbling throat. Dark blood squirted over his face and chest, his face frozen in breathless fear.

Kat looked down at the man then up to the dome. *Shakli b'tahat! Hunting me? How dare you. I will eat you for breakfast.*

The man's bright red arterial blood continued to pulse out onto the pristine white concrete. The spurting lessened with the slowing of his heart. His eyes fixed forward. Kat knew that shot was meant for her as she looked around. No one in the quad had noticed the bodies lying dead on the ground.

A bomb could go off in this place and no one would notice ... geeks.

Kat sprang to the alcove of the doorway to the library and peeked around the corner. The barrel of the rifle was gone. There was no way for her to reach the shooter from within the quad. She ran through the library stopping at a pay phone in the library to dial a number, then left the phone off the hook. There was only one roof access, she knew it well. She exited on to Rue de la Sorbonne, headed south, and circled around to the back of the administration building.

You helped this woman kill Hannah, Avner. You hatichat harah! I'm coming for you.

Kat spotted the guitar-case-carrying black-clad figure running across the street from the roof access fifty meters away. The figure was heading east entering Place de la Sorbonne, a fountain centered street with mostly small cafes on either side. Kat was closing the distance as she pulled her suppressed Beretta upon reaching *Brasserie Les Patios* and *Café Pizzeria* firing twice, missing twice. Failure and the cold weather stung her face.

That's right bitch. I'm coming for you with a bag full of pain.

Kat's shots were close enough to get the shooter to turn, their eyes met. She could see the surprise on the shooter's face.

Good. Now you know who is going to kill you. Hatichat hara mizdayen batachat!

The shooter headed south on Boulevard Saint Michel. Kat was just getting warmed up when she pulled off her boot heels. They were now well-formed running boots. Her pace increased. Kat was now twenty meters behind the target and fired two more times, more for psychological effect than target acquisition. The bullets found an old, dying Vespa. The scooter was now dead. She could see the shooter slowing.

You are all mine. Fils de pute!

When Kat entered the fountain-centered roundabout at the intersection of Place Edmond Rostand and Rue di Medicis, the shooter was gone.

"*Harah*," she said, shaking her head as she stopped in the middle of the street.

Across the street, a parked police car caught her attention where two police officers were watching something. She followed their gaze and spotted the shooter entering *Le Jardin du Luxembourg*. Kat was back on her trail.

One of the police officers spotted Kat with a suppressed weapon in her hand. He yelled for her to stop.

Sorry guys, I don't have time to explain all this to you. Go have a croissant.

In a full sprint toward the car Kat fired a shot just to the right of the driver's side police officer blowing out the window. He ducked back into the car for cover. She jumped up and slid across the hood rotating her body to kick the passenger door shut. The passenger side police officer was standing inside the open door. His body and head slammed back against the car knocking him out leaving blood dripping from the doorframe.

The shooter headed north toward *Luxembourg Palace*, running past the *Fontaine Medicis*. Kat knew there was a parking lot right around the corner on the north end of the palace.

So that is your get-a-way location, dirt-bag. Over my dead body!

Kat ran with every ounce of strength she had left, reaching the corner of the palace. She stopped, knowing better than to come bulldozing around a corner. Pieces of concrete and dust flew all around her when three bullets hit the corner. She jumped out shooting at the first glint of metal she saw then did a forward roll crossing the path to the other side of the archway leading to the parking lot.

A male voice yelled in pain.

"One down," Kat whispered to herself.

Two shots whooshed by her head and the tree behind her splintered. She spotted a second shooter, took aim, and hit him in the leg.

Two down.

Another shot hit the concrete stanchion above her head.

What the ... that wasn't a handgun. That was a rifle.

Kat peeked out from the corner of the stanchion. She spotted the black-clad figure lying prone on top of a car with a rifle in a fixed tripod position – the guitar case thrown to the ground. The shooter took another shot demolishing a big block of concrete next to Kat's ear. A piece of concrete hit her in the head, disorienting her as blood from the cut dripped into her left eye, her dominate.

This is for Hannah.

Kat jumped out from behind her cover and emptied her clip into the general area of the shooter. Car windows were blown out and car alarms blared. The smell of gunpowder filled the air. She put the empty clip in her pocket and slipped another into her gun. The shooter jumped down from the roof of the car ducking between cars as lead, glass, and plastic sprayed the area. All three jumped into a car and raced out of the parking lot.

Damn. Damn!

She emptied her clip firing at the car's tires with heightened intensity. The trio was gone. Sounds of yelling came from behind her. The police she plowed through only seconds before brought friends. Kat sheathed her weapon and headed out the northern gate, the same direction as the shooter and her crew. She spotted an unlocked car as she walked quickly north up Rue de Tournon. Within two minutes she had the car running and was driving back toward the university courtyard.

Oh Hannah. I am so sorry.

Kat returned to the Sorbonne quad to find police, ambulances, and news trucks all over the school. She wanted to say good-bye to one of her best friends. Hannah was a person who Kat respected and craved respect from. She would never know who or what, Kat had become – a thought that weighed heavily on her as she traveled back to Rome.

Nulla è una realtà assoluta, tutto è permesso. Requiescat in pace, Hannah.

CHAPTER 23

Pantera's week was *mostly* consumed with his pursuit of the mole, trained on ISA: the people, the building, and the stories.

I wonder how big Kat's areolas are? Didn't that Iranian instructor at Peary say Arabic women's nipples were like kumquats? A single laugh tried to escape, but he caught it in his throat.

The testosterone-burdened twenty-something was laden with visualizations of Kat naked as his mind wandered briefly while walking around an ISA intelligence analyst's apartment at 2:30 a.m.

By Friday afternoon, the harassment was in full effect. Not only did every member of the platoon know about Pantera's upcoming date, but members from other platoons were participating. Some congratulated "the guy who picked up an Italian model at an embassy party in Rome" and others laid bets openly against him in the "pussy pool." It didn't matter to Pantera if they thought Kat was a model, a secretary, or super-secret Mossad agent – he did his best to convince everyone he was going to score a home run. Unfortunately, he couldn't seem to convince himself.

Accustomed to intense pressure and living by the motto – *pressure turns coal into diamonds* – he tried to keep focus, Kat was just another acquisition to be conquered avoiding the thought about what he would do after he slept with her. *Get on, get in, get off ... then flee like a male praying mantis.* He was leaving the dining hall when he noticed Grit filling his tray.

"Hey Gunny, do you have a minute?"

"Sure, I'll meet you at the Chiefs' table." Grit noticed the look of consternation on Pantera's face.

A career Marine, Grit faced a number of responsibilities that fell outside the standard job description – sometimes functioning as big brother, and at other times, as baby-sitter. Fifteen years as a Marine Reconnaissance Sergeant and on his third tour with this task force Grit was uniquely qualified to handle a whole host of situations.

"You want to discuss the *Kat* situation." Grit sat back in his chair with a pile of spaghetti and meatballs in front of him.

"Yeah. How did you know she was Mossad?" Pantera asked, cocking his head.

"When women wear cocktail dresses while sitting down, the dress rides up. If positioned correctly you can look up their dress ... *to search for weapons*, you horn-dog. It's a skill like any other," he said, as he stabbed a meatball on his plate.

"That's creepy." Pantera wrinkled his nose.

"Where you come from my young friend, there're no women to worry about. Professionally, domestic special operations teams don't combat women; and personally, American women are docile and complacent. Over here in the big world, the 'old' world, women are a hundred times more dangerous than men. Beautiful women like Kat are a hundred times more dangerous than that." He pointed the meatball at Pantera then shoved it in his mouth.

"Please. She couldn't possibly be all that bad ass," he said, leaning back crossing his arms.

Grit's spontaneous bout of laugher caused him to nearly choke. "Let me tell you a little story. About ten years ago, we're hunting this Mossad dude who went rogue – real slippery bastard. Finally found him ... dead ... with his cock in his mouth."

"No friggin' way. Who did him?" Pantera sat up, eyes wide.

"Story came back, his niece. Turns out, he was a pedophile who molested her, a couple other nieces, and friends of the family's daughters. A real piece of work this one. When she was a teenager she found him, got him all turned on and then ... cut off his raging boner." Grit gave a slicing motion above his crotch. "He bled out in seconds."

"What happened to her?"

"No one knows. Disappeared like a puff of smoke. He was just the first. Her reputation in the Middle East, Northern Africa, and Balkans is mythical. They call her *Hash-sha-sheen*. The term is old Aramaic, meaning: *Master Assassin*. If that was her as a teenager … dude." He rolled his eyes and shook his head. "I can only imagine what she's like today." He finished the first of three glasses of orange juice.

"That's great, I love it. Sure would be cool to meet her." He nodded with a smirk.

Grit noticed stars in Pantera eyes. "You're not getting the moral of the story, HB. Every woman you come across could be *that woman*. It's called a *honey-trap* and as horny as you are, you'll never see it coming. That's why I stay out of the spook world. My bad guys are men. Kill them, go home to my wife and kids," he said, spinning spaghetti around his fork supported with his spoon.

"You think Kat is going to honey-trap this Horny Bastard?" Pantera wiggled his eyebrows pointing to himself.

"What do *you* think?

Pantera frowned. "Maybe."

"Like I told you, knowledge is power. Knowledge strengthens foresight my friend. Best to die with your eyes wide open." Grit shrugged.

"Yeah, but if she wants access to this unit, then it sounds plausible to use me."

"Straight up brother, my wife is the most beautiful woman I have ever seen and better in every way than any officer's wife in any military. Last year I saw that *Kat-chick* for the first time. From experience, I can tell you, beautiful women always come with baggage. A beautiful woman with baggage, who is Mossad, who is the daughter or sister of Mossad, that my friend … is a perfect storm just waiting to be unleashed on some poor schmuck. She has the three A's that destroy normal men – she's academic, attractive, and athletic. Simply put in Kat's case ... *dazzling and deadly.*" Grit looked directly at Pantera. *Could Pantera survive a black widow attack?*

"I'll agree with you. The Mossad thing bothers me, a little, but come on, she's still a chick." He offered a half-hearted grin uncomfortably adjusting in his seat.

"Your file says you're off-the-chart smart with no empathy – typical interrogator type. That right there is what'll probably keep you breathing. If she can't get into your head through your heartstrings, she'll go through your penis." He pointed to Pantera's crotch with another meatball at the end of his fork.

"Now that is something to think about." Pantera grinned as the pictorial flashed in his head.

"If you do sleep with her, play defense – play Super Bowl level defense. You're in the big leagues now and they play for keeps."

"Got it. No allowing her on top." Pantera laughed nervously as he got up.

"Good luck. I bet against you by the way. It's five to one against. Sorry." Grit turned his attention to his plate. Not knowing if he could have made it any clearer to Pantera, he thought, *this is going to have a fantastic storybook ending ... or blow up like a nuclear bomb. How do you tell a horny young man who just wants to have an unemotional, sexual fling with a non-prudish, international woman that his infatuation is with a second-generation Mossad agent, prettier than a Victoria's Secret model, and quite possibly, could rip though his unit cover faster than a hot Miyabi knife in warm butter.*

"Thanks Gunny. You've definitely given me something to think about," he said, getting up and rubbing his neck.

Pantera walked outside staring across the grinder at the security fences to the airport and crossed over to the barracks. The unit's facilities were located in the northwest corner of the Naples airport property under heavy security. He replayed the conversation back in his head, over and over. After all, he was a logical thinker capable of remembering the tiniest detail and arriving at the best solution for any situation.

But Kat? Pleeease. This is pre-date panic, sexual cannibalism, my ass. Once I show her what I can do, she'll drag me to her place and ravage me ... with a dagger and garrote.

The first floor of the unit's main building housed the administration office, platoon offices, departmental offices, and the dispensary – on the second was the barracks.

Where's Bullseye? Need to score some inside info.

Pantera walked into the common room – passing several team members playing pool, Ping-Pong, or video games as a way of relieving their stress – to get to the TV room.

During the week, the common room had the effervescent smell of mothballs thanks to camouflage fatigues. On the weekends, the room smelled like a Turkish whorehouse with a horrible barrage of perfumes and colognes when the room became the starting line before a night on the town, since females were not allowed in the barracks.

Pantera made his way to the TV room knowing his roommate wouldn't be playing any games.

The TV room was more like an international movie theatre. There were about thirty chairs, padded and reasonably comfortable – sometimes even comfortable enough to nap in – with a large screen TV playing mostly European and Arabic shows due to the international demographic of the unit. Tonight, it was a live broadcast of Al Jazeera News. He scanned the TV room spotting his roommate, made eye contact with a slight head-tilt, turned around, and left the room.

A familiar silhouette emerged behind him. Friedrich von Herbst – also known as "Fred", or by his unit call sign, "Bullseye" – five foot eight and two hundred and two pounds with only six percent body fat. He was the second platoon sniper. The Johannesburg native had a reasonably normal upbringing. His father was a civilian cook employed by the South African military and his mother was a housekeeper for several wealthy property owners. Access to the military base gave him the opportunity to spend thousands of hours at the various ranges, all before the age of sixteen. The long-distance range was the most inviting. After enlisting at sixteen, Bullseye became the record holder for the highest number of perfect shots for time in the South African Special Forces Brigade. However, Bullseye was not a touchy-feely kind of guy and hardly ever spoke.

"You're the range master for building six, right?"

Bullseye nodded.

"I have handguns next week. Could you hook me up with a couple Walthers and a Glock or two?"

Bullseye nodded.

Wouldn't he be fun interrogating? The thought gave Pantera a chuckle. "Just out of curiosity, what happened to the last platoon interrogator?"

Bullseye gave the *hanging* symbol.

"Died? Just a little more info big guy, died of what? Heart disease?" He rubbed his forehead.

"Freak motorcycle accident."

"Why *freak*?" Pantera was now thoroughly intrigued.

"He didn't know how to ride a motorcycle." Bullseye raised his arms with palms up and a shrug.

"Whoops." Pantera cringed. *Maybe he was also CIA and poked around too closely. Why didn't Jack tell me about this?*

Bullseye signed. "Package. Room."

Pantera was getting better at communicating with Bullseye through sign language. Pantera nodded and left.

He entered the standard two-man dorm room throwing his keys down on the desk. The room had two of everything: twin beds, bookracks, desks, and lockers for personal gear. Everything was made of wood or laminated particleboard. The room was immaculate, not a speck of sand or dust could be found. A large yellow envelope on the desk caught his attention.

Addressed from ISA, he opened it. It was his alias package for the hospital ... among other things.

Just a simple Navy Corpsman. Keep the cover ... keep your life.

CHAPTER 24

"... and then I took the car I stole straight to the airport. There was nothing more I could do." Kat tilted her head and stared back at Michoel from across his desk.

"Same description, huh? Damn. You said she was about to give you a unique piece of info, where is it?" He rubbed his closed mouth with one hand placing his glasses on his head with the other.

"Yeah, she was digging for it when she was shot. It became a shitstorm after that. What I do know ... they were Middle Eastern, had significant tradecraft, and set up an impenetrable defensive barrier against me. Me! Of all people."

"That's saying something. No bullets from the tree?"

"Shattered, plus the police were on my heels." Kat's frustration echoed in her restless legs.

The intercom buzzed. "Mister Bergmann. You have a call on line one."

He motioned for Kat to stay seated.

"Michoel Bergmann." Michoel listened intently. "Did you confirm? So this now makes five? Can we assist in any way?" Michoel looked away from Kat. "We are always ready, sir. Please keep us looped in. Good-bye." Michoel slowly hung up the phone.

"Alyn," he said, looking beyond her then back at her.

He never calls me by Alyn. Five what?

"That was your Director. Nyssa was killed an hour ago. She is now the fifth Katsa." Michoel laid his elbows on the desk and steepled his fingers as he leaned his forehead against his hands. "I am so sorry. I know what she meant to you."

Kat could not believe her ears. If words were a knife, that knife just sliced through Kat's heart, as well as their future together. The emotion was so over-whelming she sat speechless. She bent over in visible pain as she put her head in her shaking hands.

Why are the people closest to me being killed? First, my brother Adamm, in Kosovo. Now Raz, Hannah, Nyssa and three others from this Katsa Killer bitch. People die at my hand, not the other way around, her mind yelled.

"Go home. You will get this woman," Michoel said, trying to be supportive.

Kat nodded, getting up gradually. Eyes filled, she walked out letting a mind numbing trance envelope her.

* * *

Pantera sat behind a fragrant trash dumpster in an alley at two in the morning looking like a homeless man. Since his arrival in Naples, he spent every other night searching the industrial area for safe sites to call his handler from. With ISA's capability of tracking unique electronic signatures, he knew staying on the phone for very long was hazardous. He pulled out the ugly bag that was home to the satellite phone with scrambler box attached.

"You've got about fifteen minutes before they sweep again," Jack said. The familiar echo of the closed metal office could be heard through the phone. "How are you progressing?"

"I've spent the last couple weeks researching. The castle is buttoned up pretty good, but stories are starting to flow," Pantera said, watching a rat run across the alley. "Next week I should get the keys to the castle and start my pursuit of *Benedict*. What do you know about my predecessor?"

"He wasn't American. British, I think. Not much else."

"Could have been on the same path. Died in a motorcycle accident, but didn't know how to ride." He flicked a cockroach away as it approached his pant leg.

"Get me his details. I'll reach across the pond to see if I can get more. Good work."

"Roger that. Out."

* * *

Kat's walk to her apartment was long and torturous. Minutes felt like days. Her head swirled with memories of Nyssa. Her body ached for the touch of Nyssa's silky hands and satin lips. She unlocked the door and heard the phone.

"Hallo, *chi sta chiamando per favore?*" she answered.

"*Achut.* What's wrong?" Alona asked, surprised by Kat's somber tone.

"Nyssa is dead." She threw her purse down and fell on the loveseat in a fetal position.

"Oh no! I am so, so sorry. Accident?"

"No," she said through clenched teeth, the pain morphing to anger, "but I have a damn good idea of who it was."

"Slow down. Taking out one of you is very difficult. Please, please be careful," Alona cautioned.

Alona was Kat's confidante and biggest fan. She knew Kat's abilities better than anyone, but also knew when something was in her paw, nothing would stop her. Absolutely nothing.

"Not one. FIVE. Five of us!" she blurted out, tears streaming down her face.

"No way. What the hell? Who can do that?"

Alona's surprise caused Kat to rethink the seriousness of the situation. It was considered luck when one Katsa was assassinated, but no one has ever had the skills or financial backing to take out five.

"Breach at Aman. Remember the handler you saved me from? His department."

"Oh—my—gawd. Seriously. He's still alive?" Alona asked, inhaling loud enough to cause static over the phone.

Kat could hear her sister plop down into her chair.

"Not for long. That fucker got me ambushed by three bastards in Paris – well-trained and well-armed. They kicked my ass!" A tear dripped off her cheek into the receiver making a buzzing sound.

"I'm here for you, you know that. Enough of this, let's switch topics. What about the boy?" she asked, trying to be upbeat.

Alona didn't want to be insensitive but her sister could simmer for days. She had to get her to focus on something else.

"The boy?" Kat paused then wiped her eyes with her sleeve. "Oh shit. I'm supposed to meet him at the Parkour Centre tomorrow. Damn. I have to call him, I'm not in the mood," she said, blowing her nose in a Kleenex.

"Now stop right there. You think Nyssa would want you to just crawl into bed and cry. That's not the person she loved ... you are not that person. This Pantera guy will be a good distraction, at worst. At best ... who knows. You are going! Now tell me more about him," Alona queried.

The stern sister transformed into the gossipy sister who Kat loved so much. The conversation continued for the next several hours and on into the early morning.

"... there's just something about him. He doesn't move like the other military guys, he vacillates between idiot farm boy, horny frat-boy and genius transcendentalist, and, he has an extremely dense muscle structure. It's weird." Kat's trembling hands become calm as the infatuation with Pantera temporarily replaced her sadness over the loss of Nyssa.

"Sounds like he could be quite a handful. Be careful. Those guys at that shadow unit have a nasty reputation, but, if anyone can handle one, it's you. Seems Cinderella did well at the ball and it sounds to me like something is lingering." She tapped K-I-S-S in Morse code with her nails on the phone receiver.

Kat said softly, "You mean the kiss?"

"Yeah, damn right I mean the kiss and ...?"

"And, I liked it, but it makes me feel guilty," she said, wiping her face with another tissue.

"You may control most everything little sister, but there are some things in life that happen for a reason. I have to get ready for work. Love you *Achut*. Have a good day." Alona's cheerfulness and wisdom could always bring Kat out of one of her moods.

"Love you too," Kat said, returning to her fetal position.

CHAPTER 25

Zero-dark-twenty-nine, moisture saturated the grinder. Another typical wintery day at the Naples base located just five kilometers from the ocean. Dressed in his PT gear, this Saturday was anything but typical. Pantera noticed the number of officers milling around laughing and joking with the other team members, but no one spoke to him. The brackish taste of isolation mixed with the salty air filled his mouth as he warmed up.

"What the hell," he muttered to himself.

He set out on the three-mile run to the obstacle course and back with the rest of the unit – surrounded, but alone. After PT, Pantera approached Grit.

"Hey Gunny, do I have leprosy or something? I'm getting the cold shoulder from everyone, including the officers. What's up with that?"

"You do have leprosy." Grit scanned to see if anyone caught the question. "It's called *Italian Model Leprosy.*"

"Excuse me? Not that shit again," he said, wiping sweat from his face with his shirt.

"The pussy pool is huge. Everyone knows it's today. The officers who're in the pool want to see who they're betting against. Some of the guys from the aviation unit also wanted to get in on the action so we gave them a *special* ten-to-one offer."

"Great. I'm a *friggin'* sporting event now. So why is no one talking to me?" Pantera asked, as they ambled up the steps to the platoon office.

"It's equivalent to a pre-jump mental prep. You know how no one talks to each other right before a jump? Everyone's gettin' in the zone – *you* have to get in the zone." Grit chuckled.

"I have to get in the zone to bang a chick? Everyone knows what type of chick this is, right?"

"Hell no, what fun would that be. Only Cracker and I know about her."

"So everyone is trying to screw with my head. Isn't that my job?" He bounced off the doorframe to the platoon office, overly concentrating on the conversation.

"Ironic, huh? The guys betting on you don't want to mess with your magic Juju. Those betting against you are hoping you'll crack from the pressure. I know you have no chance, but I changed my bet. I think you're smart enough to *get her panties*, just not *get in her panties*," Grit said, raising his eyebrows.

"Well that's a relief. I mean, what? I might succeed ..." He rolled his eyes nodding in acknowledgement of the subtle hint.

"You might succeed at getting dead. Please don't. The paperwork's a bitch."

"Wouldn't want to stress your pencil finger. Wish me luck." Pantera turned and waved.

"Luck is for rabbits." Grit smiled approvingly.

* * *

Kat woke up a few hours after the marathon conversation with her sister. She made some tea to lessen the physical and emotional pain then sat down to read the paper. The pot of water boiled at the same time the phone rang.

"Hallo. *Chi sta chiamando per favore?*" she answered.

"Hallo. *Bití ha-yafáh.*" [My beautiful daughter.]

"Mama, I'm so sorry I haven't called in a while. My travel schedule ..." she said, pouring the hot water through the strainer into the teapot.

"I know, I know. I get regular updates from your sister," Tirzah said, inserting her form of Jewish guilt. "How are you, *bubbeleh*? Alona told me what happened. Did you know this girl, Nyssa, very well?"

Kat loved her parents deeply, but the concept of same-sex relationships was revolting and anti-Judaic in their eyes.

Thank you, Alona, for not telling her. "Yes. We attended intelligence school together." Kat laid the tray on the table and sat down.

"Oh, okay. You were students together," she said, quietly breathing a sigh of relief. "You must be very sad. Your father wanted me to say 'hello' to you."

Kat knew her parents secretly wondered why, their youngest daughter, has never brought a male prospect to meet them. *No one good enough*, she thought, hearing her mother's loud-enough "sigh."

"I know he does not, but thank you anyway. He still won't talk to me, you know that, right?"

"Yes, but he will. I promise he will. He just cleaned your brother's room and donated some of his clothes and other things. He left Adamm's weapons and gear for you. See, he's trying." Tirzah said softly with great emotion. "You got the Beretta?"

"Yes, I did. I don't know what I can do for him." She chewed at ends of her hair.

"You can do nothing. You need to stay patient, calm your soul, and take care of yourself. Alona says there's a new boy? Will I get to meet this one?" Tirzah asked.

"Not yet there isn't," she said looking up at the clock. "Oh *harah*. And there won't be if I don't get ready and get out of here. I love you, *Imah*."

"*Kol tuv, bití ha-yafáh.*" [Be well, my beautiful daughter]

* * *

After breakfast, Pantera packed for the day. In addition to his Parkour clothes, he added a nice shirt, pants, and his Carhartt jacket. He grabbed the rest of his personal gear and saw a bottle of *donated* cologne on his desk.

Cologne? That shit's for peacocks – Ivory soap is the cologne of real men.

The smell of grape *Bubblicious* gum wafted in the air as he opened the door and stood face to face with his roommate.

"Good luck," Bullseye spewed in a slow, South African accent.

"Uh, thanks?" Pantera muttered in disbelief, eyebrows raised. *He speaks. Pinch me, I must be hallucinating.*

With Bullseye as a roommate their room was nicknamed, "The Zone of Ultimate Silence." At best, what Pantera could expect from Bullseye was a nod – but actual words, never.

He passed through the gate in the direction of the train station thinking about bubble gum and Bullseye's words. *No pressure my ass. Even my non-verbal roommate is giving me verbal support ... sheesh.*

CHAPTER 26

The empty train gave Pantera plenty of room to spread across the hard plastic, two-seat bench. The other passengers looked at him with "*mal educado*" on their faces, but he felt his knees were more important than their idiotic opinions. His mind became calm, his body at peace.

I am who I am and that is all I can be.

The clacking rhythm of the train was restful. He pulled his hat down over his eyes and went to sleep. It was nearly noon when Pantera woke to the proximity buzzer of the train.

"RO-MA," echoed over the loudspeaker. The train entered the station like the monorail at Disney World.

He looked forward to the new experience after a good energizing nap and was happy to be finally outside of Naples. He gave himself a pep talk.

This is a new adventure and I will do what I always do ... tackle it. Whatever happens, it will be a grand experience – good, bad, or ugly – a new experience is always a good thing ... ask Icarus.

Then the logic of reality set in. *You remember what happened to Icarus.*

The sun had burned away the clouds and the heavy lavender scent of the purple bracts of bougainvillea floated along the platform. Pantera shook off the stiffness from two hours of non-movement, adjusted his hat, and checked out the directional signs.

Kat and Pantera made plans to meet at an old industrial building on the outer edge of Rome halfway between the Israeli Embassy and the airport. It was a good location. The train station was about a kilometer down the road and still within walking distance to many cafes, restaurants, and several beautiful piazzas.

He pulled out the map he'd picked up earlier in the week at the U.S. Navy MWR office. Penciled circles contained likely cafes with a big X – *Parkour*. After taking two steps, the hair on the back of his neck stood at attention.

Hold on a sec. Am I being watched?

In a practiced effort, he grabbed his bag and pretended to rummage around in it while subtly looking around in a full 360-degree arc.

* * *

Kat watched Pantera from twenty-five meters away. She wanted to see how "aware" he was by half-heartedly blending in with a small crowd waiting for the next train. The shadow warrior stories were numerous and she wanted to see their skills firsthand. When he pulled the map out and looked around, took two steps and stopped, she became concerned.

Why did he stop? What is he doing? She realized he was acting like a hapless tourist. *How did he know? Nice feint Navy boy, good tradecraft, almost got me.*

She doubted anyone else on the platform recognized his improvisation for what it was. The connection to him became stronger in her *Kat-on-Cat* fantasy.

What caused him to start the search in the first place? Am I not as good as I think I am? Is the Katsa killer better than me? Is my father right? Could I have saved Nyssa?

She stepped out from the crowd and tried to move behind him without making it obvious.

* * *

Pantera's peripheral vision caught Kat instantaneously. He turned slowly toward her.

Sneaky little kitty, nice try. Should I check her for weapons? Gawd damn she's hot.

His mind's eye captured her approach in slow motion. She looked as if she came from a Cosmo cover in her all-white Nike tracksuit, *Feiyues* – a popular Parkour shoe, her hair up in a pony-tail, and no make-up except for the "trademark" deep red lipstick. He put his map away and contemplated the appropriate greeting. *Traditional American? No. Traditional European? Maybe. Kiss her hand? Too dorky.*

Kat sized him up. *Damn, he is a big boy. What kind of asinine re-mark is he going to pull on me this time? Can I just stab him in the eye and go back to bed?*

He moved in slowly for a two-cheek kiss.

She recognized the intent and reciprocated. *No cologne but still smells good. Okay, you're still in the game.*

Her skin against his cheek for the first time felt like silk, just like her lips he remembered from the embassy ball. She wore no per-fume. Just the gentle aroma of a flowery soap tickled his senses. *She doesn't wear perfume. Way cool.*

"*Shalom,*" he said in his best Hebrew accent. "Nice of you to pick me up at the train station. Thank you."

"*Shabbat Shalom,*" she nodded with a grin. "I was done with my errands early and thought you might need some help getting to the building. It's a nice walk along the river." She stood close to him drinking in his aroma of Ivory soap and pheromones.

"Great. I got lost trying to find my platoon sergeant's office," he said with a grin, hoping it would score him some humility points.

She smiled and turned in the direction of the Parkour Centre. *Is he trying that fake farm boy, self-deprecating humor on me, again? Bet-ter than those frat-boy sexual comments at least.*

The walk over to the Parkour building was cold and the sun was shining, representative of their conversation, empty but cheerful. All complete lies. Kat described her work day as that of a secretary and Pantera told her he was still wandering around the naval base aimlessly as a "simple" Navy Corpsman.

If she's not buying this horse manure, then she's faking really well.

There was an unmistakable attraction between them. Unfortunately, the attraction was buried so deep beneath layers of purposeful deception, repressed self-loathing, and sociopathic charm that a walk in a London fog bank would have been clearer. One was covering up emotional pain, the other, completely void of it.

Whew. Never thought we'd get here. Sorry smart guy, I gave up geeks long ago. If you have no skills here, then we are done. Maybe I should check the train schedule?

When the building came into view, the conversation turned to recapping the sporting conversation from the prior week, providing each other with a superficial history of the sports they played as kids. Some truth, some not, but no talk of Parkour.

Pantera fired the first shot over Kat's bow. "So ... you said you were good at Parkour. How long have you been training?"

Kat didn't know Americans even heard of Parkour.

Lie or truth? Why stop now? "Since last year, and you? Maybe you can help me?" she said, with a subtle coy turn of her head, trying to avoid the sexual implication.

Pantera caught the head turn and was stumped as to what it meant. *Gotcha. She's wearing Feiyues for crying out loud. Bet she's a badass.*

"Who me? Yeah ... just started. The military recently opened a place in Virginia where I was stationed last. I was hoping, could you help me?" he asked, straight faced. He reached for the door and opened it for her.

Look at him. Isn't he so charming ... whatta crock.

A small black-and-white sign over the door in Italian read:

"Parkour Strutture – Non ci sono limiti. Ci sono altipiani, ma non si deve stare lì, si deve andare oltre. Un uomo deve sempre superare il suo livello. – Bruce Lee."

Pantera looked up at the sign. "What does that say?"

Kat also looked up and translated it directly, "Parkour Structure – There are no limits. There are plateaus, but you must not stay there, you must go further. A man must always exceed his level." She looked at Pantera as she walked in, and added, "Sort of a 'Parkour' motto."

Great motto, I guess he never met Icarus, Pantera thought.

CHAPTER 27

The Parkour Centre looked to be a plain warehouse in a former life – modern compared to the thousand-year-old buildings in the center of town. It had high ceilings made completely of old semi-rusted steel and was definitely the largest indoor Parkour facility Pantera had ever seen. The equipment in the front two blocked areas appeared new and the back two areas looked as old as the building itself. He looked from one end to the other. By his rough calculations, it had to be half the size of a football field.

Kat watched Pantera as he entered the building to gauge his reaction.

Anticipation was all over his face. *I could get used to this. Hot damn!*

The sun beat down on the roof creating a hot steamy interior. All of the roof panel windows were closed. Pantera took in the musty smell of athletes mingled with hints of rusting metal and motor oil.

Kat walked to the office window. The changing area, next to the office, was carpeted with tables, chairs, and lockers for its members.

"Buongiorno Antonio, due passaggi per favore," Kat said, handing the attendant two 500 lire coins. She accepted the passes, put them in her purse, and looked up at Pantera. "Are you looking for something? The toilet is over there." She pointed to a dimly lit hallway.

"No. Not the toilet. Where do I change? Where is the men's locker room?" He continued looking beyond the changing area, vending machines, and office.

Uncontrollably, she let out a giggle – sounding more like a bird chirping than an actual laugh. "That *is* the changing area. It says, *changing area*," she said, pointing to the carpeted area and lockers with a sign above in several languages.

"Girls and boys ... together ... at once ... in the open?" he returned with an unmistakable, and unpredicted, tone of modesty.

Seriously? The virgin frat-boy is modest. I should throw the little fish back. "You are joking. I heard about the over-protected, prima donna Americans, but to see it first hand is still quite fascinating," she said, crossing her arms.

"Thanks?" He ignored the insult. *Are ... you ... kiddin' ... me? She expects me to change clothes in the open with all these people around?*

"Okay Pantera, you're going to have to buck up. You're in Italy now, not your American high school gym. We don't do modesty here." With her patience diminishing, she took the tough approach. "Let's get those Parkour clothes on and get moving," she said, grabbing his arm pulling him to the changing area, nearly breaking a nail in the process.

Last time she held his arm was during the embassy ball and he was wearing a thick dinner dress jacket. The steely, sinewy tendrils of his muscle fibers rippled under his thin nylon shirt with his lightening reaction to her touch caused Kat to pause. *Damn. Can't say I've felt anything like that before.*

Since Kat already had her Parkour outfit on, she started stretching, glancing at him periodically. He threw his jacket on the bench and pulled off his well-fitted Nike black nylon short-sleeved athletic shirt. He stopped right in the middle of taking off his shoes realizing he was undressing facing Kat and the rest of the open Parkour area.

Yikes. Showing my butt in public – okay. Showing my nuts in public – not okay. He quickly moved to the other side of the bench – failing to do so unseen.

Kat saw him change locations at the bench and smirked. *So puritanical, I wonder, are all Americans like this?* Her eyes soaked in the near-perfect crescent shape of his backside as he removed his pants exposing the exact location of the insertion of his gluteus maximus and his well-formed hamstrings in relation to his quadriceps femoris. *Oh harah, perfect anatomy, modest, and wears tightie-whities. Americans ... world power, really?*

She continued down, noticing how well defined his gastrocnemius bifurcation was when something struck her. *Look at those legs ... a moon tan? A question for later, if I don't kick his ass too hard and send him home crying like the others.*

Pantera finished dressing then started his warm-up as Kat finished hers. She stood up and observed the other athletes in the various areas of the building when a male voice yelled out from one of the areas.

"*Ehi Kat.*" The man waved. "*Bello vederti, come sei stato?*"

"*Giancarlo, molto buono, grazie,*" she said in a fluent Roma accent.

They exchanged formal cheek kisses and an awkward hug.

Giancarlo was the owner of the Parkour Centre and a former member of Col Moschin – Italian Special Forces. A good-looking, dark-skinned man in his mid-forties, imposing though just a wiry five-foot-eight, he was the reason twelve countries sent their top agents for training in stealth attacks, mixed martial arts, and his personal favorite, knife combat. He was a well-known secret in the intelligence community, but not for Parkour. On any given day nearly a dozen intelligence officers worked out alongside the over two dozen civilians in the centre. One country's agents have never used the facility – the arrogant Americans.

"Giancarlo, this is Marcus Sinclair, US Navy." She introduced the men to each other in English. Kat saw something she hadn't seen before, Pantera was reading him. *No way. He is definitely more than a 'simple' medical person.*

Pantera stood up.

Giancarlo's eyes followed up – all six-foot-two of him. He wasn't intimidated by Pantera but it did give him pause since he had never met an American military man.

"Piacere di conoscerti," Pantera said in his best textbook Italian, but too formal for this situation. *Cigarettes, Giorgio Armani cologne and look at those shoes ... can anyone say, Nutcracker?* He accepted his handshake and continued assessing him.

Kat noticed the exchange and Pantera's reading of Giancarlo. *He's trying to be charming to an Italian. Now there's a twist.*

"Good also to meet you." Giancarlo returned in broken English. "You familiar with the Parkour, or is Kat your ... *istruttore?*" He wanted to make sure Pantera was not going to end up killing himself.

"Yes, a little. I've practiced back in the States. Maybe Kat will teach me some moves," he replied, sexual connotation purposely implied, "but I've never seen a place like this." *Yeah buddy, I gave you the 'I'm gonna bang your ex-girlfriend' bitch slap with a little charm to soften the sting.*

Kat caught the reference, recognizing Pantera's realization of Giancarlo as her former boyfriend. *And the frat-boy returns, I am sooo going to make you hurt.*

Giancarlo smiled and nodded respectfully. "Grazie. Kat show you." He then turned to Kat, and said, *"Non lasciarlo sanguinare sul mio equipaggiamento."* [Don't let him bleed on my equipment.]

Kat smiled slyly. *"Ho intenzione di mandarlo a casa in lacrime."* [I'm going to send him home in tears.]

Pantera watched the exchange, knew it was about him and just grinned.

Giancarlo disappeared back into one of the practice areas.

"Let's get started," Kat said, walking with purpose to the first area of the building. "The building is broken up into four main areas: beginner, intermediate, advanced, and competition." *I should just take you to the competition area and make your eyes bleed, but what an ass he has.* She gave him an enigmatic grin. "The four sections, as you can see, are clearly marked." She pointed to the sign over each section.

Within the beginner and intermediate areas, there were various stairs, banisters, walls of different heights and different textures, poles with square plates on top, low beams, high beams, and corners. In the advanced and competition areas, in addition to what was found in the two lower areas, there were pipes and industrial equipment of all shapes and sizes looking as if they were original to the building.

"Cool. I played on oil and gas refinery equipment in Texas as a kid," he said, rubbing his hands together.

"You grew up in Texas?" Kat asked.

"Among other places." He shrugged with an aloof facial expression.

Pantera digested all the equipment – calculating angles of approach, release, and movements between each piece. He noticed pieces of different colored tape in the form of X's, O's, diamonds, triangles, and squares; all connected by solid or dotted lines of different colors.

"What does the tape mean?" he asked, playing coy.

"These are the tracer tags and routes," she said, with an instructor-like tone. "Each line represents a route and each shape represents a tag that must be touched in order to move on through the course." She spun on her heel heading back to the beginner area. "Time for action Navy boy. Are you up for a little challenge?"

Kat's movement was so fast she left Pantera's view for a moment, unsettling him. They met back at the start of the beginner's area.

"We'll first choose a shape then walk the course making sure we know the location of all the tags," she said, over her shoulder heading for the first obstacle.

"Let's do diamonds," Pantera blurted out. *Time to give the little kitty a spanking.*

"Really?" She raised an eyebrow. "Okay. In the beginning area, the course length is ten shapes. The intermediate area: twenty shapes. The advanced area: thirty shapes. The competition area has sets of tens, twenties and thirties," she said, pointing to the first tag in the beginner area. *Your funeral mister, oh harah, that's right, I need to go to Nyssa's funeral. What should I wear?*

Pantera was excited, jumping up and down in his mind, this place was a dream, challenging *and* organized. The opposite of what he was told to expect from Italians – told to him by Americans who have never been to Italy.

CHAPTER 28

They walked the beginner course then returned to the starting point. The board at the starting line had a series of ten red push buttons with a letter above and a dial to the side of each one.

"Nice board. Timing station?" He spun one of the dials.

"Correct. You rotate the dial to the shape identifying the course you are taking and you hit the button before you leave."

"Sounds simple enough," he said, brimming with anticipation.

"When finished, you hit the same lettered button on the other end. Your time will show up on the board ... on *that* board up on the wall over there." She pointed to the big board on the wall over the office – the same wall hanging the record holder board.

Oops. Her head dropped.

He turned with her to a see four huge timing boards representing each of the four areas, each with ten letters on them and a digital screen to hold the time. Something else caught his eye – another board – holding the top three times and names for each area. His focus became sharper. There was something subconsciously familiar about one of the names. His eyes were drawn to a name in the first position on the advanced area leader board.

ALYN KATRYNA DAVID.

Kat waited until the truth was revealed.

"You're such a liar," Pantera said, turning to face Kat.

"Wanna quit now?" Kat spit, becoming defensive and indignant. The stress of Nyssa's death was rearing its ugly head, sparked by his hypocrisy.

"No, but you could've been honest with me," Pantera said, taking a step back with Kat's change in behavior. *Ouch. Is this where you kill me? I sense something else going on.* He didn't feel offended. He didn't know what he felt.

Yeah Navy boy, pot calling kettle ... hello? "Sorry. You're right. I forgot it was up there and men who see it are often intimidated then they get all shitty on me," Kat returned, feeling conflicted as her mind was being pulled in different directions.

"Gosh lil' lady," Pantera said, trying some Southern gentlemanly charm on her. "Ya shoodant jaga buk by its covers."

Kat nodded. "True." *Just wait until I catch you in a lie, buster.*

He bowed. "I look forward to having my ass kicked by you, lil' lady."

Kat walked over to the starting line, turned the "A" and "B" dials to the diamond position, looked back at Pantera and winked. She hit the button under "A", and was off like a cat.

The hair on the back of Pantera's neck stood up. With the competitive adrenaline kicking in, his focus became laser sharp. He waited three seconds, hit the button under "B", and was hot on her trail. There weren't many opportunities to see her in action, but what he did see was impressive. Her moves were smooth, fluid, and practiced. He could see she had enormous leg strength giving her a jumping ability like no woman, or man, he'd ever seen. She lacked the upper body strength of a man, but there was still more than enough strength for her body weight.

Should I sandbag the first one? Pantera thought.

Kat hit the red "A" button and turned to watch Pantera move through the last couple of obstacles. She never had a chance to see him move through the course until now. She found herself conflicted. Mad at him but impressed with his skills. He was at least sixty to seventy pounds heavier than her and half-a-foot taller but his grace, decision-making skills, and confidence were apparent. *You are definitely not flamboyant.*

She watched him finish the last obstacle, cross the finish line, and hit the red "B" button – losing control of her breathing for second. *Wow you are good. Let's see how you like being called a liar.*

Nanoseconds after he hit the button, their eyes met then immediately turned to look at the board: "A" – 22.93s; "B" – 23.01s.

"YOU," she yelled, poking him in the chest, "are such a liar!" Then for no apparent reason, she smiled. *You lied to me and now I'm smiling at you. What is my malfunction?*

"Okay. Okay. I didn't want to brag. My grandmother told me it is, *unbecoming of a gentleman.* Not that I'm a gentleman. I just think it's a smart thing to do," he said with a big smile and wide eyes, instituting his charm offensive. *If that doesn't get me in your panties tonight I don't know what will.*

"Yeah, yeah, yeah ... (W)hat (E)ver," she said, giving him three widely spread fingers upward then turned them sideways.

The conflict in Kat grew. *A boy, a man, smart then an idiot. I want to sleep with you. I want to stab you in the eyeball. Infuriating! I what? I didn't say that out loud, did I?*

"Guess we know. Are we going again, here?" He anxiously awaited her reply.

"Would you like to try *this* again?" she asked, putting her hands on her hips. "Or shall we move to the next level?"

"Let us head to *your* area, m'lady," he said with a bad Victorian accent. He placed one hand over his abdomen and extended the other in the direction of the advanced area.

"Get prepared Navy boy, the schoolin' shall continue," she said, marching off in a military-like fashion. "No holding back this time. I want your all." *Oh harah. That was such an invitation. Now you think I'm going to give it up, don't you.*

"Of that I have no doubt," he said under his breath.

Kat heard it nonetheless. She gave a grimacing smile with her back toward him – *Icky.*

For the next two hours, they battled – starting at the lowest level and progressing up the difficulty ladder. Each trace had thirty locations and by far the most difficult obstacles he had ever encountered. No records were broken and no words were exchanged. There were competitive glances, mostly out of respect, a touch here, and a bump there – nothing sexual. The battle wore on and a crowd gathered.

"You wanna quit now?" Kat said, trying to regain her breath. She was feeling comfortable enough with him that she didn't think her joke would offend him.

"Not unless you want to," he responded humbly. "We have a crowd and this is the penultimate race." *Ahh, you're warming up to me. Here kitty Kat.*

"Penultimate, huh." She smiled. *Seriously? Here it comes smart guy, the ass-whippin' you've been asking for.*

Kat was weakening, but acted to the contrary. Pantera saw through the act. He was ready to make his move. They turned their dials and were off again down the track.

Kat hit the button at the finish, "3:05.65s." Pantera was right behind her, "3:05.70s." She looked up at the board. The low rumbling of the crowd echoed. She looked up at Pantera and gritted her teeth then noticed the hint of a smile on his face. *When is this guy going to tire out?*

Pantera saw her grimace. His eyes narrowed, his muscles were now fully warmed up. Something came over him. It was a new feeling he had never experienced. He searched to give it a name.

Compassion for the prey? Really ... me? Not in this lifetime. If I fake it, I could score more points toward those panties. "Hey girl, you look like you're losin' energy. Are you sure you're ready for the diamond?" He leaned in close, sharpening his acting skills. "We can call it right here. You schooled me. I'm buying dinner."

The joy of dinner was merely a prelude to what came next in his mind.

"We have one more race, Navy boy. Time for you to show your mettle," she chided. She straightened herself, readjusted her ponytail, then gave him a couple boxing moves.

No man has ever matched Kat in this Parkour arena. Giancarlo, the master instructor, stood in the corner watching this herculean battle take place with riveted interest. Thought Kat felt slighted at Pantera's compassion, phony or genuine, she relieved there was one man who could compete with her.

"You, sir, can have the privilege of going first," she said, bowing with one arm extended pointing to the starting line.

"Yes, Ma'am," he returned with a slow nod.

CHAPTER 29

Two hours since they first walked in and Pantera could move through each obstacle with his eyes closed. Every trace, every approach, every technique, and every exit out of the obstacle, microscopically analyzed. A fellow member of the *Felidae* family was about to get pounced upon. Pantera stepped up to the starting line, turned the dial to the diamond position, hit the "A" button, and bounded off like a leopard.

Kat and Pantera had captured the attention of all the other traceurs in the building. The small pack stood still, nothing else moved in the warehouse.

Pantera took off into the course, Kat cringed. *You are stronger now than you were when we started. How is that even possible?* A premonition of an outcome leapt into her mind: "*Keyshelven*" (failure). She gnashed her teeth and forced another thought into her mind ... *FUCK THAT!*

Kat turned her dial to the diamond, hit the "B" button, and was in hot pursuit. Every bit of power transferred static to dynamic energy. The intensity of her focus became sharp and unwavering. She moved through the first set of obstacles with lightning speed: foot placement, perfect; hand placement, perfect; body mass center, balanced. Giancarlo and those in the crowd who knew her, watched in awe. Out for blood, she was going to get it, no, take it.

In the zone, Pantera's conscious thought now was replaced with a subconscious, almost dream-like, state of Zen. Muscle memory synced his mind's eye to every muscle fiber in his body as he became one with the universe. Each obstacle reached up embracing him like a mother's touch.

The feeling of the crowd holding their breath was palatable.

The two combatants moved through the course with a surreal cartoon quality about them. Pantera finished the last obstacle fast and smooth. He crossed the line, hit the "A" button, and turned around to see Kat's intense scowl with the frenzied twitching of her biceps and forearms.

His personal feelings clashed with his professional responsibly. *If you win – I get some bang-bang and maybe some help in hunting my mole. Now if I win – I get no bang-bang and no help. Crap, I should have backed off.*

Without even realizing it, he let out a low grunt, "Go Kat!" He felt his body transfer the last remaining energy it had to Kat.

Kat heard Pantera's cheer and a renewed feeling of energy swept over her body like she had been enveloped by a blanket of adrenaline. Weakness left her arms, the lactic acid burning in her legs stopped, and she moved through the rest of the course with precision and alacrity. Kat crossed the line, hit the "B" button, and looked up at the board. She noticed the crowd did the same in one fluid mass movement. "A," 3:09.34s; "B," 3:09.33s.

She did it, her faith in herself restored.

The crowd gasped and cheered.

Kat smiled with a thankful nod to everyone then stared up at Pantera. *Too bad, Navy boy. If you can't beat me, you can't have me. Nothing for you tonight, except a good teasing.* She repressed the urge to jump into his arms and get the hug she desired.

Giancarlo walked up to Pantera. "You ... big man ... *toccante* [impressive]." Giancarlo extended his hand out to shake hands. "Please come back, *hanno un grande giorno*." [Have a great day.] He would also not forget Pantera's comments from earlier.

Kat did not believe what she just saw. Giancarlo, one of the most competitive men she ever knew – the ex-lover still in pursuit – embracing some guy she brought into his house. *Maybe hell is freezing over,* she thought.

"*Grazie,* for letting me play on your toys," he said, thinking, *with your hot ex-girlfriend who I'm goin' to bang tonight.*

"Good workout. You owe me dinner," she said, as she smacked Pantera on the butt. "Oh, and you can change at my place. I wouldn't want you to undress in front of all your adoring fans." She walked toward the lockers giggling, loud enough for him to hear.

"Yes, Ma'am," he said during an inhalation, making the words less distinct and more humble as they exited the building. *I love it when a plan comes together. Here kitty, kitty.*

CHAPTER 30

"How far is the walk?" Pantera asked, looking around trying to keep his bearings.

"It's about a half mile, toward the center of town," she answered, looking up at him with a little more respect than before their competition.

Kat lived in a small apartment centered between the Embassy of Israel, the Parkour Centre and the nearby train station. The sun fell fast as the plants, grass, and trees were still taking their winter nap and the river looked as if it was frozen in time. Their pleasant walk and conversation became even more reserved as their bodies, physically and emotionally drained, worked overtime bestowing the delicious pain of recovery upon them.

"Here we are. It's small, but I like it," Kat said. *Make a stature joke, you big American, I dare you.*

"What a great building," he said. "You definitely don't see this in America."

Good manners, Navy boy.

Kat's apartment building was on a quiet tree-lined street just a couple blocks from Rome's two major thoroughfares. U-shaped and comprised of red brick, it was a three-story structure with quaint balconies overlooking the street and courtyard. It had a small waist-high gate leading to the courtyard with a narrow "Hansel and Gretel" cobblestone walkway leading up to the large double-door entryway. A multitude of colorful perennial flowers lined the base of the fence and at the front doorway were enormous Grandiflora red roses, asleep for the winter. Iron grills covered the first-floor windows, no discernable way to climb up to the balconies or down from the roof, and the entry door seemed to have a metal core with an electronic double-bar locking mechanism.

Pantera continued to observe as they entered the foyer.

The interior was of *Old Italian* design – ornate crown molding and shiny natural marble floor tile. A faint aroma of old socks and Ben Gay permeated the foyer. There was no elevator, just a large spiral staircase.

Kat noticed Pantera examining the building. "It used to be the home of a wealthy noble landowner a couple hundred years ago when someone got the idea of converting it into a bunch of flats."

At the end of the hallway, they reached her third floor apartment.

Pantera took inventory as they walked into the living room. He calculated it was equal to two or three of his dorm rooms. The living room had efficient furniture, to the right an arched doorway led to another room. It was sparse, but comfortable.

"This is cool," he said, placing his backpack next to the loveseat. "I've always lived in a dorm environment."

Wow, now he acts mature. He's like a pogo stick. "Through there is the bedroom and the bathroom." She pointed to the archway as she walked to the stove.

Pantera nodded licking his lips. *Condoms are itchin' to jump out of my wallet.*

"You can take the first shower ... and I promise not to peek," she said, giving him a head to toe glance, trying to smile without the sexual implication. *Maybe I should jump him right now. Kat, stop, control yourself. Remember, you promised, no frat-boys ... and he lost!*

Pantera grabbed his backpack and sauntered in the direction of the bathroom. *Peek all you want hottie. You want it, I know you do.*

Two things stood out as he entered the bathroom. First, the shower looked like it was built for *Oompa-loompas* straight out of

Roald Dahl's novel, *Charlie and the Chocolate Factory*. Second, there were two toilets.

Pantera stood in the bathroom staring down at the toilets like a lost kindergartener. *What is this? And, I have to pee like a racehorse.* A mental Ping-Pong ball bounced between two options. *Which is more embarrassing? Asking for help or peeing in the wrong one. If I am going to get those panties ...* His grandmother jumped into his head. *A gentleman would ... that's right. Acting humble will score more points. Thanks Grandma.*

"Kat?" he yelped.

"Sorry, did I forget the towels?" she said, grabbing a couple towels from the cabinet on her way to the bathroom.

He pointed down at the two toilets as she walked in. His face wasn't red and didn't look embarrassed.

"You have never seen a *bidet* before?" she said, with an air of skepticism.

"Honestly? No," he replied, shaking his head with a protruding lower lip.

You of all people use the word, honestly? American men, they're like children. She flipped the switch on the bidet, and said, "You start on the left and finish on the right, saves toilet paper." She added, trying to compose herself, "Oh, and sorry for the shower. Italians are not a race of tall people." Kat walked back into the bedroom shaking her head.

"Thanks," he said, watching her walk away. *That could've gone better, not as many points as I had hoped. Wonder what the pussy pool is up to now.*

Despite the small size, the shower had hot water and soap. Compared to the infamous Navy "spit-bath", it was still a luxury.

Kat was on the phone when Pantera returned to the living room so he fell onto the loveseat and waited. He recognized the Hebrew but had no idea what the conversation was about. She spoke for a few minutes more and then ended the conversation.

"You didn't break my shower, I hope," she teased, as she walked past returning the phone to the corner table on her way to the bedroom.

Pantera looked around the room. *So, I'm in the nest of a black widow.* He moved to the cupboard to grab a glass, poured some water from the faucet, and returned to the warm, soft loveseat falling instantly asleep.

* * *

A shock of consciousness shot through Pantera's body as he opened his eyes to find Kat standing over him, poking his chest.

"Hey Navy boy, get up," she said firmly, smiling.

"Huh?" he said, looking up at her. *Hooray. I'm still alive and she doesn't have a knife in her hand.*

His eyes soaked her in – pale skin, black bangs ending right above her eyebrows, long straight hair pulled to one side ending at the center of her chest, long black eyelashes, and purple pastel eyeshadow. She outlined her rich red lips with a dark perimeter and conservative earrings added to the overall effect. Her breasts in the black cable knit cashmere turtleneck hugged her torso as the flatness of the red knee length silk skirt across her abdomen was interrupted by a small pubic bump. A tingle crawled slowly up his spine.

Holy mackerel, she even looks like a black widow and, huh, smells like honeysuckle? Growing up, Pantera's grandmother always placed a honeysuckle plant right outside the front door of each house they lived in. His attraction to Kat was evolving into something else – something he had never experienced before – fear baked in happiness.

"Trying to get out of buying me dinner?" she asked.

"No way," he answered. "Where are we going?"

"There's a café down the street, they have great marinara," she said, throwing her coat on heading for the door.

Pantera jumped up, still a little groggy, and bounded after her.

The café was five blocks away on one of the busiest streets in Rome. It had a wonderful view of the river, and in the opposite direction, a celestial view of the Rome Observatory.

The owner of the café waved at the striking dark-haired beauty and her large companion as they approached. *"Ciao bella, chi è il tuo bello amico?"* she said, eyeing the man Kat was with.

"Ciao Paola, un passo indietro lui è tutto mio." Kat smiled and flashed a melodramatic wink, followed by a sisterly hug.

"Paola, this is Marcus Sinclair. American," Kat said, grabbing his arm pulling him closer to the conversation. "Marcus, this is Paola Conti. She is the proprietor and is *a friend* of my boss." Kat looked over at Paola with a half lip grin.

Pantera moved in for a formal European greeting.

Paola took the opportunity to grab both his shoulders giving them a little squeeze. *"Delizioso!"* she said, giving Kat an approving wink.

Pantera had no idea why they were so giggly, but when he caught a whiff of the smell of garlic, basil and tomatoes his hunger took command of his brain.

After they sat down, Kat explained that Paola Conti was, in fact, *the friend* of Kat's boss, Michoel Bergmann. She continued with the charade about being a secretary and created quite a number of cute little office stories and melodramas.

Pantera was getting tired of these stories and decided he would confront her about her continued lies, hoping he wouldn't receive a knife in the neck in exchange, or quite literally, having his head bitten off.

The rest of the evening passed smoothly with easy conversation and laughter. Kat didn't want to give any hint at her interest in him, but she was starting to feel something more than a physical attraction – something she had never felt before – safety. *I will keep him here tonight, test him.* She looked down at her watch without him noticing. *Yes. He missed his train. I will continue to gain his trust.*

They talked until closing.

CHAPTER 31

Pantera knew exactly what time it was as they strolled back to her apartment. More importantly, he planned on missing the last train back to Naples giving him a fifty-fifty chance of spending the night. Maybe better.

He smiled, and thought, *Ode to taste her concha* [sweet bread].

The mental gamesmanship was masterful. Pantera thought he was taking advantage of her, Kat thought she was taking advantage of him – each had different reasons for doing so.

Pantera continued playing the Southern charmer as they reached the gate in front of Kat's building. "Kat, you are the smartest, most beautiful ... and *the* most athletic woman I have ever met." He reached down, placed her hand in his. "The day ... this night ... I actually don't have words to describe it ... other than to say it was earth shaking. Thank you and I hope you will let me take you out again." Slowly he brought her hand up to his lips, closed his eyes, and kissed her hand.

"Yeah, yeah, Navy boy. Do you know what time it is?" she said, raising an eyebrow with a smirk. *I will admit you gave a great performance. You should have been an actor.*

"No? By golly! Did I miss the train?" He pulled his sleeve back to look at his watch.

"Were you planning on taking a taxi home?" she asked, continuing without needing an answer, "Re-lax. Tonight—you—couch. You pay for breakfast."

"Gosh Kat, I really appreciate this. I'll be happy to treat you to breakfast," he hammed. *Perfect! Her panties are as good as mine.*

Moonlight flooded in the west window. Kat hesitated at the light switch but decided to spoil the moment then turned on the stove for some hot water. *Now how do I keep him on the couch?*

Pantera had nothing to change into so he went over to the couch, pulled off his shirt, sat down, and tried to figure out how a man of his height would sleep on a two-cushion loveseat. Just in case.

Kat changed clothes and rummaged around her closet, returning to the living room holding a large down comforter and a large pillow getting an eyeful of Pantera's chiseled chest. "Hope this is okay," she said, throwing the comforter and pillow on his lap then walked over to the whistling kettle. *What a six-pack, when he grows up he will make some woman very happy.* "I have Earl Grey, Chamomile, or Jasmine. You *do* drink tea, *don't you?*"

"Sure. Do you have any milk?"

"Milk? Milk is for black teas. You have lemon with greens teas, sheesh." *Who were this guy's parents? No refinement whatsoever.*

The lies flowed during their recap of their day sitting in the small kitchen sharing their first cup of tea.

What a weird vibe ... you want me then you don't want me? You're like a friggin' rubber band, Pantera thought, then sat up straight like he was hit with a bolt of lightning. "Crap, I have to call the Officer-Of-the-Day. Can I use your phone?"

"Yes," she answered calmly. "It is over there."

Pantera dialed and waited. "HM2 Sinclair reporting in," Pantera said with a military abruptness.

Kat watched with interest at his 'military' demeanor.

Pantera nodded then said, "Ruby."

Kat knew what that was and if she had any doubts whether Pantera might actually be a "simple medic," they were gone now.

After he got off the phone, Kat gave him a kiss on the cheek, and said, "Good night."

His half-naked body rose with abs flexing, cocked his head to the side, he asked, "What do you say we take this to the next level? I think we both could use some ... *touch*," he said, undressing her with his eyes then walking up to her, making sure she had an up-close view. *I let you win, you owe me. Lips ... breasts ... yumm.*

Kat stopped, stiffly turning around. She knew this was coming, but hoped it wouldn't. It also confirmed that her plan to keep him the night was a plan hatched by two people – Kat's emotional curiosity, Pantera's physical desire.

"Look *Jim-Bob-Billy-Ray.*" *I will give you some touch, buddy. Right in the schvantz.* "Let's get a couple things out in the open. One. You can cut that Southern charm thing you got goin'. Though adorable, I'm over it. And two, you lost, so you will not be sticking *that thing*," she said, pointing to his groin, "in me ... tonight ... *if ever.*" With a brusque about-face, she left the room, black hair swinging like in a shampoo commercial.

He plopped back onto the loveseat. *Whoa. Huh? What do I say to that? Excitingly scary mixed with a little hopium. I should just take her, yeah, the fly says to the spider ... and be dead by morning. Cut your losses, Pantera, you're being sent down to the Triple-A leagues.*

All one hundred ninety pounds of Pantera froze with some kind of amazing fear as a bead of cold sweat rolled down his back. No woman had ever spoken to him like that, especially after he took his shirt off. It wasn't that Pantera felt Kat could take him physically, but he got the distinct impression ... *she believed, she could.* A disconcerting thought as the "pool," the harassment, the panties and his primary objective for the evening floated away.

Maybe I should tell her I know she's Mossad ... perhaps tomorrow.

Pantera crawled up into a ball and stared at the front door.

CHAPTER 32

Kat woke up caressing the blade of her polycarbonate partner lying under her pillow and stared at the ceiling, relieved Pantera didn't try to push into her bed. She wasn't ready for him, physically or emotionally, with Nyssa dead and the fear of the Katsa Killer fresh in her mind. Despite her issues, it didn't stop her from thinking about what sex would be like with those washboard abs. *Unless his frat-boy perception of courting extends into the bedroom, ugh.* She shivered as she got up. *Oh well, he is still a guest after all, despite his boyish intentions.*

Pantera jumped up when he heard movement from the other room. He had stayed awake all night with Grit's words ringing in his ears – "honey trap." *If she was going to honey-trap me wouldn't we have slept together last night? This shit is so confusing.* He threw on his clothes, ran over to the kettle, and turned on the heat. He rearranged all the sofa pillows to their original position, unloaded his backpack, and repacked it – refolding all of his clothes. Clothes that were used were turned inside-out for easy identification and all his equipment was rechecked to make sure nothing was lost in the last twenty-four eventful hours.

Kat heard the sound of the kettle and knew it was about to boil. *Okay, maybe you are trainable.* She put on her robe and entered the living room as Pantera was putting his GPS locator in his backpack. *That looks like a Magellan NAV 1000, recently released to the civilian market.* She recalled him using a map yesterday, not the GPS. *Probably a tracking transmitter, likely next gen.* She was thankful hers was implanted.

"Good morning. Sleep okay?" she said, trying to get the picture of a man of Pantera's mass sleeping in the fetal position on the two-cushion loveseat out of her mind.

"I did, thanks for letting me stay. I'm *sooo* sorry for the imposition," he said, with a sly smile.

She flashed her Cheshire cat smile. "Just because you spent the night doesn't mean you can go all soft on me. You're still not getting any. I like big breakfasts, prepare for an expensive tab." *Are you really going to continue with that fake humility, or has learning taken place?* She prepared the morning black Irish Breakfast tea and opened the cupboard to retrieve a couple biscotti to place on the saucer.

"This is a morning tea … which takes milk."

After setting down the teacups and saucers on the table, Kat opened the door to retrieve the newspaper. Not deviating too far from her normal Sunday schedule, she sat down to read it.

"Is there a section you would like to read?" she asked.

"Yes. There is." *No time like the present. Where's my gun again?* "I'd like the part of the paper that talks about you being a Mossad Officer and NOT a secretary," he said, leaning forward slightly in case of an immediate attack.

The gears in Kat's mind whirred. *Wow, manly.* Caught off guard she was not ready to have this conversation. *Then again, when is there a good time to have this talk?* She contemplated reaching for the knife on the counter, but stopped. "So you know? Who told you?" *You figured this out on your own?*

"My boss, at the ball, he saw you last year and the weapon under your cocktail dress this year confirmed it." He leaned back, keeping his hands comfortably ready in front of him.

"He looked up my dress?" She knew it was normal procedure, but didn't want to lead on. *Damn dress. I told them the cocktail dress wouldn't work.*

"Stop. You know that's normal. You also know we work security for these events. Are you going to answer my question?" His temper grew as his mannerism stiffened.

"If you tell me about you and your unit, I know you are not a *simple Navy Corpsman*."

"Deal. We trade one lie for one truth." Pantera, the interrogator, sprang to life. *If you think I'm giving you the whole damn enchilada, you're crazier than a loon.* "You first."

"Okay, I am a security officer at the embassy. All security officers in all Israeli Embassies are Mossad."

"And ..." He spun his finger in a forward x-axis rotation.

"What do you mean by ... *and*?" Kat snapped.

"I mean, what do you do for Mossad, exactly?" he asked, pushing further despite envisioning her jumping up and grabbing the knife behind her.

"Not much really ... just standard intelligence gathering activities. Not any different from your CIA people at your American Embassies. You *are* familiar with the CIA, aren't you?" *That better hold him off, not that he has ever heard of Kidon.* "And what about you?" She pointed back at him.

He ignored the CIA comment. *She's holding something back, she has a 'tell'. I better stop pressing for now.* "That's fair. Me? Just a li'l ol' simple medic, working for a covert team."

"*Al ta'atzben otti!*" [You are pissing me off!] *So help me, I'm going to stab you in the neck!* She raised her hand. "Just stop. We agreed to be honest, for once. Okay, for the second time. I know you're not – *just a simple medic.* Your unit down there doesn't employ – *just simple medics.* You don't walk or act like any military guy I have ever met and you definitely looked uncomfortable at the ball, despite your little 'I'm just happy to be here' act. This makes me think you are definitely not an intelligence officer, either. What ... who ... are you?!" she asked, clenching her jaw.

"Okay, okay. I really am a corpsman—*and an interrogator*—for the U.S. Navy under contract to the United Nations." *I looked uncomfortable? She could read that?*

"Interrogator, huh? I already knew about your unit," she said, waving her index finger at him, "the UN Special Operations Group. Your unit has done work for us in the past. In reality, your unit has done work for almost everyone. We call you guys ... *Shadow Warriors*."

"We have? You do? Well there. You see, you know more than me." *Damn that was close.*

Kat switched gears in what appeared to be her natural racecar fashion, and asked, "Ready for breakfast, Navy boy?" She tossed the last bite of biscotti in her mouth. Though still pissed at Pantera for not coming clean after being outed, her own hypocrisy notwithstanding, she thought, *Hmm, you might be useful after all.* "Sorry, I do not mean for *Navy boy* to be insulting. If you want me to stop calling you that, I will."

He looked over the edge of his teacup and expected to find a grin on her face. What he found was a straight face that was cooling. He slowly leaned over to make eye contact, close enough to kiss her.

She froze.

"Well, Miss David," he whispered, "I'm not insulted, for one. And two, if anyone else even thinks about calling me by *that* nickname, pain will quickly ensue. Am I clear?" He leaned back and crossed his arms.

"Yes, sir," she replied in her best mock-military tone, adding a salute and being slightly aroused by his gesture of authority. "Guess we got all that out of the way." She jumped up heading off to the bedroom to change.

Pantera stared after her, and thought, *such pleasure, such pain.* He cleared the table and returned everything back to its original state. *There is a place for everything ... and everything in its place.* His grandfather's saying came to mind.

The bastard.

CHAPTER 33

Kat and Pantera strolled down the cobblestone sidewalk. It was another beautiful cloudless winter day in Rome. A slight breeze came down from the mountains making the air snap to attention with a crisp newness.

Pantera noticed during the walk that they were on a near-direct path to the train station. With his curiosity spiked, he asked, "Can I ask you a personal question?"

"Yes," she answered, without looking up at him.

"How many languages do you speak?"

Without slowing down from her pace, she answered, "Seven. If you don't include the dialects: Arabic, English, French, Italian, Hebrew, Spanish, and Serbo-Croatian."

Pantera grinned. *Man, this chick is beautiful and brilliant. Whatta great first asset she would make, but would Jack approve?*

The front gate of the outdoor patio to the café was open and Kat led the way inside to the dining area. The café owner greeted Kat in a similar fashion as the last. Kat introduced Pantera and the hostess seated them at a little table in the front patio. It was commonplace to seat Kat outside given her model looks. She attracted people who preferred to dine frequented by the fashionable and elite making the café aesthetically pleasing and increasing customer traffic. Kat knew this and didn't mind eating outside in the fresh air. The discount or free food was an added perquisite.

Pantera watched in amazement at Kat's ravenous appetite. *A chick who can eat. Get out. If food were sex ... nice.* He glanced at Kat, who was scrunching up her nose. "Come on, out with it," he said, thinking she was trying to play coy.

"Well ... you asked me a personal question. Do you mind?" She took a sip of her English Breakfast tea.

"No. Hit me." He lightly thumped his chest with both hands.

"Where did your nickname come from?"

He adjusted himself to a formal posture, cocked his head, and rolled his eyes upward. "You can do better than that."

"Just a place to start," she said, sitting back and dabbing her lips with her cloth napkin.

"Short story. I was a Parkour champion in Virginia ..."

Kat's eyes narrowed. *He is such a hatichat harah. I knew it.*

He spotted her flash of anger. "Come on ... did you think other-wise?"

"No. I guess not," she said, with a half-tilted nod.

"And my mother's maiden name is *Pantera*. So my lieutenant thought it fitting to make 'Pantera' my call sign." He shoved a fork full of omelet into his mouth and raised his eyebrows.

She lifted her napkin to remove a piece of bay leaf from her mouth, returning the napkin to her lap. "Pantera is very unique for a last name. Where did it come from?"

"My mother's family, they're Sephardic Jews. She was visiting family in Southern Spain when she met my father, a Scotsman. Both were twenty. He was in the U.S. Navy, stationed in Rota, Spain. So the story goes, if you want to believe it. I popped out nine months later. Of course, I have no idea what is true about my family anymore ... long story." He shook his head then took a sip of orange juice.

Kat sat speechless as her eyes went wide and her jaw dropped.

"What? Did I say something wrong?" he asked, glancing at his knife.

"You're Jewish?!" Kat's hands fell to her lap as she bounced off the back of her chair in astonishment.

"Honestly. That is another and much longer story ... preferably for another time," he said quietly in a reserved tone, confused at her response.

"I'm sorry, but, *you—are—Jewish.*" The words rang in her head like the bells at a cathedral, or a synagogue. "You *do know* being Jewish comes from your mother's side of the family, right?" She hesitated, hoping he knew this was common knowledge.

"Yes, I know I'm Jewish, 'by blood'," he said, using air quotes, "whatever that means. I was *Bar Mitzvah'ed.* No one explained the mother-thing to me though." *More shit left out by my family. Why am I not surprised?* "Let's just say, my Jewish education came at the tip of a shotgun."

Kat stared across the table. Pantera looked as if he developed an acute case of constipation.

"I did not mean to make you uncomfortable. It is just ... well ... you do not look Jewish ... I mean, not at all. And. There is this old Jewish prophecy – more story, than prophecy really – it talks about a man who is born of a Scottish Knights Templar and a Sephardic Merovingian Princess."

"What the hell does that mean? My mother ... a Merovingian Princess? Now that's a laugh ... and my biological father. I've never met him." *You're a religious nut-job ... and it was getting so good. Suck.*

"I will tell you what. You give me some skin and cheek cells. I will find out for you." Kat waited.

"Let's make a little deal." Pantera's brain jumped back in gear. Believing his future with Kat ended hours ago, he hoped he could salvage his standing in the "pussy pool." "You give me your panties and I will give you whatever you want," he said, smiling as he pushed hash browns onto his fork with a piece of bread.

"Why do you want my panties?" *You fuckin' frat-boy – and I thought I left adolescent university male pranks behind.* She wanted him to suffer the embarrassment of telling her.

Without a pause or any outward signs of humiliation, he replied, "There is a bet at my unit as to whether, or not, I slept with you. The panties would be verification. And my boss bet I could. Get your panties, I mean, not sleep with you."

She sat quietly for minutes to make him sweat. *Will men ever change? Such Neanderthals. On the other hand, I might need a Jewish protector someday … soon.* "Okay. Here." She reached under her skirt, pulled off her panties with very subtle movements without getting up – then threw them in his face.

Unfazed, he said, "Thank you. You're a cool chick, and now, you may have all the cells you want … you're sure there aren't any *other* cells I could give you?" He quickly bounced his eyebrows. *Not like I'm ever going to see you again, anyway.*

Kat gave him a disappointed look with a sneer. "No, but thank you for the offer." *Infant, I should carve out your tongue.* She grabbed a knife from the table and some clean vials from her bag left over from Athens. "I will take them right now." The knife twirled in his mouth as several café patrons gawked at this unique mating ritual.

Pantera got up, put some money on the check to pay the bill and walked out of the café. *Wham, bam, thank you, Ma'am. In the ninth inning he pulls out the win! Mission complete!*

Kat followed behind Pantera thinking she had just killed her chance at a relationship while conflicted as to whether a relationship with him was worth the effort. *Men, who needs them. I have a funeral to go to – someone who truly loved me, for me.*

The two cats stood in uncomfortable silence on the platform as the train pulled in.

"Thank you, Kat. It's been interesting." He stuck out his hand.

Kat shook his hand and gave him a quick two-cheek kiss as he turned to step on the train.

"What was that for?" he said, standing on the train facing her.

Kat was miffed. "You weren't even going *to try* to give me a proper kiss good-bye?" *You are a horny frat-boy one minute, aloof the next. You are so frustrating.*

"Maybe next time." *Maybe not ... you religious succubus. I made it through alive with panties in hand. Take that you freaks who bet against me.*

The doors of the train slammed shut.

CHAPTER 34

"NA-PO-LI," the voice over the loudspeaker rang out. The two-hour train ride seemed like it took seconds. Pantera spent the whole ride sleeping thanks to staying up all night.

Damn black widows. Damn praying mantis. Damn honey-trap.

So exhausted he tripped as he stepped onto the platform. Two shore patrol petty officers noticed and walked over thinking he was drunk.

"You okay?" The tall red-haired petty officer said, inspecting Pantera.

"Yeah, fine, little tired," Pantera answered, readjusting.

One of the men noticed a unique patch on Pantera's backpack. "We're done here, you wanna ride back to base?"

"Sure, thanks." Pantera assessed their shore patrol uniforms.

It was mid-afternoon on a cold rainy day as that familiar salty taste in the air still lingered from yesterday. Today it was not so distasteful. Pantera's head throbbed and his mind swirled from the last twenty-four hours.

"Where can we drop you?" The bald driver asked, after passing the front gate.

"Thirty-third logistics – barracks." Pantera came back into focus.

Both men looked at each other. They knew what the 33rd was, everyone on base knew. Neither 33rd ... nor logistics.

Pantera opened the door to his room and found his roommate on his bunk writing a letter, naked, as usual. Bullseye looked up inquisitively with a shrug and a thumbs-up.

Pantera pulled out the panties and pinned them to the outside of the door. "That will teach you to bet against me, you bastards!" He yelled down the empty hallway.

Bullseye smiled and nodded.

Pantera threw his bag in the corner and collapsed on his rack.

* * *

Dark clouds moved in over Rome, bringing another downpour to soak the Sunday afternoon. Kat sat next to the heater in the corner of the café and flipped through the pages of a Hebrew version of People Magazine, but the events of the preceding day occupied her thoughts. The emotional rollercoaster left her wondering.

Do you a really want to continue this? Professionally he would be good to have around. On the other hand, do I want an impudent child by my side, much less in my bed? No. Not again. Not ever.

Her mind spun with both fascination and condescension. She moved off Pantera and onto a more philosophical inner discussion – contemplating her decisions over the last year. The assignments rolled past one-by-one as she ticked off her actions and the lives affected. These people would never know. With the linear regression complete, a circular argument followed.

Did Descartes have it right or is there more to it? It's simple. If not me, it would be someone else, then why not me? Though interesting for philosophical debate, the question in itself is not very practical. Cogito ergo sum.

An outline of a man sat down in front of her. Descartes disappeared.

"*Helv, Alyn. Yevm gedvel lebyet qeph.*" [Hello, Alyn. Great day for a café.]

"Michoel. I thought you and Paola were skiing in Gstaad this weekend," she said, swirling her tea.

"We were before I got a call and this package from a friend of mine in the Maldives." He paused so Kat could recognize this wasn't social.

"I'm listening," she said, raising her eyebrows.

"In November of 1988 a group called the *People's Liberation Front of Tamil Eelam* tried to overthrow the Maldives government. The Indian president sent the *Research and Analysis Wing*, you remember, the Indian intelligence group."

Kat nodded.

"They had the support of the United Nations Special Operations Group to fight back the mercenaries and PLOTE forces. The R&AW/UN-SOG were successful, but the instigator, a man named, 'Athulathmududu', the Prime Minister of Sri Lanka at the time, was never found ... until now," Michoel said, leaning back and crossing his arms.

"Let me guess –" She tilted her head.

"This would not only be a personal favor to me, but there is a substantial fee." He smiled.

"The fee has already been deposited?"

"Yes."

"I'll be taking tomorrow and Tuesday off for this."

"Absolutely." Michoel left the package on the table.

Kat slowly finished her tea, tossed some money down on the table, picked up the package, and hurried back to her flat.

* * *

Pantera was roused by the dinner bell – but not a bell – more like an ear-grating buzzer that echoes in every hallway of the building. He arrived at the dining hall to find a couple teammates from his platoon.

After a few minutes, a brash, extroverted Australian dressed in a half-buttoned, yellow and orange Tommy Bahama silk shirt and cargo shorts plopped down at the table. The conversation came to an abrupt end as the other platoon members tried to shade their eyes.

"Yo mate," he said, speaking to Pantera. "How did the date with that Italian model go? Did cha get any poontang?" He gave him a chin up nod.

If the dumbass doesn't know, I'm not going to tell him, Pantera thought.

Pantera had never met an Australian before, much less someone from the Australian Special Air Service. He knew them only by reputation. They were neither reserved nor diplomatic and completely the opposite of their British counterparts. This Australian was a staggering magnification of that reputation. Sergeant Brandon "Brandy" White, Electronic Communications Specialist, was an exceptional example of how loud and obnoxious an Australian SAS member could be. He lived up to his reputation on a daily basis.

Without waiting for a response from Pantera, Brandy continued, "Yeah, knew it. Choked, did cha? No worries mate, there are a ton of ugly frog hogs just waitin' outside da' gate for a cute li'l Yank cherry like ya'self." He added for good measure. "If ya need some girlie mags for dat case of *blue balls*, come see me." He got up and left.

The silence in the chow hall was deafening. After a few minutes, the room returned to its normal conversational level. One of his teammates asked the question of the hour.

"Dude, so did you get *DE-jected* or what?" The teammates leaned in to make sure they could hear the answer.

Pantera knew these guys never made it to his end of the barracks to "see" the proof of his conquest. He now faced a situation every male twenty-something, or college kid, gets himself into – *did he* or *didn't he* – complete his conquest of a female. With the ensuing bet for sexual intercourse success, and thus, proving his sexual prowess amongst his peers he must provide proof or a convincing story. All men lie, some get caught, some don't. However, most are not a twenty-something genius psychopath, trained by the CIA.

He shoveled a load of mashed potatoes in his mouth to give himself a minute to review his plan, in case this topic was to come up.

The best answer would originate from two starting points of the 'did he' or 'didn't he' algorithm. He would make sure to steer the conversation to his best-desired outcome by following conversational connection patterns from everyone at the table. Follow that with who they would talk to, ten levels deep, just as any respectable Chessmaster would do. He could tell the truth about the lie or continue the lie. His "Navy SEAL" persona wanted to come clean, but his CIA training taught him to maintain cover. Starting a lie means never coming clean ... at all costs ... just be more convincing. *What about Kat ... what about her ... come on Pantera, she's in the rearview mirror.*

"Yeah baby, I did that bitch," he said. Despite recalling the truth about every second in exquisite detail, he thoroughly fabricated their sex acts with extreme accuracy – another phenomenal improvisational performance. *Fuck them. I don't owe them anything. I'm not really here.*

"Wow. Dude. You—da—man!" one teammate said, attempting to mimic the Vinnie Barbarino character from *Welcome Back, Kotter.* They all looked at each other, nodding in agreement.

"If ya gonna keep her 'round, bring her to da kill house so we can show her how badass we really are. That will keep that hot little model comin' back for more! OOORRAAHH!" the Marine yelled, giving another Marine a high-five.

Pantera exhaled and looked around the hall. Not one conversation paused. The dichotomy was hilarious. An Australian says, "poontang" in a normal tone and everyone dropped their forks. Two Marines yell, "OORRAAHH" and no one dropped a syllable.

What irony. Where am I? Pantera thought, shaking his head.

After dinner, Pantera headed back to his room to wash and iron his fatigues for the following day. After laundry came SSS then lights out.

He entwined his fingers behind his head. *Whew, my cover is still intact.*

CHAPTER 35

Monday morning started with a light drizzle. Kat had one quick errand to run before leaving for Germany. She walked out the gate and started in the opposite direction she would normally take to the embassy. Fifteen minutes later, she approached a modern-designed, shiny cement colored building with a large sign over the front doorway: "*Centro Medico dell'Università Luiss.*" She continued around the corner to a solid white door in the back. Retrieving a plastic card with an Israeli flag on it from her purse, she swiped it through the reader, and opened the door. A small sign over the door read: "*Laboratorio di Patologia.*" Her wet rubber-soled boots barely made a sound as she marched down the long sterile white-tiled hallway. About halfway down, she found the door and walked in.

"*Buongiorno, è Medico Rinaldi nel suo ufficio questa mattina?*" she asked to the woman behind the desk in a familiar, but professional manner.

"*Buongiorno signora David, è stato si aspettava,*" the woman answered, pointing to the next office.

Kat wrinkled her nose from the smell of formaldehyde and musty books. Without even slowing down, she made a right turn and strode into the next office.

"*Geb 'David. Hemh tevb leravet avetk. Ayek aney yekvel lheyvet shel sheyrevt?*" [Ms. David. How good to see you. How can I be of service?]. A small bespectacled man got up from behind a large antique wooden desk to greet Kat when she walked into his textbook-laden office.

"I need your help." She pulled baggies out of her purse laying them on his desk. "I have hair and skin samples. I need a genotype-phenotype map."

The man's face crumpled up like a prune. "What are *we* looking for?"

"Jewish alleles," she said, without looking up.

The man's face un-scrunched as one eyebrow rose. The muscles around his eyes tightened and his head tilted slightly. "I am not with the eugenics program any longer. You can go to *Dor Yeshorim* for that."

"Doctor Rinaldi. This is not for the eugenics program. It is from a man I found. It is confidential and possible Sephardi."

The man's face went blank. "A man who is a Sephardic Merovingian?"

"That's the story. You're the expert on those Jews and their bloodline. Call me as soon as you have the results." Kat handed him the baggies, all methodically labeled.

"Where did you get this from?" he asked, walking around his desk and plopping down in his overstuffed black high-back leather chair.

Over her shoulder she said, "Tell you later. Oh, by the way, father comes from a Scottish bloodline, possible Knights Templar."

The man's body went limp, arms dangled off to the side of his chair staring at the bags. "*Qevdesh harah!*" [Holy Shit!]

* * *

A book hit the floor with a loud sound. Pantera shot up as if hit with ice-cold water as a dull achy pain hit his lower gut. Trying to assess the pain, his focus diverted to the figure standing over him. Bullseye, fully dressed in his fatigues stared at him. Pantera glanced at the clock: 0530HRS.

"PT?" he asked, looking up at Bullseye wondering why he was in fatigues and not PT gear.

Bullseye signed: "You – PT ... Me – Duty. Preparing your weapons for sign out."

"Thanks buddy. See ya later." He swung his legs off the bed hitting the cold black tile floor.

All members of the platoon worked in areas that kept their skills sharp when not in the field. Bullseye, being a world-class sniper, was assigned to different ranges as Range Master.

PT chatter had returned and everyone in the platoon was back to treating Pantera as part of the team – no cloud, no leprosy. At breakfast, there was the occasional glance and point, but the level of stress on his shoulders seemed to have lifted, replaced by the pain in his lower gut. After breakfast, he headed to the Med-Shop before the 0800HRS platoon formation. The Med-Shop was next to the armory and across the hall from the communications room. Brandy worked in the communications room, but wasn't his typical self during work hours.

Walking in the Med-Shop for the first time, Pantera noticed the three sections representing the three operational platoons. The room housed all the medical equipment and pharmaceuticals needed for every possible field mission – from Band-Aids to EKG-Defibrillators and Adrenaline to Zovirax. On the board hanging high up on the wall opposite the entry door, he saw his name: Second Platoon Medical Officer—HM2 Marcus Sinclair (USN). He felt strangely connected to this cover, unlike his past assignments. He sized up the room, read the inventory list on each locker and filing cabinet then read the names on the desks. There was a desk without a nameplate. He sat down, started taking inventory of the items in all the drawers, and started checking off those items on one of his indoc sheets.

He closed one of the drawers when a U.S. Navy Chief came in – being two ranks above Pantera – he stood up sharply.

"Good morning, Chief," he said, standing at attention.

"At ease, petty officer, good Monday morning to you," the tall thin man said in a relaxed and familiar Virginian accent. "I know we briefly met at the embassy party, but I don't think we were formally introduced. I'm HMC James Lawrence, medical officer for first platoon." He extended his hand, Pantera accepted. "You can call me 'Cracker' ... or 'Chief'. This is a no-rank shop, petty officer. We like to keep it relaxed in here. The rules are in your desk. Please read them when you have a chance." He took off his cap and delicately placed it on a hook behind his desk.

Pantera didn't say anything at the ball, deciding this was as good a time as any. "If I may ask Chief ... uh, your call sign ... *Cracker?*" He gave the tall, skinny black man a whimsical look.

Cracker took a seat at his desk. "Well, it's a funny story."

Oh boy, I may need a candy bar for this. Pantera thought.

"We're in this nasty firefight, ran out of ammo, and went hand-to-hand to finish off the remaining insurgents. We cleared the rest of the building and found one of my guys down with this nasty gash in his leg – half the width of his quad – no major arterial blood, no femoral artery damage. Had no idea where my med-kit went. We were, at least, six hours from the evac site. I made everyone empty their pockets. In this pile of crap there was a string of firecrackers ..."

"Firecrackers?" Pantera interjected.

"For diversionary purposes. Didn't you use them at ST-4?" Cracker queried.

"No, but thanks for the insight."

"Hmm. Well anyway, I also had one Morphine Auto Injector left in my pocket. I tranked him with the full ten mils, making sure he was good'n gonzo'd. I wrapped the firecrackers to his leg and lit them off. It sealed the cut nicely and he had a full recovery. With a scar and a great story attached. The L-T called me, *Cracker*, ever since. It went into my file as my call sign." He ended tilting his head, a shrug, and a big white toothy smile.

"Nice. Much better than my call sign story," Pantera said, returning with his call sign story. Pantera looked up at the clock and saw it was time for platoon formation. "Thanks, Chief, gotta go."

"See you around." Cracker nodded and turned to open one of the drawers in his locked desk. He pulled out a file labeled: Top Secret–CIA.

CHAPTER 36

Grit stood in complete control of second platoon. The room went quiet as he spoke.

"Good morning, gentlemen. We made it through the first quarter of the year and Black Cycle – the training rotation will officially terminate at the end of this month, seven days from now. Blue Cycle – the operational rotation will begin."

Loud whistles and applause echoed throughout the room.

"Please double and triple check all qualification and evaluation records – or no bang-bang for you. Teammates training in other countries should return by the end of the month, except for Echo and Golf squads. We'll start Blue Cycle with four full squads – Alpha, Bravo, Charlie, and Delta. The platoon should be at full strength by the end of next month. If an assignment requires a larger contingent, we'll pull from third platoon. They're going into Black Cycle. This leaves first platoon in Red Cycle – the operational readiness rotation. They are NOT deployable." Grit paced back and forth with his clipboard in his hand.

Low grumbling and hisses filled the room. Second platoon was sympathizing with first platoon at the mere mention of 'operational readiness.'

"The CO reminds you that pagers are to be worn at all times. This will be your first and only *friendly* reminder. So help you, if you lose it. Once Blue Cycle starts, you cannot be farther than one hour from the base without a signed request-chit from me. Once paged, you'll have sixty minutes to be in the ready room at G-2." A stern look came over his face.

"Yes Gunny," the group mumbled in unison.

"And lastly, if every swingin' dick hasn't already done so, introduce yourselves to HM2 Sinclair – call sign, Pantera. Our new platoon medic, interrogator, and resident expert on Italian models."

Whistles echoed in the room.

Grit continued, "He has to sign everyone's medical records AND make sure you don't have any STDs ... not that I care. In addition, he will be working his ass off to complete his quals by the end of next the month. Squad leaders get with your team and help him get up to speed, A-SAP. Any questions see me in the office." Grit snapped to attention. "Dismissed. OO-RAH."

The platoon, including the Foreign Service members, out of respect to Grit, stood up and yelled, "OO-RAH!"

Grit took a step back, did an about-face, and disappeared back upstairs toward the office. The rest of the platoon dispersed, heading off to their training assignments. A couple guys approached Pantera and introduced themselves. After the introductions were finished, Pantera grabbed a ride with them to his training range.

They dropped Pantera off at a converted aircraft hangar bay. There was no sign, so he walked in anyway.

"Sir, I'm HM2 Sinclair. Here for small weapons qualification." He introduced himself to the back of a civilian clothed man.

"Cheers, petty officer. I'm Sergeant Markum, British SAS, and I'll be your evaluator for the next three days. Bullseye has already registered your weapons."

"All this gets reported to SFC Fountain, right?" Pantera asked, wanting to make sure nothing is missed.

"Yes. The schedule for the next three days is as follows. You will zero your weapons each morning and shoot for qualification each afternoon. In addition, you'll break down each weapon blindfolded, for time, then finish with a test on common materials for improvisational suppressors and explain their design and capabilities. Are we clear?"

"Yes sergeant. Let's rock this house."

This is tougher than domestic special ops teams. OORAH! I'm with the big dogs.

* * *

The back door of the Regent Hotel in Berlin swung open as Kat walked through. She picked the lock to the employee locker room and grabbed a housekeeper uniform from the stack. In one of the lockers, she found a universal room key card, needed to open the presidential suite private elevator. Dressed and moving. *I should be in and out in ten minutes flat.* She approached the double doors to the target's suite with a purloined housekeeping cart. There were no guards outside. She swung one of the doors open to hear two weapons cocked.

"*Guten Abend.* Turn-down service," she said, acting like a horrified maid.

"*Wir brauchen keine Nacht-Service,*" one of the men said in a gruff tone.

She put her hands up. "*Peut-on parler en français?*"

"*Oui. Sortez, s'il vous plaît.*" [Yes. Get out, please.] The other man spoke to Kat in a softer, but equally forceful manner.

"*S'il vous plaît, je ne veux pas perdre mon emploi,*" [Please, I do not want to lose my job.] Kat begged.

"*Faites vite.*" [Make it quick.]

Kat rushed into the bedroom to perform her housekeeping duties keeping an ear on the two men. Within minutes, the phone rang. The man on the phone repeated the address to the change of guard location aloud. The problem for Kat, it was in German.

In German, really? Well I am in Germany, duh.

With Kat's language skills, she closed her eyes and replayed the words until she could repeat them. Pretending to be finished, she waved on her way out the door and was on the phone in the hallway. There was only one person she could ask who she trusted without question – who spoke German.

"Alona. It's Kat. I need your help."

"Assignment?" Alona gave Kat her full attention.

"Yes."

The sisters' conversation was fast and efficient. Alona gave Kat the exact translation and Kat knew where and when to hit the target. She had less than an hour.

Back to my hotel then to the riverfront, this will be close.

The walk along the Spree River was cool and refreshing. A storm of freezing rain had just passed through. Dressed in all black leather with her specially made rubber soled boots, a chill breeze slipped in through the elastic strip down the side of Kat's leg sending a shiver down her spine. Kat found a bench on the Riverwalk just off to the side of the *Marinehaus* restaurant with a good view of the front. There were very few walkers and scarcely any tourist charters on the river this time of year. Out of the corner of her eye, she spotted a large Mercedes Benz Maybach pull up to the front of the restaurant. The target got out and walked inside. Two security guards pulled up chairs under the awning. She looked at her watch.

Are these pseudo-dictator types ever on time?

Kat hopped over the short chainlink fence and crossed over Märkisches Ufer to enter a small arched alleyway to the left of the restaurant entrance. She spotted the target inside as she walked past a window. After entering the back door, she found a server.

"*Die Toilette?*" she asked.

The server pointed toward the dining room.

Kat crept down the hallway, withdrew her Beretta, and screwed on the suppressor. The target was now less than ten meters away.

At the other end of the restaurant, a black niqab-clad woman entered with a baby carriage. She left the baby carriage just inside the front door and marched through the dining room.

The dining room opened up as Kat turned the corner. Weapon drawn she spotted the dark figure approach her target. Time slowed. Without seeing Kat, the dark figure fired three rounds, center mass. He slumped over and fell out of his chair. Others at the table dove for the corners of the room. Kat froze staring at the dark figure. Mixed signals caused her a fraction of a second of indecision.

Two assassins for the same target? How? Was this a warning or double contract?

The dark figure immediately turned toward Kat and pulled out, what looked like, a garage door opener. The dark figure crouched down into an alcove and hit the button.

Paris ... Sorbonne? Oh harah ... the Katsa Killer!

CHAPTER 37

The explosion rocked the building, spreading the target's security guards and a dozen civilians to all corners of the restaurant. The shock wave blew Kat back down the hallway. Her mind scrambled, she shook off the dust and looked up. The Katsa Killer threw off the black niqab and strode confidently toward her.

Arrogant bitch, let us dance, you and I.

The Katsa Killer fired spraying plaster all over the hallway. Kat dodged and returned fire. Her vision still blurred and dizzy, she rolled into the kitchen. Kat grabbed a stack of full-sheet cake pans and used them as a shield. Two shots hit the heavy pans spinning Kat around and bouncing her off the walk-in freezer door.

I'm gonna shove my knife so far up ... this lekn kalba [crazy bitch] is a tornado.

Kat regained her balance and bolted out the back door. Two more shots hit the door right behind her. Not wanting to harm innocent civilians, Kat knew she couldn't head to the front of the building. She turned down the alley toward a wall holstering her weapon on the run and getting ready for a Parkour escape. A three-meter cinder block wall loomed ahead. Kat ran to one side of the corner thrusting to the opposite wall. Catapulting back to the first side, she was able to grab the top of the wall. With a quick pull up and pivoting her hip on the top of the wall, she hopped over the fence – landing ass-first in a commercial trash dumpster on the other side.

You think you are so good, my ass. Kat, you are running from her, remember? The devil's advocate in Kat's mind barked, *Your point?*

Kat hopped out of the dumpster and ran to the first short building she could see off to her right. She scaled the wall, ran across the roof, and leaped off the other side landing on the sidewalk of Am Köllnischen Park. The Katsa Killer didn't follow, but Kat knew she would be circling around the building. After crossing the street, a car window blew out to her right. Another shot hit a tree behind her as she ran through *Köllnischen Park*. Kat crossed over Wall-strasse and into Märkischer Platz running past the Brazilian Embassy. Another shot hit the large plate glass window shattering it and the nerves of everyone in the embassy foyer.

Who is this Katsa Killer ... how did you know I was here? Kat's mind spun wildly. She was running through an unfamiliar city and couldn't speak the language. *What the hell did Michoel get me into – this had to be a set up. Did he set me up?*

She looked over her shoulder noticing the distance to her attacker decreasing. *So she is faster than me? Harah, I just need a couple more twists and turns, a couple cool moves, and I can escape.* The map of the area jumped in her head. She made a left turn on Märkisches Ufer as the pedestrian bridge up on the right came in to view. Bullets ricocheted around her as she s-curved down the street. She jumped the fence to the Spree Riverwalk. Another stray bullet hit a child bicyclist to her left. The young girl dropped to the ground screaming. Kat had no time to look. To her right she saw an eleven-meter Penichette Riverboat motoring up the canal in the same direction she was running. The boat was her chance. Adrenaline still rising as her energy fell, she flashed to the last time she was this tired.

Sure could use Pantera right now.

Her attacker, relentlessly in pursuit, was now closing on her. She mapped her path to jump on the boat.

This better work.

At full speed, she swung around in a two-hundred-and-seventy-degree arc landing on a stationary boat anchored in the canal. She ran along the gunwale of the boat gaining enough momentum to jump from the boat to the edge of the pedestrian bridge, seven and half meters away.

"Aaagh."

She caught the lower edge with her fingertips. The bridge moaned with the newfound strain, her legs dangling over the water. Two more shots hit the concrete above her head spraying concrete dust into her eyes.

Déjà vu. Again with the concrete?

Kat squinted over her shoulder at the boat approaching. She had two options, and one of them would surely get her killed. With a ten-meter fingertip crawl to her right, like a swinging duck at an amusement park shooting game, she could drop down onto the boat. The other option – climbing up over the rail – would put her in the protected position behind the rail of the bridge. However, jumping over the opposite rail without knowing the exact location of the boat could leave her in the murky water below – open to an indefensible attack. She didn't think she had enough energy to keep crawling along the edge.

Option two it is.

She climbed over the rail onto the bridge. Two more shots, one grazed her right thigh. Blood dropped in a steady line from one side of the bridge to the other. Another two shots hit just to the left of her hand, spraying concrete into the water below, as she pivoted over the rail. In mid-air she looked down. The boat was not where she thought it would be.

Did it change direction? Ohhh ... noooo.

The boat finally appeared from under the bridge. It was a ten-meter drop to the water and half that to the roof of the boat. Using a practiced Parkour landing, she slipped on the wet roof with a loud, "THUD," coming down hard on her left side.

Breathe Kat, breathe. It will only sting for a little bit.

A series of German expletives exploded from within the cabin below.

Kat rolled off the roof bouncing onto the deck of the boat. Her attacker screamed down in defiant Arabic from the bridge as she emptied her weapon into the roof of the riverboat.

Two very large, very angry men approached Kat.

Body racked with pain, blood staining the white fiberglass, she lay writhing on the deck of the boat. Despite being stunned, Kat pulled out and pointed her Beretta at the two big men. "Don't even think about it," she growled in English. "I'm not in the mood. Drop me off downstream."

The two men raised their hands and nodded. *"Dumme Schlampe!"* one man yelled.

I better not have broken anything. "Pantera will spot a broken rib in a heartbeat," she said under her breath. *Now why did I say that?*

* * *

Kat drove straight back to Rome and directly to the home of her boss, Michoel Bergmann.

"Michoel! C'è qualcuno alla porta!" [Michoel! There is someone at the door!] Paola shook him.

The gears in his head whirred to life as his eyes opened slowly. "What?! It's four-frickin-clock in the morning, honey. What the hell!" he spit his Hebraic accented Italian.

Michoel heard the loud banging at the front door. He rushed downstairs to the foyer with Paola bounding after him. Kat stared back through the door-viewer, brow furrowed, with scrapes on her face. He opened the door, let her in, and stared with surprise. Kat was guarding her left side with a tightly wrapped blood soaked bandage on her thigh.

Kat limped inside – sore, tired, and very grumpy.

"Miss David … Alyn, what is so urgent … did you fail the contract?" He pointed to a chair in the front sitting room.

166 · JD WALLACE

"Hell no," she said, grinding her teeth. She squeezed out, "Sorbonne ... again."

Michoel's face turned white. "Paola, we are going to my office. It is okay. Please go back to bed." Michoel rushed Kat to his office, turned on the radio loud enough to obscure their conversation.

For the next twenty minutes, Kat recounted all the events in Berlin then rested her head in her hands. Her speech slowed as she reached to her back. "Now you can understand my concern. Did this contract come directly from the client to you? Or did someone else see it?"

His concern changed to fear. "Kat, please, let me explain. I know what this looks like."

"Explain fast. I am on my last nerve," she spit, repositioning herself, her hand on her polycarbonate partner on her back. *Damn the consequences.*

"You, me, and the client were not the only people who knew." He rubbed his neck nervously.

"You gave me the impression that this came *directly* from your friend, to you, to me, but it did not ... DID IT MICHOEL?" Kat's body shook but her hand was steady. The faces of Raz, Hannah, and Nyssa floated in Kat's thoughts.

"This was not *off-book*, not exactly. I had to get your Director's approval. You know me ... I am by the book. If I get caught issuing an off-book assignment to a Kidon member without clearing it with the Director ... I would be sent to a Kibbutz, or worse. I do not have Aver's lineage," he said, shaking his head and holding himself.

"So this assignment was cleared by the Kidon Director?" Kat asked, removing her hand from her back.

"I had to have his approval." Michoel rolled his eyes.

The conclusion came to them both, like a clap of thunder.

They spoke the words simultaneously. "Mossad has a mole."

Kat took it one step further ... "And that mole set up Avner and broke into Aman."

CHAPTER 38

Kat woke up in physical and emotional pain. The last two encounters with the Katsa Killer left her questioning her abilities and doubting whether the very organization she dedicated her life to, could protect her. The idea of her confidence being challenged made her angry. The devil cat American flashed in her mind. An internal argument ensued.

You need help – No I do not. He would make a good bodyguard – No friggin' way. You have no one else you can call – Sure I do. Who? – No one. Fine, but if he tries anything, I will cut ...

Kat tossed a couple *Vicodin* in her mouth, chased them down with some Chamomile tea, and reluctantly dialed Pantera.

* * *

Days of carbon-based testosterone infused from the firing range gave Pantera a renewed since of purpose as he laid staring up at the ceiling. His long, quiet nights of reviewing schematics of the ISA building, tapping phones, and tracking a number of ISA employees had so far been fruitless. Nevertheless, even negatives in the intelligence world are positives. Just more people who didn't appear to be the mole could be crossed off the list. He would have to check-in with Jack soon.

The sound of the phone startled him. "Hello." He rolled back onto his bunk.

"Hi, it is Kat."

Didn't ever think this would happen. What do you want? "Hi? Nice of you to call, I was going to call you, but ..."

What a crock of shit. "Yeah, yeah, yeah," she broke in. "I get it, you're real busy," she puffed into the phone.

"Just trying to get acclimatized. How are you?" He could hear some hesitation in her voice.

"Enough of the small talk. I need your help. Can you meet me in Florence on Friday?"

He stopped playing with the phone cord and sat up. *Wow. Seriously? Hmmm. Pussy pool over. Maybe we trade services, professionally.* "What do you need?" he asked, in a confident monotone.

"Florence. Noon. I will send a courier with the details. Thank you."

"Yes Ma'am, whatever I can do to help." He slowly put the receiver back in the hook.

Pantera felt a "damsel in distress" vibe from her, something he never expected. It wasn't emotion that moved him. He didn't know what it was, maybe curiosity, but she did smell like his grandmother's honeysuckle.

I will help ... for a favor.

* * *

Gawd damn ... what the hell!

Pantera woke up feeling as if someone kicked him in his nutsack. From the fetal position with his hands pinched between his legs, he looked over at the clock – 0453HRS. He hobbled to the toilet wanting to make sure he could micturate. He could, with little relief. Normal morning movements made the pain lessen somewhat, so he figured PT should help. Going to sick call was not an option.

PT was uneventful and didn't lessen the pain, but the hot shower helped.

Maybe this is some weird abdominal muscle strain – got to find Cracker.

He staggered to the Med-Shop hoping Cracker wasn't on duty in the sick bay. About to enter, he spotted Cracker walking down the hallway toward him.

"Chief, can I speak to you for a minute?" Pantera asked, subtly looking around to see if anyone was watching, and added, "In private."

They entered the Med-Shop and Pantera locked the door.

"I have something private and I don't want it in my medical record." Pantera was leaning forward slightly with a grimace on his face.

"Understood." Cracker looked at Pantera with professional concern leaning back against his desk.

"I've had this pain in my lower abdomen for nearly a week and it radiates down to my testicles," he said, trying not to use any grandiose visual gestures. "And no pain meds, Chief."

Corpsmen speak the same "inferred" language. If it wasn't said, it didn't apply. Cracker knew the pain was neither from trauma, nor a bacteria or viral infection – no physical exam would be needed.

"Give me a little history. You've got some chick you're dating and haven't had intercourse with her yet? Which is curious considering the panties ..." Cracker crossed his arms tilting his head to the side.

"No. Well ... this conversation falls under the corpsman code of silence. Right?" he jumped in, walking over to his desk and gently sitting down. *Either my balls ... or the lie about Kat. Whadda choice.*

"Of course." Cracker said, under the impression he was talking SEAL Corpsman to SEAL Corpsman.

"That Italian model babe – we didn't do it." He shook and bowed his head.

"Hmmm ... She *gaaave* you her panties. I knew it." Cracker laughed.

"Hey. Can you get on with this and diagnose me. Please." Pantera was getting pissed he couldn't diagnose himself. "And it better not be some weird genetic disorder."

"Simple. You have Epididymitis – better yet, Epididymal Hypertension." Cracker moved around his desk, sat down, and gave Pantera a big smile.

"Wait one friggin' minute! I have inflammation AND high blood pressure in my ballbag. How the hell did I get that?" Pantera's voice became a low growl.

"Do you want the quick-and-dirty version, no pun intended, or the full and thorough version?" Cracker adjusted himself preparing to get in teacher mode.

"Oh pleeease. I have to hear this." Pantera delicately leaned back weaving his hands behind his head.

Cracker took a deep breath. "Here we go – understanding the anthropological history of the variability of testicular function. In short, sperm maturation speeds up and slows down based on many environmental and psychological factors."

"I know all about ice cubes and the cremaster muscle, including its function during hot and cold weather. I was awake for that class," he said, giving him the – *I know more than the teacher* – rebuff.

"Sure. That's one of many systems that go on down there. What I'm talking about is the direct effect females have on males. You have a new female who has not only entered various areas of your brain, psychologically – but also physiologically."

"No way. Okay, maybe. She's really hot. But ..."

"The *buts* don't matter," Cracker cut in, "it's about proximity. We dudes can look at chicks in magazines all day long, but there's nothing like being in close proximity to someone we think is really attractive. That's the FIRST switch that gets turned on. The SECOND switch is the enormous quantities of pheromones and other hormones women give off that we men absorb. If she is in estrus ... the number goes up exponentially."

"I'm with you. She's got my two switches flipped on. I'll concede that." Pantera was listening intently while spinning a pencil in his hand.

"Now you're psychologically turned on AND physiologically turned on. Switch one and two cause the THIRD switch to turn on – the sperm-hyper-maturation switch. Remember, we're still mammals ... *animals*. We'll never be able to escape that. Anthropologically both of your bodies are getting ready to mate. Whether you're mentally or spiritually ready – your body doesn't care. And to procreate requires lots of sperm." Cracker gave Pantera a half-grin and a big melodramatic wink.

"I get it. My sperm count is going through the roof." He nodded.

"Where do you think all that sperm is sitting ... waiting to burst forth?" Cracker asked, raising his eyebrows hoping Pantera could see the punchline.

"In my epididymis." He nodded and stared off into space.

"Exactly – being stretched painfully beyond its normal capacity with three hundred million little wiggling Spartans of Thermopylae waiting to venture forth and conquer." Cracker laughed at his own joke.

A realization came like an *AHA* moment to Pantera. "You have got to be kiddin' me," he exploded, "I have ... fuckin' BLUE BALLS?!" He snapped the pencil in his hand. "I thought it was some guy's weak attempt to get his girlfriend in the sack."

Cracker tried to control his laugher, and continued, "Yes, in the crass vernacular. Been talking to Brandy?"

"HA. So this is going to happen every time I see this chick?" A bolt of pain shot through his body when he thought of Florence.

"No. Eventually levels return and people who aren't really in love, get divorced. You're now part of a fifty-thousand-year-old mating dance and according to Grit – *a deadly mating dance* – at that."

"And the prescription?" Pantera asked, leaning over the desk, intent on finding an answer.

"Sorry. I can't help you with that," he snapped, as a bout of un-controllable laughter burst out echoing in the room.

"So either heal thyself or go find a chick outside the gate and fill'er up."

"Marriage has its benefits." He looked at his wife's picture on his desk.

"Just a thought ... why have I not experienced this before?" He shrugged.

"Isn't that the ten million dollar question. You've probably never met a woman who has turned on your psychological *and* physiolog-ical switch at the same time. Some call it *love*." Cracker shot Pantera with his phantom bow and arrow, then winked.

"No way. Love is a myth, just like Santa Claus." *There is no way in hell. I'm just horny. Plain and simple.*

CHAPTER 39

"*Achut.* What's wrong? You sound horrible." Alona answered the phone to hear a tormented sister on the other end.

"I just got back from Nyssa's funeral," Kat said, pacing in her living room, forearm rubbing across her forehead, dressed in her full-length red silk housecoat.

"Oh. How are her parents? They are such nice people." She was trying to keep the conversation upbeat.

"I promised them I would rain down revenge on her killer, *Operation Wrath of God* style."

"What's wrong with that? That's what you do."

"I do not know Alona. I have met the Katsa Killer, twice. Both times, she kicked my ass. I just do not know." Kat's emotional turmoil vibrated through the phone.

"Well, I do know. I have known since we were kids when you saved me from that bully bitch. What was her name? Bina? Ya, Bully Bitch Bina! I will never forget that day," Alona said. "You sound funny. Please tell me you're not ..."

"I am. I had to. I broke three ribs getting away from her," she cried, grabbing the edge of the loveseat spinning into it.

"Please, Kat. Not again. NO! Please don't." Alona could now sense how far Kat had fallen emotionally and wished she could be with her.

"I am okay."

"No, you are not. What are you taking?"

"*Vicodin,*" Kat answered somberly, as her head fell into her arm.

"Oh, *Achut.*" Alona sighed, her disappointment palpable.

Kat closed her eyes and took in a deep breath. "Look. I need father's help. Can you talk to him, please?" Kat pulled the big, thick, rainbow blanket her mother made for her as a child, over her as mascara infused tears streamed down her cheek onto the blanket.

"You want him to look into the Avner-Aman situation?"

"Yes. Please. And anything you can find, too."

"What about the Navy boy? Is he still in the picture?" Alona refrained from probing the girl-girl versus girl-guy relationship discussion, but needed to change the direction of the conversation.

"You mean that *devil cat* American? I did not want to ask for his help, but I had to. I cannot trust my own people and he seems capable – despite being ambivalent about everything. The guy does not have an emotional bone in his body." She blew her nose in a tissue.

"Maybe that's what you need right now. Someone who will protect you ... unemotionally." Alona needed something drastic to raise her sister's spirits. "Jacques and I have set a date!"

"A wedding? Finally. Please do not tell me it is next year?" Kat's emotional pain was slowly dissipating as the physical pain returned.

"Nope. This year. The temple in Montreux became available." Alona's energy helped Kat stay on the phone.

The two sisters talked for another hour until Kat couldn't hold the phone any longer. *I love you, Achut.*

The receiver fell to the floor.

* * *

Weeks of planning comes down to this. In the lion's den, Daniel. The Hebrew painting flashed in his mind.

Pantera stood in front of the ominous building. He remembered the first time he saw the haunted house at Disneyland. A similar eerie feeling washed over him. With his body racked with pain causing brain-fog, he lifted his chin and approached with confidence.

If these killer whales smell my pain, they will eat me alive. I don't know if I can take these guys at my best. I'm definitely not at my best.

The sign above the door read: "United States Army Intelligence and Security Command."

Welcome to 'The Activity.' So this place is owned by the Federal, fucking, Reserve.

The Activity – also known as – INSCOM, DoD-ISA, Department of Smoke and Mirrors and more recently called, *Grantor Shadow.* An organization so secret it changes its name every couple of years to stay out of reach of the U.S. Congress.

Pantera opened the door and walked into a monochromatic bright white ten-by-ten room with one bulletproof window directly across from the door. The musty stale air hit him first followed by a new paint smell.

A kill box. How appropriate.

"HM2 Sinclair, here for my indoc briefing," he said into the microphone at the side of the window.

"Yes sir," the petite woman on the other side returned. "I will notify your team leader."

Several minutes went by when a short chubby ponytailed American opened the door to the left of the window greeting Pantera with a wide smile and an extended hand.

"Sinclair ... can I call you ... *Pan-ter-ra*," he said, speaking his call sign like an announcer at a monster truck rally. "It's my favorite heavy metal band."

With a slight hesitance, Pantera said, "Sure. That *is* my call sign after all. And you are?"

"Sorry. I'm Gaston Leroux," he said. "One of the analysts assigned to your team." He waved Pantera through the door escorting him down the hall.

"One of? There's more than one?"

Pantera was unfamiliar with the concept of multiple analysts. On his last assignment, SEAL Team 4 had only one intelligence officer who was also the analyst – sometimes the position was billeted by a Navy officer, occasionally by a civilian.

"Yes. There are two analysts and one senior analyst assigned to your unit," he said, speaking over his shoulder.

"And you're all civilians?"

"Yep," Leroux said, turning into a doorway leading to a conference room. "Here we are. That is Alexandre Dumas and that is Mary Shelley our Senior Analyst." He pointed nonchalantly at each person.

Dumas, dressed in a white *Ralph Lauren* button collar shirt, *Kiton* green cashmere-silk knit tie and a black two-button, qiviuk and vicuña wool, *Brioni* jacket, nodded at Pantera. Shelley gave a weak smile to go with her black polka-dotted, white dress and black leather knee high boots. Something familiar about Shelley's boots tingled Pantera's senses.

Pantera smiled and nodded back at them both. *Look at those shoulder pads … maybe you're a linebacker in your spare time?*

Though extremely smart, Pantera was not formerly educated, or well read. All ISA analysts use classic authors' names. Primarily used for subterfuge and safety, it had a secondary benefit. If someone like Pantera possessed more academic background than supported by their military personnel record, the analysts would be able to read the person's reaction and know they were not who they pretended to be. If Pantera had an Ivy League education, as most CIA and NSA officers do, even the slightest acknowledgement would give his background away as fake, putting his life in grave danger.

Pantera nodded. "Nice to meet y'all." *I'm just another run-of-the-mill interrogator. Nothing to look at here, keep walking.*

Mary Shelley spoke with a hint of an accent, Pantera didn't recognize it. "Please. Sit. Let us get to know one another. Tell us about yourself."

Here we go – the soft interrogation. If I fail this, I could also end up as roadkill. "It's all in my record. Dad was a thirty-year career U.S. Naval Supply Officer and my mom was a domestic engineer. All pretty normal. You're all American?"

Dumas glared at Pantera. "No. How did you get along with your sister?"

Pantera stared back. *I was expecting ... well ... more. Maybe your name ... Department of Smoke and Mirrors is also what your reputation is made of. Pfft.* "You mean my brother? We got along fine, of what I saw of him. We were fourteen years apart. How many people work in this building?" He batted the ball back across the proverbial net.

"It used to be over three hundred," Leroux jumped in to dampen the flames shooting between Dumas and Pantera, "but when our name changed, a little over a hundred personnel were transferred."

"Yes. Sorry. Your brother, I mean." Dumas shrugged, acting as if the question was a mistake.

"Your father retired from the Navy shortly after you were born? Isn't that unusual to have such an old father?" Mary Shelley tried to pierce a hole into Pantera's shield of confidence with her large black pupils.

Pantera wondered if they found his grandfather's real military record and were handing him rope for the inevitable conclusion. "If you're asking if I felt it was strange, yes I knew, but we moved around a lot so the topic didn't come up that often." *Lies based on truths, the easiest to remember.*

"Are we ready to get started?" Leroux grabbed one of the binders. "Please open to the table of contents. Let's go over today's talking points. Also inside the binder is your security badge. You're cleared for all doors except one."

"What door is that?" Pantera asked, trying his *innocent-but-curious* act.

"A-TAC. The Army Tactical Action Center – for live-action satellite observation. There isn't any reason for an interrogator to be in there," Dumas snapped at Pantera.

Pantera's muscles became rigid. *You're getting on my nerves, douche. Oh please, be the mole working for the Federal Reserve.*

"Gentlemen, I think you can take it from here." The tall thin Mary Shelley stood up and extended her hand to Pantera. "Welcome aboard, operator."

"Thank you, Ma'am," he returned, using an exaggerated Texan drawl as he stood up to accept her hand. *Damn. She is spoo-oo-ky and her hands are so cold. I wonder … is she the Ice Queen everyone talks about?*

Pantera, Dumas and Leroux sat in the conference room all day. The binder was over three hundred pages and covered everything from detailed procedures for document burning to where the toilets were. With Dumas and Leroux playing good-cop-bad-cop, Pantera left the building with his head spinning. He couldn't tell if his muscles were quivering because of the pain in his lower abdomen, because it was so cold inside the building, or because he had just been skinned alive and was being toyed with.

They're killer whales alright and I'm the hapless seal pup. Lay on, Macduff, and damn'd be him that first cries … he thought, regurgitating Macbeth.

CHAPTER 40

Kat had just fallen back asleep when she heard a loud knocking. Numb from *Percocet*, she got up and answered the door. Her vision so impaired from pain medication she couldn't see through the viewing hole. *If it's the Katsa Killer, she can have me. I am done.*

It was Giancarlo.

"Oh *harah*. What do you want?" Kat whined, leaning against the door.

"*Bella*. You no come for days to work out. Want make sure you okay," he said, taking her leaving the door open and not slamming it in his face as an invitation. "You look *terribile*. I make you some tea."

Without acknowledging his comment, she closed the door and returned to the loveseat throwing the blanket back over her.

"What happen to you? Did a *classificatore* fall on you?" He gave a nervous chuckle.

"Yes. A very big filing cabinet," she said being more agreeable than she felt.

After more than a year of dating Giancarlo, Kat never told him what she did for Mossad. She considered the relationship purely a physical distraction and never intended to introduce him to her family.

"Here, your tea, *bella-mia*. What did you do? Did you hurt your leg?" He knew she had deathly ticklish feet.

Deathly – to the person who tried. Tickling her feet would have only sidetracked his true intention.

"No. My legs are fine," she said, feeling his warm strong hands rubbing her shin and calf muscle.

"Where is the *ragazzo*? No come care for you?"

He used the term denoting friendship, not relationship, not that it mattered. Giancarlo was fully aware of Pantera's comment at the Parkour Centre. He hoped Kat and Pantera were involved. Kat was just as much a plaything to Giancarlo as he was to her. *Making love to Kat will teach that 'spavaldo',* he thought, eyeing her legs.

"No friend. No boy." Kat could feel his hands rubbing her thigh – reaching ever higher causing a predictable sensation nearby, something she hadn't felt for a long time.

Half dazed and completely numb, Kat wanted to feel ... something ... anything, other than what she currently felt. Giancarlo's tongue reached dark places allowing her mind to escape the midnight of emotional nothingness. She could feel him inside her ...

Why are you doing this to me ... I hate you ... I cannot move.

She knew it was him, but didn't care. Her nerves were like bees stinging her whole body. Her dry vagina hurt, but she deserved it. She retreated deeper into the recesses of her mind – spiraling down a staircase of bad dreams that weren't dreams, they were memories.

Kat woke up naked in her bed, with her ribs screaming, but didn't know how she got there. Giancarlo was lying next to her, also naked.

How did he ... what did we do? Her mind yelled. "*Figlio di una cagna!*" [Son of a bitch!]

Giancarlo jumped up. "*Bella mia ...*"

"Don't you fuckin' *bella mia* me ... you *capra stronzo!*" [goat fucker]

Kat still woozy and very weak reached for the nightstand and pulled out her Beretta.

Giancarlo had a choice, offense or defense. Offense: to jump on her back and take the gun away – easy to do in her current state but the long-term consequences could be very hazardous. Defense: jump out of bed, grab clothes, and run.

"*Bella* stop! I go! You sleep. Get better. We talk. Later." He jumped off the bed, miscalculating the location of the furniture, and smacked his penis on the dresser. "*Oui!*" he yelled, trying to gather his clothes as he stared down the barrel of her pistol. "Yes. We talk ... *molto più tardi.*"

"No! We not talk later ... *STRONZO!* If you even look at me funny I will gut you like a fish!" She could hear the door slam. "Agh!" she yelled, rolling out of bed in a fetal position falling on her knees then stumbled to the bathroom cabinet, bent over holding her ribs. She cradled the *Percocet* bottle as if it held the elixir of life – in reality it was Pandora's Box, holding the demons of her past. She tossed two into her mouth without water then fell to the floor and cried into her hands.

* * *

By the time Pantera approached the dining hall it was dark and he completely spent. The day with "The Activity" had been more draining than all three range days combined. The culinary specialists were about to break down the food line and he had to scramble to grab whatever was left. He scraped Chicken Tetrazzini from the bottom of a stainless steel pan. The smell of overcooked Brussel sprouts didn't help his appetite but he scooped hardened Velveeta cheese sauce over them to help hide the taste. It was *barracks-gawd-awful* fine dining at its worst.

"*Bon appétit,*" he said to himself digging his fork into his chow.

After dinner, he took his HUMINT materials to his desk in the Med-Shop then passed the platoon office and noticed Grit still working.

"Hey Gunny, still here? Long day, huh?" he asked, diverting his path toward Grit's desk.

"Yep, have to get all this paperwork done before we enter Blue Cycle, because if history repeats itself ... *ugh.*" He sighed. "Don't forget to take your pager from the box over there. By the way, is Florence a professional or social call?"

"Professional. I think. I mean. I like her and all, but like Churchill said, 'she is a riddle, wrapped in a mystery, inside an enigma.' Perhaps there is a key, you know, to turn her lock, so to speak." He rubbed his temple, shook his head, and plopped down in a chair.

"Maybe the best tactic is to stay just close enough to help, but not close enough to get burned," Grit said, implying more than physical distance. "You make me cherish what I've got with my wife and kids every single day." He gave his omniscient 'Gunny' grin.

"Sounds like good advice, Gunny. What do you know about our intelligence team?"

"The writers and the *Frankenstein Ice Queen*? What do you want to know?" he asked, giving Pantera a sideways look.

"So she *is* the Ice Queen? Now that makes sense. What do you mean by writers?" Pantera furrowed his brow.

"Dumas, Leroux and Shelley? Come on. Did you even go to high school English class?" Grit wondered, "Did someone fake your IQ scores in your file?"

"Ha, Ha. High School? Had better things to do." He smiled back at Grit.

"Of course you did. Alexandre Dumas, Gaston Leroux and Mary Shelley are all famous *dead* writers. That's not their real names by the way," he said, raising his eyebrows. "One of the other analysts told me one day that *dead* is what someone will find themselves if they're fucked with. You know how I feel about spooks." He lowered his chin and peered over his glasses.

"Oh, missed that." *I knew it – killer whales.* "I understand they're civilians. Not even Americans?" he probed, trying to get what he could from Grit.

"Yes and no. Leroux is former CIA, Dumas is former NSA and Shelley is former Mossad," he said, pushing his glasses back up his nose.

"No shit, Mossad?" A cold pain shot up Pantera's spine exploding in his head. "What is a Mossad agent doing at ISA? That can't be normal."

"Above my pay grade. She was highly ranked, then something funky happened and ISA took her in as a civilian contractor. Does anybody ever know what goes on over at spook central?"

"Guess not. Thanks, Gunny." Pantera got up and headed for the door.

"And a piece of advice … don't expect she'll pick up the tab for your room, or that she'll share hers with you. Get your own room," Grit said, adjusting the pen in his hand returning to his paperwork.

"Roger that." *Hmm. Didn't think of that. Cool Beans.*

CHAPTER 41

"Alyn, ath yekvel lheykens lekan?" [Alyn, could you come in here?] Michoel's voice rang out over the intercom.

Over compensating for her medical condition she walked in cheery, and said, "Yes, sir? I was just finishing up before lunch so I could make the train on time."

"I read your report on your new American contact. He's from that UN shadow company *and* you think he's Jewish. Have you done any genetic testing?" he asked, speaking matter-of-fact through the bottom of his glasses.

"I asked him for DNA. He gave it willingly, and yes, pending as we speak. Results should be available in a couple weeks." She tried not to sit in a way that would give away how serious her injury was.

"Will you be using him this weekend?"

"Not for tonight's meeting, but given the security risk with to-morrow's asset, I will ask him to shadow me to the meeting to test his covert perimeter security skills. He'll meet me at the hotel at noon. This will give us enough time to make the meeting by two o'clock," she grimaced.

"How are your ribs? Any problems I should be aware of?"

"No, sir," she said, her *Guy Fawkes* mask securely anchored. "Doctor said they're just bruised, nothing to slow me down." *He won't call the doctor. He trusts me.*

"Thank you, Miss David. Looks like you have everything well in hand."

"Yes, sir." Kat jumped up and turned quickly so Michoel wouldn't see her wince.

* * *

Pantera's groin pain was becoming unbearable. Cracker's conversation from earlier resonated. He decided to visit Brandy's room. The door swung open with a blast of heat mixed with the smell of peppermint sex. A towel wrapped Brandy stood half-naked in the doorway with a naked Italian woman lying on the bunk behind him. Pantera couldn't look at her, being afraid of a spontaneous reaction in his pants.

"Unless you're here to shoot me in the ass, I'm guessin' we've got some business to discuss. Come in and close the door behind ya." He sauntered over to his bookshelf, grabbed a stack of magazines, and threw them on the desk.

"Damn dude, you're a porn store," he said surprised. "And out in the open like that. I can come back if you're busy." Pantera not only had never seen a porn magazine, he never saw so many at one time.

"Tally-ho prude. Peruse Mister Sinclair, only 5000 lira per magazine. And oh, the French ones are the best," he said, sitting down on his bunk giving the girl a swat on the ass.

"Are you freakin' crazy? *You* are going to charge *me*?" Pantera said, in a fit of anger.

"Yo mate, ya didn't think I was gonna to give it to ya for free? So ya could spew on it and give it back. You virgin yanks, you *muy loco*," Brandy said, whirling his finger around his ear ending in bad Australian Spanish.

"Okay, Okay. I've got a deal for you. You give me one mag then I won't lose your fuckin' medical records AND the next time I have to give you a shot ... I won't shove my biggest, square-shaped needle into your freakin' penis hole. Do we have a deal?" He raised his eyebrows.

Brandy's eyes went wide. "Who knew you yank medics were so vicious?" He paused contemplating the concept of the square needle. "I like you. Sure, you've got a deal. One mag in exchange for no shots into my very large, very long penis," he said, turning to the Italian girl and winking. "Oh. And another thing, make sure you put a washcloth on your door handle so your roommate knows you're spankin' the monkey." His face lit up with a crooked smile.

"Yeah." Pantera turned back to the desk, grabbed a magazine, and left the room.

Gawd damn chicks, nothing but sperm-swallowing baby machines.

* * *

The clacking of the train lulled Pantera into a hypnotic state. He looked at his alias badge and identification documents before putting them away after spending the last twelve hours on shift at the Naples hospital.

Do I even look like a Joshua Nun, PA? More like Joshua, Son of Nun. Those freaks love irony.

Pantera mentally reviewed his time at the hospital, reassessing all his patients, their various maladies, and the orders he wrote for them. He felt confident he performed adequately for his first rotation at the civilian hospital. The hospital didn't have the rigid protocols the Navy Hospital did so it became a relaxing end to a long stressful week.

The train ride droned on for five hours. The clanging ceased as the train rolled into Florence station. Pantera disembarked from the train taking in the sounds of bustling people and greetings, then walked outside to hail a taxi.

When he arrived at *Hotel Helvetia & Bristol* in the heart of Florence, Pantera took in the distinctive style and grandeur of the hotel – he took a moment – the gravity of the situation hit him like thunder. *I get to protect a badass Mossad agent. I'm a big dog now.* He grinned.

* * *

Kat looked at her watch, it was 1:35 p.m., and she had been waiting since noon. A fashion magazine in her lap, she sat in the lobby. If she were to act rushed or stressed it would give Pantera the impression the meeting was far more important than she wanted him to believe it was. She also knew it was not his fault. The untimeliness of the ItaliaRail system was well known.

"Miss David, you look nice," Pantera said, walking into the foyer with his one, well-used green bag slung over his shoulder.

They gave each other a formal two-cheek kiss. Pantera laid his hand on Kat's side and felt her flinch.

He said nothing. *What's wrong with you?*

"The meeting is at two o'clock at the Basilica," she said, making every attempt to mask the pain.

"That's good. I'll get a room and you can come get me after your meeting," he said, turning toward the reception desk.

"Sorry buster, we start now. You can stay in my room ... on the couch," Kat said, surprised at how easy the words came out.

Thanks for the advice, Grit. I doubt I could afford a broom closet in this place. "Okay." He turned back toward her.

"For the meeting I'm going to need you to handle perimeter security, centered on me. Can you manage that?" It came out more brusque than she intended. *Let's see that Katsa Killer-bitch fight off both of us.*

"Security shadow, no problem." Pantera could see the pain, understood it, and went with it. *I'll let that snappish comment go, for now.*

"Give your bag to the valet. Room five-o-six," she replied, giving him a quick nod.

CHAPTER 42

Kat was out the lobby doors and down the street. Pantera crossed to the opposite side of the street. He watched her walk toward the *Laurentian de Medici Library.* When the facility came into full view, he noticed the *Basilica di San Lorenzo* farther off to the left. The area was familiar to Kat, but Pantera viewed the surroundings with a virgin-esque acknowledgement. It was a quick walk to the palazzo, especially at Kat's pace.

He thought as he walked. *Didn't I read that Michelangelo designed this library and it became one of his most important architectural achievements? Look over there ... the Basilica, one of the oldest churches in Florence. Wow. Hundreds of books have been written on the Florentine architecture and here I am, smack dab in the middle of it. Cool Beans.*

The semi-circular palazzo had a single line of benches over fifty meters in length. Kat moved to a specific spot on a bench and sat down. She turned her body to the side directing him where to sit. The position she chose gave her direct eye contact with Pantera, which would subconsciously direct the asset to sit with his back toward Pantera.

Pantera grabbed a newspaper from a vendor, calculated the angles, and figured out the safest distance to protect her without being too close. He had a near 360-degree view. Eight minutes later a short fat man with glasses wearing clothes from the seventies walked by Pantera toward Kat. Kat nodded at the man with a quick glance at Pantera.

He doesn't look Italian. What is that smell? What nationality is he? He thought looking over the top of his newspaper.

The asset appeared sweaty even with a cool breeze blowing. He repeatedly pushed his glasses back in place as he approached Kat. Pantera caught the smell of fish inwardly cringing at the thought of anchovies as he noticed the man's mannerisms didn't fit the situation. Slightly nervous, a bit awkward, and he was definitely not a tourist.

She stood up and he kissed her hand, caressing it lovingly. The muscles in Pantera's jaw clinched then relaxed. *What am I jealous of? She doesn't even like me.*

Kat returned to her seat and the man sat exactly where she wanted him. Pantera was too far away to hear whole words from their conversation and thought back to the languages Kat said she spoke fluently. He was familiar with all but one, Serbo-Croatian.

The man got agitated and stood up flailing his arms.

"Radovan, sit down. You are perfectly safe," Kat barked, trying to gain control over her asset. "You're being well compensated for this information. His death will not blow back on you. Instead, it should raise your stature within the party."

"No, it won't. It will throw the party into turmoil," the man cried, scrunching his face, sitting back down, and holding his elbows tightly.

"Turmoil that YOU can take advantage of. This is good for the both of us. All I need is his schedule for the next two weeks." Kat patted his arm softly.

Kat calmed him down and they continued conversing. She moved her bag to the opposite side of her body from the man. This usually meant the man could not be trusted or there was something in the bag she didn't want him to see. The conversation looked like if it was winding down.

"Here. This is what we agreed upon," she said, pulling a yellow envelope from her bag.

The man pulled a small white envelope from his inside jacket pocket.

Pantera let his guard down somewhat feeling the danger level of the situation was decreasing when something caught his eye. A teenager he noticed skateboarding aimlessly in the area earlier was now on a direct line to Kat. He came from the opposite direction moving at a high rate of speed. Pantera definitely didn't have time to play offense. The teenager was a couple meters from Kat. She turned, noticing the teenager, and made sure he wasn't attacking her or her asset.

"Radovan, get down!" Kat yelled at the man.

The teenager reached down grabbing Kat's bag and headed down the row of benches in Pantera's direction.

Pantera noticed Kat and the man hurriedly exchange their envelopes as the teenager moved toward him. Not wanting this situation to bring any attention to himself, the man walked away without looking back. The boy's approach didn't cause Pantera to change position or ruffle his paper. When the boy was close enough, Pantera swung his arm out. With fingers straight, palm down, he hit the boy square in the throat with the index side of his hand. The skateboard never slowed down. The teenager hit the slick concrete walkway like a sack of wet flour.

Pantera calmly bent down over the boy. "*Idiota*," he said, making sure he made eye contact.

He picked up the purse and walked over to Kat. "Excuse me darlin', I believe this is yours." He offered in his best Texas tourist accent – not wanting to try his unperfected Italian accent – giving her an imperceptible nod to follow along.

Kat watched in amazement. Pantera, from a sitting position dropped a full-grown teenager moving at high speed without even batting an eye – then approached her like he had never seen her before in his life. *You are either a great actor or a ... nooo way.* A strange thought struck her.

Kat accepted the bag from Pantera. "*Grazie signore, tu sei il mio eroe.*"

She headed back to the hotel. Pantera sat down and continued to read the paper. The boy recovered and left. When everyone went back about their business, he stood up and started his leisurely walk back to the hotel.

Kat met Pantera in the lobby.

"Did my performance meet with your approval?" he asked, keeping his manner and tone professional.

"Yes. You did well. Thank you." Kat panted, the adrenaline, and *Percocet*, was wearing off sapping her energy.

"Let's go up to the room. I need a nap," she said, looking for some type of sexual acknowledgement, but none came. *Maybe Navy boy left the frat-boy at home?*

Kat opened the door and walked in showing him around. It was the biggest hotel room he had ever seen and surprise was all over his face. He surveyed the room floor to ceiling – windows, massive bedroom, grand parlour, couches, big screen TVs, and the bathroom with that second toilet, giving him a smile.

"You will sleep over there. And ..."

"Why don't you show me your ribs?" he interrupted and pointed, "You flinched, I noticed." He gave her stern authoritative stare.

"They're broken. I already know," she snapped.

"Come on. Just let me see. I'm a medical professional. See, here are my credentials." He pulled out his medical identification badge and hospital key card.

"Joshua Nun? You're joking. The Hebrew King of Spies?" She laughed, raising an eyebrow and tapping her foot. *Is that some type of hint his analysts are giving? Probably just a coincidence.*

"Pleeease, like you don't have twenty aliases. Not the name silly, the credentials. I'm a *real* Physician Assistant, eighty-percent of a medical doctor, and better than most," he said, with open arms trying to show his honesty.

"I know what a P.A. is. We have something similar in Israel. Okay. Fine, but *so-help-you* if you try anything." Her eyes narrowed pointing her index finger in his face.

"Nothing sexual. Promise." He started rubbing his hands together vigorously.

"What are you doing? I said ..." Kat took a step back.

"Shut up. I'm warming my hands so the temperature difference doesn't increase your apprehension, tightening your muscles, and cause you more pain." Pantera stopped looking at Kat as a sexual objective. She was now a patient.

Maybe he does know his shit. Kat lifted her shirt exposing her left side. The bruise had the circumference of a basketball wrapped around her body with deep purple and blue hues.

CHAPTER 43

"Damn girl. A man twice your size would be on the ground crying with that kind of damage. This is going to hurt." He slowly traced each rib to find each break without pressing too far into the subcutaneous tissue. "Congratulations. You have two breaks on each of three ribs, six fractures in total. By definition, you have a flail chest injury. Lucky you didn't blow a pneumothorax along with it. And this is common for *paper-pushing* Mossad officers?" he teased.

She ignored the Mossad comment. *His hands are so warm, strong, and soft.* "I figured it was at least a couple ribs." She relaxed.

"You need pain medication. I can call a local *Farmacia* if you don't have any," he said, standing up looking down at her.

Kat walked over to her purse a pulled out a bottle. Staring at it, the last time she opened it was still fresh in her mind. "I can't," she said, speaking softly to the bottle.

"Look. You have a major injury. I'm very anti-pain meds too, but in this case ..."

"I can't." Her eyes moistened as her lower lip quivered.

"You need the meds, dammit. Take the meds," Pantera growled, but wasn't seeing what was right in front of him.

"I CAN"T!" With the yell came a twitch of pain. Every nerve ending in her body detonated and her legs buckled. Pantera's reaction was to grab her. When he did, it caused her even more pain.

Dazed and confused, her mind flashed to Giancarlo's face superimposed over Pantera's.

"NO! I WON'T!" she yelled.

Without warning, she slammed her fist into Pantera's chest. He saw it coming and absorbed it without stepping back. The punch still gave him pause, this was no ordinary woman. A tornado of fists followed a barrage of kicks. Some he deflected, some he didn't.

Gawd damn. This is a desk-strapped Mossad agent? She could kill somebody. Ouch, that'll leave a mark, or two ... or three.

"I WILL NOT GO THROUGH THIS AGAIN!" she yelled, as she squeezed the glass bottle, "NEVER!" The prescription bottle shattered. Blood, fists, and feet continued.

Pantera could do nothing but watch and occasionally block. He protected himself as best he could, but never struck back – nor did he feel the need. He held his position watching the minutes tick away. *Oh man, you're fighting addiction and who knows what else? Grit was right ... baggage.*

"What is wrong with you, Pantera?! Hit me back. Hit me damn it!" The physical and emotional stress was dissipating along with her energy.

In a soft voice, he said, "I don't hit women."

She stopped. Eyes red and puffy, cheeks streaked with black as the pain and frustration melted away – something new replaced it. "What? What do you mean – 'I do not hit women'?" *You condescending son-of-a-bitch! Pull that "men are better than women" crap on me. I dare you.*

"Exactly what I said, there isn't a woman on this earth who can hurt me." He stood unflinching.

"Physically or emotionally?" she asked, curiosity caused the lines between her eyebrows to deepen.

"Both."

Kat felt something change inside, feeling more connected to Pantera. "We can address the physical part of that discussion later. Why cannot a woman hurt you emotionally?" Her Hebrew accent elevated as her curiosity peaked. *Does tin-man have a heart after all?*

"I'll tell you, if you're done trying to kick my ass." He moved around the bed and stacked the pillows, then grabbed Kat on her healthy side. Lifting her like a doll, he laid her gently down on the bed. *Am I really going 'there' with you? So much for the professional distance.*

"I am listening. Why no emotion toward women?" she continued, adjusting herself on the bed.

"It isn't all emotions, per se. I just don't understand the emotions that relate to empathy." He pulled the comforter from the other side of the bed folding it over her like a burrito.

"In essence you are not a tin man, completely. You can feel your own emotions, but not toward others."

"Well said. If you have your own emotions and I have my own emotions, why should I care about your emotions?" he said, tilting his head.

"Very logical. Let me understand from a practical application perspective. A woman can break your heart and you can break a woman's heart, but you do not feel bad about breaking the woman's heart? You are void of both affective and cognitive empathy?" Kat was straining to remember her university psychology.

"Yeah. For example, guilt is a form of cognitive empathy. I have no guilt for any actions I perform when torturing someone. I make logical decisions based on a certain amount of information I'm given. I can read facial expressions and fake empathy toward a prisoner to gauge my intensity and get them to talk to me, but I could care less about how they feel. They're bad people and bad things should happen to them. I am that ... *bad thing*. Whether they die fast or slow is *their* choice, not mine, and is of no consequence to me. If a decision turns out bad, then either my logic was faulty or the information given to me was, but I don't feel guilt about my decision or the outcome. I was told it's just the way I was built." He sat down at the end of the bed.

"Let me guess. Something about genetics?" she asked, focusing on him with intense interest.

"I guess. I have an unusually high IQ – the higher the IQ, the lower the ability to grasp empathetic concepts ... as you know ... genetics," he parroted, told to him when he finished his psychological testing at the Agency.

"So what. Everybody is smart. I started college at fourteen. Big deal," she snapped, being dismissive so he would tell her more.

"Now that's cool. High school was so boring I rarely attended. Graduated with a two point three then joined the ... Navy." *Whoa, almost said Army.* "During the week of my Bar Mitzvah ... I memorized the *Haftarah*, earned a Grandmaster title in chess, and was tested by some university psychology professor who sent me a letter saying I had the ninth highest IQ Mensa ever recorded. All that still doesn't mean much to me." He shrugged.

"Sounds like the education system in America cannot handle smart kids – just one big cattle farm. Israel has massive genetics and intelligence programs. Did the professor tell you what type of intelligence you have?" Kat couldn't believe she was having a lucid stimulating conversation with this man, and it was also making her pain subside.

"He said I scored highest in logical and spatial, the third was kinesthetic."

"My highest was linguistic and my second was kinesthetic. Look at that, we have something in common." She smiled at him.

"And that's why you can speak seven languages, a slew of dialects and started college at fourteen. Where did you go? Was it fun?" His eyes showed genuine interest.

Kat flashed back to Hannah and winced. "I studied languages at the Sorbonne in Paris. It was a rocky road, but overall a great experience. If it wasn't for my mother ..." Kat stopped. "Did you get your intelligence from your mother? How did you and your mother get along?"

"My mother? Which one? I lived with my grandmother, who I was told was my mother, until I was ten – a non-dramatic first ten years of life. Then, God spit on me, and sent my biological mother. From ten to eighteen I had to live with an uneducated, granola-eating-Birkenstock-wearing hippy who thought she knew everything, but couldn't even keep a job. All the while, she was married to a dead-beat musician who worked once a month and drank beer all day. Bio-Mom was an idiot. There is no way I got my intelligence from her." His manner showed his frustration.

"You hated your mother. Is that why you hate women?" She raised an eyebrow.

"I don't hate women. I love women." He shook his head.

"You do not. Treating women like inanimate objects for your pleasure is not ... *loving women*. Physical love is nowhere near as satisfying as emotional love. You just told me, you have very little empathetic capability. I think it is more than that. I think you hate your mother and project it on every woman you meet. I saw it at the ball when we first met."

"So you're head-shrinking me now?" Pantera said, crossing his arms in a defensive posture.

"No. If we are going to work together, I have to know I can trust you. To trust you, I have to understand you – and vice-versa. Am I right?" Kat attacked with common sense. "From a purely logical perspective, think about it, do you think you are projecting your mother onto women and then objectifying them as a defense mechanism?" Kat asked, raising her eyebrows.

Pantera sat and stared.

CHAPTER 44

Pantera paused to absorb what Kat asked. "My mother was verbally and physically abused every day by a *dead-beat* musician after coming home from a *crap-ass* job. She stayed married to, and supported, that *putz* for six years. I don't understand why women don't stand up for themselves. If they have no respect for themselves, then why should I have respect for them? She should have left after the very first hit or insult." He tilted his head and stared at the first woman who wasn't anything like his mother.

"So ... this robo-automaton-sex-starved-teenager act is a defense mechanism so you will not have to deeply connect with a weak woman." She adjusted herself under the comforter and grimaced. "And all women are weak ... in your eyes."

He thought about her comment for a moment. "Yes."

"Do you respect me?" she asked, pointing at herself with an, *I dare you,* look on her face.

"Most definitely." He readjusted himself on the bed. "Now I have a question for you?"

She paused looking at him sideways. *Tread carefully bucko. I can still jump out of this bed and ...*

"Why are *you* such a man-hater?" he asked, in a respectful monotone.

"Oh. Is that how you see me?" Her eyes went wide.

"That's how I *saw* you, until just now, when your defensive wall came down. Talk about defenses."

"It is a short story. I had a touchy-feely uncle. My father would not do anything about it. I got mad one day and did something about it myself. Man-egos, man-pride, and man-fear-bullshit quickly followed, etcetera, etcetera. End of story. Any man who thinks they are better than a woman better not cross my path." Her flash of temper passed.

"Why don't more women feel the way you do? Women in America like gender inequality. I told one she should move to Saudi if she wanted to feel helpless." Pantera looked down and shook his head.

"American women have only been fighting suppression for a couple hundred years – European and Middle Eastern women for thousands of years. The world covets the physically strong, not the mentally or emotionally strong," she said, wiping the black streaks from her face. "I grew up in that male cockeyed world of thinking. I am tired of it. It is time for women to rise and take their rightful place as leaders on this planet."

"Wow, sounds like your childhood was as shitty as mine. I like the logic behind your belief. Women need to stop being subservient to men. I guess we can blame western religion for that, among other *man-designed* ideologies." He nodded and smiled.

"Yeah. Two peas in a pod. Think we can work together?" Kat's mind was whirling. *Here goes nothing. I certainly hope I am making the right decision here.*

"If you're a little more straight with me ..."

"Pot ... meet ... kettle," she interrupted. "Hel-looo." *If he thinks I am giving up my Kidon status, forget it.*

"Yeah, yeah. Maybe we both could be a little more honest with each other. Assuming we're going to move this ... relationship, for lack of a better word, forward." *I'm still gonna need more from you before I tell you I work for the CIA.*

"I need your help," she said, lowering her head in a humble manner.

"Name it. I'm here." He lifted his chin up preparing for another blow of a non-physical nature.

"Someone is hunting me. I do not know who it is. I do not know who they work for. I do not know why they are hunting me. I asked you here because, as you can see, I was really banged up after the last encounter and I am just not sure I can take her on myself." Kat didn't know what was more painful – the pain in her body, the pain of admitting failure, or the pain of admitting failure to a stranger.

Gawd damn, whatta prize. I can hunt a hunter. What if you're being hunted by the CIA or ... the Federal Reserve? Could I use you as bait to trap 'em? "No shit, it's a her? Seriously. What do you chicks eat in this part of the world?" Pantera was trying to imagine another woman more dangerous than Kat. *That is freakin' off-planet scary.*

"Yes. She has skills AND money. I have never seen ..."

"Done," he jumped in before she could finish. "I'm in, but I have a small favor of my own to ask of you." He decided her help would be beneficial to him and there was no way Kat could be a Federal Reserve mole. *Do I tell Jack I'm going to recruit her, if so, when?*

"What is it?" Kat started thinking. *If you turn out to be Jewish, my boss should have no problem accepting you as an asset.*

"Soon. Say we take a little R&R for the next couple of days. Can we move our situations forward by taking it one step at a time?" He stood up as his logical nature took over.

"I like that plan. I think we should get to know each other better. This is a good start." Kat let out a slow breath relaxing her muscles causing her pain to return. She shrank back into the bed.

Pantera noticed her cringe. He left the room without a word.

* * *

Pantera came back about an hour later. "What did you do with the pain meds?"

"I flushed them down the toilet," she said, lying on her uninjured side, face half buried in the pillow.

"Now we're cookin' with oil. Like you implied, 'emotional strength is stronger than physical strength.' The psychological addiction is much stronger than the physical addiction and it was your will that broke the habit. I respect the fuck out of you for that. I've seen what it can do. *No bueno, muy no bueno.*" He plopped some bags on the end of the bed.

"Thank you. Sincerely, *thank —you.* What is all that stuff?" Kat asked, staring at the bags.

"Natural healing stuff. I had a friend – a long time ago – addicted to painkillers. We studied natural remedies for healing different traumatic maladies. Western medicine doesn't know shit, except money. Unfortunately, he got hurt again. The hospital gave him the wrong pain meds. He relapsed, drove while on *Percocet,* and died in a car crash. I'm very anti-pain meds, but I know they have a use, sparingly. There are better ways during recovery," he said, unpacking.

You keep getting more complex, I am beginning to like you. "What are you going to do to me this time?" she said, feeling comfortable he wouldn't take it as a sexual comment.

"Lift your shirt. This is Arnica. Put it on your ribs a couple times a day. It will reduce vascular congestion and the pain associated with swelling." He softly rubbed the Arnica directly on her side.

"Damn, that's cold!" She twinged.

"Now you know why I rubbed my hands so hard before I first touched you. Over here, we have comfrey, ruta, calcarea phosphoricum, and eupatorium perfoliatum to put in your tea. I also bought some tea ..."

You were listening to me about tea. She sat up, enjoying his bedside manner.

"Directions on the label. They will speed bone and connective tissue healing and keep the pain down that comes from muscle soreness and swelling. During recovery, pain is from the healing process because your body wants to rush all this fluid to the area

causing the stretch receptors to go crazy. The flip side of that coin –
we need all that fluid to speed healing. I love the contradictive nature of physiology." He thought back to the fun and challenging
times he had in the advanced military medic schools.

"Anything else, doc?" she said respectfully.

"Let's put the heating pad on so you can get some sleep. You've
had a long day," he said, tucking the blankets up to her chin and
kissing her on the top of the head.

Now you are becoming someone I can connect with. Amen, she
thought.

CHAPTER 45

Cloistered in a brown and charmeuse satin goose down comforter on a king sized bed Pantera watched as Kat slept. It was nearly eight o'clock and past his normal dinner hour. He crept from the bed and out the room without disturbing her, just in case she was serious about him sleeping on the couch. They had made significant progress and he didn't want to lose what was gained. He picked up the phone in the grand parlour.

"*Concierge, per favore* ..." he said in a hushed tone. "Hello, can you get me a table at *il Latini* for nine o'clock?"

"*Sì, sì, nessun problema* ... of course," the concierge replied.

He hung up the phone when he heard Kat getting out of bed. She entered the living room, and asked, "So, what are you up to?"

Her hair was a mess, clothes disheveled, and her make-up askew – or in some places non-existent.

He couldn't help but laugh. *Man, she's still so unbelievably beautiful. Reminds me of that Black Jaguar down in Florida. What a creature.* "How are you feeling?" he asked.

"Better, thanks to you," she said, hobbling to the refrigerator.

"I made arrangements for a table at *il Latini* for dinner. Fodor's recommended it. I hope you don't mind?"

"No. That's great. What's the dress code?" she asked, using terminology he could understand. "I will take a shower and get ready while you figure out what I'm supposed to wear." *Training the man, to be a man, no time like the present.*

He stood looking at her as she picked up her toiletry case and headed off to the bathroom. She knew the restaurant and the attire. If he was going to work in her world, she had better teach him about clothes, food, drink and the psychology of all three.

"You want me to find out what *you're* supposed to wear?" He already knew the answer but decided to ask anyway. "Because you don't know?"

"Of course I know, but if we're going to be a team ... professional, or other, you need to know how to operate in *my* world. I will teach you about the finer things in life. In exchange, you will keep me safe."

... or other? ... finer things in life? In order to get one, I have to learn the other. American women are so much easier.

Pantera called down to the concierge and the minor catastrophe was adverted.

The walk to the restaurant was refreshing and relaxing for both. No further discussion of addiction, man-hating, women-hating, or spy tradecraft took place. They walked down the normally busy Via della Spada, then Via dei Federighi which, this evening, was quiet. The tourists were resting getting ready for an evening that usually started at 11 p.m. on a Saturday night. It was a perfect time to walk past the *Marino Marini Museum* and the *Ventidodici Gallery* on their short leisurely walk to the restaurant.

Finer things in life, not so bad, Pantera thought.

When they arrived at the restaurant it was crowded. It was a favorite of the locals and one of the best restaurants in all of Florence. The warm aroma of tomatoes, garlic, and basil sent their taste buds blazing. With Pantera's size and Kat's looks added to her passable northern Italian accent, the hostess seated them rather quickly near the kitchen. Hours went by and the dinner rush had passed. Kat caught the eye of every waiter to such a degree that several had made not-so-subtle advances toward her.

You call me a horn dog. These guys keep trying to hump your leg.

Kat told Pantera about each one. They laughed about it and though quite flattered, she would give each advance a definitive answer.

"And you called me a ... what did you call me? A horny fratboy?" he said, with eyes wide.

"I did, you were. I like this ..." she said, using her index finger to point from head to toe, "man, much better. You don't see me being interested in them, do you?"

"No. I do not."

After dinner, they walked past the *Basilica di Santa Maria Novella*.

When they got back to the room Pantera grabbed his old, green bag and moved it closer to the overstuffed red velvet couch in the grand parlour.

It looks more comfortable than my bunk back at the barracks.

While picking up the phone and calling to the OOD's office to perform his security test he undressed. He placed his GPS locator and pager on the table next to the couch and left his weapons in his bag.

Kat watched all this from the master bedroom with enjoyment. It had been a long time since she felt this safe.

"What is that electronic stuff on the table, if you don't mind me asking?" she asked, entering the grand parlour.

"The bigger rectangle is my GPS locator. The smaller square is my pager. For the next four months I have to stay within one hour of the base," he said, holding them nonchalantly. "I'm sure you're familiar."

"And you still have to do that security test while on the pager?"

"Yeah. Can't let the bad guys get too far away with one of our people. We protect our own and leave no one behind."

After finishing her evening routine, she strolled back into the grand parlour with her hair up in a ponytail, no make-up, wearing a black lace, *La Perla*, mid-thigh-length silk negligee with panties. Pantera, in the middle of drinking a glass of water, spilled most of it down the front of his T-shirt.

"You don't have to sleep on the couch, but this is *not* an invitation. You get me?"

He looked up at her from the couch with the water penetrating his shirt showing the exact outline of his pectoral muscles in relation to his flat, nearly visible, washboard abdomen. He could not help but gawk at the extreme inward angle of the tip of her breasts to her abdomen, the slight protrusion of her hips, and the soft slope of her thighs. The smell of honeysuckle and the feeling of *home* washed over him.

"Come on," he said, flashing back to the 'blue balls' discussion with Cracker, "are you sure you couldn't find something else to wear ... like a freight container?"

"Sorry. I prefer the finer things and this," she said, pirouetting, "is a finer thing. If you can't handle it, stay on the couch."

This is probably another one of those psychological tests Mossad is famous for. Sorry black widow – you aren't eating off my head tonight.

"Yes, Ma'am," he said, punching his pillow, "I'll stay on the couch."

Wow. What depth of character. Navy boy never ceases to surprise, in a good way.

CHAPTER 46

The sun broke through the crack in the drapes and hit Pantera in the face. The perfume-like fragrance of the couch swathed him in a warm embrace, arousing in him a feeling of relaxation.

He looked in the bedroom at Kat's space on the bed. It was empty. He found her sitting on the balcony with a cup of Irish Breakfast tea in her hand, crouched up in a chair staring out over the bustling city of Florence.

"You know," she said, in a relaxed voice, "This is the third time I've been in *Firenze* in the two years I have been posted in Italy. I have, not once, taken the time to see all the sites." She picked up the teapot and poured him some tea.

"I sure would like to know more about the city," he said. "I read this book about Florence right before I got on the train. Would you be interested in having an escort around the city? Ya know, to keep you safe, of course." He accepted the cup of tea and adding a couple pieces of cheese and salmon to the saucer.

"That's a deal. And in exchange, I will teach you about tea." She nodded for him to sit down.

Oh gawd. Didn't think the education proposition was going to start right away, Pantera thought.

"Breakfast and dinner are the two best meals to assess someone. Dinner is much more complex ... and revealing. We will start with breakfast."

"What about lunch?" he asked, sitting down while trying to organize the lesson in a logical format.

"Lunch is a crapshoot and can't help, except for one thing. If someone wants a lunch meeting and not a breakfast or dinner meeting, then they are hiding something – even subconsciously. They are purposely avoiding the chance they will be assessed by their drink selection."

"Damn. That's impressive." He gave Kat an intense look of fascination on a topic never covered at the CIA Farm.

"For breakfast ninety-nine percent of earth's population drinks coffee or tea – tea drinkers out number coffee drinkers. What is your preferred breakfast drink?" Kat wanted to use this opportunity to get to know him better and for him to get to know himself better.

"Orange juice ... and milk." He slurped up a whole piece of Salmon at once.

"Uh-huh. Now that explains a lot." She raised her eyebrow at his tactless attack of the Salmon.

"Like what?" A piece of Salmon flew out when he tried to shove in a piece of cheese.

"Juice means you miss your childhood, probably the *under the age of ten* part, and ... let's not get into the milk and mother discussion." She couldn't tolerate the unmannered eating. "Stop shoving food in your mouth like that. Were you born in a *nikud*, um, English, a barn?"

"Let's not talk about my mother. Sorry, just hungry." He gently placed his saucer on the table.

"When you are with me, do as I do. Now, coffee and tea. Coffee is simple and over time has become the preferred drink of the common people, or proletariat . Tea is complex and has become the drink of the aristocracy, or bourgeois."

"Should I be taking notes?" he said, sitting down.

"You are a smart boy. Just listen. Coffee dates back only about six hundred years as tea dates back a couple thousand years. Coffee comes from the Middle East and tea from China. Coffee can be traced back to a goat herder and tea to an Emperor. Coffee comes from one plant and has one primary drug, caffeine. Tea comes from many plants and those plants offer a wide range of medicinal uses. Coffee is toxic and tea is medicinal." Kat took a sip and watched to see if Pantera was following.

"Wait one second. There are all kinds of variations of coffee. I know that." He watched her and took a sip with his pinky finger in the air.

"Yes. Variations of the same plant. Welcome to modern genetic manipulation. It's funny, people fighting genetically-engineered food, drink one of the most genetically-engineered foods on the planet, coffee."

"Didn't know that. Cool beans," he said, laughing at his own comment. "Aren't human beings a weird bag of nuts?"

"Now about tea," she continued, getting back to her lesson, "The benefits of tea are more numerous than the types of tea. There is a hierarchy to tea drinkers largely based on how people make their tea. The bottom-feeders: people who can't tell the difference from breakfast tea and afternoon or evening tea."

"That was a jab at me, huh." Pantera shrugged.

"Live it, own it. Next: the people who drink tea using a tea bag. Very bitter. Nasty stuff. Next: the people who use a tea infuser. The top of the hierarchy are those who use a looseleaf teapot or cup. This is where the concept of *reading your tea leaves* came from."

"Let me get this pecking order straight in my head. The bottom of the food chain are the toxic coffee drinkers, then uneducated tea drinkers, then tea-bag drinkers, then tea infuser-users and on the top are the loose leaf drinkers." He cut a piece of Salmon, placed it on a piece of cheese, and tossed it in his mouth.

Kat nodded. "Perfect. Now for the real fun. The discussion of tea leaf choice as it relates to the psychological intentions of the person. The four most common teas are White, Black, Green and Oolong – with various blends and herbals following ..."

Pantera sat mesmerized by Kat's knowledge, poise, and luminescence. In the past the only way he learned was for him to read it, see it, or do it. He finally found someone who didn't offend him, who he knew wasn't inferior, and he respected. Most importantly, the person was a female. They sat and talked for hours.

* * *

The train slowed. "RO-MA," the voice on the loudspeaker rang out.

Kat was curled up on the bench in front of Pantera.

"Miss David?"

Opening one eye, she said, "Still calling me by my last name? We have spent two nights together, you can call me Kat." She secretly liked the fact he was still being formal.

"I'm working on it, just wanting to be respectful." He stood up and gave her his hand.

In reality, Pantera had only two ways he spoke to women. He had no reference as to what laid in the middle.

"Well, I will teach you the difference between respect and disrespect of a woman. Won't I?" She stood up and grabbed him by the shirt edge. *You big, strong, emotionally-stunted brainiac. I've done more with less.* "Listen to me, Navy boy. You will now kiss me and give me a big hug." She directed him with sharp comportment.

"Yes, Ma'am," he said, reaching around Kat enveloping her in his arms, yet mindful of her injuries then plowed his mouth on to her lips.

"Whoa. Whoa!" she barked, tilting her head back. "Nice shootin' Tex. What the hell was that?!" Kat gave him a Southern accent looking him square in the eye.

"You said to kiss you," he said, offended.

"Yes. Kiss me. Not attack me with a cross between a vacuum cleaner and a blender."

"I guess this is where you teach me how to kiss, too?" He said straight faced. *You mean I've been doing it wrong all these years? Why didn't some American chick tell me?*

Over the loudspeaker: *"Prossima fermata: Napoli."*

"We will pick this up later. Yes, I will teach you how to kiss," she said, giving a small giggle as she walked off the train.

He grabbed her bags and placed them on the platform.

"Oh, by the way, I have to go out of town for a week or so. I will know in a couple days. It will probably be from the middle of this week to the middle of next week. We can discuss our *partnership* sometime after that."

"Sounds fine. I still have some more *research* I have to do before I can discuss my situation with you anyway."

They made plans to speak later in the week and Pantera disappeared back onto the train.

CHAPTER 47

"Sergeant Fountain. What's on my scheduled this week?" Pantera felt rested entering the parachute hangar for his weekly meeting with his T&E Officer.

"Pantera. Good to see you made it through last week," SFC Fountain said, as he finished packing a parachute.

"Let me guess. No riggers. You guys do the Parachute Jump and Helicopter Rope Suspension Technique rigging also?" He leaned up against the packing table with a Coke in his hand.

"Yep, with a few other special ops rigging certs, for extra measure. Need something to do after I retire." He grinned with a sideways look and spit a dark-leafed liquid into a Pepsi can.

"I'll have to look you up sometime. Would love to do some jumps up in those Apennine Mountains," he said, staring out the hangar door at the mountains to the north.

"Alright." Fountain finished the last tie on the parachute he was working on. "Your schedule will be getting more intense this week. Monday: Automatic weapons, including suppressors. Tuesday: High-Altitude/Low Opening and High-Altitude/High Opening. Wednesday: SCUBA – Open Circuit Diving, Closed Circuit Rebreather Diving, Closed Circuit Mixed Gas Rebreathers, and Night Operations with Submersible Delivery Vehicles. Thursday: Hand-to-Hand and Non-Projectile Weapons. Friday: Performance/Tactical Diving with Vehicle Mechanics and Hot Wiring of Electronic and Analog Systems." He put the parachute next to six others on a side table.

"Nice. I like, but doesn't some of my quals from the Teams at Little Creek cover some of this?" He finished his Coke and threw it into the fifty-five gallon drum in the corner.

"No. If you were in a Navy unit, then yes, maybe. This is a UN run unit so there's a whole new set of qualification records and paperwork to be filled out. Now head over to building nine and talk with Sergeant Huckabee. He's former Canadian Special Forces – Joint Task Force Two. You'll be working with him today."

"Full auto. Love it. See you tomorrow for some parachuting, Terry." Pantera hit the air with his fist.

* * *

Pantera's parachuting day was so long he almost missed chow. The amount of food on the chow line was minimal, the smell was unappetizing, compared to Salmon and cheese. The culinary specialists were familiar with him as they could always use the help of a medic and let him behind the line to fill his own plate. He quickly finished dinner headed up to the room for a quick SSS before he called Kat.

"Hallo?" The voice clicked over.

"Miss David?" he said, in a more professional tone than usual.

"Mister Sinclair?" A small giggle echoed on the other end.

"Okay Kat. I get it." What she said on the train hit him.

"Good. Pantera." The women's voice turned into a laugh. "This isn't Kat."

"Oh. It isn't?"

"No, but I could be ..." The voice trailed off.

"Give me the phone, sheesh." He could hear Kat approaching the phone. "Pantera. I'm sorry, my sister seems to think she's being funny." Kat paused and Pantera had an idea of the dirty look Kat was flashing her sister, from his own experience. "Alona, my sister, decided she is going to use my flat while I'm gone for the week.

Without asking, may I add. She just showed up on my doorstep a couple hours ago."

In an attempt to skirt out of the situation, Pantera returned, "I'm sorry to bother you. Just wanted to call you and wish you a safe trip. I'm goin' to be underwater all day and tomorrow night. I wouldn't be able to call you like we planned."

"It's good you called because I will be leaving tomorrow afternoon and won't be home tomorrow night either."

"Where are you off to, if I may ask?" He wanted to test the waters.

"I can tell you. I'm off to Serbia for a little harmless discussion. All very boring." She knew giving a plausible lie, or cover story, is better than saying nothing. "What have you been up to?" She was genuinely interested in what the shadow warriors do when not hunting terrorists.

"Yesterday was automatic weapons qualification and today was parachuting," he said, making it sound very rudimentary.

"Now that sounds fun. We'll have to meet up when I get back and further our discussion," Kat said.

"I have an update coming and should be prepared to provide a descent report," he said, being purposely cryptic.

"Thank you for the call, Navy boy." Her smile could be heard over the phone.

"Okay. Have fun with your *discussions*. Talk soon." Pantera hung up.

* * *

Kat put the phone back on the hook and noticed Alona staring at her.

"What's going on there?" Alona had one eyebrow raised.

"I told you. I asked him to help me. We're going to get together and compare notes. It seems he wants my help with his ... situation," Kat replied, giving Alona an innocent smile.

"*Achut,* you are playing with fire." Alona shook her head. "You need to be very careful. Very, very careful. You get killed and Mossad considers it a professional hazard. If he gets killed, the whole unit takes it personally. And you will be first on their off-book hit list."

"Mossad? Mossad has left me and five of my sisters flapping in the wind. Who do you think I should call? Ghostbusters?" Kat opened the refrigerator pulling out a bottle of white wine.

"I'm not saying you're making a mistake by asking for his help." She took Kat's hand reassuring her. "I'm suggesting caution. That's the deadliest unit on the planet. That's all."

"Anything from father?" Kat asked.

"No." Alona set two wine glasses on the table.

"Didn't think so. What would make me think ..."

"Stop right there," Alona cut her off, "He's working on it. It takes time."

"Yeah, well. Time is what I'm short on. This bitch could be standing in the courtyard right now as far as I know." She poured each wine glass half full.

"Slow down. We'll find her."

"Sure. Or she'll find me ... again." Kat plopped down on a dining room chair. "Oww," she yelped, holding her ribs, a firm reminder of the last encounter with the Katsa Killer.

CHAPTER 48

"How did you do with the *stealing cars* part of your indoc?" Staff Sergeant Harry Franklin, Charlie Squad Leader waved Pantera over to sit down with the rest of his team in the overly white dining hall as the smell of bleach and bacon filled the air. Harry Franklin was another of several U.S. Marine Reconnaissance Sergeants making up the three platoons of UN special operators. He stood six feet tall, sandy-blonde high and tight with a unique rope burn encircling his neck – a gift from a high value target half a decade in the past.

"Good. Definitely not part of the operational readiness training at the Teams," Pantera said, sitting across from Harry.

"No kiddin'. I spent ten years with Marine Force Recon and none of that prepared me for this. Did you have that NSA dude, what's his name? Chamberlain?"

"No. Some guy named ... Shattuck, Muckluck, ahhh, kiss-my-butt, I don't remember. Names don't mean anything. He was such a dick. I just dropped my nose to the grindstone and got outta there as fast as I could." Pantera shoved a heaping spoon of scrambled eggs in his mouth.

"How was Florence? Another weekend of rough and tumble nakedness?" Harry asked.

The whole team turned their attention to Pantera waiting with baited breath.

"What can I say? When you have the meat, the women can't help themselves. What sperm-guzzlers they are, too. So listen to this … we're sitting at this bench suckin' face, ya know, a little PDA and this freakin' skateboarder swoops by and tries to steal Kat's purse." Pantera gave a grand skateboarding gesture.

The team was captivated by Pantera's storytelling.

"Before even thinking about it I swung my arm out, hit the punk in the throat and dropped shithead to the pavement," he said, using a gesture to recreate the action.

"Dude. That was sweet," a voice said, coming from one of the team members.

Harry jumped in during all the congratulations. "Saving the damsel. Very good. How 'bout a little business? I know you still have one more week of individual quals left. Are you going to be on base this weekend?"

"Yup. No chitty-chitty-bang-bang for me this weekend," he said, thrust his index finger inside the "O" of his index finger and thumb of the other hand.

"Why don't I see if I can grab a unit training location and we can help you get a couple of those unit training quals signed-off," Harry offered.

"AB-SOL-FUCKIN-LUTE-LY," Pantera howled, excited that something finally presented itself. Otherwise, it would have been a long weekend.

"Roger that, Doc. I'll check in at the OOD's office to see which range we can use and call Top-Shirt and Gunny for their approvals. John, you come with me to get the comms list for the evaluators and see what kind of deal we can strike. Pantera, you may have to prostitute your girlfriend to one of the evaluators. Is that going to be a problem?"

Huh? Girlfriend? Pantera paused with a deer-in-the-headlights look.

"Just kidding, peace out gentlemen. Let's go high speed, OOORAH," he bellowed, jumping up to put his plan in motion.

"Let's form up at zero eight hundred hours on the grinder tomorrow after PT and chow."

* * *

Kat exited the plane and read the sign over the airport terminal:

MEĐUNARODNA ZRAČNA LUKA ZAGREB
("Zagreb International Airport")

The airport was a small single flight line airport. Kat traveled on a diplomatic passport and moved through customs quickly. Walking through baggage claim with her one carry-on bag she spotted her handler leaning against a parked car in the immediate loading zone. They exchanged pleasantries and got in the car.

Twenty minutes later·the car pulled into an underground parking structure. A fancy sign over the doorway read, "*Esplanade Zagreb Hotel – Presidential Suites.*" Two men, Kat, and her handler entered the elevator. The driver passed a card over a box above the buttons and the elevator moved, passing all floors and stopping on the seventh floor, the top floor.

In a deep guttural Hebrew with a distinctive practiced authority, the handler directed, "Miss David. Your room is at the end of the hall, second door on the right. Briefing in one hour. Your clothes, hair and make-up requirements have already been delivered." He looked in the direction of the room.

"Thank you." She said in a professional Hebrew, as she sprang down the hallway.

Kat entered the suite and recognized it, not as *a presidential suite*, but as *the presidential suite* – the hotel's largest suite. A tingle went down her spine.

She trained for this, she worked hard for this and this is what would make her father proud. The closet held three skimpy dresses, a long overcoat, and matching shoes. At the vanity table, she found a full make-up case, three distinctive wigs, and a large jewelry box.

She opened the jewelry box and immediately recognized that everything was faux jewelry– but good costume jewelry.

A large dossier sat on the dining room table. She grabbed the file, kicked off her shoes and went to the kitchen. With a hot cup of Oolong tea in hand, she retired to the couch in the living room and read. It was early morning when Kat finished the dossier when her handler and the two other men walked in.

Kat had never worked with this handler before. She could tell he was "old-school" Mossad. He was in his mid-sixties, short and balding with a combover. The dumpy brown polyester pants showed his droopy socks, reminding her of the Greek on the plane not so long ago. She smiled at the significant difference between the two.

At least his shoes are laced up, she thought.

With soft rubber soles and leather uppers Kat knew her handler's intent was to appear nondescript. It was very effective. These men were the old-school Kidon assassins – the deadliest. They look exactly the opposite of how they are portrayed in the media and why they are so effective.

"Miss David, you can call me, Ariel. This is Saul and Amir, Shin Bet. They will be responsible for your security, surveillance of the target, and will be your escorts until the end of this assignment." His dark brown eyes were penetrating, his Hebrew gruff.

Kat nodded and they nodded back.

"This is a straightforward kill-order assignment. The target is Major General Rade Dragic, Serbian Commander of Užice Korpus. His criminal history is in the dossier," Ariel began.

Kat pulled the photo out and gave it a long look.

"He is responsible for the death of thousands of Jews in Serbia and the surrounding areas. He is one of the top weapons traffickers in the Balkans with several of the largest organized crime syndicates as his clients ... and he is a ghastly sadist."

A sadist? My favorite. Kat clenched her jaw and entered her *I dare you* mindset.

"Every three months, Dragic reports to the Embassy here in Zagreb to brief the Ambassador. He will get a suite at the Hotel

Dubrovnik and will normally not hire a prostitute until Friday night. His modus operandi – he beats the prostitute, has intercourse with her, then kills her. He leaves the cleaning to his security team. He will arrive tomorrow and the suite has already been reserved."

One more pseudo-macho man is going down. I am making the world a better place, one man at a time. Kat grinned.

"We will intercept his call to his source and Miss David will be inserted as his prostitute. The last three times he has asked for women of different color hair and features. We have to be prepared for whatever he asks for. Let me be clear. If something goes wrong, Saul and Amir will be right next door and will clean the room. Miss David, the remainder of your supplies will arrive tomorrow. Do you have any questions?" Ariel paused waiting for a question – knowing he didn't miss anything.

My first high value target, finally.

"Is there a pager or something so I can walk around?" Kat was not going to miss the opportunity to see the sights and go shopping.

"Yes. Your pager is on the table. We will contact you when we are ready. Dismissed."

Being somewhat overwhelmed, she leveled herself quickly. *Doesn't matter their position. They all bleed. Now after five years in the Kidon, I made it.*

Kat had officially graduated to the highest level of assassin. She was truly, in Mossad's eyes, a Master Assassin.

Adamm, I hope you can see me. Please help father understand.

CHAPTER 49

Kat was in the hotel store when her pager went off. The thrill shot through her body as she walked calmly to the elevator.

Ariel met her in the hallway. He stopped his conversation with Saul and Amir. "The requirements are on the vanity."

The note read: "Red hair, brown eyes, and armpits shaved. Ready in one hour."

Kat knew there was probably more to the list, but Ariel knew the General wasn't going to make it that far.

Don't forget the black chalk for the teeth. Don't want that to happen again.

Kat had a bad past experience playing a prostitute. Zagreb prostitute means poor dental hygiene. Showing up with her perfectly straight white teeth could end her life. She slipped into the black skimpy dress and black knee-high boots. In another box sitting on her dresser, she found every conceivable, concealable, instrument of death.

Toy box.

Saul and Amir met Kat at the elevator. They all jumped into the car and were off. Saul stopped a block from the hotel. "We will be in the room to the left if ..."

"Got it," Kat interrupted, "Now let's drop this fucker."

The two men smiled and nodded.

Kat entered the lobby area and noticed a man approach her with a Serbian military pin on his lapel. In her best lowbrow Serbian accent, she got his attention.

"здраво уопште, где је наша странка?" [Hallo General, where's the par-tee?] She acted inebriated.

The man sneered. "I'm not the General. You follow me."

Whew. Kat relaxed.

Balkan dialects are extremely difficult, so she had to try it out on the "help" before speaking to the General.

The man led her to the elevator getting in with her. Saul and Amir stepped up next to the other elevator as the doors closed. She felt reassured. Her confidence grew with every step as she strutted down the hallway.

Sadist huh? Looks like you're hitting women days are over, General Douche-bag.

She could see another man standing in front of a set of double doors at the end of the hallway. They stopped. The man at the door spoke a deep raspy Serbian.

"Give you purse him. I now search you. Face wall, bitch." The guard moved closer and Kat could smell mackerel.

Ever heard of soap?

Kat handed the other man her purse and raised her arms out to the side. He forcefully pushed her up against the wall. With one foot, he kicked each ankle to the side to get her to spread her legs farther apart. He grabbed both breasts – more in the pursuit of sexual groping than trying to find a weapon.

Kat caught his vicious grin. "Hey, hey, not for free bastard."

The man continued groping her until he got to the edge of her dress. Realizing she wasn't wearing panties he reached up and under. He found what he was looking for – where her legs stopped. He proceeded to take one hand and slide it forward – penetrating her slightly. She groaned faintly for the act, but clinched her jaw muscles.

Well fucker you just made my list ... right after the General.

The other man didn't find anything he could identify as a weapon. He handed the bag back to her and then knocked on the General's door.

The General answered the door with an unfiltered Russian cigarette dangling from his lips and his military shirt unbuttoned with a thin white T-shirt trying to hold back the grizzly he had underneath. He looked her up and down, gave her a predatory smile, and motioned for her to come in.

Kat assessed the General immediately. He was monster huge, standing at least six foot five and weighing over two hundred and fifty pounds. Wealthy by Balkan standards, he wore crappy cologne mixed with a strong low-end tobacco smell that could have put a lorry driver's sock to shame.

Qevdesh harah, I wonder what would happen if men could actually smell themselves?

Kat strode in and sat down on the bed. The General did not speak a word. He prowled toward her. Before she knew it he slapped her so hard across the face it knocked her into the bedside table – cutting her cheek on the corner.

That's going to leave a mark.

Wincing in pain from the rib fractures she reacted quickly, but acted slowly – giving him the impression she was disoriented. The feint allowed her to pull her first weapon. She got up slowly. His attack continued by grabbing the shoulders of her overcoat and pulling it straight to the floor. This caused her to spin around and face him where she could have kneed him in the face, but didn't.

"Pleeease ... don't hurt me," she begged, acting out in a mousy Serbian.

The General, in a grating tone through a masochistic smile, said, "I'm goin' to beat you to a pulp and then," his eyes gleamed, "fuck your brains out."

He reached up under her dress forcefully grabbing her crotch throwing her across the bed. The bottom of her dress rose up to her navel. One side of it ripped, revealing her left breast.

Okay General Douche-bag, look what I have for you.

She flipped over to a crawling position, hoping he didn't realize her muscle tone was far greater than any Balkan prostitute. Already winded, he unbuckled his belt.

There is no way I'm letting this scumbag hit me with a belt. "My turn," she said in English, so he would understand.

She crawled a couple feet across the bed toward him and jumped on his chest. With her legs wrapped around his diaphragm, she grabbed his chin with her right hand as if to kiss him.

His eyes widened and he smiled, "Ah, yes!"

He opened his mouth in anticipation of a kiss, instead he got a whole lot more than he bargained for. Her right hand stabilized his open jaw while her left hand held a small canister the size of *Binaca* breath spray. She pumped the button three times spraying something into his mouth. She sealed her lips over his and breathed out as hard as she could. This forced him to inhale deeply. The canister dropped to the floor. With one hand holding the back of his head she forced his mouth closed with the right – sealing it tight.

"If the *Ether* wasn't exciting enough for you, General, just wait 'til you see what comes next." Her legs vice gripped around his rib cage staring into his eyes.

She saw his man-ego fronted by a masochistic grin morph into unadulterated fear. His massive hands reached up to grab her throat in an attempt to throw her off. She was far too strong. Ankles locked, she squeezed his mid-section so hard she felt a pop. After ten seconds, she felt the muscles in his body go flaccid. She rode him to the floor like a cowboy riding a dying bull.

"Night, night Richard Cranium," she said, flashing her Cheshire cat smile. "Now, I've got fifteen minutes."

She snatched two pillows and placed them on top of each other in the middle of the bed. With all her strength she lifted the two hundred and fifty pound General onto the bed face down with his pelvis on the pillows. She pulled his pants down to his knees leaving his butt sticking up in the air.

What is it with men and tighty-whities?

CHAPTER 50

She retrieved a small speculum and a syringe, withdrawing some fluid from a small vial. She inserted the speculum into the General's rectum, opened it wide, then inserted the fluid into one of the large veins of the external rectal vault.

"Have a little *Succinylcholine*, you fuckin' bastard," she muttered.

She picked up her tools, tossed the room, and positioned the General into a supine position. After straightening herself, she re-assembled two plastic air guns. The General stopped breathing.

"Help! Help! The General!" she yelled at the top of her lungs.

The two security officers rushed in. She shot them with a tranquilizer dart and within three steps they dropped to the floor. Saul and Amir arrived from next door.

"Throw them off the balcony and wipe down the room while I write the note." She directed.

The note said: "The General died having sex. We failed the General. Please forgive us."

She wrote in a barely readable Serbian scribble. Kat and the two men ran down the stairs and out the back of the hotel to the loading dock where the car was waiting.

The next day the Zagreb *Večernji list* paper read:

"FOOTBALL GAME ERUPTS, ENDS IN BLOOD SHED"

and on page six,

"MAJOR GENERAL RADE DRAGIC, DEAD FROM HEART ATTACK, SECURITY GUARDS COMMIT SUICIDE."

Kat read the paper, poured herself a cup of tea, and walked out onto the veranda. Her handler appeared in the doorway as she was looking out over the park and art pavilion.

"Good improvisation with the guards. Very good. His guards were never outside the door before. Your tickets for Tel Aviv are on the vanity. You leave tomorrow morning. Did you put everything you wore in the bag so Saul and Amir could burn it?" he asked with a hint of satisfaction.

"Yes. It's in the closet," she replied, turning to look at him.

"And your cut, will that be permanent?"

"I don't think so." Her body ached as yesterday leapt into her mind, but thanks to the medicine Pantera gave her the pain was now tolerable.

"Good working with you." Ariel left the suite.

Kat finished her tea and reflected on the recent events. *I need a spa day.*

CHAPTER 51

"CLEAR," the last man yelled.

Harry looked up at the evaluator. "TIME?"

The evaluator looked at his stopwatch and turned his gaze to Harry. "One minute, thirty two seconds ... PASS. Gentlemen, you're quals are done at this house. Your eval sheets will be sent to your platoon sergeant."

The six men unstrapped their helmets and cheered.

Harry yelled, "Guys, bring it in."

Pantera said to the team, "Just wanted to say thank you for taking time on a Saturday to help me get caught up. And next time I have to update your tetanus, I won't shoot you in the *ball sack.*"

The men roared. They all slapped Pantera on the back as they walked out of the kill house.

Harry walked over to Pantera. "Ya know. You could bring that fine Italian model of yours around next Saturday. I'm sure Grit could get one of those intel-spooks to sign-off on her clearance. Just sayin', it would be nice to share with your fellow teammates." He shrugged with his hands in the air as he walked away.

* * *

"*Hallo Imah*," Kat yelled, dropping her bag in the foyer. "I'm home." She walked into the sitting room of the house.

"Kat? Kat!" Tirzah got up to give Kat a big loving embrace as she noticed the centimeter gash under her eye. "Aw, are you alright?"

Kat nodded.

Kat's mother knew what she did as a profession, but rarely saw any injuries.

"Come in here and sit down. I want to hear about your new gentleman friend. I had to hear about this from your sister," she said, dragging Kat onto the couch with a pseudo-pout staring intently at her. Kat's mother was a tall thin stereotypical Jewish mother.

"There isn't much to tell. We've seen each other twice – a couple dinners and a couple breakfasts." She took her mother's hand. "Nothing really to tell."

"Will you bring him to Alona's wedding? You haven't had a boyfriend in so long."

"I don't know, *Imah*. That's still a long ways away. Where is *Abba*?"

"Alyn?" Her father walked into the room. Gideon David, Director of the *Sherut haBitachon haKlali*, better known as – Shin Bet – one of the three intelligence agencies of Israel. And husband to Tirzah David (Herzog), daughter of the former Director of Mossad. Kat's father was a medium-height, heavy-set man with a permanent brooding scowl. By current society's standards, he was significantly older than Kat's mother.

Kat jumped up out of either fear or respect, she never knew. "Father, it is good to see you."

They gave each other a formal two-cheek kiss.

"Your Director informed me of your success." He nodded approvingly.

"Yes, sir. The mission went well," she said, in a humble tone.

"And I understand you have a debriefing on Tuesday morning. I will see you there. Get some rest." He turned to leave the room.

"Did Alona talk to you about my situation?" She rubbed her hands together behind her back.

"Yes. The Avner-Aman breach. The investigation is still on-going."

"Has there been anything? I have lost five friends and fellow Katsa, *Abba!* And! I have had my ass handed to me twice. There has to be something you can do?" she yelled, her emotions bubbling to the surface.

"Are we still talking about the Katsa Killer or is there something else you would like to talk about?" he asked, speaking in a calm monotone.

"Don't HANDLE me!" she shouted.

"Is there something you want me to do or is there something I haven't done? Which is it? There is nothing in the Aman system that leads to a mole. It was a highly skilled intrusion by someone who knew our system and they created their own access."

"And ...?" Kat knew her father was deflecting.

"And what?"

"When are you going to stop hating me for Adamm's death?"

"I don't hate you." His shoulders dropped.

"Of course you do. Your precious Kidon son got killed and you leave your *whoops-of-a-daughter*, the second senior level Kidon female ever, out in the cold. Stop ignoring me!"

"I have not left you out in the cold. You could have been so many other things." He said in a grating tone.

"What? A housewife? An analyst like Alona? You got the genetic report. I'm doing what I was genetically built for – and serving a country who can't protect me," she said, pointing out the window.

"Mossad is doing everything it can do. You are so impetuous! Men are so much ..." His anger broke through.

"Men are what?" Kat broke in. "Better at what? Is that it? Only men can work for Kidon? How dare a female do what a man does?" She pushed harder.

"Yes! There are places women have no right to be, this is a man's world! Ever since that day with your uncle ... so embarrassing." Gideon exploded.

Kat stopped. She did it. The resentment she thought was about her brother's death wasn't about his death at all. It was about her father's embarrassment behind the death of *his* brother at hand of *his* daughter.

"Over a decade, and your dead pedophile brother is more important than your living daughter," she screamed, the pain was almost too much for her to stand. "Please don't come to the debriefing. I don't have your support – never had your support – so please don't bring that charade to my promotion ceremony. I have lost faith in you." Kat grabbed her bag and stormed out of the house.

Tirzah stared up at Kat's father from the couch. "Gideon. You will fix this ... by God!"

* * *

Deep into the night, Pantera sat staring at the computer screen in the ISA building – in the heart of the beast. He rubbed his neck more out of frustration than to relieve the stiffness.

Where are you? You slippery little bastard.

He looked at his watch and realized it was almost midnight. His mind wandered from the stress and missing dinner and lunch.

Over a dozen offices searched. Nowhere? Absolutely no ... where.

He turned off the computer and was getting ready to leave the building when he heard something down the hall. Before turning off the computer, he remembered looking at the badge entries. There were no badge entries for this part of the building. This is Spycraft 101: Know Your Surroundings.

Pantera got up and moved slowly toward the sound in a conscious effort to hide the sound of his footsteps. Halfway down the hallway he smelled smoke. He cautiously approached the room from which the smell was emanating. He pulled his favorite blade and readied himself for confrontation. He stuck his head around the corner as his eyes swept the room. It was empty with smoke rising from the trashcan. Just as he entered the room, he heard someone run down the hall and exit the building.

Don't worry my friend ... I will get you. I always do.

CHAPTER 52

Pantera rummaged around the empty unassigned office and discovered a lot of miscellaneous binders and non-classified documents – nothing of real interest. The trashcan had a few pieces of unburned paper in the ash. One small unburned section of a letter remained. Pantera carefully picked it up. All that remained was the header. The logo read: FEDERAL RESERVE SYSTEM. He placed it carefully in his pocket taking note of the time and exact location where he found it.

Time to call Jack.

Pantera pulled out the phone and unhooked the scrambler. He hooked up the scrambler to the phone of the desk and made a call.

"Making any progress?" Jack answered the phone.

"It is freakin' slow. It's a desert out here." There was irritation in Pantera's voice.

"Patience my friend, slow and steady wins the race. They will make a mistake. Don't worry about that," he said.

The slow Bostonian accent became calming to Pantera.

"I met with the three analysts. No one knows their real names – two guys and an older chick. One former Agency, one former NSA and the woman, I understand, is former Mossad."

"Mossad? That is unheard of. I've never heard of anyone being *former* Mossad."

"I can't do anything about the Agency guy until you get me a name to check out unless ... you can get me a photo of him? I can do facial recognition." Jack was trying to push Pantera's creativity.

"Yeah. That's it. I'll just walk up and snatch a badge from an ISA intelligence analyst. Thanks Jack, sure you couldn't get me killed any faster? What did you find out about the Brit?"

"He was MI-6 undercover as British SAS with the unit. I was told he gave some information to his wife, who is also MI-6. She won't turn it over, but they agreed to send her to Naples to speak to you. Maybe you can get something out of her."

"Anyone else looking good as our mole?"

"No. This place is zip tied tight. I've engaged a female Mossad officer from the Rome Embassy. I think they also have a leak." Pantera wanted to see Jack's reaction to bringing Kat in on the investigation.

"A Mossad officer? You know how fierce they are. Just make sure she doesn't double you over." Jack paused to make sure Pantera understood.

"I know. I know. But when she gave me her situation she looked, quite frankly, scared. I haven't told her anything, yet. We'll meet this weekend and see how we can help each other."

"Alright. Call me after your meeting with the MI-6 woman."

"Deal. Ciao." Pantera threw everything back into his bag and left the building.

* * *

"Congratulations. You made it to your third and final week," Fountain said, leaning back against the parachute packing table as Pantera entered the hangar bay.

"Thanks. What cool shit have you got for me this week?" He took his cap off and plopped down in a chair throwing his boots up on the metal desk.

"All illegal, of course. The analysts have asked that you come back in, but they never told me how much time they wanted. I as-

234 · JD WALLACE

signed you to HUMINT the whole day today. Tomorrow: Standard Explosives and Unconventional Explosives. Wednesday: Breaching and Surreptitious Entry Operations. Thursday: Apprehension Avoidance. Friday: Navy Hospital." Fountain missed his Pepsi can and cleaned his hand on his pant leg.

"Do I use my same alias package for the Navy hospital as I did for the Naples civilian hospital?"

"Yes. That's your permanent NOC (Non-Operational Cover). That's what it's there for. I understand Grit will sign-off your unit training. You're almost operational. If you need anything give me a call. You know where I am," he said, pulling out the wad of tobacco, throwing it the can and wiping his hand in a paper towel.

"Thanks Terry. It's been a blast working with you." Pantera shook Fountain's hand and walked out of the hangar bay.

It was a short half mile walk to the ISA building with the night's events fresh in his mind. He could only wonder bad thoughts. *Did I miss one of their surveillance systems? Was I on camera going through someone's desk? Why would they want to talk to me? I'm not operational yet.*

He marched into the building catching the tubby outline of Gaston Leroux coming down the hallway.

"Pan-ter-ra," Gaston yelped in his effable manner.

"Mister Leroux. I understand I was summoned?" Pantera asked, acting irked to cover his trepidation.

"Yeah, yeah. Let's talk in my office." Gaston turned around and the two men walked back down the hallway to Gaston's office. "Could you close the door behind you?" He moved around behind his desk. "You worked in the building last night?"

"Yes?" he answered all prepared with his story.

"Did you see anyone else?"

"No? Should I have?" he asked, playing the *you-tell-me-first* game.

"Well. There was a second heat signature on the tape, but there was no badge entry." Gaston opened a binder on his desk.

"Gosh. You have a thermal system? It wasn't in the indoc binder."

"We don't put *everything* in the binder, Pantera. Just in case." He gave Pantera a big wink.

"If that's it. I'll be going."

"Oh, one other thing. I had you checked out. You were pretty hot shit at ST-4 from what I hear. Did you know anyone at the Farm?"

"The Farm? I milked a couple cows once, but that was in Kentucky. Do you remember the name of that Farm?" he asked, taking a long pause. "I hear you worked at the C ... I ... A. Where did you work?"

"Sorry. Maybe I was mistaken. Have a good day." Gaston gave Pantera a lazy salute.

"Yeah. You too." Pantera ignored the salute and waved instead. *Whatthefuck, over. Was that a fishing expedition or what?*

From the ISA building Pantera walked to the platoon office with thousands of reasons behind the conversation with Gaston. Unexpectedly he had the rest of the day off.

"Good morning, Gunny. Thought I'd stop by before heading to the Med-Shop."

"Got cut early, huh? Good work taking initiative with Charlie Squad," he said, nodding approvingly. "Harry tells me he asked you to bring Kat by next Saturday. Are you considering it?"

"Considering it ... you think the CO would approve?"

"Yeah I think so. Barring any complications," Grit said, with a slow upturn in his voice.

"I'll ask if she's interested. Could you arrange for me to work Thursday night at the Navy hospital instead of Friday so I could get *a jump* on the weekend?" he asked, raising his eyebrows at the insinuation.

"What would be the purpose of this?" He slid his glasses down his nose.

236 · JD WALLACE

"I thought I'd invite her up Friday so I could possibly *seal-the-deal*," he replied. "Then Saturday we both show up at the kill house."

"Wow, still working on bedding her?" Grit paused for moment. "Your funeral."

"Let's just say, we've come to an understanding." He shrugged with palms up in the air.

"I'll put the request on the CO's desk. I think Gaston handles the clearance requests. And if you need a quiet place to hang call Rosina at the *Residenza le Rosa Bed and Breakfast*. Tell her you're friends with Chris and Rose, she'll treat you right."

Yeah, what else do I use as a cover if she and I are spotted in Naples?

CHAPTER 53

Kat reflected upon the events over the last week staring out the plane window into empty space. A stunning homage of images flooded her mind. The images summarizing the debriefing stood out as the least painful debrief she could ever recall.

A feeling of exhausting exhilaration came over her as she opened the door to her flat. She dropped her bag, jumped into bed, and fell fast asleep. In her dream, she heard a telephone ring far off in the distance. The electrical conduction of every nerve ending in her body rang out in unison.

That's my phone. Kat sprang from bed and ran into the next room.

"Hallo?" she answered, forgetting what time it was.

"Kat?" Pantera was pensive since his last call.

"Ah, Navy boy. Nice of you to call," she said, spinning around and falling onto the couch.

The conversation continued with complete lies about their week. When they were both out of lies Pantera thought it would be a good time to discuss their next meeting.

"Do you have any plans for the weekend?"

"Actually. No," she said, knowing it was coming, but wanted to see if he would trip over his tongue.

"How about we meet at a small secluded bed-and-breakfast over-looking the ocean and a nature preserve? I doubt anyone will find us and it should be reasonably safe." He was taking it slow and methodical.

"Safe, huh." *He is certainly upping his game. Let's see where this goes.*

"We can start Friday morning and go through Sunday," he continued.

"Do you have a car?"

"Uh. No. I can borrow one."

"No. That's okay. I have a car."

"However ... there's a training session I have to attend on Saturday. You can come if you want."

"A training session? Really?"

"I'm almost done with my indoc so I can be operational. To speed up the process they have me doing some training on Saturdays."

Kat's paused. "And you, or they, won't mind if I show up?" *Of course he doesn't. He has probably told everyone we've been banging like rabbits.*

"No, but you don't have to if you don't want to," he said, reversing direction then adding guilt, "but my boss would like to meet you."

"Your boss? The guy who knew you couldn't *get IN my panties*, but instead bet that you could *get my panties*. That boss?"

"Well. Yes."

Kat's paused again. "Okay, I will come meet all your superfriends, but you will owe me ... big time."

"Whatever you want. Oh. One more thing. You have to be cleared to travel on our part of the base. Grit didn't think you should have a problem getting a pass since you work at an embassy. Expect a call from a Gaston Leroux, he's the ISA intelligence analyst assigned to our unit," Pantera said, breathing a sigh of relief.

"You said ... Gaston Leroux? The guy who wrote, *Phantom of the Opera?*"

"Yeah, I didn't know that when I had my first meeting. They're a weird bunch. I know."

"Okay. See you Friday morning." Kat was worried. *Do you think ISA can burn through my embassy cover? Who knows nowadays, I certainly hope not.*

* * *

Kat had been driving since five in the morning and was relieved to pull in to the Navy hospital parking lot. *I certainly hope you know what you're doing. Agreeing to this could give him the wrong impression. On the other hand, no risk, no reward ... and no regrets.* She looked around and realized the hospital was actually located inside a volcanic crater, but the surrounding area was green with an artistic sprinkling of white. The B&B was closer to the hospital in *Agnano* than it was from the Navy base over at the airport, so she agreed to pick Pantera up at the hospital.

She was leaning on the edge of her car when Pantera walked out the emergency room doors. He stood tall in his blue scrubs and long, bright-white lab coat, with his pockets filled with pens, papers, and little books with a backpack slung over his shoulder. Her heart skipped a beat. For a moment, she envisioned herself married to a doctor with two kids and a white picket fence.

Now there's something that will never happen.

Pantera walked outside into the bright rays of sunlight and was simultaneously hit with the Aphrodite brilliance of a black-haired beauty wearing a full-length, black, winter-wool dress coat with fur-lined hood and black Prada knee-high-mid-heel leather boots leaning against a red Italian sports car. The contrast of colors against the backdrop of the snow-capped mountains and clear blue sky gave Pantera pause.

"Hello princess. Are you sure you're here for me? Maybe there's an Italian doctor I can find you?" Pantera said, feigning sincerity.

"No. You will do for now," she said, giving him a grin and a wink. "How are you ..." she stared overtly at his name badge before he grabbed it. "Joshua?"

Here you go again joking at my alias. I'll return the favor one day.

240 · JD WALLACE

"Funny. Nice shiner. Another paper cut?" he asked, reaching for her cheek.

She slapped his hand away.

He knew the force needed to create that wound must have been substantial, but had faith that she would tell him when she was ready – hoping it would be sooner rather than later.

She spun around the car and got in on the driver's side, purposely ignoring him. He threw his bag in the back, got in and they sped away.

CHAPTER 54

"Where in the hell is this place?" Kat barked, turning down a small dirt road off a main thoroughfare.

"Grit says it should be down this road," Pantera said, peering down the road praying they weren't lost. "A-HA, there it is!"

The *Residenza le Rose* was a small, white-washed, 1920's converted villa off the beaten path surrounded by lots of plush greenery and a beautifully manicured orchard. The inside walls had many colorful, cheerful paintings and photos. Walking upstairs to their room the attendant swung the door open revealing an apartment larger and more colorful than they had anticipated for a typical bed-and-breakfast.

This guy ends up getting us an apartment better than what my employer usually gives me. Sheesh. Alona needs to see this place.

With large windows and a veranda looking out over a small courtyard surrounded by dense landscape and the ocean beyond the bedroom had an almost postcard feel being lit with only natural light and candles.

"Alright, Navy boy. What do you want to start with?" Kat threw her bags down and faced Pantera.

"Huh?" he asked, looking at her as if hit by a herd of buffalo.

"Don't look at me that way. You know what I mean." She put her hands on her hips.

"Are you saying you're not ruling *it* out?" *Did I actually ask that?*

"Let's build some trust here and we can discuss *it* ... later. Business first." She gave Pantera a quirky smile.

"Where do you want to start?" Pantera was still coming to terms with their emotional barriers to intimacy.

"You tell me why you need my help. I gave you an outline of my story already." Kat said, rummaging around in the kitchen.

"It's a bit convoluted, but here goes ... the US Federal Reserve is owned by non-US interests. Common knowledge, I know. One of the largest and most corrupt privately-controlled corporations in the world they use a financial process called 'forfaiting' or 'trading' to maintain money flow. In order to keep their financial control they have to manipulate politicians in many governments, including the U.S. and Israeli governments. Similar to what the Vatican does, but they use money instead of God."

"Wait. Who do they report to?" Kat walked over and sat down on the red Victorian tufted chaise settee.

"They report to no one. Well ... except to their owners – foreign financial institutions. Recently we've received information that a couple of the owners of the Fed have been financially exploiting situations in a number of countries. To do this they have moles planted throughout many governments, including the U.S. One mole was tracked to the U.S. Department of Defense. A group called, "The Activity.""

"Okay. I've heard of them – considered the United States version of Mossad."

"Um, yeah, maybe worse. Like a Mossad within a Mossad."

Kat nodded. *Oh, so you mean a type of Kidon group, within Mossad.*

"The mole, and there may be more than one, has been peddling intelligence information to further the interests of their employers which is leading to a lot of people getting killed. Technically, it's treason, as their interests are often counter to the U.S. government's interests. I have to find this person and find out what they know and who they report to – without getting dead." Pantera found the snack bar. "They have Snickers. I love this place."

"And I thought I had a problem. You have to find *this someone, this mole,* inside a non-existent group who is ... inside the largest military industrial complex in the world, who is ... being funded by one of the largest private corporations in the world, which is ... owned by a group of even wealthier foreign corporations. And the UN gave you this assignment?" Kat asked, crossing her arms in disbelief.

"Yup," he hastily answered, picking a peanut from his teeth. "It's like trying to find a needle in a stack of needles, all with poison on them." *UN? Please don't ask that question again.*

"Where are you so far?"

"The cast of characters is down to about a half-a-dozen. My leading candidates are those that interface with our unit. It makes more sense when I say it out loud." He opened a bag of peanuts and downed the whole bag at once.

"Why is that?"

"My predecessor was killed mysteriously." He nodded at Kat to show how serious his situation was. "Enough of me, what about you?"

"Definitely not as convoluted. Someone broke into the Military Intelligence Directorate's system and absconded with a list of female Mossad officers." Kat rolled her eyes.

"Are you on that list?" Pantera asked, his protective instincts roared to life.

"Honestly. I don't know. Taking the conservative route ... I would say 'yes' for lack of a better answer." Kat opened the screen to the terrace and took a deep breath of the moist salty air.

"Didn't you say someone was chasing you during an op? I would say, *yes*, also. Do you have any leads?"

"None. And the most frustrating part is that it's not just me. This woman has taken out five of us and two in the last month," she said, walking back in and laying down on the settee.

"You've engaged her twice? And with your mad-Parkour skills you couldn't catch her?"

244 · JD WALLACE

"My mad skills won't get past a three-man defensive position and she has always had the jump on me."

"Gol-ly. Sorry to switch gears but let's talk about those mad skills for second?"

Here we go. You are going to get all shitty on me about kicking your ass in Parkour. Freakin' men. "Look. I attended a French boarding school called, *L' Ermitage*, just outside of Paris. Parkour was an everyday event. And you, you certainly didn't just *pick up* Parkour in the last year." She snapped back.

"Whoa there Skippy. Just like you, I was downplaying my skills. I started rock-climbing and doing Parkour with a couple friends in high school. It was better than going to school. The Navy added it to their physical training curriculum. Before I was shipped to Naples I was the command Parkour champion. Not much else to tell."

"Aren't we quite the pair?" *Okay, not so shitty. When do I come clean with him?*

"You mentioned something about genetics ... you called it u-netics or gen-u-nets? Something like that."

"Eugenics."

"Yeah, that's it. What's that?" he asked, taking a sip of Coke then realized it was warm. "Eek."

"I'm surprised the U.S. doesn't have a program like ours."

"Obviously not. Go on, I'm listening." He took off his shoes laid down on the bed ready to be engrossed by Kat for many more hours. She was like a drug. A drug he didn't feel the need to have sex with any longer. She was like a song you can't get out of your head.

"In the late 1940s a group of very wealthy Jews calling themselves *Zionists* bought the current Israeli area from the British. They also paid members of the United Nations General Assembly to give them the area calling it the *State of Israel* – forcing the Palestinians, the indigenous people, from the land or putting them in internment camps. You know the internment camps today as the *West*

Bank and *Gaza Strip*. Jews from all over the world came to live – the first all-Jewish country." Kat pulled the throw over her legs.

"Jews never had their owned land? Where have they been all these centuries?"

"Jews have always been gypsies, small communities within other people's countries. The biggest in number were the *Ashkenazim*, in Germany, and *Sephardim*, in Spain – and of course the *Mizrahim* in the Middle East," she said, answering his question and continuing her story. "All the Jewish scientists who lived through WWII moved to Israel. Hitler allowed these Jews to live because he was focused on genetics and developing a *master race*. The Jewish scientists were the best at manipulating *bloodlines* as it was called then. The concept of bloodlines dates back to 1850s Germany with a priest named, *Mendel*."

"I didn't think a lot of Jews made it out of Germany. Then again I didn't go to my high school history class that often."

The adorable self-deprecating humor. Whatta mouth-breather. "Funny. Within a few years of Israel establishing a State the concept of DNA was discovered by Watson and Crick in 1953 England. That's when the Israeli eugenics program really took off. A select group of Jewish families participated. Eugenics combined with arranged marriages made those families genetically superior to the rest of the population. This is where most of Israel's leaders and spies come from." She pointed to the bottle of water on the nightstand, of which he returned by airmail.

CHAPTER 55

"Your mother and father were *arranged*?"

"Yes, they were. Right now the wealthiest families in the world are Jewish, and the wealthiest family in the world, who founded the concept of banking ... is Jewish. Within the next generation, or two, the Jews will no longer be a dismissed race or religion. The truth about the Vatican, Christianity and Islam will soon be revealed to the world." Kat took a long swig of water.

"I don't know about all that *Jews take over the world stuff*, but you are the most fantastic woman I've ever met. That's all that matters to me," he said, mesmerized and relaxed as he laid unguarded gazing at her.

"Let me guess. That's a pure logical and objective statement?" she said, raising her eyebrows.

"Not entirely."

Well look at that. Tin man has a heart. "I'm being straight with you. I'm not telling you all this as part of some conspiracy theory. Since you're Jewish, I thought you should know, all Israeli Jews know."

"I am?" He laid his chin on his arm lying in a prone position on the bed.

"Yes. I received your paperwork the other day."

"What about all that Merovingian-Knights Templar stuff?"

"That's going to take a little longer. There are only a handfull of people who know about Jesus' wife and child. What really tickles me ... Jesus was a Jewish Rabbi. So his bloodline is going to be Jewish, too. I'm sure the two-point-four billion Christians and one-point-six billion Islamists love the fact their religions are, fundamentally, a branch of Judaism. Something they don't teach in bible school I am sure." Kat gave Pantera a smile.

"Yes. I've a heard a little about a couple Jewish-owned Banks. Maybe we can save that conversation for another time."

Shadows moved across the room as the sun fell from the sky with Pantera on the bed and Kat on the settee. They both continued to talk about a smattering of topics until they fell asleep.

You may be a mouth-breather, but you make me feel safe.

* * *

It was dark when Kat awoke. She was fully encased in the thick Chenille throw as she lay on the comfortable settee. Quietly walking past the sleeping behemoth on the bed she made her way to the kitchen to make some tea. She sat drinking her tea in the candlelight when Pantera walked in.

"What time is it? Is there any lemon for my tea?" He grinned.

She looked up relieved at his newfound knowledge of tea. "It's almost seven and yes, lemon should always be available. Otherwise, what's the point?" she said, nodding at the tray then continued reading the paper.

"As you always are. Dinner's at eight," Pantera replied, pouring a cup and reaching for the lemon slices.

"Oh, really? When did you make that reservation?" She was surprised at his ability to get up without her knowing.

"At the same time I laid the throw over you. Must say, you were really out."

"Guess that means I trust you – don't lose it. Where are we going?" she asked, without looking up.

"We are going to *'A Fenestrella*. A little restaurant down the road – and yes, you brought the correct outfit. The long blue dress with the black Italian pumps should work just fine and the long black dress coat if it's too cold, which it will be," he stated sharply, taking a sip of his tea and pretending to read the paper.

Kat didn't know if she should be pissed that he looked through her suitcase or happy that he's taking initiative to learn about civility.

Oy vey. Developing a heart AND taking an interest in the finer things. Will wonders never cease.

* * *

The short drive to the restaurant wound through the deep green *Posillipo* neighborhood and ended at the small seaside fishing village of *Marechiaro*. There was still a chill in the air, especially with the top down, but not overly so. The restaurant, *'A Fenestella*, was not much to look at from the street. After descending the stairs, the quaint and protected little harbor opened up as the cool salt air hit them like a wall of Lily-of-valleys.

"Who recommended this restaurant, may I ask?" Kat was caught off guard at the beauty of such a rustic fishing village.

"Grit, just like he recommended the B&B."

"Definitely must thank him tomorrow. He's a good man," she said, trying to reconcile that a large *military-man-slash-Neanderthal* had the refinement to find such places. *There must be a woman behind the man.*

Approaching the entryway, they met Victor and David, the second-generation owners, and were whisked away to their table. Kat and Pantera were given a table in the corner of the bustling restaurant. On one side, the smell of a honeysuckle-covered bannister, and on the other, a view of the rising full moon as its shimmering reflection danced across a calm ocean surface.

Kat and Pantera just finished ordering dessert when a tall dark-haired woman approached their table. She came into Pantera's view walking stiff and professional. Kat's back was to her.

"Pantera. Gaston asked me to give you a message," the tall woman said, before Kat could turn around and look up.

"Kat. This is Mary Shelley. The senior analyst assigned to our team. Mary this is Kat – a friend." Pantera pointed back and forth.

Kat turned, looked up and froze. The blood drained out of her lips. Mary Shelley stopped with a deer-in-the-headlights look. Their they stood – face-to-face – the first female to ever become a senior level Kidon Katsa, and the recently assigned senior level Kidon Katsa and the youngest ever. They were two of the most dangerous women in Mossad, if not the world. They had a history; a history that was for the most part, good, but a chance meeting could change a relationship.

There was a nano-second of pain on both of their faces then it was gone. That was all the time Pantera needed for the exchange between the two women to register.

"Hi. Mary Shelley from the Intelligence Support Activity – Naples," she said, extending her hand.

"Hi. Kat. I work for the Israeli Embassy in Rome. Nice to meet you," Kat said, forcing a natural smooth motion of her facial muscles.

"Nice to meet you, too." Mary turned to Pantera. "Your platoon deployed this afternoon. Gaston asked me to make sure you knew and I have a message from Grit." She ignored Kat.

"My pager never went off." Pantera checked his pager.

"You weren't paged because you don't have all your quals completed. You're assigned to third platoon for now. You should be operational for the next mission. Here's Grit's note. I think it's about tomorrow." She forced a smile and left.

Kat and Pantera both sat for minute lost in their own thoughts.

Kat's head was spinning ... *Mary Shelley?*

Pantera was blind, his mind's eye took over ... *They left me behind, bastards. And, what was that between Kat and Mary Shelley?*

"How is that Tiramisu?" Kat asked.

"It's good. I thought you didn't like coffee?" Pantera returned, recovering from his blindness.

"I think our next lesson will have to include *pairings*. There are foods that require a certain drink. Italian desserts, except for maybe Gelatos and Italian Ice, require an expresso. It's just the way things are. Guess no macho-manly stuff tomorrow ... hmmm, what shall we do with ourselves?" She smiled. Kat knew that if Pantera caught their facial expressions it was now mandatory that she distract him with sex.

Pantera snapped back to life and looked at Kat with her half smile.

"I guess we can *discuss it*," he said, throwing the earlier conversation back in her face as he opened the letter from Grit:

P –

Don't worry my friend. You will be in the game shortly. Didn't want to bother you on your, what I hope is a monumental weekend. Give your girl a hug and kiss from the platoon. Tell her our day at the kill house has been postponed, definitely not forgotten!

Peace,
Grit.

Pantera smiled and handed the note to Kat.

"I really have to meet this guy. Is he married? Let's get the dessert ... to go," she said, tucking the note into her purse.

CHAPTER 56

They were not in the room two minutes before Kat jumped on Pantera like a jungle cat going in for the kill. Pantera caught her in mid-air.

"Is this where you kill me?" he said, with a plain expression on his face.

"What?! What are you talking about?" Kat asked, sliding down off him like a sulking puppy climbing off a couch. "I was giving you what you've wanted, my body."

"Yeah. Not so much. Thanks to you, I'm not only interested in your body. And if you think distracting me with sex will make me forget what just happened back there, then you don't know me at all." He opened a Coke from the snack bar.

Qevdesh harah! The boy just became a man. He's sooo attractive right now. "Okay. It was worth a try. What do you want to know? Be careful, you repeat anything I tell you and we're both going to end up being hunted for the rest of our lives." She unzipped her dress.

"Fair enough. I was told she's former Mossad. No one will give me her name," he said, taking off his shoes and going over to lie on the settee.

"Not *former*. Her name is Tal Cohen." *If I give her up as a Kidon, I give up myself. That is not going to happen.*

"Wait one friggin' second. She *still* works for Mossad? Fuck-a-bag-o-donuts."

"I just saw her at a debriefing in Tel Aviv last week. I have no idea why she's at *The Activity*. Maybe infiltrating it? That's what I mean. If I give her up and my *Director* finds out. *Oy vey!* A kill order will be issued for me ... and you. That statement use to mean more, than it does now. They can't even keep me safe from that damn *Katsa Killer,* anyway."

"Stop. There's no way I'll give you up, but it certainly lights up my spidey-senses."

Let me show you what will light up your spidey-senses. "Does that mean she's one of your targets?" Kat asked, dropping her dress to the floor.

"Yeah, she is – and rising in the polls as we speak." *Gawd damn. That's not the only pole rising right now,* he thought, as he stared at her purple silk bra, garter and panties.

"I hope you understand what kind of shitstorm you and I are in," she said, slowly walking over to the settee and taking off her Italian pumps as Pantera took off his button-down shirt.

"Y-Y-Yes. We are in a hea-vy, heavy shitstorm." He could feel his heart pounding in his chest.

"Glad we are in agreement. Looks like we are stuck with ..." she stopped, slowly climbing over him as her mouth reached his and her tongue slowly traced his lips. Her tongue flittered like a butterfly seeking nectar from a flower. "... each other."

Pantera grabbed her breasts.

"Whoa there cowboy. Caress, don't grab." Her strong hands encircled his stout neck with delight. She held his head like a cup between her hands to drink from, her mouth seeking the long draughts of his nectar breath.

They were frozen, filling each other with languor. Pantera carried Kat to the bed and threw her down, exciting her further.

She threw her body back and closed her eyes to better feel the movements of his warm, incisive hands. Pantera dared to touch her voluptuous body and follow every contour of her rich silky curves. Her nipples hardened as he lightly caressed her breasts.

"That's good. Slow-ly," she instructed. *Why is it that all macho guys think a woman's body is like an American muscle car?*

Kat undressed Pantera exposing his well-defined physique. The same body she remembered from the day at the Parkour center. She pulled off his T-shirt exposing his clearly curved biceps, striated pectoral muscles, and v-shaped contoured lower abdomen that entered his jockey shorts.

"No more tightie-whities, I like the boxer-briefs. Much better," she said, rubbing her hands all over the fabric and feeling the movement within.

Uncomfortable with the sexual repartee Pantera tried to participate. "The bra and panties are very ... um ... accentuate your form," he said, spilling out like lumpy pancake batter.

"That's it Navy boy. Talking is good. Sex is much better if we communicate our likes and dislikes," she continued, kissing and groping him through his underwear.

He looked back to her. Her pale thighs, slender and silky, gleamed. The shadowy folds of her sexual secrets taunted him.

Under their bodies was a big satiny down comforter calling to them to frolic in its whiteness.

They fell back, two bodies in accord – moving against each other to feel breast against breast and belly against belly. They ceased to be two bodies – all mouths and fingers and tongues and senses. His mouth sought her mouth, her nipple, her clitoris.

"Hey Mister Tongue. I'm more than a vagina. There's just as much fun on the fairway as there is on the putting green," she said. "Slow down. Pretend you're licking a slow melting ice cream cone. Y-Y-Yes. That's a good jungle cat."

They were entangled, moving very slowly. They kissed until the kissing became a torture and their bodies grew restless. Their hands always found yielding flesh, an opening. The candles and incense gave off a sweet, musky odor – which mingled with the odors of sex.

I wonder when your tongue will give ... OUT! Wow! There it is ... that's the spot!

Pantera had Kat lying on her side, with one leg thrown over his shoulder, kissing her between the legs. Now and then Kat jerked backwards, away from the stinging kisses and bites. His tongue was hard and wonderful. When she moved her buttocks it rubbed against the satiny coolness of the comforter – creating a balance of hot and cold. With his hands enjoying the shape of her, he inserted his finger into the tight little damp aperture.

"There ya go. Slowly in ... slowly out. Now lift up a little ... no ... a little more. Perfect. Rub that spot right behind the pelvis bone ... baaack and fooorth. Puuuurrfect."

He could feel every contraction caused by his simultaneous kisses, movement of his tongue on her clitoris and his finger rubbing her *Gräfenberg* spot. Her pleasure was expressed in melodious ripples of her voice. Like a savage being taunted, she bared her teeth and tried to bite the one who tantalized her. When she was about to orgasm and could no longer defend herself against her pleasure Pantera stopped – leaving Kat halfway on the peak of an excruciating sensation, half-crazed.

Pantera looked up at her – smiling at her exquisite pain.

"Aren't you the tricky little bastard. Let's see how you like it," she said, reversing positions with him.

Uncontrollable, now like some magnificent maniac, Kat threw herself over Pantera's body. Ripping his underwear off she parted his legs placing herself between them and gluing her mouth to Pantera's manhood – moving with desperation.

Look at that, not too much hair and smells like soap. I can work with this. I'll shave you later.

"Yikes woman. Those things are sensitive," he cried.

"I know, just wanted to see if you would say something. I'll bring ice later," she said followed by a mischievous look.

"Ice?" Pantera was now scared.

She ground against him feeling the blood flowing into his genitals – throbbing, soldering. When she felt his pleasure about to climax, she stopped, to prolong it. She opened her mouth to his burning love sacks that were bouncing up and down yelling out to be caressed.

"No way! That's not fair." The blue ball nightmare still vivid in his memory.

"This may be new to you, American, but we Israeli women want to orgasm at the same time as our men. If you want to continue having sex with me, you better get used to it," she said, giving him a smile that almost glowed in the dark.

Pantera was now in the frenzy before orgasm. He felt her firm hand grab him, a hand he could trust, slide his member into her warm, moist, life-generating grotto. She wanted to throw herself on this pulsating shaft until it made her cum, but wanted to prolong her pleasure. Her rhythmic movement ceased. Pantera's man muscle pounded inside her. He softly clutched her voluptuous pointed breasts feeling the brushing of her sexual hair against his pelvis. Kat rubbed against Pantera, then slid her hips up and down, slowly, knowing the friction would force him to feel her breasts and belly.

Hands everywhere at once.

"Control yourself Navy boy, not until I tell you." Kat buried her pointed nails in his strong, rock-like shoulders, between his pectorals and underarm – hurting him with a delicious pain. The tigress took hold of him, mangling him. Kat's body was burning hot and she feared one more touch would set off the explosion. She was begging now to be satisfied, spreading her legs while still mounted on top of her Navy boy.

She sought to satisfy herself by friction against his body.

"Come on Kat ... I'm gonna explode!" Pantera was using every ounce of prostatic control he had. This was new for him – a physical sexual challenge.

CHAPTER 57

Kat's orgasm came like an exquisite tidal wave. At each spasm she moved as if she were being stabbed. She cried to have it end. Sitting rhythmically atop his undulating body they both tried to orgasm in unison, but Kat came first. Kat moaned mercilessly as she continued until Pantera's body tightened in orgasm. The veins in his neck engorged. He arched his back contracting and yowling, consummating their overwhelming desire. She fell onto his chest wanting to feel him withdraw from her body ... slowly. They fell asleep in a loving embrace.

* * *

The ride back to base was quiet. Kat and Pantera sat mentally exploring a two-and-a-half day visual montage.

"Hey, Navy boy. How do I get on base or do I drop you off at the gate? Like the rest of the *Italian and Arabic women* you sleep with," she said, goading him out of his trance.

"Huh? Oh. Gaston at ISA gave me your pass," he said, pulling the pass from his bag and tossing it into her lap. "You're free to come and go as you please. And if you're going to do something spooky, please know that my name is attached to your pass." Pantera looked over for an acknowledgment.

"I've been at this a long time, sir. I know what's at stake," she said, insulted.

"Didn't meant to offend, just throwin' it out there. Left turn over there. Pull up to Gate 4. Make sure you turn off your lights when you drive up to the gate," he directed.

"Roger that, sir," she said, smiling at him with a sideways look.

* * *

Pantera had just given Kat a small tour of their part of the base and airport. They pulled up to the parking lot across the street from a building with a sign out front: United Nations – 33rd Logistics Company. Behind the parking lot was a large fenced in area with dozens of white trucks and oddly designed vehicles. Written on the side of each vehicle: "United Nations."

The couple sat on the hood of Kat's car as he finished pointing out the surrounding buildings ending with pointing up to where his room was in the sea of windows on the front face of the building.

Wouldn't a midnight rendezvous be fun? Kat thought.

A tall Black man heading toward the building saw the couple and changed direction approaching them. "What are you two beautiful people doing out on a glorious Sunday night?" He said in an almost aristocratic Virginian accent.

"Chief Lawrence, I would like you to meet ..."

"Let me guess," Lawrence cut in, "the *Italian model* who has had this unit buzzing for the last month." He requested her hand to give it a light kiss. *"Piacere di conoscerti, bella."* He gave the body motions of a flamboyant chivalrous knight.

"Perché grazie, non sei così affascinante." She returned with a small curtsey.

Pantera proceeded with the introduction. "This is Kat. Kat, this is Chief Lawrence, also known as, *Cracker*. He's the medical officer for first platoon."

"Cracker, huh? You guys certainly come up with some unique call signs. Your wife must love you." Kat was combining Grit's ability to find great locations with Cracker's civil refinement and rethinking her belief that the men at his unit were as *Neanderthal* as Pantera.

"I certainly hope so. My wife and my children are the center of my world. If not, what's the point in living?" he said, eloquently and confidently.

"What are you doing on base on a Sunday night, Chief? Shouldn't you be home with the family?" Pantera inquired.

Cracker stepped back from Kat with a thankful nod. "Damn operational readiness evaluations start tomorrow and we were assigned that *bastard*, pardon my french, Tokahara. Captain Tokahara from the Japanese Special Operation Group. I thought I would spend a couple hours going back over my fake inventory and protocol binders. I scored perfect last time and I'm not about to let *him* bolo *me*. Besides, my wife is working with the kids on their homework, which is her field of expertise. Why are you still here? Didn't second platoon have a mission?"

"I didn't finish my quals in time. I'm in third platoon until second gets back," Pantera said, looking disappointed.

"Enjoy the time off. Once Blue Cycle starts ... hold on to your hat. It's a wild ride. Third platoon are good guys. Just watch out for Crispen, he's the practical joker. Y'all have a good night now," he said, turning toward the office building he walked away.

Kat and Pantera spoke for a few more minutes and turned to give each other a kiss.

"Let's talk Wednesday night." Kat gave Pantera a stern look.

"Yes Ma'am," he returned, unfazed by her pseudo-directive and giving her a big long sensual kiss.

"You're getting better at the kissing. Very good." She winked as she turned to get in the car.

He watched yearningly as she drove away with the conflicting emotions of his desire to be on that deployment with his platoon swirling with his desire of being with Kat, haunting him, chewing at him.

* * *

Pantera leaned against the wall in a seedy part of Naples called, "Chiaia." Pitch black, no moon and surrounded by hundred-year-old buildings, he thought about how his relationship with Kat had been progressing over the last four weeks and what she would think of what he was doing right now.

I'm turning into a freakin' cliché. Spy meets spy in dark alley. Criminy.

He heard steps in the distance.

It's about time. I've got a couple dickheads to school in pool back at the barracks.

The sound disappeared. Pantera leaned back into the shadows and ducked down against his favorite trash dumpster. Out of the shadow across the alley a woman appeared. She was tall, five-foot-ten, blonde hair falling down each shoulder outside the black hood she had over her head. She looked at her watch stood in the light for about thirty seconds then disappeared back into the shadow.

Pantera looked at his watch. *You're twenty minutes late. Damn 'sun never sets' Brits.*

He stood up and walked across the alley standing in the street lamp light facing her direction. She walked out of the shadow and approached.

"Why are Brits always late? Or is it women?" Pantera said softly but loud enough to be heard.

"Why do yanks always think they're the *center-of-the-universe?*" She countered with a sharp Yorkshire accent.

"Marcus Sinclair. CIA." He nodded.

"Christine Brown. MI-6, I understand you're investigating corrupt bankers and their relationship to ISA?"

"Yeah, and not getting anywhere. What can you tell me about my predecessor?"

"He was investigating a link between an ISA analyst and the Rothschild Bank." She pulled out a pack of Benson & Hedges Silver and offered one to Pantera.

He shook his head to the cigarette offer. "What do you mean *link*, exactly?"

"His original assignment was to find an information peddler working out of this ISA office. It took him a year. He finally found a deleted electronic transmission on an unused server in the Naples ISA office between the analyst and Rothschild Bank. It was a money transfer from a Rothschild Bank numbered account." She lit up the cigarette with a small butane torch.

"Okay. Good. Rothschild Bank is one of the owners of the US Federal Reserve *as well as* the Bank of England, among others. What happened to him?" Pantera looked like a big cat sitting on the limb of a tree.

"He must have screwed up. A week later there were two attempts made on him. Immediately after the second he stole a motorcycle and tried to get back to London. He was run over by a truck right outside of *Basel*," she said, her voice became somber.

Noticing the change, he asked, "Who was he to you?"

CHAPTER 58

"He was my husband. You *will* find this bastard and end him. For my husband … and me," she said, through a clenched jaw and watering eyes.

"That's the plan," he said, unfazed by her emotion. "How can I get hold of you?"

"This is my *personal* sat phone in Copenhagen. It's with a friend. Leave a number and I'll get back to you. I'm currently on my way to Kuwait City. Anything else?"

"That's it. Wait. One question. Did he ever give you the analyst's name?"

"No, but he always referred to the analyst as *him* so I will assume it's a man."

"Excellent." *And the number drops to two.*

"Good luck. If you get the opportunity to interrogate this guy, I want in. Cheers."

"*If* that happens. I'll call you. Ciao."

The woman turned and was back in the shadows walking down the street as Pantera walked back into the alley to call Jack before heading back to the barracks.

* * *

Exhausted, Pantera entered the dorm room after a long Thursday of sick call and Advanced Trauma Life Support teaching, ending with the meeting with Christine Brown. He saw the answering machine light blinking. It could only be one person.

"Hey it's me, call me back," Kat said.

He picked up the phone and rang her straight away.

"Hallo?"

"Hey Princess. Got your message, is there a problem?" he asked, tucking the receiver into his shoulder as he undressed.

"No. I just wanted to tell you I'll be traveling for the next week or so. I leave tomorrow. I know it is last minute. I'll call you as soon as I get back," she said, sounding as normal as possible.

"Okay. Be safe. No more shiners," he pressed, still trying to get her to talk about that event.

"Uh-huh. Any progress with your ..." she paused, making sure nothing could be picked up by the keyword recording devices.

"Had a good meeting. Down to two male candidates. Will fill you in later. And you?"

"Nothing. Damn desert. At least you're making progress. I'm chasing a ghost," she said, frustrated.

"Agreed. Now, go knock'em dead. And ... *thank you*," Pantera said, reinforcing the last two words.

"And to you." *Knock'em? Naw, Slice'em!*

* * *

A bolt of lightning shot through Pantera's body as the door swung open and a huge bag flew in the room. He jumped to an upright position banging his head on the bookshelf above his bed. His eyes wide open as adrenaline cursed through his body looking over at the door.

"What the fuck, over!" he yelled.

It was 0237HRS and four-and-a-half weeks since second platoon left on deployment. He knew who it was, he didn't understand the attitude. It was very unlike his roommate.

Bullseye was *Minotaur* pissed. "Fuckin' recon. *Basrah*. Only TWO kills! Burqa. *Vir 'n fokken maand!*"

After spending a month as Bullseye's roommate, Pantera was getting pretty good at deciphering his abbreviated form of communication and the *Africaan* language.

"Let me see. You were watching the Iraqi Army in *Basrah* in a burqa and only got two kills for the whole month. Yeah, I would agree, that sucks," Pantera said then smiled, not at Bullseye's situation but at successfully deciphering his cryptic language.

Bullseye nodded with a half grin.

"Yup. My month sucked too," he said, visualizing his weekend trysts with Kat. He grabbed his blanket and jumped back into his bunk. *Yes. My team is back. I'm done with my quals and I can finally go hunt and kill something I can see.*

* * *

Kat sat at the gate waiting area staring at her ticket:

PRISHTINA INTERATIONAL AIRPORT

Kosovo. Ocean waves of memories flooded her mind. Here she stood looking back in time at her most heart-wrenching assignment – an assignment that in order to succeed, she had to lose her brother.

"For the love of country," she heard as tears welled. *"You all know the risks ..."* the Director of Mossad said, at Adamm David's funeral.

She bit her lip. *Whatta asshat!* She saw Adamm's happy face and a glass of Chardonnay in his hand from the Orahavoc region, right down the road. How he loved wine. *He could have been a sommelier.*

Conflicting emotions raced around inside her like a couple of mating swallows. She meandered through the baggage claim section with her usual one carry-on bag. Across to the other side, she spotted a man wearing a white button-down shirt with an open collar and a blue single-breasted suit – Israeli conservative. They looked at

264 · JD WALLACE

each other. She could immediately tell he was not a typical intelligence contact – he was wearing oxfords.

Another emotional vignette from her past punched through to the front of her mind's eye. It was lunch with Tal Cohen, her instructor; and Nyssa, early in their relationship. Kat was back in Mossad intelligence school.

"Ladies. Let me give you an unofficial lesson that could save your life one day," Tal said.

Kat and Nyssa gazed at Tal in awe – the highest awarded female Mossad Katsa.

"The topic is men's shoes."

"What?" the ingénues said in unison.

"The simplest things are what trip people up, especially men. They don't pay attention to details and think women don't either. The best women intelligence officers pay attention to the details," Tal said, pointing to all three women. "Men's shoes are broken down into two basic forms: Oxfords and Loafers."

"Does this work with boyfriends?" Nyssa interrupted.

Kat looked at Nyssa with a furrowed brow.

"What? I might want one, some day," she retorted.

"This is especially true for potential male mates – if you're into that. Now let's continue. Oxfords require some effort, meaning: they must be tied giving a clue as to the type of man who wears them. *Real men* make an effort regarding their appearance. Oxford men roll up their sleeves and pitch-in when the situation calls for it. Oxford men will go the extra mile and often come from humble beginnings." Tal took a sip of tea, pinky finger in the air.

"Like most of those *old-school* officers?" Kat asked looking around the lunchroom for an example, but couldn't find one.

"Yes, most do. Loafers on the other hand as its name implies, have no laces and you slip into them like a slipper. Here is an easy mnemonic: *Loafers are worn by loafers.* Loafer men are lazy and spoiled. Loafer men expect everyone to do their work for them. And worst of all Loafer men are all about themselves and run the opposite direction if things get too hot. Americans call them *Ivy-*

Leaguers, the British call them *Fagged Officers*. Loafers are worn by the worst intelligence officers ..." The concept of loafers and oxfords was engrained in Kat's memory from that moment forward.

Kat's focus returned from the past with the thought of her handler the last time she was in Kosovo. *Avner, you loafer-wearing, babaganoush-eating-puss-bag piece of anal-rectus meat.*

The oxford wearing man swiftly and quietly walked toward her.

She noticed the lapel pin. It wasn't Mossad. It wasn't Shin Bet. She mentally scrolled through the visual list of lapel pins. She recognized it. It was ... *Sayeret Matkal.*

Oh harah.

CHAPTER 59

She continued walking toward him trying to maintain her composure as if walking toward her grave. *I would prefer the Katsa Killer now.*

Sayeret Matkal: Israeli Special Forces. They held a reputation as myth, smoke, and vapor – second only to Pantera's unit in the level of secrecy for a military unit. The saying goes, once you see the face of a *Sayeret Matkal* it will be the last face you'll ever see, but unlike Pantera's unit, these guys are all Israeli and are often sent for "in-house" cleaning.

Kat was staring death in the face and she knew they feared ... *nothing*. It wouldn't matter that she's Kidon. A *ninja* cannot take on a *samurai* directly. Her mind wildly searched her memories for anything out of the ordinary, anything she did wrong and every minute over the last month and a half with Pantera.

Could they have been following us ... and both of us didn't notice?

She traced every face in every hotel, bed and breakfast, tourist attraction, park, walk, and beach they ever visited. Nothing stood out. If her agency wanted her dead this would be the group they would use. Her temperature rose as a bead of perspiration crawled down her temple. Her clothes became scratchy. She made eye contact. He blinked twice.

Is this their warning before they strike? A respectful good-bye?

She blinked twice in acknowledgement. She looked to his hands. Nothing there.

He'll pull it at the last second. I'll never see it coming.

Kat noticed a glint. Something in his left hand. Something she overlooked.

Something brass?

He turned his palm just enough for her to see a key. A locker key.

Her pulse slowed ... it was not her time.

She continued to walk toward him. They passed each other on the left side. She let him drop the key into her hand as she walked by. They never slowed down and she continued to scan the area to see if anyone was watching.

All clear. Whew, time to change my panties.

The locker had a small envelope – her ID support package: passport, Serbian Dinars, and the name of the hotel. From the airport locker are she strolled down the concourse to the bus terminal. From the bus station, she waved down a taxi to the hotel.

"Хотел Приштина, молим вас." [Hotel Prishtina, please.]

Assassins never check in to hotels themselves, handlers do, and always stay on floors without cameras. This was not going to be a normal assignment.

"Thank you for staying with us, Ms. Oseku. Your deluxe suite is ready and the valet is waiting for you with your boxes that arrived earlier," the petite blonde desk clerk said from behind the counter.

"Thank you," Kat said, with a patrician Serbian accent.

The suite was comfortable, but small compared to more modern hotels with one exception. It had a Jacuzzi. She tipped the valet, closed the door, and walked over to the Jacuzzi.

Yes. If I'm working with Sayeret Matkal – I'm going to need this.

Kat searched the room for envelopes in the usual hiding places. Nothing.

Time for a nap. They know where I am. Who knows when I will sleep again.

* * *

Kat awoke from a sound sleep to knocking at the door. It wasn't the man she saw at the airport as she peered through the peephole. She let the man in. Without saying a word, he circled the room with an electronics detector then handed her two large envelopes.

"I'm Eli Siegel. We will be back for the briefing at nine o'clock tomorrow morning. See you then." The squat dark-featured Israeli eyed her then left.

Kat called down for tea service and a cheese and fish tray, found a comfortable place on the couch, and pulled out the paperwork from the envelopes. The standard dossier package included photos and a couple audio tapes with poor sound quality.

Where are the videos? How in the ... oh, whatever.

For the next several hours and two pots of Bai Hao Yinzhen tea, she went over and over the information. She played the tapes a hundred times – listening for every nuance and inflection in the woman's voice.

Finally. I got this.

It was nearly midnight by the time she looked up at the clock. She felt comfortable with the material and her ability to mimic the voice of the target. The bed was big, soft and warm, she fell fast asleep.

* * *

The sound of the breakfast tray being placed outside her door woke Kat. She looked at the clock. It was a little after seven and she felt rested.

She picked up the tray and went into the bathroom to start up the Jacuzzi. Comfortably situated in the Jacuzzi, she continued with the tapes while eating her breakfast for the next hour. Still studying the dossier on the couch, a knock at the door broke her concentration.

"Good morning, Miss David," Eli said, as four Sayeret Matkal men entered.

"Good morning, gentlemen," she returned. "This is a heavy team mission?"

"Yes," Eli said over his shoulder as he turned the desk chair to face the center of the room. The rest of the men sat on chairs and the bench at the end of the bed. No one sat next to Kat on the couch.

What the ... do I smell?

"As you should have read, this is a surveil-kill-infiltrate mission. The target is Lule Troshani. An Albanian-born Israeli National living in Kosovo. She traffics Serbian and Israeli girls to the Middle East. It has taken over three years to get what little information we have on her. No one has been able to infiltrate her organization." Eli paused as he could see Kat had a question.

"Why hasn't law enforcement investigated her?" Kat was curious as to why Kidon wanted an easy-to-find criminal.

"First. There is no law enforcement in the Balkans. That is why she's here. Second. She is Israeli. The *Yamam* investigated her for three years and came up empty. They handed it to Mossad. Mossad gave it to Kidon. Killing her would be easy, but then another white-slaver would take over her operation. We need to kill the buyers. We will finish it ... we always do."

Kat loved old-school, oxford-wearing handlers. They were good and they knew it.

"Before you arrived," Eli continued, "we identified her main operational location and three stash-houses in this city, but she rotates so we have to move fast. The buyer's list is the target."

"What are we doing different than *Yamam*?"

From what Kat knew of *Yamam*, they were good.

"They have no women. Every man sent in, ends up dead. No one knows why. You're the only woman in Israeli intelligence who can fill the role of Troshani, Miss David. Our way in is that no buyer has ever seen her. They have only heard her voice. In my opinion, it should take us a week to complete surveillance on her.

We only have three weeks until the next auction to prepare for the buyer takedown." Eli opened a file folder referring to it while he spoke.

"How do we get close to her?" Kat turned one of the dossier pages and took a sip of tea.

"She starts her day at a little Albanian coffee shop around the corner. We will set up there. Comms check at seven o'clock Monday morning. Unit two, you take overwatch position. Get some rest gentlemen, and lady, this is going to be a long three weeks. Any questions?"

The answer came almost in unison. "No sir."

Kat closed the door behind them and remembered what she had told Pantera about being "just a week or so." Unfortunately, she couldn't call Pantera directly in case the base or ISA traced all calls. She would have to ask Alona.

CHAPTER 60

"Hallo, Corriere della Sera. Come posso smistare la telefonata?" the receptionist at the Italian newspaper answered.

"Alona David, *por favore*," Kat returned.

"Hallo, Alona David."

"Alona ... I need your help," Kat said with urgency.

"Of course, little sister, what do you need?" Alona heard the stress.

"Call Pantera. Tell him I'm all right and I'll be home in about three weeks. This is going to take longer than what Michoel told me. His number's in the safe."

"Do you need anything else?" Alona asked.

"Yes. What do you have on my KK problem? Did father find anything yet?"

"I just heard this from a friend. The breach was followed by a worm-virus. It ripped through several operational systems destroying the access monitoring software. That route to the KK is gone. You know *Imah* gave *Abba* an ass-chewing after you left. She told me she gives him an earful every week. He'll come around. What about Pantera and his situation?"

"He's down to two guys. Remember when I told you about meeting Tal at dinner and what Pantera said about her? When I looked at her I felt something was off. If the mole's a man ... *oh well.*"

"Then why is Tal working for ISA *and* Mossad? Maybe I'll ask around on that." Alona scribbled something down on a piece of paper.

"Who knows? Above my level. Could you find everything you can on a Lule Troshani, an Albanian-born Israeli white slave child trafficker? You know – from your *special sources*." Kat asked, feeling better. If Alona couldn't find anything on this woman, there wasn't anything to find.

"Stay safe, *Achut*."

* * *

"Francesco, I'll be in Rome at my sister's for a couple weeks. I'm taking my laptop and the mobile phone with me. I'll fax in my column, *Addio*," Alona said, walking out her boss' office and moving swiftly down the hall.

"*Che dire di che cosa mi ha promesso?*" A disconnected voice rang out from the corner office.

"I keep my promises. You will get it when I get it," she yelled back, throwing her bag over her shoulder she walked past her office toward the elevator.

The sign on her office door read: Alona David – Editor – Metropoli.

"Bianca. Call the train station and get me a ticket from Milan to Rome. First-class please," Alona said as she walked by.

"It'll be waiting there for you. Have a nice trip!" Bianca yelled from behind the receptionist desk as Alona boarded the elevator.

Alona David, an Associate Editor of *La Repubblica* newspaper and in-charge of the weekly section on multicultural issues in Italy, was strategically placed by Mossad to handle southern European and Balkan information gathering for the Mossad Intelligence Communications network. The third of four genetically-enhanced children of Gideon and Tirzah David, Alona spent many years as a *Sayan* and was now a full Katsa.

Remember last time Kat called from Kosovo? Adamm dead and handler missing. It better not repeat. Alona shivered just thinking about it.

* * *

The door to Kat's apartment flew open and Alona raced to the bathroom.

Charah be'leben, I have to pee. I really need to stop drinking a bottle of Champagne on a three hour train ride.

Alona returned to the kitchen to put the hot water on.

Please don't tell me Kat doesn't have any coffee. Ah-huh, in the back. Good girl.

Alona looked at her watch and thought Pantera should be in his room by now.

"Hellooo." A half asleep voice came over the phone.

"Navy Boy!" Alona practically yelled, being hyped up on caffeine. "Get up! We have to talk."

"This must be Alona ... it's one o'clock in the morning and my roommate is going to suffocate me for waking him up." Pantera was lying in bed with the blanket and pillow over his head.

"How have you been? Oh, I have a message from Kat." Alona was pacing in the living room with the cord fully extended.

"I'm good. Take a valium. What's the message?"

"Her trip has been extended by a couple weeks. You sound tired. Why are you so tired? Kat tells me you have great *stay-ing* power."

"Wow. It there anything you two don't talk about? I spent all day bandaging natives at a Navy base public relations event after getting themselves ripped up during a five kilometer mud-run competition. For me, sunburn."

"Oh, that sounds ... interesting," she said, wrinkling her nose. "Anyway, sorry for waking you, but if you need any help with your situation, give me a call."

"Very good, I will. Good night," he said, dropping the phone to the side of the bed leaving it off the hook. He could hear Bullseye grunt. *I think I now have whiplash.*

* * *

"Comms check." Eli came over the radio.

"Unit one check."

"Unit two check."

"Jasmine?"

"Jasmine check," Kat replied into the radio.

"Let's see if we can place the radioactive tracer on her today. Kat let's take advantage of the chaos in the coffee house," Eli directed.

"Roger," Kat answered, moving from her position across the street to a position inside the coffee house.

The coffee house was an ordinary Albanian business with the smell of coffee mixed with dust and rotten wood. Old beyond its years, the building had a crumbling whitewashed plaster façade with large gaps showing red brick. The chairs and tables were rustic and rudimentary and the equipment was turn-of-the-century.

Two hours later.

"Target spotted. Coming from the northeast," a voice came over the radio.

Everyone slowly turned and watched.

Lule Troshani was a dirty blonde with green eyes in her mid-fifties and had the facial cracks of someone in their seventies. She dressed in average clothes: a plain blouse, a knee length skirt, wore no make-up, and wore no jewelry except for a pendant necklace.

The radio, "Entering the building in ... three, two, one."

Kat caught her out of the corner of her eye wearing sunglasses, a hat, and red boots. She thought to herself, *she's got the fashion sense of a six-year-old.*

The radio, "Security is staying outside. Jasmine you're a go."

Kat sat and watched as Troshani ordered her coffee. Kat spotted the cup that would be used for her coffee and followed it. Simultaneously she freshened her make-up while making sure she knew where the security guards were. From within her large handbag she took out a small white tube and squeezed a small amount of clear gel on the middle finger of her left hand.

It doesn't even feel greasy. Cool stuff.

CHAPTER 61

"Jasmine is going in," Kat said, speaking into her purse.

Troshani picked up her coffee. Kat stood up and took the earpiece out of her ear placing it in her purse while walking toward her. Just when she was close enough, Kat mocked a trip and with her right hand tossed her coffee on Troshani – hitting her across the shoulder and down her chest.

Troshani recoiled.

Kat quickly let out a screech, immediately started apologizing, and reached for a bunch of napkins, as Troshani stood stunned. Kat moved in to help wipe away some of the coffee from Troshani's blouse while spreading the radioactive gel down her sternum including the pendant around her neck.

She recovered and shoved Kat away.

Kat continued to humbly apologize to her, pretending that she also spilled coffee on herself.

Trohshani stopped and took a hard look at Kat. Her demeanor changed from anger to acceptance. "That's okay. It was an old blouse anyway," she said, wiping her arms.

Kat spotted the change and rolled with it. "I'm truly sorry. That is a lovely pendant you are wearing." She took the opportunity to move in closer.

Two men, Troshani's security guards, ran up. She waved at them to stop and go back outside. "Yes, handed down to me through the generations. I never take it off," she said, ogling Kat like a child watching a merry-go-round.

"You must let me make it up to you. Can I buy you another coffee sometime?" Kat flashed her eyelashes. Kat felt something she had never felt from a target.

"Why yes. You can buy me a coffee ... tomorrow morning, right here, same time. And maybe you won't spill it on me," she said, giving Kat an impish grin before turning and leaving.

Kat suddenly realized. *Troshani is gay. Eeeww.*

After Troshani left the coffee house, Kat looked at one of her security men across the street. He shook his head faintly. She moved to a chair occasionally glancing at him. After a few minutes, he nodded. Kat walked out and placed her earpiece back in her ear.

"Good work, everyone. Unit one continue surveillance. Unit two take second shift. Jasmine, back to the hotel," Eli charged.

Kat loved being bisexual but was repelled at the thought of Troshani being gay. She had to stew in the Jacuzzi for a while. The slimy schmegma wouldn't come off. Kat was sitting on the couch with a cup of Jasmine tea when there was a knock at the door.

Eli walked in and sat down in the office chair. "Excellent work today, you really believe she's a lesbian?" The old Mossad officer gave a look of disbelief.

"Yes. It's a strong feeling, let's say," she said, knowing where the conversation was going and didn't like it.

"Do you think you can get her to ask you back to her place tomorrow?" Eli raised his eyebrows and leaned back in the chair.

"Why? Aren't the bugs in place?" Kat was trying to hide behind her teacup.

"A dinner at her place gives us opportunity to become familiar with the location. We don't have to go in blind."

Kat knew this. She just didn't want to go in. "That's a tall order. She's hugely distrustful. I will try."

"See you tomorrow." Eli left the room and Kat returned to the couch to take a nap.

* * *

A couple hours later the phone rang.

"*Achut.* Did I catch you at a bad time?" Alona was chomping on a biscotti.

"No, I was taking a nap." Kat recognized Alona's concerned tone. "What's up, you sound stressed."

"I'm worried about you. Remember what happened last time you were in Kosovo."

"Thank you. I'm fine. This situation is completely different. This handler wears oxfords." Kat grabbed a notepad and pen to take notes.

"Good. I found some info on your girl. According to my sources she's cunning, been at her current career for over a decade, hates men, and uses her own product. She has caught and killed over a dozen male law enforcement and intelligence officers," she said in a professional intelligence reporting manner.

"She uses her own product. Yuck! Now I'm really creeped out. I found out about the lesbian thing today. She makes my skin crawl." Kat was contemplating another soak.

"Sorry. And I spoke with Pantera, he's fine. I think he doesn't like me very much."

"Oh *harah*. What did you do?"

"It's your fault. You buy that damn Indonesian *Kopi Luwak* coffee. You know it's too strong for me. I called him at one in the morning. I forgot what time it was."

"Pleeease. I'm not buying that Italian crap you normally drink. I doubt he doesn't like you because of that. It's probably something else."

"Okay. Stop using those Jedi mind tricks on me. You know I hate that. What was the outcome of your *Jewish* conversation with him?"

"Oh yeah, it went good. He was even curious about the Merovingian legend. Depending on how the relationship goes ... I could recruit him," she said, adjusting herself on the couch.

"For Mossad? You're joking. No. You're not joking. Does that mean if something happens to you ... I can call him? You know, considering all that's going on?"

"Uh," Kat paused, "Yes. You can call him. We're almost there now. I just don't know how to finish the story. He's been completely honest with me, but ..."

"Please." Alona jumped in, "I'm begging you. Please don't make me be the one to tell him what you *really* do for Mossad, for the country." Alona up-ended her mug of coffee.

"I won't. It's not for you to tell. I have time. Plenty of time. Talk to you later."

"Au revoir, Achut."

Her mind whirled at the thought of telling Pantera the rest of the truth. She threw her track suit on and went down to the gym to run it off.

* * *

"Okay gentlemen, Jasmine is without comms today. Unit one, you're on the target. Unit two, get eye contact with Jasmine."

Kat walked into the coffee shop about fifteen minutes ahead of schedule to peruse the area for the best place to sit. She wanted Troshani's back to the window. Within five minutes Troshani arrived.

Kat waved. "Miss Troshani, over here," she said in an earthy Serbian accent.

"Oh please. Call me Lule."

Kat noticed her hips swung more vigorously than yesterday.

"I hope you don't mind, but I went ahead and asked the barista what your drink was and ordered it for you," she said, giving a shy, but affectionate grin.

"No I don't mind, many thanks," she returned with her crooked, coffee-smoker smile.

280 · JD WALLACE

Kat and Troshani started with the usual female pleasantries, giving each other compliments about each other's clothes while probing with small sexual innuendoes and flirty glances.

"Do you live in Kosovo?" Troshani inquired.

"No. I work as a buyer for retail chain and I'm here looking at new products. I'm guessing you live here. What do you do?" Kat leaned over the table caressing Troshani's hand.

"I live here ... and Abu Dubai. I own a small import-export company – mostly mechanical parts."

So that's the euphemism for child trafficking these days. I'm looking forward to exporting your tortured soul.

CHAPTER 62

The conversation went on for nearly an hour and a half including light hand-touching and ended with several toe touches to Kat's inner thigh.

"I would like you for dinner." The pariah smiled, double entendre intended. "My place, seven o'clock Thursday night, wearing something sexy." She wrote her address down on a napkin.

"Why not tonight? I'm available tonight." *Please don't drag this out any farther.*

"I'm sorry kitten. I have to go out of town today. I'll be back Thursday afternoon ... in time to eat you, uh sorry, eat with you," she said, subtly sliding her finger from her crotch to her mouth. Troshani winked at Kat, got up, and left with her braless breasts bobbing.

Kat glanced over at her shadow who was now sitting a couple tables down. He gave one barely imperceptible shake of his head and returned to reading his paper. She received the all-clear signal and a few minutes later, she met Eli in the hotel bar.

"*Arak Kawar*, neat," she said, giving her drink order to the bartender. "This assignment just keeps getting creepier and creepier." She sat down next to Eli.

"Yes. It does. For the better," he said, giving off the unmistakable spark of contentment. "We've got the best of both worlds. We can pull all the intel from her place surreptitiously tomorrow. If anything gets missed we have dinner on Thursday where we end her quietly. All wrapped up by Friday. Right on time. I have to admit, despite having the reputation you have as a loose cannon, you do get the job done." He raised his glass in her direction.

"It is not *loose cannon*. It is im-prov-i-sa-tion ... something your fellow lethargic loafer-wearing, watered-down-coffee-drinkers forgot since leaving the front lines. See you tomorrow," she said, finishing her drink. She slapped the glass down on the bar and stormed off.

* * *

The target's house was three kilometers southeast of Prishtina city proper. It had a ten-foot cement wall capped with three lines of razor wire and a wrought iron gate. Three stories in height, the house was made of white stucco and had a red-tile roof.

Kat walked down the street, she noticed the team was set up just on the other side of a large hedge of Night-Blooming Jasmine, she smiled, *there's a good omen*. The field was three houses down from Troshani's house.

Eli was briefing when Kat walked up. "There are four guards: two walking the perimeter, one watching TV on the first floor, and the fourth is on the second floor sleeping. There is one maid and she's in her room on the first floor."

"Where's the office?" Kat looked at the diagram on the cold, wet grass.

"The third floor. There's no phone line to it that we could find. We will get her mobile phone tomorrow. Let's remember. If we take down one, we have to take them all down – taking Thursday dinner off the table." Eli folded up the diagram and gave each member a nod.

No moon, my favorite night for these types of operations, Kat thought.

Kat was in all black with a full complement of communications gear and weapons, including her favorite assassination tools, devices, and gels. She followed two men as they approached the fence at the back of house. They threw a blanket over the razor wire and cleared the wall.

"Guard status?" Kat said quietly into her radio.

The radio hummed, "All clear."

Kat stepped onto the back patio. She recognized it as an old wooden structure.

This place is going to squeak like a dying mouse.

She placed her feet strategically on the joints to prevent any sound from being created. The door had a simple six-pin deadbolt. Before opening the door, she pulled out a small squeeze bottle of oil and squirted it on the door hinges. After a couple minutes, she opened the door and listened for any sounds or movements from the first floor. The TV in the living room was on and a radio was playing in the maid's quarters. The house smelled like cooked cabbage as she slid the door closed leaving it unlocked.

Kat squawked her mic twice. "Jasmine is inside."

A rack of high-end knifes sat on the counter. She continued to the living room and spotted the guard sitting on the couch watching TV with his back toward her. She crept up to the corner of the kitchen and peered into the living room. The staircase was to the left about six meters away. The path to the stairs would take her within one meter of the guard.

If I crawl on all fours to get past him, I'll be in a very bad position if I get caught.

She crouched down on all fours and slowly approached the sofa where the guard was sitting then turned to move toward the stairs avoiding his field of vision.

I should thank the inventor of carpet runners for stairs. Whew.

With muffled sounds, she tiptoed up the stairs then looked down into the maid's room. The maid was not in her room.

Eli you ass-face, you didn't do a thermal scan before sending me in here.

She reached the second floor and heard moaning sounds from the room ahead. A room she had to pass to get to the next set of stairs.

Maybe Troshani's product is in there? One catastrophe at a time.

Purposely stepping on the floor joints, she leaned up against the wall next to the moaning room. Slowly peeking around the corner she saw a large bump on the bed moving up and down. Her night vision struggled to get more details on the bed movement. A woman's body and two large breasts rose straight up from under the blanket. Kat pulled her head back.

I know where the maid is now. She grinned.

She took one more look to make sure the two lovers were not facing the door then hopped to the other side of the doorway. Up the next flight of stairs she pranced. The frequency modulator's numbers spun as she approached the keypad, tuning it to the frequency stolen off the fob at yesterday's coffee. Within seconds a number popped up on the screen, she punched in the code and one door bolt slid back. The inner mechanism of the *Mortise lock* flashed in her head as she withdrew her lockpick tools.

Not a cylinder configuration, a lever mechanism. Don't break your lockpick.

It took Kat over five minutes to open the lock. She shook her head in disappointment as she swung the door open and examined the room. The room was completely square – approximately 10 meters by 10 meters – full of old-world oak desk and furniture.

Something is off. There's got to be something else. Remember the rule, if there is two devices, there will the a third.

She heard the moaning continue below as she took out a laser, pointing the beam into the room and rolled it across the floor of the doorway.

Floor is perfectly even. Hmmm.

She sprayed a fine mist into the room and the floor lit up like a Christmas tree. There were tiny hidden laser units at the base of the bookshelves on one side and mounted to the unique molding on the other. The grid squares were one meter by one meter and about ten centimeters off the floor. It was five meters across to the desk. *The safe is probably behind the desk. Cunning, but not cunning enough.* Kat took a minute to calculate her approach. *Too far for a single jump. My only option is to step over the grid lines one by one. Not all that difficult in the whole scope of things.*

She was about to step into the first square when Eli's voice reverberated in her ear, "Jasmine, report."

"In office. Battling laser security system, if you don't mind," she hissed back.

Her parkour skills jumped into action. She looked back across the floor at the lines. *Pantera could move through that without even thinking about it.*

CHAPTER 63

Kat put a small flashlight in her mouth, searched the desk drawers, and flipped the switch on the computer. There were several letters to various Middle East companies, but nothing informative. A search of the directory of the computer revealed two spreadsheets. One was a five-year list of all transactions, but the buyers' names were coded. The second spreadsheet held bank accounts, deposits and withdrawals for the last five years.

All this crap is coded. Mother-fraggal-rock, you pune-eating, pedophile with cottage-cheese-thighs!

She pulled a disk from her bag and made a copy. After turning off the computer and putting the disk in her bag, she turned her attention to the picture behind the desk. It swung out and revealed a *Gardall FB-1212.*

Whew. I didn't bring a digital reader.

With ultrasound monitor plugged into her ears, she opened the safe in less than four minutes. The safe stored stacks of dinars, pounds, dollars, francs, shekels, rials, a gun ... and one black book.

Damn right. I got you ... you, did I really think cottage-cheese-thighs? How original.

Kat grabbed the book and read through it. This was the book – addresses to all the stash houses in four different countries and the codes to the bank accounts and buyers' names. She snapped pictures of all the actionable information. There was a sound ... or lack of sound. She froze.

I can pick up the book on Thursday.

Kat returned the book to the exact location in the safe, grabbed the gun, and emptied the bullets into her bag. Everything was put back exactly where it was and retraced her steps. She wiped down the door behind her, and radioed, "Coming out."

She leaned against the wall to the side of the moaning room door and peeked around the corner to find an empty room. Pausing a moment she heard two male voices downstairs in the living room. After taking a couple steps down the stairs, she saw the maid getting dressed in her room. Her exit was blocked.

She checked each window on the second floor – all had a magnetic lock. The window over the terrace was the best route. She bypassed the security wiring to the window and stepping out on the terrace squawking the radio twice. Her guys were directly below in the grass next to the fence.

The radio buzzed, "All clear."

Kat closed the window and stepped down the angled roof to the corner making a standard Parkour drop onto the corner brace of the terrace. Her feet hit the stanchion perfectly then to the bannister which gave a small groan as she jumped to the ground and rolled to a flat position. She had thirty meters of open grass stretched out between her and the location of the blanket exit.

Over the radio, "Two men, front porch, all clear to exit."

She took a deep breath and swiftly ran to the exit. Without slowing down, she planted her foot square in the man's cupped hands and vaulted over the fence.

* * *

Kat noticed the breakfast tray had already been delivered. She grabbed the tray, placed it on the stand next to the Jacuzzi and flipped the switch. The adrenaline from the night's festivities was wearing off – and soreness always followed, now together with the never-ending pain from her broken ribs. After a long hot soak in the Jacuzzi, she put on her robe, crawled into bed, and slept for the rest of the day.

Kat peeled one eye open to look at the ringing alarm clock. *Five o'clock? Are you kidding?*

Since yesterday's debrief also covered the briefing plan for this evening there would be no knock on her door. She could take her time getting ready.

The closet was filled with clothes, the vanity with make-up and disguise kits, all from headquarters. She thumbed through the closet and found the perfect short LBD and a pair of calf-high boots. The boots were specifically made to hold a whole host of ghastly items.

Panties or no panties ... that is the question. Something I can burn when I'm done.

She laid everything on the bed and measured them up and down to make sure they would distract her target. The dress looked good with the boots as she took in a deep breath, sat down in front of the vanity, and started getting ready.

She waving down a taxi in front of her hotel and thought how unusual this was. *When was the last time I got in a taxi in front of my own hotel?*

Not only a breach in protocol, it was an enormous safety hazard. This situation called for an overt presence in case her target decided to check her out – which she did, thoroughly.

The taxi dropped Kat off in front of Troshani's house . The gate was unlocked, so Kat strolled up the pathway and mentally reviewed everything she saw the night before making sure nothing was missed or left behind. Before she stepped onto the stairs leading up to the front door a man emerged from the shadows at the top of the patio.

"Oh!" Kat gave a little screech in mock alarm.

"Ко си ти?" [Who are you?] The man said in a gruff Serbian accent.

"I am Jovana Oseku. Ms. Troshani invited me to dinner," she said, adding a hint of flirtiness.

The man radioed. A couple minutes later, the front door swung open.

"Jovana come in. Don't mind him." Troshani gave a big open arm greeting. Kat overcame the internal feeling of repulsiveness and returned the greeting. The two women walked into the big living room.

"Let's sit and talk until dinner is ready," she said, motioning for Kat to sit on the large couch she crawled past last night.

Whoa boy. Looks like appetizers are going to be served on the couch.

Troshani started with light touches outlining Kat's arm with a stolen touch to the side of the breast. Kat would touch her knee and slide her fingers up to three-quarters of her thigh and stop.

Where in the hell is that dinner bell.

Kat was having a hard time getting motivated and tried to focus on Troshani's body, not her face. Her body wasn't bad – reasonably in shape, flat stomach and strong thighs. She wore a loose-fitting purple, silk sleeveless top with no bra showing her larger than average breasts and sharply pointing nipples; a very short tight-fitting, black-lace-trimmed skirt; and black Italian pumps with a quite obvious red satin thong. Kat was desperately refraining from touching any erogenous zones.

Oh no, here we go ... the fashionless, styleless, Albanian hooker wants me to ... agh.

Troshani grabbed Kat's hand and pulled it to her damp panties.

"You see. I shaved just for you." Troshani closed her eyes and moaned.

She rubbed Kat's hand forcefully against her fleshly mound and guiding Kat's finger inside her. With her other hand she groped Kat's breast when the maid rang the dinner bell.

A little earlier would have been nice.

Troshani stopped, readjusted herself, and stood up – extending out a hand to help Kat up off the couch. Kat entered the dining room noticing dinner was traditional Albanian.

"Do you like Albanian food?" Troshani looked over at Kat.

"Yes, I do." Kat sat down and placed the cloth napkin in her lap.

The meal started out with bread and *Dolma* as an appetizer. The main course was *Tarator* with baked lamb and stuffed peppers – ending with *Kanafeh* and a good amount of *Konjak Skënderbeu* to drink.

"How do you like the drink? I get it custom." She winked at Kat.

"Very good." Kat was thinking she should grab a couple bottles after and take them back to her room. "Another glass would be nice."

When dinner was over Kat was surprised at how good the meal was. *I vote this assignment with the best food. Four stars. The maid is going to be unemployed in a couple hours – maybe I can take her home with me?*

CHAPTER 64

Kat was tired and trying not to yawn. She decided to turn up the charm and flirting to get Troshani to invite her upstairs.

"I have a very comfortable room upstairs where we can have more dessert," she said, standing up and taking Kat's hand.

Kat grinned. *Glad I didn't have to perform a striptease on the table to get her moving.*

They walked past the moaning room from the night before and into a large richly decorated bedroom. The canopy bed with plum curtains had an enormous burgundy and gold duvet. Troshani approached the bed and swung Kat around lifting her up on to the center of the bed. Without warning she quickly followed.

Not aggressive, are we?

Troshani straddled Kat grinding her pelvis while pulling Kat's dress down exposing her black lace *La Perla* bra. Kat reciprocated by lifting Troshani's top over her head and taking one of her breasts into her mouth – giving it a little bite on the nipple.

"Oh, yes! That's my girl. I want your panties," Troshani called out.

Troshani became more aggressive – pulling Kat's panties down, then her own, grinding, squirming, and driving flesh-on-flesh contact.

What an octopus, this is worse than that first time with Pantera. I didn't think that was even possible.

Kat had a breast in each hand, her tongue moving from one to the other, nipping each one driving Troshani into a frenzy. With one swift move, Kat switched positions with Troshani and was now on top. Troshani let out a moan of submission as she allowed Kat to continue grinding against her. She took one of Kat's breasts with both hands and started sucking on it with enough force it could have withdrawn her sweet, life nurturing juice.

She's a damn Hoover on steroids. If I say something, she will just get turned on more.

Kat reached back behind Troshani's leg lifting it up exposing her dripping wet forbidden fruit continuing to lift her leg over her head. She flipped Troshani over, face down.

In order not to raise suspicion, Kat took her middle finger and forced it deep into Troshani's anus.

"OH ... You are *sooo* good. Yes, more!" Troshani gasped.

Kat slid her tongue up from the small of her back. With the other hand, she withdrew the twenty-three centimeter high-density polycarbonate stiletto knife from her boot.

Troshani squirmed in ecstasy. She lay face down and completely at Kat's mercy. Mercy was definitely not on the menu tonight. Kat slowly removed her finger from her anus as her hips rose up begging for more. She grabbed Troshani's hair, forcefully lifting it out of the way. Kat's lips left her neck when she whispered in Troshani's ear.

"Night, night, you fucking pedophile. May you burn in hell."

In one smooth practiced motion, she thrust the knife deep into the foramen magnum at the base of Troshani's cranium. The body shook like an epileptic child. The knife stopped upon reaching the hilt. With a strong, short lateral motion she severed the spinal cord from the brain right above the C1 cervical disk. The body went limp as its electrical system was cut.

Cleaning the planet ... one dirtbag at a time.

Kat jumped up from the bed, straightened herself, and ran to the window taking out a small ultra-violet laser pointer from her other boot. She pointed it out the window into the trees, turning it on and off three times. Within seconds she heard the thud of four bodies dropping in near unity. A couple seconds later, the maid's body dropped to the floor.

Well damn. No maid for me. They better leave me some food. I can't live on hotel food for three weeks.

A minute later two bags were thrown into the room. The small bag had a small spray bottle. She sprayed a type of *polyfoam* into the knife wound. *Don't want the cleanup crew yelling at me because her body fluids drained out all over the bag during transport. My ass still hurts from the last ass chewin' I took.*

She wrapped the body up in the duvet and shoved it in the body bag and prepared it for transport. From the small bag she pulled out the earpiece and throat mic.

"Jasmine on comms. Target ready for transport." Kat ran upstairs and pulled out all the cash, books, and computer files from the safe.

"Jasmine, please make sure you get all her IDs and personal information. This could be a good NOC for you down the road."

Eli's voice was now irritating.

No shit. Whatta tool.

"Gentlemen, let's pull the bugs and the phone tap from the outside line."

Kat now had high quality audio tapes of all the calls to and from the house over the last couple days. The mobile phone was now in her possession. "Can we get tech services to forward all the house calls to the mobile phone?" Kat was thinking aloud in the van on the way back to the hotel.

"They're on their way," Eli said, looking back with surprise at Kat's strategic thinking skills. "Good work tonight ... everyone."

* * *

Grit stood proud in front of his full platoon as they stood in PT clothing after a long eight-mile run. All the pagers went off.

"Okay gentlemen, looks like we have a full platoon mission. SSS and meet in the G-2 briefing room in one hour. Please maintain relaxed grooming and uniform standards. And for crying out loud Sam, when are you going to grow some facial hair?" Grit said in a buoyant tone. "Dismissed."

Pantera stowed his personal gear and called Kat's phone hoping Alona wouldn't answer.

"Hi Alona," he said, trying to be upbeat while he tossed his clothes in his locker.

"Hi Navy Boy, how are you?"

"I'm good. Kat's not back yet?"

"No, not yet, still a couple weeks to go."

"How long are you staying in Rome?"

"Until Kat gets back, then I'm going to take her on a vacation. What's up?"

"Could you tell her I'm heading out and will call when I get back. Oh, and tell her I'll have a four-day weekend pass when I get back," he said, his voice trailing off.

"No problem. That sounds great. Stay safe."

"Thanks. Have a good weekend." *She's much easier to talk to without the caffeine.*

Setting the phone back on the hook, he turned to see a wet Bullseye walk in, naked.

"Aw dude, could you give your roommate a warning?" Pantera knew there would be no answer. He considered it rhetorical and left.

* * *

"... No, thank you for calling, I have you down. See you in two days." Kat said in Arabic, hit the off button on the mobile phone, and turned to Eli in Hebrew. "That makes the sixth buyer confirmation. Looks like a full house."

"Your Serbian and Arabic accents are improving." He sat at the desk updating his report.

"It helps there are no brokers and I only have to speak to the overworked assistants – much easier than I anticipated. Are you sure we can't take all this to *Yamam*?" Kat tossed the mobile phone on the bed and walked over to the bar. She hated long missions.

"If we brought these billionaires to the Israeli legal system, since Kosovo is out of the question and the International Criminal Court is a joke, they would find someone to contract against us – you and me – we'd be dead before ..." He turned in his chair and placed his glasses on top of his head. "You know, and you're already being hunted by this *Katsa Killer* woman. Do you want even more heat? You know intelligence and law enforcement can't work together. It always goes bad ... for us."

"You're right, just another couple days. I am *sooo* going to need a vacation," she said, dropping her shoulders and looking at the ceiling.

CHAPTER 65

"Platoon Sergeant O'Malley. Grit? ... is everyone here?" A man behind the podium at the bottom of the mini-amphitheater stood all of five-foot-eleven, weighing one hundred eighty pounds in his very starched and pressed British Special Air Service uniform. He is Commanding Officer of the 33rd Logistics Company – United Nations Special Operations Group and his name is Major William McFarland. A highly decorated SAS officer, McFarland's last command was the SAS Counter Revolutionary Warfare wing and he brought with him a reputation for being strategically brilliant and enigmatic.

Pantera looked up at the podium and smiled. *And he lost money on me too, teach him to bet against me.*

"Yes sir. Second platoon are all present and accounted for, sir," Grit barked from the top row.

The room had a steep angle down toward the podium and consisted of modern plastic cloth-padded chairs about one hundred in number. Each chair had a pull-up half table not unlike a university classroom.

"Are the analysts ready?" McFarland looked over at the two men and one woman sitting on the bottom of the right side of the room.

Leroux smiled. "Yes sir, we are."

Pantera stared down at them. *Huh, the dead writers. One of those dudes is a Federal Reserve mole. And you ... Mary Shelley, or Tal Co-*

hen, or whatever your name is, I may take you out just for shits and giggles.

"Then let's get started. Twenty-two hours ago, the Kuwaiti Ambassador to the UN was kidnapped along with his two top aides, his wife, and child. We believe an unknown number of soldiers from the *8th As Saiqa Special Forces* unit of the Iraq Special Republic Guard under the command of Qusay Hussein are responsible. Whether the direct orders were from Saddam Hussein we have no knowledge at this time. The UNSC has received a special *sealed* request of assistance from the Emir of Kuwait ..."

Pantera whispered in Grit's ear. "Think we'll get the contract for Qusay and Uday, someday?"

Grit smiled and nodded. "Hope so."

"... Your unit has been tasked with the hostage rescue and a secondary objective of interrogating the unit commander. We believe the ambassador was taken in an attempt to force the hand of the Kuwaiti government to turn over control of the northern oil fields to Iraq. Several armored units have been seen moving toward the Kuwaiti border in recent days and we believe this is the early stages of an attack on Kuwait."

"Sir." Grit stood up. "We were in Basrah for a month and didn't see anything. Where is this intel coming from?"

"Yes Grit, I know. This just came to ISA in the last day. I confirmed it by satellite." The blonde haired man sporting round gold-rimmed glasses peered back at Grit.

"Thank you, sir. Didn't want to head out on some wild-goose chase like last time," he said, sitting back down he gave the analysts a sideways look.

The analysts sat stonefaced, not looking back.

"I completely understand platoon sergeant and I agree with you wholeheartedly." McFarland nodded and continued, "By our approximation, Iraq will have a seven-to-one advantage over Kuwait even if they were prepared – which they're not. The capture and apprehension of the unit commander will be of great significance."

Pantera stood up. "Sir, do we have any idea who, or what, the unit commander is? I know Iraqi commanders have no education much less strategy training. They often hire out mercs to function as unit commanders."

"Very astute Pantera, guess you'll have to figure that out when you catch him, uh?" McFarland spoke in a calm and reassuring manner. "Now back to the matter at hand. According to ISA the unit has stopped at a small school to the southeast of Amarah – two hundred kilometers from the Kuwaiti border to the northwest. It's possible there will be a larger contingent traveling down from Baghdad to supply and support them. There's only a small window of time before the supply units arrive." McFarland flashed a map up on the wall behind him.

Leroux stood up and McFarland acknowledged him. "Sir, if there are no questions for us, we would like to get back to work and leave the operational planning to you."

"Does anyone have any questions for the analysts?" McFarland looked up into the crowd.

A general head shaking could be seen.

"Thank you analysts, have a good day." McFarland waved the analysts away and turned back to the platoon. "Due to the lack of actionable-intel, this briefing will be short and I'll expect your typical high level of improvisational skills. There are two possible routes to Amarah from Baghdad – routes 6 and 17 – as you can see here and here. Route 6 is the more probable route, but I want Route 17 covered also. This is a HAHO authorized combat jump insertion. Captain?" McFarland looked over at a British pilot standing off to the side. "Do you wish to do the air-control briefing?"

"Yes, sir. Good morning gentlemen." The Captain said, taking over the podium. "Transportation to the drop zone will be by civilian-coded C-130 aircraft from a height of twenty-eight thousand feet. Based on a half moon, low wind night jump you will exit about thirty miles from the landing zone. It should be a great night but watch your shadows. See you on the flight line." The Captain waved a half salute and walked out of the room.

"Just a couple additional points gentlemen," McFarland said, jumping back behind the podium. "To confirm: One. You will surreptitiously obtain ground transportation with minimal casualties. Two. There are no restrictions on weapon choice but suppressors are mandatory. Three. The *Kahlal Bridge* is your FUBAR location. Four. Uniform is Iraqi traditional civilian or throbes with keffiyehs. Five. Emergency code phrase is *ducks on a pond*. Be on the flight line at 1400HRS. Department heads prepare and distribute your gear per company directive. That is all. Platoon Sergeant, do you have anything?" The CO looked up at Grit.

"Squad Leader meeting to follow, sir," Grit said, with an unusual forcefulness. Pantera saw him turn on his *game face,* as he called it.

"Gentlemen, be safe out there." McFarland nodded and gave a side-grin before walking out of the room.

CHAPTER 66

The warm dry air tickled Pantera's face like the silken scarf of a wood nymph as he slowly floated back to earth – reminding him of motorcycle riding in the Arizona desert as a teenager. Pantera hit the soft warm sand of the Iraqi desert with both feet. He dropped his harness and stepped back and away from his ram parachute unstrapping his oxygenation mask. He could smell the pollenating date palms in the cool breeze of the cloudless night. He rolled up his parachute returning it back to its harness and glanced across the desert seeing the outline of two groups forming to his two o'clock. With his gear under his arm he walked over to the group and put on his mic and earpiece. Within a couple minutes he could hear Grit's voice.

"Radio check and status."

All the team leaders radioed in with the same response.

"We are a go," Grit said. "Mike-One. Status?"

"Mike-One is a go. I'm about one click from the rally point." Pantera responded to his designation. Pantera was the last out of the plane, and with that, the last one to hit the ground.

"Comms, radio in our status."

"Roger that," Brandy's unmistakable Australian accent bellowed.

When Pantera reached the rally point, Charlie and Delta teams were in full combat gear.

Grit issued the orders. "Alpha, Golf and Bravo, Echo you know what to do. Charlie, create a defensive line along the east side of the river, south of the bridge. Delta to the north of the bridge. The school is two hundred meters directly ahead to the west-north-west."

"Delta, take point, prepare to move out."

Over a dozen soft clicks from the locking and loading of their submachine guns could be heard. Both teams were ready.

Delta moved across the bridge forming a wedge on the other side to defend as Charlie crossed over. Grit and Pantera moved with Charlie – three operators in front of them and two behind. Delta team approached the school.

Delta team leader called over the radio, "Grit to my location."

Grit moved up and knelt down next to the Delta team leader.

"Grit, there are only two tangos on thermal. These guys are in the wind," he said, handing Grit the thermal unit.

"Motherfucker," he said, gritting his teeth – another reason for his call sign. "We're going to track these MF'ers down. Let's clear the area. Move out."

Delta team leader radioed, "Delta-Five ... Tango-One. Delta-Four ... Tango-Two."

Within minutes, the sound of two thuds could be heard as two bodies hit the ground. Charlie team, Grit, and Pantera remained in their position waiting for the "all clear" signal from the Delta team leader.

KABOOM! An explosion rocked the ground throwing everyone back. Smoke and dust filled the air.

"Delta-Two and Delta-Three are down. Medic stand-fast," Delta team leader squawked.

After regaining his night vision and shaking off the ringing in his ears, Pantera spotted the location of the explosion. He couldn't move. Running into an area before it's cleared could lead to finding more devices – the hard way.

"All clear."

Charlie moved into one of the buildings as Delta set up a perimeter.

"Brandy, get that tango's radio." Grit's orders came swift.

Pantera moved to the explosion site. Delta-three was dead, he moved to Delta-two. He was alive. He nodded to Grit, who was on the other end of the building.

"Brandy, get us an evac – one down, one out," Grit ordered.

Delta-two had a strong pulse. His breathing seemed impaired, but was functioning and regular. Half his face was blown off with thermal burns. Chest, arms, and hands had minimal damage thanks to body armor.

"Grit, I'm going to need a hand," Pantera radioed.

"On my way," Grit replied, moving to Pantera's location.

Delta-two's left leg had third-degree burns, but was intact and the right leg was hanging by a couple knee ligaments. Without thinking, Pantera grabbed a tourniquet from his pocket and strapped it around Delta-two's right leg giving it a jerk with all his might.

"Get me a burn sheet and some water from my bag." Pantera pointed.

Grit reached into the bag pulling about a large cotton sheet folded up inside a plastic bag and tossed it to Pantera. He laid the sheet over the burned leg and poured water on it.

Moving back up the body, he started his secondary survey. He arrived at the face and neck. The right side of the face was burned to the bone.

"The blast sealed all the blood vessels on his face. His right eye is gone," he said to Grit over his shoulder.

Brandy radioed, "Evac in niner-fiver mikes."

"Another burn sheet," Pantera said. He cut it to fit the face, but not cover the airway, then carefully poured water over it. Pantera's direction was fast and assured, while Grit was grabbing and throwing.

"Anticoagulant." He sprayed the remaining injuries on the upper torso and arms.

"Bronchodilator inhaler." He sealed Delta-two's lips around an inhaler and hit the button.

"IV tray and Plasmanate." He slid a large bore catheter into the left external jugular vein and hooked up a bag of plasmanate shoving it under Delta-two's left shoulder.

Pantera took his vitals again. "Stable ... Done!" he yelled. He raised his hands in the air as if he had just finished roping a steer at a rodeo. "Ready for transport," he radioed.

"Comms, bring me the satphone." Grit's voice was calm. "Bill. We're FUBAR'd. No Tangos. I repeat. No tangos. We've got one down and one out with evac in niner-fiver mikes. Request further orders." Grit rubbed his hand over his face.

"Understood Grit. Alpha and Golf to these coordinates ... Bravo and Echo to these coordinates ... Charlie and Delta to these coordinates. Your mission now is to hunt these guys down and make sure they don't get resupplied. Be advised, we have no assets in the area. You're on your own, Grit. Keep me updated. Out." A tone of controlled anger could be heard in the major's voice as he thumped the control desk in the A-TAC room of ISA.

Grit pulled out his map to see what the Major was planning.

"Squad leaders. Listen up. We're creating a net for these bastards. We're going to block their access to each major city – then squeeze them. Put your HUMINT collectors to work. You'll have to work the natives." Grit got off the radio with the team leaders. His eye muscles tightened and a sneer came over his face as he whistled, "A-Hunting We Will Go."

Pantera recognized the Thomas Arne song from the 1777 production of *The Beggar's Opera*.

CHAPTER 67

Kat sat trance-like writing her report which she hoped would speed up the debriefing process and get her back home *to him* and a much needed vacation with Alona. A knock on the door shook her out of her daydream.

"Target number six just checked in at his hotel. Sheik number four. Saudi Arabia is going to be missing four sheiks when tonight is over," Eli said as he walked in.

"Serves them right, no one should have so much money." She finished her thought on the report and shuffled her papers back into the folder.

"Congrats. You made it the full three weeks. Are you ready?"

"Ab-so-fuckin-lute-ly," she said, using her first Pantera term. The intensity was more than she anticipated. "Sorry. A friend of mine says that – thought it was appropriate."

"A bit rambunctious in my opinion for an academic such as yourself," Eli said, looking at her with a wrinkled nose and narrow eyes. "Let's go." He turned and walked to the door, Kat followed. They took the elevator straight down to the parking garage.

* * *

Kat sat quietly in the van staring at the monitors as unit one, unit two, and Eli prepared the auction site. It was an hour until auction time. Kat looked over the checklist in her mind of everything they did in the last few days.

All stash houses cleared, check. Rescued forty young girls, check. Killed eight guards, check. Recruited a few girls as bait, check.

The monitors came online one by one. Kat could view each buyer, their guards, and her team. Her voice was all that was needed to kick off the auction – and the attack. The van was fifteen meters from the exit, just in case.

This no-radios thing kinda sucks.

It was nearly auction time and the first buyer arrived in a Silver 1930 Maybach DS7 Zepplin. Over the next hour, the remaining five buyers and their security detail either showed up in specially built Rolls Royces or Bentleys.

When did a shit-hole like Kosovo have so many expensive cars? Oh yeah, these idiots' cars travel with them – and their people lie starving in the streets. "Loafers," she said under her breath.

Once all the buyers arrived, they starting *reviewing* the merchandise as Kat's temperature rose.

Look at those two old bastards ... they are checking to see if they are virgins.

Her skin crawled as she watched these old men grope, squeeze, poke, and prod these little girls – some as young as eight years old.

I will wipe you Saffron-saturated-McFalafel-eating scumbags off the earth.

She put her headset on and spoke into the microphone.

"We will get started." Kat's voice reverberated throughout the warehouse. Kat started counting all the guards.

Outside: twelve guards against unit one. Inside: six buyers against unit two and Eli. Hmmm.

About to give the kill command she noticed one of the unit-two guys heading for the door. *Going to help unit one, good work.* She paused – allowing him enough time to get into position to assist unit one with the guards.

Six against two on the inside, I certainly hope Eli can shoot straight.

"Item number one up for bid," she said, over the loudspeaker.

Eli and the remaining unit one man stood behind the six buyers. Kat could see the glint of their suppressed Model 70 Berettas. The unit-one man fired two shots to the back of the head of the first three buyers in rapid succession. They fell against each other. Eli hit the first two buyers with single shots but missed the third buyer. The third buyer dropped to the ground and rolled. Eli shot two more times. Missed. The buyer jumped up and threw off his throbes. The unit-one man turned and hit the buyer square in the back. After the throbes came off, Eli and unit-one saw the bullet-proof vest.

Kat watched in amazement. She trusted Eli to do what he was supposed to do. Her trust in him was gone. "Dammit Eli!" Kat yelled, bolting out of the van.

The buyer was heading for the back of the building. Both men were on the heels of the buyer as he sprinted away.

She passed the firefight with the guards and ran to the warehouse next door. The two large sliding doors were open as she slipped in noticing the two doors on the other end were open.

Little trust-fund baby will come in from the other side and hide behind those crates. Oh this will be fun.

With a number of quick Parkour moves, she scaled the crates and had a 360-degree view of the warehouse from one of the ceiling crossbeams. She stopped and listened for the sounds of his princely leather-soled shoes. Within a couple minutes, she heard him as he entered the warehouse tiptoeing along the opposite wall. She spotted a large crossbeam spanning the whole width of the building.

I can drop right down right behind him right over there.

She spotted Eli and the unit-one standing in the doorway as she crossed the beam. She shined her ultra-violet laser at their faces. They looked up to shoot her. She motioned for them to stay back. The beam was extremely rusted making gripping the beam difficult, but she was able to drop down just as the buyer tiptoed under her. She jumped from the vertical wall beam to a stack of crates. No sound.

The visual of her crashing through a crate with a weakened top popped into her mind. From the crate, she jumped to the ground. Ten meters separated her and the buyer as he continued along the warehouse wall. She predicted where he was going and went to a set of crates about five meters in front of him.

The T-junction will be perfect for an ambush, she thought.

She leaned up against a large crate and slowly withdrew her second most favorite weapon – the thirty-centimeter, ceramic, single-blade *Wakizashi* short sword – a gift from a real Samurai.

Hello, my old friend. I know it has been a while. Let us draw blood together.

The Saudi prince's footsteps grew closer.

Her breathing slowed counting his steps. Without warning, she leapt out from behind the crate and watched as the buyer's eyes grew to the size of balloons as all the blood drained from his face.

"Good-bye pedophile, say hello to Troshani for me," she said, her blade in a high attack position.

In one smooth dynamic motion, the blade sliced through the Saudi prince's neck as if it were made of soft, warm *Tzfat* cheese. The blood from his neck sprayed upward like the *Strokkur* geyser and his head hit the ground like a melon in springtime. Within seconds, two men were standing behind her.

The unit-one man smiled and nodded approvingly.

Eli had a morbid look on his face. "A tad melodramatic ... don't you think?"

She shrugged. "No. Justified." She cleaned her bloody blade on the dead man's clothes and turned toward the van.

CHAPTER 68

"Grit to my location." The unmistakable voice of Charlie team leader, SSGT Franklin came over the radio.

Grit walked into the room where half of Charlie team was standing. He saw Harry crouched down looking at something.

"Look at this. These are *Al Sherek* cigarettes ... these are Syrian, not sold in Iraq." Harry picked one up and showed it to Grit.

"That explains the well-placed pressure plate. I was having a hard time believing that bomb was of Iraqi Special Forces design, looks like ol' Qusay is ratcheting it up a notch. I'll kill him one day," Grit said, standing up and leaving the room. "Let's move out."

* * *

"On three ... three, two, one." Pantera and Delta team headed off carrying their wounded and deceased teammates back across the bridge to the evac site.

"See you at the rally point." Pantera nodded at Grit.

By the time Pantera and the rest of Delta reached *Mijar Al-Kabir* – rally point November three-four – it was daylight. Charlie team had found an abandoned hut to crash in.

"Charlie take first watch. Let's get some rack time," Grit charged, turning to Pantera, "I have a feeling this mission could take some time."

"Comms, anything on the airwaves?" Grit's voice broke the silence over the radio.

"Sorry Gunny. Dead air. I'm working all channels." Brandy's voice seemed uncommonly focused.

"They knew we were coming ... damn," Grit said, under his breath.

* * *

Back in Tel Aviv, Kat ducked into one of the offices after the debriefing and ceremony to call Alona who was still at Kat's apartment.

"Where have you been? You were supposed to be back last week." Alona sat with nails chewed to the nub.

"I know. The debrief was a pain. It took way longer than anybody thought. Details later. Can you please call Pantera and tell him I'm on my way home?"

"Kat." Alona hated giving Kat bad news. "Pantera is gone. He has been gone over four days. He gave me a message, but it's probably outdated by now."

"Damn. Okay. I'll call Cracker and find out."

"He's probably fine. What about a trip to Monaco for a small hiatus?" Alona tried to calm Kat down.

"Let me make sure this weird feeling I have is nervous energy, or hunger, and not a bad omen. See you in the morning for breakfast?"

"Of course *Achut*. See you tomorrow. Have a safe flight."

After Kat got off the phone the queasy feeling in the pit of her stomach intensified – the same one that nagged her since finishing the assignment. Something was wrong with Pantera's team and she knew it.

* * *

Kat opened the door to her flat to find her sister typing on a laptop and talking on a mobile phone. Two pieces of electronics Kat didn't know Alona had. She headed to the bedroom to unpack and take a shower.

"Glad you're home." Alona gave Kat a big hug and kiss as she walked into the living room.

"Glad to be home. I hate those long missions. And this Troshani woman ..." Kat shook her body trying to remove the touch memory from her mind. "... so gross."

"Now that it's over ... I was thinking ... Monaco!" Alona raised her hands in the air in excitement.

"I can't. Not right now. I need to make sure Pantera is okay." Kat shook her head.

"Who are you going to call? Ghostbusters?"

"Pretty much. I wanted to call Tal Cohen, but ..."

Alona interjected, "I found out."

"You found out what, exactly." Kat stopped preparing her tea and turned to face her sister.

"I found out that Tal still works for Mossad and she has orders to infiltrate the ISA office in Naples. She's looking for an information peddler."

"Seriously? She's doing for Mossad what Pantera is doing for the United Nations?" Kat leaned against the kitchen cabinet and looked at her sideways.

"That person must be really good. I mean, *WOW-good*. Able to remove CIA officers, an MI-6 officer, hiding from a Mossad officer and works for Rothschild Bank ... you don't think?" Alona stopped and looked at Kat.

"No way!" Kat's eyes widened.

"It couldn't possibly be ... the same person ... who orchestrated the Aman breach and is feeding information to the Katsa Killer? Come on?" Alona shook her head.

"Let's sit on this for now. I'm going to call Cracker and see if I can find out what's going on without interacting with Tal. Pantera said he narrowed it down to one of two guys, *two men*. Like Pantera says, *two birds, one stone.* If I go in looking for information about Pantera's team, I get closer to the mole ... which hopefully, gets me closer to the Katsa Killer. It's a long shot." Kat finished preparing her tea.

"That is quite a plan there super spy. Did you forget the part about mole-man having access to the Mossad system? That *man* will know who you are, what you do, and where you are? You are at such a disadvantage." Alona dropped her elbows on the table putting her chin on her hands.

"Well ... looks like I'll have to smoke him out. Let me call Cracker and get the ball rolling." Kat walked over to the phone.

"Med-Shop, Chief Lawrence speaking."

"Cracker? It's Kat. Friend of Pantera's," she probed, hoping he remembered.

"Sure, I remember you. What can I do for the *Italian model?*" He put his boots up on his desk.

"Yeah, thanks for that. I would like to know about second platoon. There's something wrong isn't there?"

"Well ... yes. They're on day five of a mission that was supposed to take twenty hours. It's been over forty-eight hours since they've checked in. That's about all I can say over the phone."

"Read me in?" Kat asked in a firm but pleasant tone.

"I'll have to contact our CO. I think Gaston Leroux will be your contact. It will take a few hours to get the approvals. When can you get down here?" Cracker actually liked the idea of having Kat in the A-TAC room.

"I can be there this afternoon. I have to get to the office and speak to my boss."

"Have Gaston page me if you need anything else."

After hanging up the phone, she turned to Alona. "Ready for breakfast, I'm starved."

"You still want to go to breakfast with all that's going on?" Alona asked, sounding surprised.

"Yes. One. I am hungry. Two. There is nothing I can do at this second ... at least not until I am cleared. Three. I am still hungry!"

With a big smile, she grabbed her sister and her bag on the way to the door.

CHAPTER 69

"Alyn David, how nice to see you again," Michoel greeted with mock formality.

Kat did not "officially" report to Michoel so they acted the parts they were assigned to play. Michael, Head of Diplomatic Security Service, supported Kat under the guise of "Diplomatic Security" which is acknowledged, respected, and protected worldwide.

"Good morning Michael, I'm heading to the Navy base this afternoon," she said, speaking pleasantly.

"Yes, I hear. A fine gentlemen named, Gaston Leroux, called me. They have a strange sense of humor down there." He slowly removed his spectacles.

"While I'm down there I was thinking of dropping by Pantera's boss' house and speak with his wife. I'm curious about what she knows." Kat had too much energy and paced the floor.

"Sounds like good research. Anything else?"

"Do you know Tal Cohen?" Kat sat down staring intently as her legs bounced restlessly.

"I know *of* her, but then again, who doesn't. Why do you ask?"

"Alona told me Tal infiltrated ISA in Naples to find an information peddler. Seems like a weird coincidence. Don't you?"

"So you think ..." He leaned back in his chair and rubbed his neck.

"Not yet, but I'm not ruling it out. Keep your ear to the ground. I may be walking into a hornets' nest. Have an extraction team standing by. Please." She got up, waved, and walked out of the office.

* * *

"Mommy, there's a pretty woman at the door." Kat could hear the little boy and see him peeking through the door window talking to his mother over his shoulder.

"Christopher to your room," Rose said, grabbing the top of the boy's head with one hand then turned him nudging him in the direction of his room. "We will discuss doors and strangers later." She opened the door.

"Hi. I'm Alyn David, a friend of Marcus Sinclair's." Kat smiled hoping there would be some type of acknowledgement.

"I know exactly who you are. You are far more ... than Marcus had described. Please come in." Rose directed Kat to a chair in the dining room. "Can I get you something to drink?"

"Tea?" Kat replied.

"So Kat, I hope you don't mind if I call you that."

Kat shook her head.

"What brings you to our little neck of the woods?"

"First. Let me apologize for just showing up. Why I'm here is curiosity. I would like to know how you do it. Do you *know* what Grit and the others do? How do you cope with what Grit does, not knowing where he is or if he will ever come home? And for fifteen years?" Kat the *Mossad agent* left the building and Kat the *girlfriend* just walked in.

"Those are some interesting questions. The easy answer is – I have no idea what Chris does. I'm not sure I want to know. If I was a wife of a hedgefund manager stealing millions of dollars from normal everyday people – do you think the hedgefund manager tells his wife what he *truly* does for a living? She probably doesn't care either. It's a man's world. So from my point of view, what's the difference? There are certain things you just don't need to know," she said, pouring hot water into a teacup and then placed a bag in it.

"So then by not knowing, it is easy to cope?" Kat was getting the *see-no-evil* vibe from Rose.

"Yes. I cope by thinking he goes to an office, and on business trips, and he comes home. If there comes a time when he doesn't come home, I will deal with that ... then. Can I ask *you* a question?" Rose asked before sitting down in the dining room. "Are you in love with Marcus?"

Kat paused tilting her head back. "I don't know. We are just starting to develop a strong connection. I admit that." Kat looked away summing up all their time together.

"You're here because you heard something about the team, *missing in action* or *not checking in on time* or *overdue for a rendezvous* or something like that." Rose gave Kat an omniscient grin.

"Yes." Kat stiffened up.

"The platoon wives love to talk and some want to know everything. I used to be one of those women. Then I stopped. It was an emotional rollercoaster. I trust him, he trusts me. End of story." She took a sip of her coffee.

Kat relaxed somewhat. "I still can't get this feeling out of the pit of my stomach."

"Probably because you're in the same line of business I would gather." Rose smiled.

"How do you know ..." Kat was concerned that this woman knew more about her, than she knew about this woman.

"It's okay." Rose gave Kat a grandmother pat on the thigh. "Chris and I may not discuss missions, but we do discuss the social lives of his platoon. You can consider me an unofficial ombudsman. I help handle the platoon wives, kids, military issues, money, etcetera, etcetera ..."

"And Grit told you I work for Mossad?"

"Yes, but honestly," she said, leaning toward Kat giving a mock whisper, "I have no idea what that means. Sounds like a great chicken dish."

Kat nodded. "How did you and Grit meet?"

"Chris and I were high school sweethearts – the cheerleader and the football star. He enlisted and we got married soon after. We had no money, nothing. Two stupid kids hugging each other for dear life wrapped in the blanket of the US Marine Corps. While Chris moved up in rank, I went to school and handled the house. When his assignments increased in difficulty, I had the opportunity to meet some truly astounding women. The advice I'm about to give you is the same advice they gave me when I was sitting where you are now."

Married after high school? People do that? Kat thought.

"You ... must ... have ... faith – and not that monotheist-type from western religion. You must have complete faith in your man, your partner. You must have faith in what he does and how good he is at it. Anything less and it will crush you."

"You trust he will come home after every one of those *business trips*?" Kat was having a hard time with the *trust-your-man* philosophy. *Why is it the woman always has to trust the man?*

"Yes. I have to. Otherwise, I wouldn't be able to function. Chris and I grew up in a little town called, Gatlinburg, Tennessee. It's referred to as the Bible belt – where everyone believes in some omniscient extraterrestrial alien that controls everyone's destiny. We weren't into all that. It was too esoteric for us. We believe in the energy of people and all living things ... and their interconnectedness. And most importantly," Rose said, eyes glistening, "we believe in each other."

"You guys are students of Eastern philosophy then?" Kat raised an eyebrow taking a sip of tea.

Rose's speech slowed and her voice cracked. "Yes. In a way. Let me give you a practical example. When he's home, he gives me some little touch during the day, he takes out the trash, he fixes things and he spends every second he can fully-involved in the kid's lives. Even better. Every day when Chris wakes up he whispers, *thank you,* to me. I never ask him why, deep down I think I know. For that reason and that reason alone, I will stand next to him for the rest of my life ... *or his.*"

"Wait. Pantera does that to me also and I never asked him what it meant. *Oy vey.* You're giving me the *wife talk,* aren't you?"

"Yeah, of a sort. You and Marcus are really guarded. I don't know what's in your past lives, but I can see there is some negative baggage. The two of you need to avoid using your past to block your future with each other."

"Very profound for a housewife," Kat said, prodding for Rose's resume.

"Not just a housewife, a woman with a Master's in Social Work and counselor to hundreds of military wives, girlfriends, kids and officers." She winked. Rose's ombudsman hat was firmly on her head.

"Rose, you have given me a lot to think about. Thank you for letting me take up so much of your time." Kat got up and moved to the door.

"Kat, you have to do *me* a favor, now." Rose was somber in her approach.

"Of course." Kat was piqued at what Rose would want from her.

"Because I know you now and what you can do, promise me if anything ever happens to Chris you will be the first person to come see me. Not call me, *come see me.*"

Kat could see the tears forming in Rose's eyes. She turned to look Rose square in the eye. "Ab-so-fuckin-lute-ly."

Rose smiled wide, being extremely familiar with the term.

Kat felt good saying it.

They gave each other a big hug as the tears rolled down their faces.

The military wife bond was sealed.

CHAPTER 70

"What do you mean you can't cross the damn border?" Major McFarland yelled into the phone as Kat opened the door to the A-TAC. "I've got thirty men who have been up there for five days and are running out – if not already ran out – of supplies and *you* are telling me you can't steal a truck and drive to a supply coordinate for your own Ambassador who *we* are trying to find? YOU FUCKIN' IDIOTS DESERVE TO GET INVADED!" McFarland slammed the phone down and then noticed Kat approach.

"Sorry you had to hear that. Who are you?" He gave Kat a sideways look.

"Alyn David ..." she said, hesitantly.

"Oh, Miss David, over here." Gaston Leroux stood up, waved, and quickly walking over extending his hand in a harried-professor manner. "Nice to meet you." He looked over at the Major. "Bill, this is Alyn David ... she's a contractor."

McFarland looked at Gaston and then turned to Kat.

"Ah, yes. I remember – another contractor from Israel. Now that I see you ... I'm guessing my number's not up," he said over the top edge of his glasses, trying to lighten the mood.

Kat shrugged. "The day is still young."

McFarland laughed. "I like her." He turned back to the situation board.

"Miss David, let me fill you in." Gaston motioned for Kat to come over to the desk.

Kat walked over and thought, *Pantera thinks this guy is one of the moles? Really? He doesn't look the part. Maybe that's what makes him so good.*

* * *

"Damn it, we missed them again." Grit kicked the dirt. "This guy is really pissing me off."

Not only frustrated at the fact they missed the kidnappers for a third time, but the team was out of supplies and low on Dinars.

"We've covered every freakin' piece of sand from *Basrah* to *Al Windh*." Grit flipped the antenna on the satphone. "Pirate-one to Mother Hubbard."

"Go for Mother Hubbard." McFarland's voice came over the phone.

"SITREP. Strike three – low on ding dongs – otherwise golf-tango-golf." Grit's voice was slow and stressed.

"Pirate-One. No ding dongs in the cupboard. Need to use bow and arrow," McFarland replied, showing physical pain as he spoke the words having been in Grit's situation before.

Gaston looked over at Kat. Kat nodded. She didn't know exactly what was said, but she had an idea.

Grit squawked his radio twice. "Well gents. Our dicks are in the wind. Bows and arrows." Grit looked over at Pantera shaking his head. Pantera raised one eyebrow and shrugged. The universal sign for ... *no surprise there.*

Hours after the check-in call, Brandy woke Grit.

"I did it," Brandy said, his eyes lit up like a Christmas tree. "I fuckin' did it, I found their asses!"

"What, where, how ..." Grit was trying to shift his brain into gear at one-thirty in the morning.

"They just called for supplies. They're hiding out at a farmhouse outside Mehran." Brandy paused, hoping Grit would understand the significance.

"Mehran ... Mehran?" Grit repeated. It took a minute. "In Iran?!" Grit sat up. "How did they ..." His brain was fully engaged.

"Yes, Gunny. They're in Iran." Brandy wanted to solidify the thought in Grit's head.

"What a huge set of elephant balls. Man o' man." He rubbed his month old beard. "An Al-Qaida–trained Syrian terrorist leads a team of Iraqi Special Forces over the border into a country that hates Iraq more than we do." A thought jumped into Grit's mind. *I don't have anyone who speaks Farsi. Ah, who cares, they're outside of Mehran, not in Mehran. A recon and destroy mission. That just jumped this thing up ten notches.*

Grit reached for the satphone. "Pirate-One to Mother Hubbard."

"Go for Mother Hubbard."

"Tangos possible location November three-three dot one-one by Echo four-six dot one-five. Out."

* * *

"Where in the hell is that?" McFarland turned to one of the specialists in the room.

"Tracking sir ... Mehran ... IRAN."

Kat was uncurling herself from one of the chairs listening intently.

"You mean to tell me ... an Iraqi Special Forces unit took a Kuwaiti Ambassador across the Iranian border? Wow. If anyone catches wind of this – the newspapers will have a field day. Okay, what do we have in Iran?" McFarland looked intensely at Gaston.

"Bill, we have nothing in Iran. They shut their borders long ago. Told the UN to go – you know where. If they really did cross the border, they either paid someone handsomely or they crossed covertly." Gaston shrugged.

* * *

"Gentlemen. We have a three hour drive ahead of us. Let's try to get there before the sun comes up. See you at rally point November two-two." Grit's calm voice directed over the radio.

Rally point November two-two was twelve kilometers north of road 13 between the road and the town of Mehran – an Iranian town just north of the Iran-Iraq border.

"Alpha and Golf set up your ambush about twenty clicks from the border in the riverbed just off the north side of road 15. Take channel two. Everyone else on channel one. Let's finish this and go home." Grit looked haggard. *Here's the difficult decision for the day. It's going to be 106F by midday. We either sit and wait for nightfall or go in now. Twelve hours in blistering sun will fry the best of us.*

It was hot and dry as a bone. They were very close to being exposed in hostile territory several times so far. A covert unit that gets exposed – gets dismantled. It is career ending. The platoon was living on goats and dogs for the last three days. Another twelve hours of no food with only a small amount of water wouldn't kill them. However, sitting under a desert camouflage net in the hot summer sun with grains of sand crawling around in every orifice leads to mistakes. Mistakes lead to lost men.

Grit made his decision. "Brandy advise Mother Hubbard. We're going in. Everyone switch to desert camo and use the rest of your water. Bravo and Echo set up on the barn. Charlie and Delta set up on the house. Considering what we've been through I doubt very seriously if any of the farmers are alive. Let's keep in mind this Syrian bastard could try to get us to buy the – I'm-the-civilian-farmer bullshit. Kill all obvious tangos, hog-tie anyone who surrenders. We'll sort them out later. Sniper two, what does thermal say?" Grit was back in the game and this was the fourth quarter. His platoon was about to punch it through the uprights.

Sniper two thought, *other than it's freakin' hot out here?* He decided not to say that. "We have a total of thirty-six tangos. Twenty-five in the barn – mostly horizontal. Eleven in the house – all over the freakin' place. Unable to tell who is a friendly and who isn't, Gunny." The voice came from sniper two, also known by the call sign, "Baby-face", Staff Sergeant Sam Wilkinson, U.S. Marine Corps.

"Let's get set up." Grit directed the four squad leaders.

Shortly after Bravo and Echo had moved down to the last desert berm, they followed along its back side until they were about fifty meters from the barn. Charlie and Delta had to wait because their access to the house was a hundred meters of wide-open farmland leaving them completely exposed.

Bravo team leader radioed, "Bravo and Echo in position."

"Snipers one and two take out all window dressing once we breach." Grit's voice became almost mechanical. "Charlie breach the front. Delta breach the back. We all breach at once. Move out."

Charlie and Delta slowly moved past the barn to set up on the house. Bravo and Echo were in position ready to breach the barn. Grit looked around, noting each man and his position.

"GO, GO, GO!" Grit's voice rang over the radio.

CHAPTER 71

Bravo and Echo jumped up moving on the barn and Baby-face performed two perfect melon shots on the guards. No one in the barn stirred as the doors of the barn flew open. In a matter of seconds everybody in the barn was dead or dying.

The front and back doors of the house swung open simultaneously. Bullseye took out two targets standing near a window. Charlie came in the front and dropped the first two targets before they could raise their weapons. Delta dropped their first two targets entering the back.

Grit heard rustling upstairs and pointed for Pantera to follow.

Halfway up the staircase Grit saw the glint of a metal barrel peek out from a corner. He put two rounds straight through the thin wooden corner. The gun dropped to the floor. There was silence. A muffled scream and rustling came from a room at the end of the hallway. Grit and Pantera cleared each room moving toward the last room. They stood at the last door. Grit signaled he would breach. Pantera kicked down the door. Grit rushed into the room. No doors, no windows and no one standing up – just four bodies tied up with duct tape.

"Clear!" Grit yelled.

"Clear!" It echoed a half a dozen times throughout the house.

Pantera and the remaining men of Delta team entered the room with the hostages. Grit pulled out his photos of the hostages and knelt down next to each one.

"Ambassador, check. Wife, check. Daughter, check. Ah, who might you be?" Grit motioned to have those who were identified cut free and removed from the room. He took a long hard look at the fourth tied-up person. The unknown man motioned to have the tape removed from his mouth so he could speak.

When the ambassador's tape was removed he yelled, "That's the leader, he killed my aides."

A black-clad balaclava masked man nodded to the Ambassador and upheld an open palm.

"We know sir, we know. We found your aides a couple days back." Grit sniffed the taped man. "He even smells Syrian."

Sweat poured off the Syrian's face and the smell of Syrian tobacco laced with Hashish filled the room.

Grit leaned in close to the Syrian and pulled down part of the balaclava covering his nose and mouth. "You really didn't think we would fall for this ... did you? You've been watching too many American movies, dumbass. Should have run when you had the chance, but then again ... you never really thought we would find you, did you?"

The Syrian sneered back at Grit.

A couple guys from Delta team searched the Syrian for weapons and also found him to be void of anything that would identify him.

"And it's good." Grit got up with a look of pure satisfaction on his face raising both arms in the air.

The whole masked team started laughing.

Grit turned to Pantera. "Mike-One, check out the ambassador, his wife, and the kid. Check the injured in the barn. Prepare them for transport. Then ... this piece of shit is all yours. I'm going to see how in the hell we're going to get out of this fuckin' sand pit." Grit helped the team escort the battle-beaten civilians out of the room and down stairs.

In the presence of hostages, or hostiles, it is extremely important to maintain their anonymity – the reason why Grit called Pantera

"Mike-One." No names and the use of masks are simple and effective tools so no government or intelligence agency can find them – except through the limited access single channel.

* * *

"I'll evaluate them downstairs," Pantera directed. "Take scumbag here, to the barn."

Pantera was walking down the hallway when he heard the unmistakable pop and smell of bubble gum. Bullseye was standing over one of his kills folding up a Bazooka cartoon in his hand. He was making something with the paper in a strange way, something Pantera had never seen. Every move of his big hands on the tiny paper was precise and impressive.

"What're you doing?" Pantera asked.

"Offering." Bullseye's focus unbroken.

Pantera knew this conservation was going to be challenging.

"What are you making?"

"Origami swan."

"Ah, to hold the soul of the person you killed in the hope they can become something better in their next life. How did I do?"

Bullseye tapped his index finger on his nose and placed the beautiful origami swan on the chest of the dead Iraqi soldier.

Pantera knelt down next to the body. "May you be a better person in your next life."

Bullseye looked at Pantera, nodded and winked, then walked away.

* * *

Ever since Brandy's call Kat's nerves were as raw as meat in a butcher's window. *I hate this. Is this what Alona goes through when I'm gone? I owe her so much.*

Kat heard whispering over her shoulder. It was Gaston speaking to Tal. *Oh harah, here we go.*

Over the loud speaker, "Pirate-one to Mother Hubbard, do you read?"

The room went silent.

"Go for Mother Hubbard," McFarland grabbed the microphone bending the wire post.

"SITREP. Three friendlies recovered. One hostile being interrogated. Two injured. Thirty-five tangos down. Ready for extraction. Over," Grit said with more inflection than usual.

A huge yell and sigh of relief came from the room.

McFarland paused, waiting for the room to return to silence. "Pirate-one, can you remain at your location until nightfall, over?"

"Roger that, Mother Hubbard. Will call back at two-one-zero-zero hours. Pirate-one, out."

Gaston walked over to Kat who had a stone expression. "I arranged for you to have a room at the BOQ. Come back at 1800 hours. Mary Shelley said she would like to buy you dinner and speak with you."

Kat raised her eyebrows and nodded.

* * *

Grit turned off the phone. His second radio squawked twice. "Alpha-one to team leader. We have engaged three hostile vehicles. Six tangos down. We have obtained two more trucks with supplies. ETA to your location is three zero mikes, coming through rally point November two-two. Out."

"Roger that. Alpha-one." Grit returned.

Grit squawked the channel one radio. "Thanksgiving has come early guys. We'll hunker down here until nightfall to wait for the extraction plan. Alpha and Golf have obtained supplies with ETA in thirty mikes. By the way, please ignore the screaming. Our little Syrian friend is going to find out the penalty for screwing with us."

Grit's little side note was unusual, but then again so was the whole mission.

CHAPTER 72

"Hello Ambassador. I'm the medical officer. I'll take your vital signs and ask you a series of questions." Pantera sat down next to the ambassador and rolled up his sleeve to attach the blood pressure cuff.

The ambassador whispered, "What do I call you ... what country are you from?"

Pantera looked up at him with the stethoscope in his ears and balaclava over his face, "We do not have names. We are not from any country, but at the same time, we are from every country. As far as you are concerned, we do not exist. Your government will debrief you and come up with a plausible story as to how your aides were killed. Their bodies will be retrieved and sent back." Pantera thought his Scottish accent came out well.

Pantera finished his assessment and walked outside to meet Grit.

"They're in good health, moderately malnourished and dehydrated – but ready for travel. I'll head to the barn to sew up our guys and speak with our little Syrian friend. Want to come?"

"Ab-so-fuckin-lute-ly. I hope you're as good as the last guy."

The two men walked to the barn as the rest of the platoon set up defensive positions in case they were found. The Syrian was face-down, half-sitting in a chair and half-lying across the long side of a rectangular wooden table. His arms were strapped to each corner. Pantera reached into his bag and pulled out an Epipen and stabbed him in the rhomboid muscle, between the left shoulder blade and the spine.

Pantera started by speaking in Arabic. "My friend and I do not actually believe you have anything we want to hear. I'm just going to torture you to death because I've nothing better to do. We'll mail your rotting corpse back to Qusay Hussein as a gift."

"Nice." Grit nodded looking at Pantera with half-amazement and half-satisfaction.

"You like? Just getting warmed up," Pantera said, smirking at Grit then turning back to the Syrian. "I have three more of these needles. They will lower your pain threshold making every nerve in your body hurt and make your heart race like an Arabian horse. That's not a good thing by the way. If you tell me crap I don't want to hear I will stick you with this other needle." He pulled a long thin syringe from his backpack. "It has a time-released toxin. If I don't give you the antidote it will start burning the tissues in your lungs until you start coughing up your insides. You'll look like a bloody geyser, from a cheap horror movie. It takes hours to die. I hope you have dreamed of drowning to death in your own blood because that is where you're headed, my friend."

The commander struggled and cursed at Pantera.

"However ..." An evil smile came over Pantera's face as he looked around the barn. "Before I give you the toxin I'll take this little drill. You see this ... it's called a *Dremel.* I'll drill straight through each of your fingers – through the nail bed, through the bone, and out the other side. After I do that I will spray the hole with this," he said, continuing to pull tools out of his backpack, "and it will make sure you don't lose too much blood. I can perform this procedure on every finger." Pantera pointed around the barn. "If I have enough time I'll take those rusted nails over *there* and stick them through each of the holes in your fingers. I'll then tie them to that rope over *there* and hang you from the rafters up *there*." He sat down on the edge of the table. "Gosh, with you hanging in mid-air, well, that's when my imagination will really get creative."

"I don't know ... those crossbeams look pretty weak," Grit said, looking at the ceiling of the barn supporting Pantera's performance, "but it sure would be fun to see. Guys let's tie a hand to the table for Pantera."

The Syrian turned his head to give Pantera a look of hatred.

"Grit, I think that's the look of impudence. Step one from the torture handbook. We're going to just fly through the physical interrogation steps."

"*Aleklab alameryekyh!*" [American dogs!].

Pantera leaned over the Syrian. "Oh sir, no need to thank us, this is just part of our ... *Welcome to Being a Terrorist* gift package."

The Syrian's muscles twitched uncontrollably.

"I guess to be fair – not that you were fair with the Ambassador's aides. We saw what you did to them. I'll ask just once. Do you have anything you would like to tell us about Iraq moving armored tanks and troops toward the Kuwaiti border?" Pantera stood back with his arms crossed.

The Syrian spit at Pantera as he finished his sentence.

"You see Grit, you were right. He doesn't know anything," he said, acting like a game show host.

Pantera revved up the drill and drilled through the Syrian's left thumb. The Syrian let out a bloodcurdling scream. With the high speed of the drill very little blood squirted out from the hole. Smoke started coming out of the hole and the smell of burning bone filled the barn.

"Wow that stings the nose, never can get used to that burning bone smell." Pantera laughed.

The Syrian tried to scream loud enough to get someone from the road to hear him. Unfortunately, the team took all the hay bales and lined the walls of the barn. The barn was virtually soundproof. No one could hear the screams in the house, much less the road.

Pantera felt the wood as he reached the other side. The Syrian was covered in sweat, shaking like a scared horror-film heroine and panting like a dog on a hot day.

After spraying the hole with the coagulant, Pantera continued, "Just think Mister Terrorist, I have nine more fingers. Gawd, I love fingers."

Waiting for the pain to subside, Pantera watched to see if the Syrian's mannerisms changed. They didn't. He walked over to get a drink of water.

This gave Grit the opportunity to play good cop. "Just give us a time, date, location, how many units, anything, and all this can stop. You're Syrian for fuck sake. You're protecting Iraq. What for? They couldn't be paying your family that much money. Trust me when I say this, we will hunt your family down and wipe them out, too. No descendants, means no one will remember you."

The Syrian laid his head down on the table. His breathing slowed.

Pantera returned. "No comment? That's okay, I like no comment."

He grabbed the *Dremel* and proceeded to drill a hole through the index finger. The Syrian screamed so hard his nose bled and his body shook violently. Afterward, Pantera stabbed him in the back with another Epipen and waited a few minutes.

"You know Mister Terrorist, I've never had anyone make it to all five fingers. I would really like it if you could hold out to all ten fingers because that swinging-from-the-rafters thing ... I *just* made that up," he added, leaning down to make sure the Syrian heard every word with a masochistic smile on his face.

Pantera was almost done with the middle finger when the Syrian passed out.

"Damn. Doesn't look like I'm going to make it to five, Grit," he conceded, looking over at Grit then asking, "You think we could get a contract to catch one of those monster Russian KGB bastards? Maybe they can make it to ten. I really want to try my hanging-from-the-fingers idea on someone." Pantera's eyes twinkled.

"You're a sick bastard. Glad you're on my side." Grit laughed as he grabbed a chair and leaned against one of the support columns of the barn.

Several hours later it was getting dark. Alpha and Golf teams had returned. Everyone ate chow and were preparing to "run for the border." When Pantera and Grit returned the Syrian's demeanor had changed.

"I will talk ... but please kill me quick," he begged.

Pantera and Grit looked at each other in wonder as Grit asked, "Hmmm, okay, what information would you like to imbue upon us?"

Grit continued to quiz the commander as Pantera pulled up a chair, sat down on the other side of the table, pulled out a Snickers bar and started eating.

"Hey buddy. Want a Snickers? It does a body good," Pantera jeered at the Syrian.

"That's milk, dude." Grit chuckled. "Seriously now. What's Hussein's plan?"

CHAPTER 73

"Iraq to invade Kuwait in August. All Army forces. Take control over oil fields. Wipe out all wealthy people in Kuwait. Army can keep whatever they take from Kuwaiti people." The Syrian looked up at Pantera, pleading for him to shoot him.

"Well boss, would you like fries with that?" Pantera stood up and pulled out his weapon.

"Nope. I'm good." Grit walked out of the line of fire.

Pantera shoved his Glock into the Syrian's ear. "Don't move. Any last words?"

Bang. The Syrian's brain exploded into a small pile of hay. His head bounced against the table like a bowling ball hitting a floor. Grit pulled out a sheet of paper and a sharpie and wrote something on the paper, folded it up, and put it in the Syrian's shirt pocket.

It read:

TO QUSAY HUSSEIN –
THIS IS A GIFT FOR YOU FROM US.
WE ARE COMING FOR YOU.
MUCH LOVE,
SHADOW KNIGHTS

* * *

Walking back from the BOQ Kat saw Tal standing out front of the ISA building.

Time for the talk, Kat thought.

"Do you mind if I buy you dinner?" Tal approached Kat in a calm manner.

"Sure. Let's go."

Kat and Tal sat quietly in the corner of the BOQ café.

"So, you and Pantera are an item? How's that going?" Tal said, softly.

"Good. You know, as could be expected. We really haven't done much." Kat took a bite of her pepper-coated pastrami sandwich, purposely being vague.

Kat knew she was in a highly dangerous position. If she gave Tal the impression she was withholding or guarding and Tal was connected to the Katsa Killer, Tal would speed up whatever plan she had and send her attack dog, or dogs. If she was too open or provided lies that were too far from the truth, Tal would spot the deception in her facial expressions and mannerisms. One wrong move could lead to certain death for her and Pantera. It was a perilous tightrope walk to mystery-ville.

"How's your sister ... and your father?" Tal had tension in her voice.

Asking only about Kat's sister and father and not her mother was a signal. Unfortunately, it was a signal Kat couldn't figure out.

"They are good," Kat responded. *This is so unlike Tal. What are you trying to do?* Going on the offensive, she asked, "What about you? What are you doing with the Americans?"

"You know me, just another assignment," Tal rebuffed, blowing on her hot coffee.

"Will you be returning to the office, maybe back to the school soon?"

"No. It's about time for me to retire. I don't know what I'll do next." Tal stood up. "Let's see if the boys can get back safe."

Kat had a thought she sprang on Tal. "Can I bring Grit's wife and kids to the flight line?"

334 · JD WALLACE

"I don't think that should be a problem," Tal responded. The two women continued talking on the way back to A-TAC. The loudspeaker buzzed just as they walked into the room.

"Pirate-One to Mother Hubbard," Grit's voice flowed out into the room.

"Pirate-One." McFarland read from a piece of paper in his hand. "Extraction coordinates are NO-VEM-BER three-three dot zero-four-six-one-one by E-CHO four-six dot zero-nine-six-four. Prepare Lima Zulu for two mike-india eights. Extraction in one-two-zero mikes."

"Roger Mother Hubbard, loud and clear. Out."

Tal turned to Kat. "You can go get Rose if you wish. Please keep in mind. These guys have never, and I mean never, had anyone waiting for them on the flight line after returning from a mission. It will be, to say the least, a shock."

* * *

Rose was sitting in the living room reading when she heard footsteps coming up the walkway. Kat took in the well-kept, red brick, four bedroom on-base structure with a small front yard and a carport. It was a standard military tract home that sat on a nice quiet cul-de-sac street.

Rose got up, walked over to the door and noticed it was Kat. Rose's face went ashen.

"Is he ... are they?"

"Rose it's okay. They're fine." She held the screen door and followed Rose inside.

"Oh thank God." Rose gave Kat a big hug. "Please have a seat."

"I'm sorry. I didn't mean to scare you, but thought you should know the boys are on their way and will be back on base tomorrow morning." She sat down on the couch.

"I'm guessing from your face this was a more difficult mission than usual?" Rose sighed.

"Much more. The original plan was for twenty hours. As you

can see, it took over six days." Kat nodded.

"And Chris ... is he ..." Rose put her hands to her face.

Kat forgot the pact they made last time she was here.

"Grit is fine," she interrupted, "everyone is fine. I asked the Senior Intelligence Analyst and the Commanding Officer if I could escort you to the flight line to watch them get off the plane. It will be a bit of a shock for you both, I am sure. After sixteen years and never having seen them return from a mission and deplane, I thought this would be one of those *once-in-a-lifetime* opportunities. Consider it a *thank you* from me to you. I also don't think they would mind ... that much." Kat raised her eyebrows giving a half grin. She had absolutely no idea how this gesture would go over with Grit and Pantera considering what Rose said during their last conversation.

Rose was still, contemplating. "Okay, let's do it," she said, pensively. "Where do I go? I've never been to that part of the base before."

Kat paused for moment. "Go to the gate and someone will escort you to the parking lot. I'll meet you there." The reaction was better than she hoped.

"Can the kids come?" Rose's face lit up. "You have to meet our kids. Jesse, Shawn, Christopher ... come down here please," Rose yelled up stairs.

Kat froze and she heard the stampede of feet bounding down the stairs. Her first impulse was to run. Of a small list of fears Kat had, kids topped the list. She stood there as if a tank was about to run her over, not having met someone's kids before. It never entered her mind about having kids. Her palms moistened.

Oh harah, kids.

"This is Christopher, our youngest, who you met this morning. This is Shawn, our middle child. And this is Jesse, our oldest." Rose pulled her daughter close and put her arm around her. Kat stared at Jesse with fascination. Jesse was an exact replica of Rose – equal in height with the same pure blonde hair.

"Kids? This is Kat. She is a friend of Uncle Marcus and she has arranged for all of us to go see your Dad get off the plane tomorrow." Rose stared into the faces of her children waiting for a response.

Christopher bolted forward jumping on Kat like a bouncing rubber ball. Jesse and Shawn were rather reserved and slowly approached Kat to give her a big hug. The processing of what they just heard showed on their faces. Initially Kat felt uncomfortable, but the feeling changed and a sense of *home* came over her.

They have no idea what I do for a living. No idea where I come from. No idea of my relationship to Pantera – and they hug me anyway. Hmm.

Their hugs were unconditional. These hugs came from the heart.

"Okay gang, let's get ready for bed. We have to get up early tomorrow ..." Before Rose could finish her statement all three looked at their mother.

"What about school?" they said, in unison.

"No school." Rose finished her thought. "Kat needs to get going. I'm sure she has a lot of things to do also."

Untethering herself from the children, Kat headed for the door. Rose met her at the door.

"Kat. Thank you. The kids have never, in their entire lives, had the chance to see their Dad at work. This is the biggest present anyone has ever given them," she said, hugging Kat as tears dripped from her cheek onto Kat's coat.

"For you Rose ... anything," Kat reciprocated.

Kat wiped the tears from her eyes and walked back down the path toward her car while trying to remember the last time she felt this way. The last twenty-four hours had been the wildest emotional rollercoaster ride she had ever been on.

Can I do this? Could I live this way and still be good at my job? Would he try to force me to give up my job ... once he finds out?

Her mind turned to the next eight hours. She only had one pair of clothes, no personal gear, and had a room at the BOQ. She banked a quick left and headed for Rome.

It's only four hours up and back.

CHAPTER 74

When Kat pulled up, Rose and the kids were standing at the back of their car. Rose gave Kat a big tight hug.

"Kids are you ready?" Kat looked in each of their faces.

The kids were not as intimidating as they were yesterday. They greeted Kat warmly with a *thank you* and a two-cheek kiss.

"Follow me guys. Let's go to the hanger bay where they store some of the other planes your Dad uses to do his job."

"Does my Dad know how to fly?" Christopher looked up at Kat.

Kat looked down at Christopher with a big smile. "I'll bet he is a very good pilot. I'm sure he's not flying today," she said, hoping she wouldn't have to delve further into the topic of Grit's occupation.

Gaston was standing at the back door of the hangar bay when Kat noticed him. She excused herself from the kids and walked over.

"Good morning Mister Leroux. Hope I'm not breaking any regulations." Kat smirked.

"No, not at all. How are the kids?" Gaston gave a big smile.

"The kids are good. Inquisitive as hell."

"Okay, well, just wanted to see if everyone was all right and to tell you that the plane is on final approach." Gaston put his palms together and gave Kat a respectful monk-like nod, then left.

Kat proceeded back to Rose and the kids.

"Why does my Daddy have so many planes?" Christopher tugged on Kat's skirt.

"Since your Dad's work is so secret the planes must have very different paint." Kat got down on one knee.

"What? Different paint?" He wrinkled his nose.

"You see those over there? Those are for flying at night because they are painted black."

"That's cool." Christopher's eyes widened.

A memory flashed in Kat's mind – one of her first memories of her father. He was showing her all the bladed weapons used in combat. Kat knew she was genetically chosen for what she does. She was *predestined*. Kat flashed back to Christopher's face.

Am I setting in motion something that Grit and Rose don't want for Christopher? Are they aware of that moment when a destiny is bestowed on a child. A destiny that motivates a child to perform certain work in the world? They're American, probably not.

"The plane your Daddy is flying in today will have two colors. On the bottom half will be painted blue. So people looking up at it can't tell the plane from the sky. The top is painted tan, so the people flying above the plane can't tell it from the ground." She watched Christopher's face light up in understanding.

"How do you know all this stuff?" Christopher looked up at Kat.

"Because I went to college," she said, tousling Christopher's hair and grinned at Rose.

"I can see it," Jesse yelled, her voice stretching upward. "It's so big!"

Kat looked up and saw an L-100-30 with civilian flight numbers and design. The workhorse of the CIA – which made her pause for a moment. *Why a CIA plane? No tactical air unit available or they didn't want the civilians at Kuwait airport to notice.*

The plane rolled up to the flight line and turned around with the rear cargo door facing the hangar bay. The engines shut down. The wind from the turbo-propellers almost knocked the kids down. They laughed hysterically – making all the adults laugh with them. Kat looked around.

There's no one here. So this is what a secret military unit comes home to.

Other than Kat, Rose and the kids, no other families stood waving banners, no friends throwing confetti, no glitzy military officers patting themselves on the back for a job they had no part in. Only the usual support crew to help unload the plane and medical personnel to take the injured men to the hospital.

Not this time guys, Kat thought.

It was a couple minutes before the cargo door slowly opened. It hit the ground with a loud noise shaking the windows in the hangar bay. The support crew ran up into the plane to carry the two stretchers down the platform. Blood soaked bandages covered the bare-chested men. Kat looked over at Rose. She didn't cover the kid's eyes.

Life unfiltered. That is a brave woman.

Kat could see Pantera giving a report to the medical personnel, pointing to their injuries, and then signing a paper on a clipboard.

Look at him. So professional. This is turning out better than I expected.

He walked back up into the plane. The platoon hobbled down the ramp. In a broken single-file formation they approached the hangar bay where the kids were standing. With dumbfounded looks on their faces they all recognized Grit's kids and either gave the kids a "high-five" or patted them on the head as they walked by. The kids looked happy and awestruck as if they were standing at the entrance to a football field when the football players entered the stadium.

Thirty dirty-dusty, battle-worn men in full-armed combat gear walked off that plane. The anticipation pouring from Rose and Kat was palatable. Grit and Pantera walked somberly down the cargo door together. Rose instantly covered her mouth and nose with her hands. Kat watched as Rose tried to say something to the kids but she was too overcome with emotion.

Wow. Guess fifteen years will do that to you.

* * *

All Rose could do was point with a shaky finger. After fifteen years of Grit always walking in the door – pressed and clean shaven – just like he had come home from a *business trip,* this was in stark contrast to what she saw before her now. Blissfully unaware of what Grit really did and how unbelievably dangerous it was, she watched him in heart-wrenching awe get off a plane with all those heavily armed men who looked absolutely demolished. Men who came to the house for a plethora of reasons, unarmed. A feeling of relief descended on her like a bolt of lightning and a freight train colliding.

* * *

Kat saw Rose's reaction through her own blurred vision. She was unable to determine if it was empathy for Rose or her own feeling of relief at Pantera's return that was triggering such emotion in her. Kat put her arm around Rose and the two walked slowly toward the two men.

"Something's wrong." Pantera's sixth sense took hold. "Incoming!" he yelled.

Grit's defenses went up. He reached for his weapon. Three high velocity celestial bodies were rapidly descending upon him.

"Kids?!" Pantera shouted.

Grit spun his weapon around behind him so the kids wouldn't get hurt. Pantera grabbed his weapon and unclipped it from his harness stepping to the side to avoid the ensuing avalanche like a Spanish matador. All three kids hit their Dad like a bag full of bricks shot out of a cannon. Christopher hit first, planting his head square in Grit's lower abdomen, almost doubling him over. He tightened up and sucked up the pain – this was the best kind of pain. Jesse and Shawn each took a side of him burying their heads in his chest and wrapping their arms around him so tight that he didn't know if he would ever get another breath. Rose watched this unfold and let out a giggle from behind her tear-soaked hands. Even Kat thought the scene was pretty amazing.

Overcome with emotion, Kat let go of Rose and ran toward Pantera.

Pantera's internal motion detector went off. He picked up Kat running toward him.

How unlike her. What did I do to deserve this? he thought.

He clipped Grit's weapon to his harness behind him and prepared for Kat's attack. Unlike the last time she jumped on him, this time he allowed her in. Her breasts hit him in the face as he grabbed her backside. They stood frozen in time.

I definitely need to know what I did so I can repeat this. Ahh, who cares, it feels good.

Rose walked slowly up to Grit. The kids moved out of the way to allow their parents some *mommy-daddy-alone* time. Rose took Grit's grimy, tear-soaked face in her sodden hands creating a most tender, passionate muddy kiss. Casanova would have blushed.

"How in the ..." Grit stopped, looking into Rose's eyes Grit struggled to find the words.

"Kat." Rose said, as they both looked over at Kat and Pantera.

Grit turned his attention from Kat and Pantera to the whole platoon standing in formation in the hangar bay – a very uncommon event. When the platoon saw him notice them, they yelled out their platoon motto:

"Second platoon, second to none, if we can't do it, it can't get done! OOORRRAAAHHH, Gunny O'Malley!!"

CHAPTER 75

The postcard moment drew to a close and Pantera let Kat slide down his chest.

"Alright Navy boy, what's the plan?" She batted her eyes and gave him a huge inviting grin.

"I've spent six days in the smoldering sand pit of hell with one spit-bath. Trust me when I tell you, you want none of this," he said, pointing to himself with self-deprecating humor.

You do not smell so bad. I've smelled worse.

The smell of his body odor unlike any guy she has ever dated actually did not bother her. She did catch the smell of burnt flesh and bone mixed in with gun powder residue which perked her up.

"How did you know?" he asked, keeping his hands firmly on her waist.

"Long story," Kat dodged.

"So, you and Rose are best buddies now?"

"Oh yes, we've spent hours talking about you and Grit," she said, with a mock melodramatic tone while rolling her eyes. "Again I'll ask," she said, kicking him in the shins, "what do you have to do before you can leave for the day? And I should add ... I have a room at the BOQ." She turned to walk away looking straight ahead increasing her pace toward the car.

"Oh, you do, dare I ask how?" he said, chasing after her. "I have to stow all my personal gear, inventory all weapons and ammo, and check them back in. Medical equipment needs to be stowed in the platoon medical locker. Then I can SSS, grab some chow, and write my report. Then the debriefing, which could take days ..." Pantera slowed down his pace.

She stopped and turned with a pout on her face.

"Okay. Okay." *You really want me? Wow. This is cool.* "I'm kidding. New plan. I'll stow all the gear. That will take about an hour. I'll ask Grit to page me for the debriefing. Let me grab my stuff and meet you at the BOQ and I can take a shower over there. How's that, Ma'am? Satisfied?" he said, tilting his head back.

"Listen up Navy boy. It's been over a month. I need a *hot-beef-testosterone injection* – definitely more than one – right now. So I'm going to need the whole damn weekend, better buckle-up, buttercup. Oh, you and I are going to take a shower and you're getting shaved," she barked, the Cheshire cat smile glowing.

"Shaved?" Pantera gulped. "You mean down ..."

"Yup," she cut in, "Sorry it's taken me so long, but I thought it was about time. I'm not into man-jungles. I like smooth and soft." She kissed him on the cheek and walked back to her car.

Why is it you still induce fear in me? Pantera thought.

* * *

Pantera looked at his watch. It was 0217HRS. *Man, this is getting really old.*

For the last month since the wild weekend at the BOQ, Pantera has taken one night a week to search the ISA building for the illusive server Christine Brown told him about. He was on his last hallway of offices.

The risk on this is getting really high. Stay strong brother ten more offices.

Pantera methodically searched each office for hidden compartments, false bottom drawers and fake books for a "server." He entered office number seven. This was the empty office he found the burned piece of paper with the Federal Reserve System logo. Nothing was out of place. He turned his attention to the desktop computer and an idea flashed before him.

You think Christine meant storage disk instead of server?

He crouched down behind the desk and slid the desktop out from the wall just enough to look inside the box.

Son of a bitch. I found you, you little bastard.

Inside the desktop was a small black box. He had never seen this type of computer equipment before. The one female connector on the thin side was also unfamiliar.

There must be a cable somewhere nearby. But where? I've been in this office twice now. I can't suck that bad.

Pantera moved back out from behind the desk and sat in the chair scanning the small cube-like office. Something suddenly looked out of place. It wouldn't look out of place for a cube. Pantera wasn't a cube – he didn't work and live in a cubicle.

Why would a can of air freshener be needed in an empty office?

He walked over to the can, picked it up, and tried to spray the office. It didn't work. He pulled on the top and nothing happened, then pulled on the bottom. The bottom popped off and a black cable fell out.

Well, well, well. Let's get you plugged in.

Pantera sat at the computer for over two hours. Everything was encrypted. He looked at his watch. It was 0547HRS.

Damn it. The cubes will be returning soon ... I need something.

He searched the directory – pages and pages of encrypted files. He wanted to take the box, but knew how dangerous that was if there was a tracking device in it. He finally found a hidden directory partitioned from the rest of the drive. There were two picture files. He printed them out and returned everything just as it had been.

Yes. You little prick. I'll give you 'good cop' you pint-sized turncoat. I'll have to call Jack later. Crap. Someone's coming ...

* * *

Pantera sat quietly in the dining room eating breakfast.

"Hey wake up!" Cracker jabbed Pantera as he sat down. "Romanticizing about the girlfriend?"

"Oh hey. Yeah. Of course. How is op readiness going?" Pantera asked, refocusing on the conversation and away from his find and the complicated web of trouble he was about to get into.

"Very good. We're on unit training objectives and what-such. Heard you finished your first United Nations debriefing?"

"Yeah. Definitely different than those arrogant, stick-up-their-ass, United States Judge Advocate General jerkoffs. Bastards can't hit the broad side of the barn with an elephant gun but somehow think every move in the field should have their friggin' approval and give us an SOS (Special Operator Skewering)." Pantera still had bad memories of his past SEAL debriefings.

"Second that. I had some butter-bar ask me one time. What socks was I wearing? I thought *numb-nuts* was hitting on me. Don't you love these United Nations barristers though? They support our mission, know we have to be creative to get our mission completed, and are about as cool and understanding as they come." Cracker smiled reminiscing about his last debriefing. "Did they buy beers afterward?"

"Hell yeah, got the barley smelling shirt to prove it." Pantera lit up. "I've never had a beer with a JAG-ass."

"Hello gents." SSGT Franklin sat down with Cracker and Pantera. "We're still on for this Saturday at the kill house, right?"

"Yup, Kat says she can't wait." He looked off into the distance. "Somehow, I get the impression she gets more turned on by gun power than sex oils."

"Okay brother, T-M-I," Franklin said, trying to wave away the thought.

"I hear the *Shootout at the OK Corral* is not going to be just our unit this year," Cracker said, smiling at the two men. "It seems there's a rumor about one hot *Italian model* that's going to be participating and many new international participants."

"This is going to be epic," Franklin added, diving into his pancakes.

"What the hell do you mean ... *Kat is participating?*" Pantera sat dumbfounded.

CHAPTER 76

"Thank you gentlemen, excellent run today. Somebody from this unit better take the trophy today or I will make your lungs burn during the next platoon run. See you at the OK Corral at 0900 hours. Dismissed." Grit walked away with a roguish grin on his face.

When Pantera entered the dining hall the sound level was an octave higher than usual. The glances at him by people from units he didn't recognize was unsettling. He knew the reason and he had grown to accept it.

"Hey buddy, who's your partner for the shoot-out?" Baby-face sat down.

"Bullseye and I are buddying up," Pantera said, looking up and chuckling.

"What is it? Do I have shit on my face or something," he said, trying to remove some phantom schmegma.

"Dude, you really have to do something about that facial hair. Just because we're on relaxed grooming standards doesn't mean *not shaving* is the only option. We're not embedded like the *silly fellows* – Special Forces. Honestly. Even if you had facial hair no one would buy the ruse you were of Arab descent anyway. Do what I do. Shave. We're just a pair of white boys from Hicksville, America. Just accept it." Pantera returned to eating.

Sam nodded in agreement. "You're right, who am I kidding. Why are you and Bullseye buddying up? I thought you were Grit's buddy. I hear you and Grit work pretty well together."

"Grit told me he had a partner." Pantera shrugged.

"I just came from the OODs office where the sign-up sheet is, Grit's name is not on it. You think he's bringing in a ringer at the last minute? Like his old partner? You know they're the record-holders," Baby-face asked, giving Pantera a look of surprise.

"I thought this was a *Naples only* competition?" Pantera shot back.

"Oh no. It's always been open to the sixth fleet and allied forces. Let's be honest, who in a thousand miles of this place could even beat our worst team? Nobody comes out any more – until now. See you at the Corral." Baby-face got up, took his tray to the dishwashing area, and left the dining hall.

Pantera remained, thinking in a *Rodin* pose.

* * *

"Hi guys." Kat smiled as she walked into the big man cave. Everyone stopped and took a long hard look.

"Damn," a voice said, from someone in the room.

Kat couldn't tell who. She continued walking farther into the common room of Pantera's barracks. Kat felt like a clown fish moving through the tentacles of the most dangerous sea anemone in the world.

Exhilarating. I'm so turned-on right now.

Kat giggled to herself as she continued through to the TV room. She stood in the doorway as if she was Kelly Lebrock in a scene from *Weird Science*. There were two men intently watching an Al-Jazeera broadcast of April Glaspie speaking with Suddam Hussein about his military buildup at the Kuwaiti border.

"Guys? Helloo?" She waved.

Both men stood up.

Bullseye looked at Kat and let out a gasp. He remembered Kat from the flight-line greeting in the hangar bay, but not this close.

"Bullseye, you remember Kat? I know I didn't formally introduce the two of you back then."

Bullseye nodded.

"Kat, this is Bullseye, sniper and roommate." Pantera pointed to Kat and back to Bullseye.

"Hi Bullseye," she said, extending her hand.

Bullseye nodded and took her hand to shake it. His hand enveloped hers. Kat inhaled. Her hand disappeared into his like Fay Wray and King Kong. She thought, *Feels like 12-grit sandpaper.*

"Umm, you're in the Israel Army now?" Pantera questioned.

"Sweet boy, everybody in Israel is in the Army. I was recruited from the *Talpiot* program when Mossad found out I was better than the *Sayeret.*"

Bullseye raised an eyebrow and shook his head.

"Okay, whatever that means. Anyway, love the boots. I look forward to having you in the stands cheering me on. Ready to go?"

"Were you expecting me to wear a short, tight, white dress with no bra and panties?" She steamed. *Boy is he going to be surprised.*

Kat and Pantera followed behind Bullseye as they approached the car. Upon reaching the car, Pantera swung her around and wrapped his arms around her – locking her arms behind her back.

Careful Navy boy, you could get hurt.

"I just wanted to say, *I'm sorry*. I didn't mean to insult your uniform or what you did before joining Mossad. I hope you will tell me about it later." Pantera looked into Kat's eyes with a serious look ending with a smile. "And ... *thank you.*"

Kat nodded and accepted his kiss. *And accepts his failures, good Navy Boy.*

Bullseye waited a minute then cleared his throat. The couple chuckled and got in the car.

* * *

"That building over there?" she asked, rhetorically. There were no other buildings around.

She could not believe her eyes. It was much larger than the Parkour Centre and easily the largest "kill house" she had ever seen.

"Welcome to the largest shoot house in the Eastern Hemisphere. There is a bigger building in the desert outside of San Diego. These places run twenty-four hours a day, three-sixty-five ... for both public and military." He unsnapped his seatbelt.

"Why is it I've never heard of this place?"

"I can't answer that. Why did no one from my unit know about the Parkour Centre until I told them?" he said, looking at her and shrugging. "Inside, you will find over one hundred thousand square feet or about two and half football fields. The walls and targets are moveable so the design can be changed daily. The catwalks also move. I actually thought you and I could have fun on a shooting range, but I'm going to guess this is more your speed. I hope you like."

Kat turned off the car glared at Pantera. "You *sooo* get me."

Kat, Pantera, and Bullseye walked into the building and after regaining their vision they looked at all the people in the front foyer, up on the catwalks, and in the stands. The heads of the crowd turned and a short hush came over the area as all caught a glimpse of the *Italian model*. Pantera thought he spotted a couple flag officers in civilian clothes up in the crowd. There were definitely some agency types lingering around. Grit met them in the foyer and gave Kat a two-cheek kiss.

"Are you ready?" Grit looked directly at Kat.

Kat nodded and looked up at Pantera. "I am. I don't think he is," she said, tilting her head toward Pantera then waiting for him to catch up.

"Wait one freakin' minute ..." he realized, pointing between Grit and Kat, "you mean you're taking Kat as your partner to uphold your title?" Pantera looked as if he had just been punched by Iron Man.

"Yup," Grit replied, nodding with confidence.

"You knew about this?" Pantera turned to Bullseye.

Bullseye shook his head.

"Kat. Let's get you checked in and check out your weapon. We have a safety briefing in about fifteen minutes." Grit ignored Pantera surprised look and thumbed in the direction of the office.

"You're right ... this is *sooo* my speed." Kat gave him a big kiss on the cheek.

"Alright missy, time for you to get spanked *BIG DOG style*," he barked, increasing his tone at the end of the sentence as Kat walked away.

"Bring it on, Navy boy," she said, over her shoulder.

The nearby crowd hissed and laughed as they watched the exchange.

Pantera stood frozen like a guy who got hit with a paint ball in the nutsack.

Bullseye smacked Pantera on the back pointing to his head and signed the word, "G-A-M-E."

"I know. I know. Get my head in the game. I will. Count on it," he said opening his bag and pulling out his Cordura thigh holster.

CHAPTER 77

The range master jumped up on a large box looking out over a sea of bodies – all with loaded weapons in their hands – with a microphone in his hand.

"Ladies and gentlemen, welcome to the fifth annual ... *Shootout at the OK Corral.*"

The crowd cheered and howled.

"Since you have had your safety briefing let's get down to business. The weapon for today is the HK VP70M nine mil with suppressor. This is a two clip, single elimination, winner-take-all competition. For your one-hundred-dollar entry fee you will compete for the prize of six thousand, four hundred dollars. At the completion of each round the walls and targets will be relocated. Those of you with eidetic memories will have no advantage." There was hissing from the crowd. "No use of verbal commands. Competitors cannot be in the stands or on the catwalks at any time. Please look up at *that* wall. Note the current record holders and last year's champions. Their time: 7:22.35." He looked down at Grit at nodded.

The crowd turned to see Grit standing with his new partner, a female with a long ponytail in an Israeli Army uniform. The whispers echoed throughout the building.

"One of those record holders is in the house today, but with a new partner. We will see how that turns out. For all you mathematics majors out there – only the walls and targets change, not the course distance. Meaning: the time to get through is consistent ... no griping that you can't beat the current record because the course keeps changing. There are thirty hostiles and an unknown number of friendlies. Each friendly shot is a five-second penalty and missed hostiles will result in a one-second penalty. Good luck, gentlemen ... and lady. Let's keep it pointed down range!" The range master jumped down from his box and returned to the office as the crowd cheered and clapped.

* * *

It was a full house. Pantera had never seen this many people in the building before and the stands had never been pulled all the way out. He narrowed his vision in Kat's direction.

Kat saw him and smiled. The Parkour "date" fresh in her mind. She turned to focus on Grit and his review of their hand signals.

"Thanks for being my partner," Grit said, in a humble tone to Kat. "I hope this won't be too much of a problem. Did you tell him you came up a couple times to practice with me at the other kill houses?"

"No, I didn't. Don't worry. I have a nice present for him," she said, giggling as she looked back at Pantera and Bullseye.

Pantera and Bullseye looked at each other with an intense stare. They had been buddied up numerous times before, but most importantly, they had a distinct advantage in the area of non-verbal communication. Everyone knew that Bullseye was fluent in American Sign Language, as well as a number of African variants, but no one had been on the receiving end like Pantera.

Bullseye signed, "Dead meat."

Pantera nodded.

From the stands came a series of low murmurs; looking up at the clock they noticed all the times were in the mid-to-low ten minute range.

"Sinclair and von Herbst on deck," the loud speaker blasted out.

Pantera and Bullseye jumped up, fist-bumped, put their protective eye gear on, and strolled over to the entry point. Like a knight about to charge into battle Pantera glanced over at Kat, nodded, and smiled.

He is such a big boy. I like competing against him, she thought.

The buzzer sounded and Bullseye was into the first room like a flash: *pop ... pop-pop*, three down. Bullseye indicted he would breach. Pantera entered and moved to the right, *pop-pop*. Bullseye entered when a target jumped up from the left, *pop*. He hit it before it finished rising. Next room had two friendlies. Three hostiles swung down behind the hostages, *pop-pop-pop*, all melon shots. Next room was a bigger room with lots of boxes, chairs and tables. Two hostiles on the left and three on the right, *pop-pop-pop*, Bullseye hit them with one shot each.

Pop-pop, Pantera turned, *pop-pop*.

Pantera then had a funny feeling about this room. He had a real-life experience just like this. He signaled for Bullseye to lead into the next room. Just as Bullseye cleared the door two hostiles from the room behind which they just cleared jumped up near the other doorway.

Pantera knew it. *Pop-pop*. He hit them almost instantaneously.

Within seconds, four more in the next room jumped up. Bullseye started from the left. Pantera was right behind him shooting from the right – dropping the first one ... then Bullseye, then Pantera.

The next three rooms Bullseye and Pantera nearly ran through. In the last room Bullseye swept from left to center shooting the hostile before he was even two steps into the room – but didn't see the last target to his five o'clock. Pantera entered sweeping from right to center and nailed it.

The buzzer went off: 8:33.94.

Bullseye and Pantera gave each other a fist bump and a simultaneous nod, no words were spoken. They were first place for the first round with Kat and Grit still to come.

The crowd let out a gasp.

* * *

Because Grit signed up at the last minute, Kat and Grit were the last to challenge the course.

"Here we go." Grit put his glasses on.

Kat nodded.

Instead of moving back to the foyer, Bullseye and Pantera decided to stay at the exit point to watch them come out. Kat and Grit's names were called overhead in the foyer.

The buzzer sounded.

Kat followed Grit into the first room and the only thing she could think was how to keep up with this guy. *This guy is a machine.*

Kat tightened her belt and stepped up her game. She was on his heels, always covering his six – keeping one eye on him and one eye in the opposite direction. Her weapon was a too big for her. She was used to a .32 calibre and this 9mm was like carrying a cannon.

Wow this rubber floor is cool. The bounce gave her an extra boost as they moved through the course.

The buzzer sounded: 9:12.16 – second place behind Bullseye and Pantera.

Grit turned to Kat before noticing Pantera and Bullseye walking over. "Kat ... that is a damn good time. We'll get them."

"Oh you will, will you, Miss Parkour champion?" Pantera said, with a mock air of arrogance he extended his fist out to Kat giving her a wink and a smile for encouragement.

Batting her eyes, she fist bumped him back. "Damn Skippy. You can count on it."

Snapping an about-face, she grabbed Grit's arm and stomped off. After a couple steps she leaned into Grit and softly asked, "I *did* say that Skippy-thing correctly, didn't I?"

Grit started laughing. "Yes, you got the *Skippy-thing* correct."

CHAPTER 78

The day wore on and the heat inside the non-air conditioned metal building rose. The fatigue could be seen on the faces of the remaining contestants. The crowd would moan if someone was too slow on the draw. So far no one hit a friendly. Rounds two and three went by and the times remained basically the same. Only four teams left. When the first team took off into the course Pantera motioned to Bullseye to follow him into the office. Pantera grabbed the trauma kit and threw it on the table. He took out one of the smaller bags in the kit and opened it. It was full of chemical ice bags.

Pantera grabbed a couple and cracked them. "Put these up to your neck on each side of your larynx, ah ... your Adam's apple. I don't have enough time to lower our core body temperature, but I can get our cerebral temperature down."

Kat peeked around the corner, then straightened up and walked in. "Whatcha doin'?" She smiled at Pantera and jumped on him placing her hands on both sides of his head giving him a big wet kiss.

Bullseye stepped to the side – ice packs still on his neck – with his eyebrows raised.

"Love the enthusiasm. Is there a reason for this jubilation?" Pantera was confused.

"Situational awareness and improvisational intelligence, you are really good." She nodded with a wink.

"Please. Everyone out there knows that placing an ice pack on the carotid arteries lowers the cerebral temperature making your thinking more efficient." He didn't understand what she was all happy about.

"They probably do, but how many are actively taking advantage of that knowledge?"

Bullseye nodded and shrugged.

He looked at Bullseye. "Okay. Maybe she has a point," he said, turning to Kat. "I'm not doing anything I wouldn't do in the field."

"Exactly." Kat leapt down and smacked him in the chest.

The two most important skills in the spy world were improvisational intelligence and situational awareness. Combined, they are the ability to use one's surroundings to one's advantage. These skills cannot be taught and nothing gets an agent killed faster than someone who cannot take advantage of their surroundings.

I found my MacGyver, she thought.

* * *

The crowd roared with disappointment. Team 2 hit a friendly making their time over fourteen-minutes. They were out. Team 1 came in a half-second behind Kat and Grit on the penultimate round. After a brief rest the championship would start again.

Grit caught the smirk on Kat's face as she meandered over to Pantera and Bullseye. He followed.

"Alright Navy boy, shall we wager a little side bet?" Kat said, acting cocky.

"What do you propose, Princess." He crossed his arms.

"If Grit and I win ... You are my manservant for a full weekend. You will wear whatever I want, cook whatever I want and wear whatever sex oils I want."

"Oh gawd ... not the peppermint," Pantera groaned, louder than he should have.

Grit and Bullseye took a step back.

"This is the real shootout, for sure," Grit said.

"BUT! If you and Bullseye win, I take you on an all-expense paid, four day trip to Switzerland. If you would be so willing to use your four-day pass," she declared, crossing her arms and tilting her head to the side.

Grit and Bullseye watched in disbelief.

"Damn dude. She's not bashful is she?" Grit couldn't help himself as Kat and Pantera squared off against each other.

"By cooking you mean stay in. Correct? None of this, *parading the boy-toy around outside naked,* in some small Italian town to freak out the locals ... like before ... right?" Pantera's eyes went wide. He realized what he just said and who he said it in front of. "Crap."

Grit and Bullseye looked at each other.

"No. You wear whatever I want ... in *my* apartment," Kat answered.

"You already know the answer ... since you're calling me out in front of my boss and my roommate." Pantera flashed back to the embassy ball not so long ago.

"You ... are ... ON ... Princess!" He extended his hand to shake, sealing the deal. *Oh gawd. What are you up to now?*

Kat shook his hand. *Oh Navy boy. You are so much fun. Wait 'til you find out what I have in store for you.* "Get prepared for a spanking of a lifetime," she snapped, giving him a mock sneer.

Grit grabbed Kat around both shoulders, turned her, and marched her away.

"Puttin' it on a little thick, don't ya think?" Grit said quietly in her ear.

"Yeah, probably, but my sister's wedding is in Switzerland in a couple months. Didn't want him to have an excuse to get out of it." She gave a big smile but facing away from Pantera so he could not see it.

Grit stopped and almost fell over laughing. "Lady, you're nothing but a bag full of surprises. Absolutely priceless."

* * *

"Sinclair and von Herbst to the entry point." The names echoed throughout the building.

Bullseye and Pantera had their game faces on. Pantera looked over at Kat. Took his two fingers and pointed to his two eyes, then took one finger and pointed it at Kat. She gave him a grin in return.

Buzz.

Bullseye was off and Pantera was right behind him. Bullseye's weapon in his left hand and Pantera's weapon was in his right. Kat and Grit stood motionless listening for the sound of their weapons discharging, timing the rate of fire and gauging the reaction of the crowd.

"They sound like they are on fire," Kat said, breaking the silence.

"They do." Grit nodded.

Kat and Grit knew it would take a herculean effort to beat these guys – but absolutely would not concede.

Buzz.

The whole building held their breath. It was a perfect run.

Time: 7:43.21.

Not a record, but the fastest of the day. It would be extremely difficult to beat and was faster than anything Kat and Grit put up so far. Bullseye and Pantera looked at each other, nodded, and stood over to the side in anticipation of watching Kat and Grit come through the exit.

"O'Malley and David to the entry point."

Grit turned to Kat. "Why don't *you* take point?"

"Are you sure?" Kat cocked her weapon.

"Yes, I'm sure. I already have a record. Besides, I think I've been holding you back. I'll do my best to keep up," he said, smiling modestly.

"Yes, sir," she said, giving him a mock salute.

"By the way, don't call me sir. I work for a living," Grit said, straight-faced.

Buzz.

Kat's reaction was so fast it made Grit feel like he was standing on his heels. Before he could blink she was through the first room had two kills and was deep into the second room with two more kills before he fired his first shot – all her shots were center mass. He realized – assassins' targets don't wear armor – he knew her real occupation now.

Kat was moving at a faster pace than her predecessors and the crowd felt it.

The tension was mounting.

Grit caught up and was now in the fourth room. He was finally able to anticipate Kat's movements and counterbalance the field of fire. Kat's speed and reflexes were lightning fast.

How could I shoot her if I could barely see her? Grit thought.

He struggled to keep up. They entered the five-man room and Kat took out four leaving one for Grit. He paused for a nanosecond in recognition of this fact and Kat was already out of the room and firing in the next room.

Buzz.

CHAPTER 79

The crowd watched in amazement. The whole building fell silent and everyone took a deep inhale. It was an eternity for their time to flash up on the screen. Bullseye and Pantera didn't even notice Kat and Grit as they came through the exit. They heard the rate of fire and thought it was definitely faster than theirs.

Time: 7:49.83. It was Kat and Grit's best time of the day.

Grit and Kat hugged.

"I slowed you down. I'm sorry. You're the best I've ever seen. I hope we get to do this again," he whispered in Kat's ear.

Kat looked up at Grit and mouthed the words. "Thank you, me too."

Finishing the hug with Grit she ran over to Pantera and jumped into his arms as the whole crowd cheered.

The overhead speaker rang out: "Will von Herbst and Sinclair come to the office to collect your winnings as champions of this year's SHOOTOUT AT THE OK CORRAL! Everyone, thank you for coming."

Grit walked over to Kat, Pantera, and Bullseye, and said, "Dinner my house. 1800 hours. BYOB."

* * *

"Where are you going? Sneaking from my bed in the middle of the night," Kat asked, rolling over to see Pantera putting his clothes on. "And that is definitely un-sa-tis-fac-to-ry."

"I have to check in with my handler," he replied, having trouble with his zipper.

"From the UN? Should I ask?"

"Yeah, the UN, I will tell you later. I found the mole."

"Tell me now," she said, jumping up from under the covers.

"No. I have to check in. I need authorization for a catch-and-rendition or catch-and-kill," he said, talking through his shirt as he pulled it down over his head.

"I need to talk to this guy. He may know about my situation." Kat jumped out of bed.

"Kat. Stop. Let me find out what I'm authorized to do. I also told the MI-6 chick I would give her a call. Let's just slow down and take a breath."

"I'm trusting you, don't let me down." Kat gave him a big hug and kiss.

"Come on, really, aren't we past that?"

Pantera walked out of the Navy Lodge and took three cabs to his favorite conversation location.

* * *

"I found the mole," Pantera said, quietly hunched down behind the dumpster.

"You did?" Jack's breath was audible.

"I'm sending you two photo files. One is the Rothschild Bank receipt with the numbered account and the other is the letter from the Federal Reserve with some name I don't recognize."

"I can check out the receipt. Who is the letter addressed to?"

"Ray Smith ... also known as ... Gaston Leroux."

"How did you find out Gaston Leroux is Ray Smith?"

"I did a second, more thorough, search of his house and found his go-bag. He had his old CIA badge and passport in it." Pantera was hitting the outside of his thigh with his other hand. "I will check him out." The sound of pen scratching across paper could be heard.

"What am I doing? An interrogation with rendition or do I end him when I'm done?"

"We didn't spend money on you to perform rendition interrogations. You know better. Remember what the director said? If we retire our detainees, then discussion of advanced interrogation techniques need not take place with either the Senate Select Committee on Intelligence or the House Permanent Select Committee on Intelligence of Congress. The SSCI and the HPSCI only reviews interrogation of living bodies, not dead ones."

"Understood, can you get me the number to the clean-up crew?"

"Sure. Is your girl under control?" The squeak of Jack's chair told Pantera that Jack was leaning back – relaxed about Kat's involvement.

"She wants a piece of this guy, too. I'm guessing everyone does. I'm holding her off at the moment."

"Smart. Good luck." Jack hung up.

Pantera brushed himself off and walked down to the corner taking three more cabs back to the Navy Lodge.

* * *

"Well?" Kat was pensively waiting for Pantera.

"They want him retired after I'm done," he responded, sitting down in the chair across from the bed.

"Are you going to let me in, or what?"

"Yes, of course. I'll call you when I have a time and place. Can we go back to bed now?"

"No. I'm going to need some more testosterone to counteract all this adrenaline," she said, with an upturned smiled.

* * *

Two bodies were lying on the bed in complete exhaustion when the pager vibrated across the night stand. It was 0235HRS.

"Damn." Pantera looked at the number on the screen.

He rolled over to face Kat softly moving some hair out of her face and whispered, "*Thank you.*"

He paused for a moment to soak up her beauty and have a mental snapshot in his head – an enormous motivator to return.

Kat was awake, just playing possum. She hated saying good-bye.

Pantera ran downstairs and asked the clerk to call a shuttle for a ride back to his unit's location at the airport. A twenty kilometer ride south. The Navy lodge was on an official Navy base – pure Americana – in the middle of Italy. The villa was a two-room suite, balcony, bigger than the rooms at most B&Bs, with a small kitchen.

Kat got up, made herself some Irish Breakfast tea, and grabbed the paper. It looked like she would have Sunday all to herself.

CHAPTER 80

The platoon shuffled into the amphitheater when McFarland took his position at the podium and looked up at them.

"Good morning gentlemen. I am sure you are aware Iraq invaded Kuwait a couple days ago. It was a complete disaster – even after the intel you obtained. *Emir Jaber* left the country and flew directly to the UNSC to request aid. Kuwait has agreed to place a fifty-billion dollar gold deposit with the UN to pay for any country's military assistance. Planning and movement of hundreds of thousands of troops from around the world is going to take months. The director of the UN-SOG has received word that there are several death squads ransacking, raping, and murdering wealthy residents. These death squads are being led by a group of Ba'athist Secret Police from the Ministry of Interior called, "Black Crows." The Emir has placed a bounty on each Black Crow head. The UNSC has issued a sanctioned kill order for all Black Crows and any Iraqi militia found violating the rules of the Geneva Convention. We have over a dozen reports coming in now." McFarland paused for questions.

Grit stood up. "Are you saying, sir, that all Black Crows and those under the command of a Black Crow are live targets? Are we photographing them for proof?"

"Yes, unless you can catch one and interrogate him. By all means, have at it, but don't leave him alive," McFarland continued,

"Ops Plan is as follows. Second platoon, you will break up in to three hunting parties: Alpha/Golf, Team One. Bravo/Echo, Team Two. Charlie/Delta, Team Three. This is a HALO authorized insertion from a height of thirty-three thousand feet and your DZ will be these three skyscrapers at these coordinates." He pointed to the map behind him. "Your plane will be disguised as a private plane of a Ba'athist high-ranking official in case you are challenged by the Iraqi Air Force."

Pantera caught Bullseye's hand signal to give to the Iraqi Air Force ... *the bird*.

Now that's the perfect signal.

"Isn't most of the power off in Kuwait city, sir? And are there any assets in country?" SSGT Harry Franklin asked respectfully.

"Most of the power in Kuwait City is off. You'll have to rappel down from the top of your assigned building. Further instructions will be provided by an in-country intelligence asset. If anyone believes you have captured an HVT call for the interrogator who will be assigned to Team Three. Let me reiterate, this is NOT a capture mission, hunt ... interrogate, if possible ... dispose of ... end of story. Gunnery Sergeant O'Malley, do you have anything to add?"

A voice bellowed out from the crowd.

"Team leader meeting to follow."

McFarland stood at attention and the whole room stood up.

"Dismissed."

* * *

Kat sat peacefully in her office with Sunday on the Navy base still on her mind as she prepared reports from the last few days of embassy activities, lost passports, visa background checks, and information obtained from various contacts around Rome. She felt no feelings of anxiety or trepidation at Pantera's absence. She met the diplomatic carrier on her way out to have lunch. He handed her a package. She reversed direction and returned to her desk. The first three words on top of the page stood out:

"SANCTIONED ASSASSINATION CONTRACT"

Putting all the paperwork back in the envelope she walked into Michoel's office. "Michoel, I'm heading out of town on a contract. Want anything back from Serbia?"

Michoel gradually raised his head and slid his glasses to the end of his nose. "We're finally going to take out that genocidist – about time. Have a good trip."

Kat went home, got into her comfy pajamas – despite it being mid-afternoon – and poured herself a cup of English Breakfast tea. The dossier of Boris Petrovic, the Serbian presidential candidate, laid across her lap.

* * *

"Ready to increase your body count?" Grit said, looking forward.

"About damn time," Pantera sneered.

Pantera and Grit stood in silence as they watched their fellow teammates shuffle up the ramp of the cargo plane.

The flight was smooth, the night was calm, and the moon was half full. The platoon was in the zone. Grit and Pantera were in the back of the plane along with the rest of Team Three. They would be first out since their DZ was the farthest north. The trip took two hours longer than usual. The pilots felt it was safer and less congested to fly up from the southeast over the Persian Gulf. By passing Kuwait on their left they could make a one hundred and eighty degree left turn and fly directly over Kuwait city from north to south. Team Three consisting of Charlie and Delta squads would take the northern quadrant of the city.

The red light started blinking.

"Here we go." Grit nodded to Pantera.

The platoon took off their pre-jump oxygen masks that were connected to the plane. In nearly one motion the platoon pulled their jump oxygen masks down over their faces. Creating a seal,

368 · JD WALLACE

they tested their system for the third time since boarding the plane. If the oxygen unit fails – they die – physics is inflexible.

Grit glanced down the length of the plane and saw everyone with a thumbs-up. He nodded and gave the thumbs-up to the flight engineer. The cargo door opened. The pressure dropped and everyone cleared their ears. The sting of the minus thirty degree wind hit the small patches of exposed skin around the outside of the *Gentex* full-face oxygenation mask. It was cold and dark with the smell of pure oxygen filling their noses and the view of the full moon shimmering off the deck of the plane, their minds buzzed with excitement.

All heads turned when the yellow light started blinking.

Team Three stood up, turned to their right, and shuffled forward in a tight group – affectionately called, "nut to butt." However, carrying over one hundred pounds of equipment on their chest and down their front makes the whole physical connection impossible.

Grit stared at the green light waiting for it to go on. He would be the first out the door and Pantera right behind him. The rest of the team could not see the light. They would just shuffle as fast as they could out the door right behind the person in front of them.

The green light started blinking.

Grit launched himself off the cargo-door ledge and Pantera took one step to the right and followed. Charlie and Delta's muffled yells could be heard as bodies were flinging themselves out the back of a one hundred and twenty mile an hour plane.

"One, two, three ..." Pantera started counting to himself, something he liked to do since military free fall school so he would know when he hit terminal velocity.

In a free fall a person reaches terminal velocity – the maximum speed possible under those conditions – within about twelve seconds. At that point, the speed of the parachutist is approximately one-hundred and twenty-five miles an hour.

Pantera looked at his altimeter and the needle was pointing to five thousand feet. He saw Grit in front of him pull his drogue. Pantera pulled his drogue and felt his descent slowing. It was time to find the DZ and line up for the landing. He looked down at all the buildings with all the red lights on the north end of Kuwait city. He spotted the geographic markers that would give him a good idea where he should be headed.

The needle on his altimeter continued to drop – 2000, 1800, 1600, 1500 – his mind yelled for him to pull. With a jerk his parachute hurdled out of his pack. The ram chute completely filled with air.

CHAPTER 81

Pantera reached up, grabbed the toggles, and focused on looking for the blinking green lights on top of the Holiday Inn Hotel. He turned and followed Grit's line as he passed over the beach. Grit was about twenty meters ahead of him. The temperature was warmer, there was a slight onshore breeze and the buzz of the oxygen was wearing off as the salt air hit him. He followed Grit's parachute straight forward and found the blinking green lights. He pulled down on the toggles just slightly to give Grit enough space to land without jamming up the guys behind him. Grit hit the northern edge of the building and started running to the other side as he collected up his parachute.

Pantera pulled down hard on the toggles and his descent slowed. *Three, two, one. BAM.*

He hit the same puddle Grit did and he started running to the other side of the building pulling and gathering up his parachute as hard as he could to get it out of the way of those behind him. The last man hit the edge and cleared his parachute. The whole team landed safely.

By the time the last member of the team had hit the roof, Pantera and Grit already had their abseiling harnesses on and finished anchoring off their ropes. They cocked their Heckler & Koch MP5SD weapons, locked in on the rappelling rope, and *Geneva* rappelled down the glass hotel face. Surveying the surrounding area as they descended the west side of the building, they noticed there were two tank units to the south at the *Dasman* roundabout and nothing to the north.

They hit the ground and took up defensive positions to protect the rest of the team as they came down. The last two men pulled the ropes from the roof and packaged them up. Someone approached as they stowed their gear. With hand signals, Grit directed two guys to check it out. A woman in a black burqa with a green glowstick in her hand approached the two men. After speaking to her they escorted her back to Grit. She pulled down the *Niqab* and smiled at Grit.

"Hello. Christine Brown, MI-6, your host for this mission. I'm guessing you're the hit squad sanctioned by the UN Security Council?" She threw back the burqa headpiece and a mop of blonde hair flew out.

This was not Grit's first female intelligence officer in the field. It was his first that looked like she just stepped out of a salon.

"Yes, I'm Grit. What's our situation?" he said, resting his hands across his tethered submachine gun.

"I have three reports of Black Crows in the northern sector. At last report, one unit is currently ransacking the British Consulate about five hundred meters to the northeast," Christine said, sizing up Grit and the rest of the unit.

"You have a place for us to store our gear?"

"I have a safe house that can be used for a base of operations in a basement of an old apartment building about two hundred meters away. It's in the same direction as the embassy. There is also a good amount of ammo and comrats with some local food." She pointed to the northeast.

Grit made a circling motion with his index finger and pointed to the northeast.

Christine took her burqa completely off revealing a black fatigue outfit and a significant amount of suppressed weaponry. She tied her hair back in a ponytail, pulled a black balaclava over her face, and pulled the hoodie up over her head. She looked like the rest of the team.

Grit walked over to Christine. "This is Pantera. He's your escort. Do not leave his side."

Christine gave a blank nod at Pantera.

Pantera nodded back despite recognizing her. *Damn she's good. She didn't blow my cover.*

Grit directed over the radio, "Squad leaders make sure everyone is on channel three. Charlie take point. Move out."

Pantera and Christine threw on their backpacks and got in formation.

They walked past the *Farah Motel* and they could hear rustling in the building – no one was outside. Their building was the next over and the path to it looked clear. Christine pointed to a door on the south side. The team swept the area and set up a perimeter. Grit directed Pantera and Christine to the south side door. Christine removed her lock pick tools and opened the door swiftly. The door opened to a significant storage space.

"Where's the owner?" Grit said, more curious than concerned.

"I'm the owner. I killed the owner last week right before the invasion and told everyone in the building the Iraqis were coming and they needed to get out of the city. The building has been mine ever since," she replied, using a gruff attempt at a Southern American accent in an attempt to mimic Grit.

"Drop and go gentlemen. We have some hunting to do. The embassy is two hundred and fifty meters to the northeast." Grit stood at the door.

* * *

"Contact, fifty meters. There are three trucks and two SUVs parked outside the main gate on the south side of the building. I can see four Iraqi Special Forces soldiers loading one of the trucks," Baby-face could be heard over the radio.

The two squads stopped.

The Embassy of the United Kingdom, Street No. 11, was a large six and half acre facility with a two story, thirty-thousand square foot residence surrounded by seven smaller buildings in the southeast corner circling a moderate sized courtyard. There was a two-story twenty-thousand square foot office building in the southwest corner and a tennis court in the northwest corner. The swimming pool and recreational area were located in the northeast corner with a large grass lawn in the center. The compound was surrounded by a ten foot high cinder block wall with only one way in, the main gate on the south side.

"Charlie-one. What's your twenty?"

"We're on the west side. Across the street from the *Dasman Diabetes Institute,*" Harry responded.

"Delta-one. What's your twenty?"

"We're on the east side in the ruins of the old Saudi Embassy."

"Leader, Mike-one and *host-ghost* are on the south approaching the parking lot. Stand-by for further orders." Grit peered through his binoculars surveying the area.

"Baby-face, what's on thermal?"

Sam crept up on the wall in the southeast corner to get a view of all the buildings in the south portion of the compound. "The southeast main residence: Ten verticals on the first floor and four verticals and six horizontals on the second – no one in the smaller buildings with two verticals in the residence courtyard. The southwest office building: Six verticals on the second floor, none on the first floor. Oh, wait a second, looks like we also have a three-on-one gang rape in progress in the central grass area."

"Charlie-One: Take the four at the truck. Secure the office building. Snipers clear the grass area. Delta-One: Secure the residence building. Team Leader, Mike-One and host-ghost will pull up behind Delta Team." Grit's voice was fast and firm.

A series of nearly inaudible pops could be heard. Charlie squad could be seen dragging the four men out from the line of sight of the front gate.

374 · JD W<small>ALLACE</small>

"Charlie-One to Leader. All clear and snipers are set up on the southeast corner."

"Delta move," Grit radioed, slow and smooth.

Christine moved to get up but Pantera put his hand on her shoulder and shook his head.

Delta moved through the gate. Half the team moved to the front door and the other half ran north to the other end of the building. Pantera and Christine stayed with the front-door group.

CHAPTER 82

The compound was eerily quiet, even with a rape going on outside. The front double doors to the residence were wide open.

Grit directed Delta-one and his team straight into the building to take out the ten guards who seemed to be focused on boxing up antiques and artwork. He pointed to Pantera and Christine to follow him upstairs. Christine pulled her suppressed Uzi as Pantera and Grit prepared their suppressed HKs. Grit directed Pantera to sweep right to left and gave Christine the center. They moved up the large circular staircase, one step at a time, listening to determine the locations of the verticals.

Grit was point.

Four men came into view. Two were standing together talking and the other two were guarding what looked like the British ambassador. One man was directing his anger at the ambassador. Three staff members sat in the corner hugging and shaking. Grit stopped and turned to Pantera using hand signals. He directed him to take out number four, farthest to the right, Christine to take out number three, and he would take out number one. This would leave number two for interrogation. Number two seemed to be senior to number three. Both were Black Crows.

Pantera and Christine nodded.

Grit, Christine and Pantera lined up and slowly walked toward the four men.

376 · JD WALLACE

Unlike law enforcement training which teaches to shoot from the staircase, intelligence officers are trained to walk up, close as possible, with their eyes on their target and wait until noticed.

They were about five paces into the room when Pantera's target turned. *Pop.* Pantera dropped his target and within a fraction of a second there were two more pops. The three men fell into a humble repose.

Downstairs Charlie team heard the suppressors and their dropped seven. Within a couple seconds three more bodies hit the floor at the other end of the building.

Grit, Pantera, and Christine swept into the room after their shots. One man left standing. An older, pepper-haired Senior Black Crow official stood quietly as if he just had his Bourbon glass shot out of his hand. With his body half-turned and hands in the air, he slowly turned his head to see three black figures standing less than five meters away pointing suppressed submachine guns with red lasers at his face.

"*Kent alekhetwh aletaleyh yemken an tekwen alakheyrh fey heyatek. 'Ela rekbetyek, 'eber alekahelyen, wed' yedyek 'ela rasek, wetshebyek asab'ek.*" [You're next move could be your last. On your knees, cross your ankles, put your hands on your head, and interlace your fingers] Pantera said, speaking slowly from behind his balaclava.

The man complied.

Christine walked over to the ambassador pulled down her mask to show just her face. "Ambassador, I'm MI-6. Your security code is *Pound Sterling.* We'll get you and your staff to safety."

"And ... who are they?" The ambassador straightened himself as he was being untied still reeling from the shock at how fast his circumstances reversed.

"They? ... They were never here." Christine stood up and winked at Grit and Pantera.

Without taking off his cover and in his favorite Scottish accent, Pantera said, "Ambassador. I'm the medical officer and I need to make sure you and your staff can travel. Would you answer a few questions for me?" Pantera reached into his medical bag and retrieved his medical testing equipment.

"Squad leaders: Collect all uniforms. I think we'll need them. I need two guys from Delta at the residence front door for interrogation. Charlie and Delta escort the hostages back to base, set up the watch bill, and get some chow," Grit's said, his voice echoing on all the radios.

"The ambassador and staff are ready for transport. Now the fun begins." Pantera turned his sights on the Black Crow.

"Can I stay and watch?" The ambassador looked in Grit's direction.

Without speaking Grit directed two team members to take them all out of the room. He motioned for Christine to stay.

Pantera grabbed the Black Crow and launched his small frame into a high-backed chair then withdrew a small bag from his backpack. "Grit, I'll need a mirror." He duct-taped the man's hands to the chair.

"Sounds like a party. Always wanted to see you black-op types do an interrogation." Christine pulled up a chair to the opposite end of the table.

Pantera took off his balaclava.

"I've found the Iraqi people as a whole, and especially the Iraqi Army and Police, the stupidest people on the planet. Don't get me wrong, they're not dumb by any stretch of the imagination. Stupid people have the capacity to learn, dumb people don't." He continued to lay out his tools.

"Yes." Christine laughed. "I agree. Like my favorite saying, 'Everyone is born dumb, staying that way is stupid' or my other favorite, 'A person who is dumb can't speak. A person who is stupid shouldn't'."

"Exactly. Iraqis, as a people, have chosen to go backwards with their education while the rest of the world has gone forward. And don't get me started on how superstitious they are. Did you know most Iraqis can't even write their own language? Let's not even talk about the unattainable concept of simple mathematics? Ninety-nine percent of the population has less knowledge than a South Korean eight-year-old. Sad really. I once read a confidential report from the Brookings Institute that Iraq was the most corrupt country on the planet. Who knew?" Pantera shrugged. "Okay. Who didn't know?"

"To be honest, most of the Middle East is lawless. Every government official's on the take. Trust me on that." Christine leaned back in her chair and put her feet up.

Pantera taped the Black Crow's head to the chair, tightly.

Grit entered with the mirror and sat down next to Christine. "Is he giving you a history lesson behind his plan for torturing this guy? And I forgot the popcorn."

"Excuse me. I thought I would give this fine gentleman – who possesses the moral compass of *Hannibal Lecktor* – an anatomy lesson. This should scare the pee right out of him. By the way ... my girlfriend and I just saw the movie *Manhunter*. Can I say 'wow'. We are *sooo* looking forward to *Silence of the Lambs*. You have to love that author Thomas Harris."

"Sorry, didn't get to see it." Christine was focused intently on Pantera's preparation.

"That's okay. I'll give you a preview," he said, turning to speak to the Black Crow in Arabic, "Just trying to give back to your backwards little country."

"You're goin' to *de-cap* this guy?!" Grit leaned back and weaved his hands behind his head.

"Give that man a prize. Can anyone say anatomy lesson? Let's see how the little Black Crow likes looking at his own brain." Pantera smiled as he doubled checked his instruments.

Sweat ran down the man's cheeks.

"You see this ... *dumbass* ... this is a butane torch. A couple weeks ago my girlfriend taught me how to make *Crème Brûlèe*. I had this idea to use it as a sterilization tool. Then, even better, I thought about using it to heat up a scalpel so it'll cut *and* seal blood vessels at the same time. I love this idea. I just need someone to practice on." Pantera heated the number-thirteen scalpel blade to a glowing red color.

Grit placed the mirror across from the Black Crow so he could see everything that was going on.

Christine, sitting fascinated, asked, "What are you going to do?" She turned to Grit, "What is a 'de-cap'?"

CHAPTER 83

"Oh, you will see, but first, to be fair, I must ask Mister Black Crow a question." Pantera turned back to the man sitting with his head and wrists tightly wrapped to a large high-back wrought iron chair.

"Are you ready to answer our questions?" Pantera said, in his academic Arabic.

Eyes wide and defiant, the Black Crow returned, "*Weswef ahesl 'ela athenteyn wesb'eyen men alhewr al'eyen!*" [I will get my seventy-two virgins!]

Pantera leaned in close. "Yes. You might, but I will rip out your soul before that happens." His eyes narrowed and a vicious grin came over his face.

The scalpel was glowing red hot and in one smooth motion Pantera cut a line around the top of the man's skull. There was a puff of smoke for each blood vessel cut. The stinging smell of burnt flesh, hair and blood filled the room. With the circumferential incision completed, he separated the skin from the bone cap of the cranium.

The Black Crow screamed like a teenager at a horror movie.

"What's that?" Pantera heard splashing at his feet and looked down. "You're such a pansy. You already peed yourself? Such a little girl."

The Black Crow had tears running down his face. He watched intently as Pantera hacked through the cartilaginous connective tissue while pulling the scalp back.

"You have been scalped ... my *Black Crow* friend. Isn't that irony? If I'm not mistaken the Crow nation was one of many American Indian tribes who scalped the white man. In my humble opinion, as they should have. Wasn't there also a Black Crow comic book character? I'm thinkin', 'Wow', are we getting some education today, or what?" He laughed as if he was the only person in the room.

Raising the one large clump of skin and hair above the man's head he laid it down on top of the Black Crow's right hand. His eyes grew to the size of saucers and his neck veins bulged through his thin, tanned skin as he continued to scream like a girl on prom night.

Pantera leaned down and whispered, "Are you *sure* you don't have anything you want to tell us? I'm just getting started." The last word dangled off his tongue like the *Tootsie Pop* owl.

Christine shook her head. "I'm learning so much. If I may ask, are these methods in the *Enhanced* Interrogation Manual?"

"Are you referring to the *FM 34-52*? That is for living detainees to keep the idiots of both intelligence committees at bay. I mean come on, who would be stupid enough to think that *waterboarding* would do anything to a Jihadist Martyr. Their goal is to blow themselves up – do you think waterboarding is going to get them to talk?" He turned to Christine and smiled at Grit. "I'm a black-op interrogator. Our rule is – if the detainee dies then no need to report the 'interrogation'. The trick is getting the detainee to realize their death is imminent, it's just a matter of when." Pantera finished cleaning his scalpel and placed it back in its sleeve in his roll-up bag.

"Wait a minute. For you guys, if the detainee dies, then the interrogation techniques don't have to be reported?" Her face creased in intense thought.

"That's correct. No interrogation took place. We just report the information obtained 'before he died' as a 'dying confession'. No

US Congressional oversight. And even better, since we're part of the United Nations, not the U-S-A, different set of rules," Grit instructed, raising his eyebrows looking at Christine.

Pantera turned back to the Black Crow, and said, "Phase two."

The Black Crow crooned and his body shook when Pantera reached for the battery-powered oscillating autopsy saw with arbor section blade.

"Christine. Please watch carefully. I must cut through the bone, but be careful not to damage any of the underlying brain tissue. I can cut through the pia, dura, and archnoid maters – or collectively known as the *meninges* – since they are not important, but if I cut brain tissue this dude will start speaking in tongues. And that would be, *No Bueno*." Pantera looked into the mirror making eye contact with the man. "Are you watching, Mister Black Crow?"

Pantera turned on the bone saw and started cutting into his skull as bits of bone dust and brain fluid flew about the room – the familiar smell of burning bone penetrating everyone's nostrils.

Christine pinched her nose. "Just cannot get used to that."

"Sorry about not warning you about the smell."

The man watched in the mirror in horror. Squealing like a stuck pig he cried to Allah. He tried feverishly to move but was unable to do so.

"You might want to believe in something a little more real. Allah doesn't want you. If he did, he would have protected you from me. Now he can't have you until I am done with you," Pantera snapped. "As I told you before, you can die fast or slow ... your choice."

When he finished cutting, Pantera grabbed the scalpel and started cutting away all the connective tissue as he separated the skull cap from the brain. He gently laid the large, single piece of bone on top of the man's left hand.

"And that Christine, is the definition of 'de-cap'd'." Pantera smiled.

The Black Crow looked at his brain in the mirror then fell unconscious.

Pantera looked at Grit, and said, "Well. That was faster than the Syrian finger-drill. Next up ... the electrodes." He took a step back and admired his work. After about a minute the Black Crow still had not regained consciousness so Pantera jabbed him in the back with an Epipen.

He regained consciousness within a minute.

Pantera leaned in, and whispered, "Good morning, Mister Black Crow. Is there anything you would like to tell us or is it time for you to start praying? Do you think Allah will mind if you miss *Fajr*?"

The man looked at his brain again in the mirror and started crying, but his eyes were dry.

"What do you want to know? Please kill me!" He repeated yelling over and over.

"And there it is." Pantera looked at Christine. "Mortality. Once they realize I can truly torture them indefinitely their whole bravado disappears and they will gladly eat a bullet. There you go, Christine. He's all yours." Pantera ambled over to a chair next to Grit, sat down, pulled out a Payday candy bar and watched Christine get the answers she needed. "Ahh, can you get enough nuts?" He started laughing as he shoved the candy bar in his mouth.

For the next forty-five minutes the Black Crow told Christine about the number of Black Crow units, their names, and to whom they reported.

"I think I have everything I need," she said, looking over at Grit; "Do you mind?"

"Save me the bullet," he returned, without stirring from his comfortable position.

Christine pulled out her Walter 9mm, walked around behind the man, and shot him through the chair at the base of the head. The brain shot straight up in the air and landed on the table like a dying Mackerel.

They all laughed.

"Isn't that a delicacy in some countries?" Pantera continued to eat his candy bar.

"Yeah. Probably his," Christine chortled, putting her weapon away.

Grit got up and wrote something down on a piece of paper:
It read:

TO QUSAY HUSSEIN –
ANOTHER GIFT FOR YOU. WE ARE STILL COMING.
MUCH LOVE,
SHADOW KNIGHTS

Grit folded up the piece of paper and put it in the man's pocket.

CHAPTER 84

The sun rose on the bleakly quiet area of Kuwait City. No cars, no pedestrians, and not a living soul stirred as Grit, Pantera, Christine, and the two Delta squad members returned from the British Embassy. They entered the basement and found Brandy in a corner with a handful of antennae wires, two satellite phones, and several radios that were taken off the Iraqi soldiers.

"Hey boss, I found a couple wires leading up to the antennae and satellite dishes on the roof and patched in," Brandy said.

"Any news?" Grit said, pulling off his backpack.

"Sorry boss, nothing. Some chatter from the armor units, but I think the Black Crows are not actually reporting to anyone." He returned to his pile of gear.

"Squad leaders to my twenty." Grit was deep in thought when the squad leaders arrived. "We have Christine on the satellite phone getting us any reports of locations on these guys. We know we have two groups left. Let's send out three, two-man buddy teams to start sweeping the neighborhoods. We have uniforms for the guys using the vehicles. Those on the perimeter use throbes and keffiyehs." Grit ripped open a MRE and laid its contents on the table.

Pantera and Christine dropped into a dark corner of the basement and fell asleep.

* * *

Christine was shaking Pantera to wake him.

"Shhhh." She placed her index finger to her mouth and pointed to Grit asleep in the corner.

They walked over to a closet, slipped in and shut the door.

"What did you find?" Christine's face was tense.

"Good to see you too. I found the *server* and documents your husband was talking about. When I get back I'll chase down our little mole and interrogate him." Pantera felt his own sense of relief in saying the words out loud.

"Good. Thank you. I'm not going to make the interrogation. Leave me a message and when I pass back through we can catch up. I'll cover any problems with Rothschild Bank in the UK if you want to handle the US Federal Reserve side of things." She raised her eyebrows, turned, and left the closet.

* * *

"Grit. Wake up." Pantera stood over him with a big smirk on his face. "We found a group. Christine is working with Brandy to narrow down the coordinates."

Grit's eyes blinked rapidly trying to focus on Pantera's face while simultaneously trying to jumpstart his brain. Grit jumped up.

"Did the ambassador and his staff get out okay?" he asked.

"Yeah, no problem," Pantera replied, walking beside Grit to the radio room.

Christine looked up as Grit and Pantera entered. "Looks like we're headed over to the *Abdulla Al-Salem* neighborhood. It's about two and half kilometers from here. We can enter the block from this end, park at the Fuddruckers, grab a burger, and walk in from there."

"Squad leaders saddle up in five mikes, Grit radioed, turning to Christine, "Quite the sense of humor you have, Ms. Brown."

* * *

"Charlie-one to leader. We have contact. They put up guards on either end of the street and are stripping every house." Harry's voice came over the radio.

"Charlie-one, let's pinch'em. Charlie to the north end. Delta, wait ten minutes and start from the south – we'll push them to the center. House-by-house search," Grit replied.

Delta waited ten minutes and progressed down the street to the first house. In the darkness, they could see four Iraqi vehicles on the street about five houses down. The street had twenty houses on it. Ten houses on each side of the street. All were two-story homes situated on a half-acre of land. Surrounded by cedar block walls and iron gates each home had a *Frank Lloyd Wright* architecture style.

Grit turned the corner to see the street in full view, he was amazed. "Damn. Look at these homes. They must be ten to fifteen thousand square feet each. And no trees or plants, just sand ... so much sand."

"No kidding, definitely not lush Tennessee," Pantera joked.

Three men from Delta took the east side of the street and two men took the west side. Grit, Pantera, and Christine followed and covered the exit of Delta-west as they went in and cleared each house.

The first three homes for Delta-west were empty. Entering the fourth house they heard a *pop*, and then about ten seconds later, *pop-pop*. Standing at the gate, the three cocked their weapons and stood ready for whatever exited. The two-man team came out with a frightened little Kuwaiti boy wrapped up in a blanket. They dropped the kid off with Christine and moved on.

"Why is he *my responsibility*? Why don't you or Grit guard him? This is just because I'm a female ... isn't it." Christine's face contorted.

Grit got into Christine's face.

"One. This is your turf. We're just visiting. And two. We kill things. We don't babysit things," Grit barked, turning and winking at Pantera as he walked by.

Grit walked out the gate and through the gate of the fifth house with the Delta-west team. Several voices could be heard from inside and on the left side of the building.

"Delta-four and five clear the building. Pantera on my six. We're going around the side." Grit moved off to the side of the building.

Grit and Pantera turned the corner of the house, there were four men standing around. A fifth, in a Black Crow uniform, was yelling down at a man, a woman, and a child. The men had their backs to Grit and Pantera. Grit motioned for Pantera to sweep right to left and leave the yeller standing. A series of shots rang out from inside the house. Grit dropped his two as did Pantera. The man swung around pulling the woman up and in front of him, to use as a human shield.

"Akhemad benadeqkem aw aneny sewf yeqtelha!" [Put down your guns or I will kill her!]

Pantera lowered his gun and starting laughing, looking at Grit, he said, "These guys really need to stop watching those ridiculous American movies. This guy is hilarious."

Grit started laughing, but didn't lower his weapon keeping the red laser pointed at the Black Crow's ear.

"Sorry dude, doesn't look like you're going to get the opportunity to torture this one," Grit said, from behind his gun sight.

The Black Crow looking confused yelled at Grit and Pantera in Arabic. "PUT DOWN YOUR WEAPONS! I *WILL* KILL HER!"

Pantera pulled out a Snickers bar and started eating it in an unfazed manner. "Yeah, yeah, yeah, we heard you the first time. Please shut up. You're hurting my ears."

Grit was waiting patiently, making the Black Crow nervous.

A common covert tactic for special operators is to just wait, as long as it takes, until the target makes a mistake.

The Black Crow tried to readjust his grip on the hostage. His head moved out from behind her. Grit hit him square in the right eyeball blowing his brains out all over the man and the child.

"Melon shot!" Pantera yelled out as he continued eating his chocolate bar. "You see, Snickers really does satisfy."

Christine walked up with the boy in tow. "Did I miss something?"

"Yeah, Grit had a great melon shot right through the eyeball. It would make a great *Polaroid*. I can send it home to your folks, Grit," he said, smiling with chocolate in his teeth.

Grit reached down to help the man up. When the man and woman saw the boy, they hugged and kissed him. They told Christine he was their son which is why they had come back to the house.

"Whew," Christine gasped. "No rugrats in tow."

They all laughed and returned to base.

* * *

Kat departed the plane and looked out over the airport before stepping down the stairs to the jet-way. It was a single runway airport with only twelve gates – all of it Russian manufacture. The sign above the terminal read:

Београд Никола Тесла Аеродром
("BELGRADE NIKOLA TESLA AIRPORT")

CHAPTER 85

She walked through baggage claim and spotted a familiar face. They made eye contact. He smiled and approached.

"Alyn David, aney shemh leshemv' shanev 'evebdeym yhed shevb." [I was happy to hear we are working together again.] The man stood six foot four and weighed two hundred twenty pounds with black well-groomed hair, dark brown eyes, manicured fingernails, and clothed old-school style. Kat recognized it as a *Savile Row, Ede & Ravenscroft*, bespoke tailored, grey vested pinstriped suit with professionally shined black cap-toed Oxfords. His name was Joseph Mendelson and was the son of a Russian journalist who grew up in St. Petersburg and joined Mossad after attending university. He was currently assigned as the Senior Security Officer attached to the Embassy of Israel in Belgrade.

Kat gave Joseph a big hug.

"How long has it been ... over five years?" He smiled showing his perfect white teeth.

Kat had Joseph as her handler for two flawless assignments. At the time, Kat was young and didn't know how bad assignments could get. Seeing Joseph was like taking in a breath of fresh air.

"We have a beautiful suite with a terrace overlooking the *Danube* and *Studentski Park*. We can talk more later." Joseph's demeanor changed. Softly, but firmly, he grabbed Kat under the arm leading her to the car waiting outside in the cargo area.

There were two men standing outside the elevator in the hotel parking garage as Kat and Joseph approached. No one spoke. The elevator stopped on the top floor. Kat could see the name on the door at the end of the hallway – *Presidential Suite.*

"That's your suite. We'll be down the hall. We have to spend the weekend setting up on the target. You have tonight and tomorrow off. Relax. Go out for dinner, study your target, and we'll brief you on Sunday morning. By the way, did you know you were being tailed at the airport? Dark features, woman, maybe Egyptian?" Joseph pulled back his sleeve revealing the *A. Lange & Sohne's Grand Complication,* checking the time.

"Damn." Kat shook her head. "She could be ..."

"Oh really?" He broke in. "The woman I've been reading about in the briefs. We'll look in to it. We lost her on the way here, but keep your eyes open." Joseph stopped at the door, gave her the key card, winked, and walked back down the hall.

* * *

"Bingo!" Brandy's voice echoed in Pantera's ears causing him to sit straight up from his deep slumber.

"What?"

"Got'em! They're in the *Al-Surra* district. Oh, one other thing ... they are not alone." Brandy's voice went monotone. "They brought friends."

"Grit. Christine. Could you come in here please," Pantera yelled, wiping the sleep from his eyes and pointed to Brandy.

Grit hurried in. "It's about damn time, we haven't heard squat for six days."

Brandy looked up pulling his headphones off. "Something must have happened with Team One and Two. The Black Crow group we're tracking just called in for support from two Special Republican Guard (SRG) units. That's in addition to the two Special Forces squads they already have. They're supposed to meet up at the Swiss Embassy. I get the idea a number of wealthy Kuwaitis locked themselves inside after the Swiss left. They told him one hour." He rolled his eyes.

"Spread the word. We're moving out." Grit stomped off and radioed, "Squad leaders, Ops plan meeting. On me."

* * *

Where is my box? Kat called down to the concierge. "Is there a diplomatic package down there that hasn't been brought up?" Kat said with an affluent Serbian accent.

"Yes Ma'am. It was labeled for the Embassy of Israel." The clerk replied.

"Can you tell me the registrant of this suite?" Kat softly asked.

With keyboard sounds in the background, the clerk said, "The Embassy of Israel."

"Thank you. Please send it up." Before Kat could hang up the clerk continued.

"Oh Ma'am. There's a man down here with an Israel Embassy credential named ... Marcus Aurelius?

Isn't he a funny guy using a Great Roman Emperor and stoic philosopher as a cover.

"That's fine. He'll bring it up." Kat hung up.

Instead of lugging bags on and off every flight and ultimately to each hotel, Mossad officers ship their "boxes" by diplomatic courier.

Joseph brought up three boxes and put them in her bedroom – her personal gear and two boxes of supplies for the assignment, then left.

"About time." Kat joked, right before the door closed. *I really hate it when my stuff gets lost.*

She opened her box and pulled out her comfy clothes, jumped into the shower to wash off the travel grime, grabbed the dossier, and made herself some Chamomile tea. She read to find holes in his defenses, weakness in his personality, vices, etc. Everyone has vulnerabilities and she would find his.

She stared at his picture. *Qevdesh harah ... is he ugly. His face looks like a wrinkled penis.* His physical features displayed a square head, protruding forehead, acne-scarred face, deep-set eyes, and an irregularly large, bulbous, nose. *Why would someone want him as Serbian president? I would prefer a donkey.*

She continued reading. Divorced with two children, an extensive kickboxing background, and former president of the kickboxing federation, he is currently a senior member of the *Arkan Tigers*.

The Tigers were a small group within the Serbian Volunteer Guard (SVG) responsible for the genocidal killing of hundreds of Croatians and ethnic Jews in Serbian territories.

Boris is believed to be the catalyst which could ignite a war with Croatia. Secondary objective: the future plans of the Arkan Tigers and the Serbian Volunteer Guard would be of use – but not a high priority. End of file.

Kat stepped out onto the terrace and soaked in the view of the beautiful park across the street. *Hope he's okay. If we were normal, what would our Friday night be like I wonder?*

* * *

The group of thirteen stood around a large table with a map on it in the musty, dry Kuwaiti hotel basement.

"Gentlemen. Christine suggested we set up a sniper team, here, up on the roof of this Mosque. You'll cover this south-facing T-intersection. The second sniper team will cover the northern entry point from this building here. Charlie will create a second perimeter line around the embassy. Pantera, Christine and I will enter from this fence line, here. These people are never going to believe we're friendly. They might believe a blonde woman with a British accent," Grit said, giving Christine a small grin.

It took the unit nearly forty-five minutes to travel ten kilometers due to the number of blockades they had to circumvent.

"Delta-four to leader. There's a tank sitting right in the middle of the south T-intersection. Looks like the SRG units beat us here."

Grit acknowledged.

"Charlie-five to leader. We have a dozen or so SRGs set up on the northern corner."

"Okay team. We've got a full moon tonight, watch your shadows. Everyone maintain your positions until the shit hits the fan. Leader out." Grit swung his HK around to his back turning to Pantera, he said, "Time to show me those cool Parkour moves you have."

Pantera swung his weapon around to his back, changed his gloves to a sturdier leather pair and jumped the wall heading east from the empty lot they were standing in. There were seven backyards to move past before reaching the embassy.

"This might be a rough and tumble route but they will never expect it." Pantera looked down at Christine. "Can you keep up?"

"Please. I'm the female James Bond. It's nothing but ten-foot-high cinderblock walls. My cat could do this." She smirked.

"If you girls are done chatting." Pantera started down the fence line.

"Charlie-one. Set up on the northern SRG group. Delta-one set up on the south group and figure-out a way to disable that tank." Grit moved his eyebrows up and down at Pantera and Christine. "What do you say we clear an embassy?"

Pantera glanced over and saw a woman staring out a window. He waved and gave her a thumbs-up.

The threesome slowly descended the wall into the backyard of the embassy. Pantera slid his favorite weapon out, sheathed behind his handgun – the *US Marine Raider Stiletto*. The stiletto, dual-bladed with a razor sharp edge and point, had only one purpose.

Some voices could be heard getting closer. All three crossed the ten meters from the grass to the shrubbery at the base of the building. Two chimney-smoking SRGs were walking the perimeter in a lackadaisical fashion. Pantera motioned that he wanted the far one. Christine wanted the near one. Grit gave the *by-all-means* signal to both.

CHAPTER 86

Pantera counted down and stepped out from the bushes in front of the two men. Their eyes grew large, cigarettes fell from their mouths as they tried to raise their weapons. The very bulky and slow AK-47s were no match for a stiletto. Pantera thrust his knife straight up through the soft palate of the man's jaw entering his mid-brain. He gave it a quick circular motion to do as much damage as possible then withdrew it. The man crumpled like wadded newspaper.

The second SRG saw Pantera drive his stiletto up into the brain of his comrade. He tried to turn and yell. With his mouth open his eyes rolled backwards as Christine plunged her knife into the back of his head. Pantera and Christine pulled the bodies into the bushes.

Grit rolled his eyes at Pantera. "A bit theatrical, ya think?"

Pantera shrugged. "I want my face imprinted on their souls."

Grit radioed. "Does anyone have a thermal on this building?"

"Charlie-four to leader. Twenty verticals and about ten horizontals, but that's not the whole building. Some of the building has iron in the walls because I'm not getting a reading." Baby-face's voice was fast and professional.

Pantera was about to step out from the bushes when Grit grabbed his shoulder and motioned for him to stop. There were several voices coming from the terrace above.

Pantera listen to the Arabic conversation. "Black Crow dude sucks. He's an idiot. Father some general."

Pantera and Grit, through a series of hand signals, devised a plan. Christine watched as they spoke to each other in some weird variation of American Sign Language. Grit motioned for Christine to follow him to the south side of the building.

Pantera moved in the direction of the north side of the building. He immediately started up the face of the building reaching the bottom of the terrace. There were three men standing in the center – weapons down, smoking. He moved to the corner where the bannister met the wall and waited. When they arrived at the south side Grit snapped a branch of one of the scrubs.

Christine froze. *What the fuck!* she mouthed, giving Grit the evil eye.

Grit smiled and gave her the – *wait for it* – signal.

Pantera saw the men raise their weapons and approach the south side of the terrace. He jumped down from the bannister, ran across the terrace and slid his stiletto into the back of the skull of the first man. In one fluid motion he pulled the stiletto out and inserted it into the second man's skull. He tried pulling the blade out of the head of second man, but lost his grip on the knife as the second man fell twisted to the ground. Without pausing Pantera left the knife in the skull and launched himself at the third man, catching him in a headlock. With the adrenaline surging he placed one hand on the man's chin and the other on the back of his head. He twisted with all his might. *Listen to that. It's like popcorn.*

The sound of the C3 and C4 cervical vertebrae being shattered permeated the silence. The man fell to the ground with his mouth still open in an attempt to yell. Pantera leaned over the balcony motioning for the other two to come up. The knife made a slurping sound as he retrieved his knife from the skull, wiping the blood on the man's shirt.

The doorway from the terrace opened to a hallway. The hallway connected several rooms. The three entered with knives in hand. Grit picked the quietest room first. It was empty. From the first room they could see into the second. Three men were rummaging through the desk and shelves of an office.

"You … handgun. Cover us," Grit whispered into Christine's ear. Grit and Pantera slipped into the room without being noticed. Grit, with a stiletto in each hand buried them into the base of the skull of the two men standing next to each other at the bookshelves. Pantera was not in the right position so he had to grab the third man as he turned. Christine had the man in her sights. Pantera reached around the top of the man's head placing his hand on his forehead. Inserting his stiletto into the right side of the man's neck he pushed it straight across from the right side of the neck to the left. The tip could be seen on the other side. With the blade up to the hilt in the neck he slashed forward – cutting open half of the man's neck. The man's head fell backward like the broken top of a Pez dispenser as the bright red blood pulsed upward like a teenage volcano science project gone wrong.

Christine lowered her weapon with a semi-shocked look. *Damn,* she thought.

Grit motioned to move on to the next room. Over the next several minutes, the three operatives were able to dispatch every soldier on the second floor of the embassy. No Black Crows.

They descended slowly down the staircase. Grit spotted a Black Crow beating a man sitting in the chair. His family huddled in the far corner.

Four hostages, Grit thought, *Where are the other six?*

Grit walked back upstairs to speak with Pantera and Christine. "We have to go in hard and clear the rest of the place." Pantera and Christine nodded as they swung their suppressed sub-machine guns to their front.

Grit radioed, "Leader to Charlie and Delta leaders. We're going *hot* in two mikes." Grit quietly prepared his weapon and took point heading down the stairs. He pointed for Pantera to sweep from the right and Christine to take center. They stepped into the room as their bullets hit their targets like a well-rehearsed ballet.

Grit moved into the room with the left wall at his back. Pantera hit all the targets on the right side of the room as he kept his right side against the wall. Christine knelt down next to the hostages motioning them to remain silent.

Pantera continued down the wall to the first room. Upon reaching the room an SRG was stepping out raising his weapon to focus on Christine. He did not see Pantera on the left side of the doorway. Pantera hit him in the ear blowing his cerebral material all over the wall. He turned the corner of the doorway and was facing two men with AK-47s aimed at him. He reversed. Not in time. A strong stinging pain radiated along his upper arm.

Oww! That's going to leave a mark.

Pantera pulled a fragmentation grenade and tossed it into the room. Immediately after he threw it, he yelled into the radio, "FRAG!" He then jumped for cover.

After the explosion he hopped up and cleared the room. He continued down the hallway in search of the six remaining horizontals. There was one last room in the hallway.

Christine caught up to him. "Thanks for that."

Pantera nodded.

Without warning an enormous explosion went off outside. The shock wave rocked the embassy.

Over the radio gunfire could be heard. "Charlie-one to leader. The tank has been disabled."

"Delta-one to leader. All north end tangos are down."

Pantera and Christine paused to listen to the announcement over the radio.

Pantera turned to her, and said, "Our turn."

They inched closer to the room. There were sounds of muffled cries.

"If I'm counting right, all the SRGs should be down. What's in here?" He thumbed in the direction of the room.

Christine reached for the door handle. Pantera stopped her. She froze.

"Something smells funny. Even an idiot wouldn't leave hostages in an unlocked, un-booby-trapped room. Right?" he said, raising his eyebrows at her, requesting agreement.

Pantera removed a small extendable dental mirror from his vest. Blood from his wound dripped down his hand onto the handle. Pantera extended the mirror, got down into a low-crawl position and slipped the mirror under the door. He looked up at the door handle and the door frame. The wire traced around the room to a "Bouncing Betty" IED in a vest with several pineapple grenades sitting in a chair located in the middle of the room. It looked as if it had significant tension.

"There has to be another way out of the room," he said, over his shoulder to Christine.

The room had no windows. There was a large air vent in the ceiling. Pantera retracted the mirror and put it away.

"You're going spelunking through an air vent," he said, giving her a confident wink.

Christine nodded. She went to the next room to climb into the air vent. Pantera entered the main room where Grit was speaking with the Kuwaiti family.

Grit looked up. "Where's she going?"

"We found a Bouncing Betty connected to a door trigger. Nothing she can't handle."

Pantera plopped down in one of the chairs, wrapped up his arm and started eating a Baby Ruth. "Hey. Did you know the Baby Ruth was named after President Glover Cleveland's daughter? Man, this baby gets you going." He laughed.

CHAPTER 87

"Do we need to interrogate this guy?" Grit asked, referring to the Black Crow kneeling in a urine puddle in the middle of the room shaking like an Elvis impersonator.

"Huh? No. I think we got all we needed out of the last guy. Besides, I didn't bring any cool tools." He continued to chomp down on his candy bar.

Grit shot the Black Crow in the noggin and walked away radioing to the team. "Return to base and prepare for extraction."

It was still daylight outside and they could not return to the base in their current black fatigues. The two families helped the team grab clothes from the embassy and enough vehicles to get back to their base without raising any suspicion. "The least we can do for the people who saved our lives," the beaten man said happily.

"Brandy. Get eagle eye on the satellite phone and have them prepare an extraction plan," Grit ordered, in his usual *the mission is over* voice as he fell into a pile of blankets in the corner.

* * *

A couple hours later Pantera woke Grit up.

"Hey Gunny. The extraction plan is in. We have to secure a couple boats to rendezvous with two British HC3s at *Miskan Island* ... in four hours." Pantera waited for a response.

Grit heard the urgency of Pantera's voice. Thankfully his ears were working better than is eyes.

"Four hours? Isn't Miskan like thirty kilometers from here?"

"Well. Twenty-five, but yeah, we gotta go."

Pantera nodded in acknowledgement to Christine as she did in return. They both knew it was for more than what just took place.

"Peace," he signed.

* * *

It was a bright sunny Sunday morning and Kat was sitting at the table on the terrace when Joseph came in. "Hey? How did you ..." she said, then stopped when she realized who she was talking to.

"Really? I can't override a hotel door ... in Belgrade? Now that *is* funny," Joseph answered. "Did you order the Israeli breakfast? It's really good here – almost right from the Kibbutz." He sat down at the table then placed the cloth napkin in his lap.

"Why yes I did. You said you were dropping by for brunch, not breakfast. This is just the juice and tea tray." Kat put down the paper.

"So how's Alona?"

"She's good, getting married in a couple months."

"I heard she's rated as a Katsa now. Oh, how our girl has grown up." He laughed. "And you, scoring a UN-SOG guy. What bar stool did you scape him off of?"

"Hey now, watch yourself, picked him up in Saigon. You know me. I only troll the good spots." She winked. "He was too easy, drunk on Cobra wine, might have to throw him back."

Sparring with her is like pulling sap from a tree with your teeth, Joseph thought.

Kat did not want to come out with a direct question as to how Joseph knew about Pantera because that would give away her lack of knowledge on the subject.

"Who put that in my file?"

402 · JD WALLACE

"Obviously it was somebody who knows ... and has the clearance. Ready to get started?"

Kat rolled her eyes at the obtuse statement, but deep inside she knew it could have been only one of two people. One of them she trusted with her life, the other she was not so sure about anymore. She shifted gears with Joseph and started the briefing.

"Surveillance over the weekend hasn't produced much. He has a four-man security detail – two on, two off. We bugged and searched the office. Nothing. He spent time with his kids all weekend so we haven't been able to access the house. Even if he had SVG paperwork we don't believe he would have it in the house. There must be another location separate from work and home where he stores his confidential information. It may be several days before we get an opening. Then we'll just honey-trap him. That's where we stand," he said, pouring himself some tea.

"You mean standing in the middle of the desert," she retorted, returning to her paper.

* * *

"Alona. You have a phone call on line two," the intercom rang out.

"Hallo?"

"Alona. It's Marcus Sinclair."

"Navy boy. You're back. Staying safe I hope?" she said, keeping the conversation light.

"I'm good. Thank you. Can you tell me when Kat will be back?" Pantera knew there was only a limited amount of information he could get from her.

"She left a couple days ago. I'm sorry, but I can't tell you where."

"No, no, I know. She wanted in on my next *special event*." He hoped she understood the subtext.

"Oh, yes. I'm sure she would like to be involved. Can you hold off a couple days until she gets back? I would tell her, but then she gets rushed and you know how that goes."

"I understand. It isn't that big of a rush. Make sure she calls me as soon as she returns." Pantera recalculated the logistics in his head, hoping he hadn't tipped anyone off which would make him – *the hunted.*

Snapping him out of his thoughts, Alona continued, "When are we going to meet you?"

"Umm, good question," Pantera stammered, "I'm thinking sometime after I get off my current rotation. I know Kat now owns one of my four-day passes and she was thinking about a trip to Switzerland. Maybe we will stop by on the way up. By the way, who is ... *we?*"

"That would be my fiancée and I," She said, speaking slowly with a question in her voice.

Oy vey! Kat didn't tell him about the wedding. "Oh, okay. Thank you and hope to see you soon."

They hung up.

* * *

The night was quiet as Kat ran along the *Danube* – one of the most beautiful scenes in Europe and the subject of many paintings and literature. Her pager went off. *Good timing,* she thought, *after four days.*

Joseph was sitting on the couch when she returned. "One of our contacts called us. The target has ordered a prostitute for this evening. She's supposed to be at the hotel at ten o'clock. Oh and get this, he's staying in the *Tesla suite.* We have no idea what she looks like, so it will be up to you to find her and dispose of her before heading up to the room. Unless you want to skip her, hit the room early and hope for the best."

Kat gave Joseph a half-grin as she entered her bedroom. "I will find her ... I always do. I won't even charge you extra for her. Did he specify any preferences?"

"He prefers shaven upstairs and *au naturale* downstairs." He laughed.

"Not like he'll make it that far." Kat started talking to herself. "Let's see ... you Balkan types love the blondes. So blonde it is."

Joseph was gone by the time Kat walked out of the bedroom. She looked in the mirror to make sure everything was in place ... blonde wig, brown contacts, yellow teeth, cheap-looking gold necklace, tight nylon red dress with no stockings, and cheap red stilettos. She threw her overcoat on and grabbed her bag of tricks on the way out the door.

Kat took the private elevator and walked out the back of the hotel. She walked almost three blocks down the street before hailing a cab. It was a little after nine o'clock when she walked in the target's hotel and sat down at the bar. Despite the unbelievably stereotypical apparel, Kat still managed to turn the head of every man in the place.

This was not the type of attention this spy wanted.

CHAPTER 88

She found a chair at the end of the bar giving her a complete visual of the foyer and entrance. Her drink untouched, she sat ready. The bartender brought her another and pointed to the admirer who bought it, who was now sauntering toward her.

Look at Mister Beer-nutz. This ought to be comedic.

He tried some pick-up line that she could barely understand, but believed it to be in Croatian or Macedonian. She turned to face him. He licked his lips as he eyeballed her breasts that were nearly falling out of her one-size-too-small dress.

She grabbed him by the crotch getting a good feel of his manhood. "*Premala, otići,*" [Too small, go away.] she said, in an earthy, louder than normal Serbian voice so everyone in the bar could hear. The crowd roared.

He opened his mouth, but could not say anything – then stumbled away. It was nearly ten o'clock and there was no sign of a prostitute coming or going. Kat decided to head for the bathroom and call her handler.

"Joseph. I have no contact. There must be a back way up. I'm going up to the room and see if he will take a second if she is already there."

"I put a man on the roof, if you have to go in that way, just in case."

"Good call. I knew there was some reason I liked you." She tossed the radio back in her bag.

Kat got out of the elevator, made a right turn, and started down the hallway. The suite was at the end of the hallway after the next right turn. She approached the corner and without making it look too obvious, she peeked around the corner. The prostitute was already being thoroughly patted down by security. She also noticed a camera above the door to the suite.

Maybe this is a good thing.

Hotel security cameras were made to capture pictures of faces. Even if Kat got past security, which was never hard, the camera would have her face for the local law enforcement to have on record.

Kat decided the last option was the only option – to the roof and rappel down. The stairwell she used had a fire door to the roof. It was chained. She retrieved the lock pick tools from her *drug case* and unlocked the frail Russian-designed lock. Her contact was waiting for her.

"All I have is gear. I don't have any clothes," the man said, looking her up and down.

"It wouldn't be the first time I had to rappel in a dress. Rig me for Geneva. Last time I tried traditional abseiling in a dress the damn harness gave me contact burns on my womanly parts." She grinned.

The man looked down and cringed. He pulled out the Geneva harness from his bag and strapped her in. The suite was only two stories down to the terrace and the roof had a small sloping angle. *The descent will be easier than going in through security.* Kat reached the suite and flipped upside-down over the edge of the terrace to see what she was heading into. The target and hooker were groping each other on the couch while drinking from champagne flutes. A large plate of fruit and cheeses sat on the table in front of them.

Tired of hanging upside down Kat decided to move to a hidden section of the patio. Turned-on by being a voyeur the idea of having sex with Pantera during an assignment colored her thoughts. *How about hanging upside-down and ...*

She refocused and calculated she had about five to ten minutes before they moved into the bedroom to get down to business. After softly landing on the patio in her bare feet, she watched the two half-naked bodies saunter into the bedroom. She unlocked the door, tiptoed across the living room, and withdrew a full eye-dropper of fluid putting half into each flute from a small clear bottle. The prostitute was making loud gargling sounds which informed Kat as to exactly where in the performance they were. *You've got to be kidding. How easy could this get?*

The woman's butt was in the air and her head was bobbing up and down. Kat pulled her air pistol as she slipped into the room, shooting the prostitute in the butt. The woman bit down hard then bolted straight up in pain still on her knees.

"Oww! Fuck!" Boris yelled.

Kat laughed as she kicked the prostitute in the head launching her off the bed bouncing her off the wall under the window, un-conscious. Jumping up on the bed she landed on the target's chest with her knees buried deep in to his elbows. The target let out an agonizing groan and tried to shake her off. Kat took the opportu-nity to spray some *Ether* into the back of his throat. She covered his mouth with one hand and used the back of his head as leverage with her other hand.

"Awww, Boris, my little puppy. Don't be mad. Lights out in ... three, two, one."

The target was out and the prostitute was lying on the floor be-tween the wall and the bed. She zip-tied Boris spread eagle to the bed frame then went into the living room to retrieve one of the flute glasses.

Kat smacked Boris a couple times, full handed, across the face. "Wake up lover boy."

Boris recovered. Kat was sitting on his chest with her dress pulled up around her waist and her feet flat against the bed above his shoulders with a flute in her hand.

He was about to yell.

"I wouldn't do that naughty boy. No, no, no," she said, waving her index finger. "You know what happens if you do that. Don't you?"

"What do you want? I have money. You want money, right?" He nodded nervously.

"Sorry schmuckatelli, bird in the hand is worth two in the bush. Wouldn't you agree?" She made sure he had a good view of her.

"What do you want?" His pitch increased when he looked over at the prostitute.

"I want you to drink this. It's very simple. Drink this and we shall have a little talk. Don't drink it and there will be no talking," she said, squinting at him.

Boris continued to look down, then back up at her eyes. His muscle tone relaxed.

"Maybe you want a little of this?" Kat slapped him. "Focus. Drink."

He drank the whole flute.

"Congratulations. You just ingested about seven milligrams of Scopolamine. In a few minutes you will do whatever I tell you and will answer any question I put before you. And you thought a don-key face like you would get a piece of this." Kat shook her head as she climbed off his chest straightening her dress.

"Fuck you, you bitch! I will kill you!" Boris yelled, as loud as he could.

"Yeah, yeah, I've heard that before. Oh sorry ... forgot to tell you. The suites in this hotel have soundproofing. That is so one crazy party doesn't bother the other crazy party. Did you know they have *sex parties* in these suites? You could probably blow someone up and no one would hear it. Now that would suck, wouldn't it?" She looked down at the tied up, half naked man. "Now shut up," she snapped.

His lips sealed in on themselves.

While the Scopolamine was taking effect Kat lifted the prostitute and carried her into the next room laying her on the couch. She stabbed her with an Epipen.

She woke up in about a minute.

Wow. Pantera was right. These Epipens rock.

"Hi," Kat said, sitting next to her on the couch, "I need you to drink this. It will make you feel better."

The woman was dazed and confused, but saw Kat pointing a gun at her. She complied.

"Good girl. I won't hurt you. I promise," she said, giving the girl a comforting smile.

Kat grabbed the girl by the arm and escorted her back into the bedroom so she could keep an eye on her until the drug took effect. The drug was in full effect on the target. Kat fired a barrage of questions at him. He answered each one in minute detail. Kat taped a complete confession of everything the target and the SVG/Arkan Tigers did for the last ten years. It included burial sites, accomplices, money transfers, and the list went on.

"That was fantastic. You are such a good boy, Boris darling." Kat leapt off the bed.

Kat knew her one hour was close to being up and the security guards would be coming in to check on the target.

Kat looked Boris in the eyes, and said, "Lay still."

He complied.

Kat turned to the prostitute. "Stand up at the end of the bed."

She complied.

Kat walked over and pulled a Glock 17 from the nightstand. *These guys are so predictable.* She gave the prostitute the Boris' gun.

"When I say, *GO* ... you will shoot him eighteen times. You will then fall asleep."

The prostitute nodded.

CHAPTER 89

Kat gathered up her stuff, wiped down everything she touched, cut the zip-ties, and put them back in her bag. She went to the sliding glass door, turned and yelled, "GO."

She heard the shots ring out one at a time as she climbed back up the rope to the roof. Then the shooting stopped.

By the time the security guards had reached the prostitute she was asleep at the foot of the bed and Boris had seventeen bullet holes in his chest.

Kat cleared the roof and gave a high-five to her contact.

"Angel is in the nest," he radioed, helping her up on to the roof.

They gathered all the equipment and took the fire escape route back down to a waiting car.

Kat threw the tape recorder in Joseph's lap. "There's the *Full Monty*, boss man. Let the analysts chew on that for a while." She collapsed in the back of the car, exhausted.

* * *

Kat kicked off her shoes, threw her bag to the foot of the bed, and fell into her fluffy satin down-filled comforter with the debriefing still swimming in her head from a couple days before. She looked up at the clock, realized it was dinner time at the Naval base and grabbed the phone.

You are probably still at work. I'll leave a message.

"Hello?" a man's voice answered.

"Marcus?"

"Yes? Kat ... you're home?!" he said, with a mixture of elation and surprise.

"I am. What are you doing in your room? Aren't you supposed to be out playing in the mud?" she said, curiously.

"Playing in the mud? Very funny. We've been home for days. I've been waiting for you."

"When are you heading to the *special event?*"

"I'm sorry. I couldn't wait. I'm leaving right now."

"I'll meet you ... where are you going?" She ran to her bag and ripped it open.

"3500 Via Girolamo Santacroce. Apartment 2."

"Don't have dessert until I get there ... please." Kat changed clothes, grabbed her bag of tricks, pulled out her gun and suppressor from the nightstand, and ran out the door.

* * *

Pantera scanned the building and studied the second floor. After picking the lock, he threw his backpack over his shoulder and walked up the flight of stairs. The door to the apartment was at the end of the hallway. He knocked.

"Yes, yes. One minute." Gaston's voice could be heard from the other side.

The door opened.

Without allowing Gaston Leroux to react, he stuck a high voltage cattle prod in Gaston's neck and squeezed the trigger. Gaston let out a small squeal falling to the floor like a living mannequin, his body shaking like a ten dollar vibrator. The smell of sage and lilac incense filled the room.

"Hello Ray. Ray Smith I believe, not *Gaston Leroux.*" Pantera walked in, closed the door and looked around the apartment.

The fear on Ray's face was obvious.

"I'm sure you know who I am. This is my third trip to your apartment and it's still just as boring as the first time, but I like the incense." He walked over to Ray who was slowly recovering and sprayed chloroform in his mouth. Ray fell unconscious.

Pantera dragged Ray's body to the dining room, duct-taped him to a chair, and took out his infra-red thermal goggles to look around the building for heat signatures. *Nobody.* He then took Ray's bed apart, putting one mattress over the window and the other over the door. *Sound proofing.*

By the time Ray woke, he was tied up, the apartment was tossed and his bed was covering the only two ways for sound to escape, much less his escape.

"What do you want? You're *sooo* going to jail for this," Ray said, testing his bonds of tape.

Pantera sat across the table eyeing his prey. "Ray Smith: Yale graduate, Skull and Bones president and former analyst for the CIA," he said, looking off into the distance; "When all of a sudden he mysteriously leaves the Agency and *voilà,* he shows up at ... *The Activity* ... in Naples, Italy."

"Thanks for the recap. Is this going somewhere?" Ray spit back.

"Let's me introduce myself, you Ivy-league prick. I'm Marcus Sinclair ..."

"No shit. I know all about you," he said, increasing his defiance.

"Black Site Interrogator for the ..."

"Yeah, yeah, yeah ... United Nations. You're such an idiot," Gaston said, shaking his head.

"Central ... Intelligence ... Agency. I bring greetings from your friends at the Special Activities Division. My chief is Jack Barnett. Who I'm sure you have heard of."

"BULLSHIT! You are so full of ..." Ray struggled. "You can't smoke me, ass-wipe."

Pantera pulled out his satellite phone and hit the auto-dialer. "Hey Jack. You want to talk to dill weed? I'll put you on speaker."

"Hello Ray." Jack's voice swam into the room like the ghost of Christmas past.

Ray froze. He stopped struggling and his eyes fixated on the phone.

"Come on Ray, don't be mad. Most people can't see Pantera coming. That's what makes him so bloody effective. *Bloody* being the operative word. And yes, some of us at the CIA can hide things from the DoD's favorite spook shop." Jack's chair creaked through the phone.

"What do you want? What did I do to you?" Ray's chin and shoulders dropped.

"Pantera will tell you, all the best." Pantera hung up the phone. "Now, if you're done posturing, can we get on with the business at hand," he exclaimed, crossing his arms on the table.

Ray realized his life was over. Tears filled his eyes as he looked up at Pantera, and said, "I have seen death and death is me."

"How astute, who do you report to?"

"Tal Cohen."

"Does Tal still work for Mossad?" Pantera asked, testing Ray's knowledge.

"No."

"You're saying you didn't know Tal Cohen, aka, *Mary Shelley*, still works for Mossad?"

"She does?" His mouth remained open.

"Who do you know at the Federal Reserve or Rothschild Bank?"

"No one."

"Stop playing with me or I'll start peeling your skin off." Pantera said, gritting his teeth.

"I don't know anything about any banks." Tears rolled down Ray's face.

"What is this?" Pantera pulled out two pictures.

"That's not me. I swear. It's a set up."

"Well. If you can't be straight with me, I'll have to get to work on you."

"Wait! This might be helpful ..."

"What?" Pantera stopped pulling tools from his bag.

"Tal told me that your girlfriend. That *Kat* girl ... she's Kidon."

"Huh? What's a Kidon?"

"Kidon is Mossad's assassin squad. Kat is only the second female to be accepted, Tal was the first."

"You're telling me, Kat, the girl you met when we were chasing the kidnappers in Iraq, is an assassin? A flat out assassin ... you guys and your stories, sheesh."

"Yes. From what I hear. One of the best. She has a master's in languages from the Sorbonne, qualified for the *Talpiot* program and *Sayeret* at eighteen, before being recruited to the Kidon. Her father's the Director of Shin Bet. He was a total badass in his day. She even has a scary legend."

"What do you mean *scary legend?*"

"The story goes. She's called, *Hash-sha-sheen,* the Master Assassin. Her first kill was her uncle at fourteen-years-old. Can you believe that ... fourteen! She cut off her own uncle's dick!"

CHAPTER 90

Pantera hid his surprise. "Let's get back on topic. Enough of this legend crap. Give me the name of your Federal Reserve contact and I will end you quick."

"Dude, just kill me now. I don't have a Federal Reserve contact." His body slumped.

Pantera heard a sound outside.

The secondary alarm code ... Damn.

Intelligence officers are given unique security systems. The system never turns off. Every time a door or window is opened the clearance code has to be re-entered.

A flurry of bullets came through the door as bedding material fluttered around the room. A bullet ripped through the side of Pantera's thigh as he jumped out of the line of fire. Ray was still sitting in the chair with his eyes closed. Pantera looked up at him.

"Peace. Ray Smith." Pantera shot him in the head then jumped up and ran to the bed covering the window. He pulled down the bed and found two men standing outside pointing red lasers at him. *Son of a bitch.*

The bed covering the door fell and a man walked in. "Get on the floor."

Pantera got into a prone position.

"Ray's dead," the man radioed, "What do you want us to do?" He waited for an answer. "Roger that."

416 · JD WALLACE

"Put him in a chair." He directed the other two men.

Pantera was now taped to the same chair as Ray Smith.

"Who are you and who do you work for?" The masked leader looked Pantera in the eye.

"I'm Fred Flintstone and I work for your mother. She says it's time to come home and do her in the butt." Pantera spit in the man's face then looked down at his bleeding leg

The leader drove his gun into Pantera's wound. Pantera yelled out in pain, "You MF'ers. I'm going to suck your eyeballs out your friggin' head!"

"Tell me who you work for," the leader said grinding his teeth then smashing Pantera in the mouth. Pantera realized the glove had brass knuckles in it. The hit dazed him.

"Okay. Okay," he said, speaking through a swollen jaw and cheekbone. "I will tell you. I will tell you." He looked up at the clock on the wall and noticed that Kat's two hours was up. *She should be here any minute. I just have to slow this down. Who's going to show up? Kat the girlfriend or Kat the assassin?*

"I work for ... the US Federal Reserve." He looked up at his captors to see if his scam was working.

The man stopped, turned away and got back on the radio.

* * *

Kat pulled into a parking space about two blocks from Ray Smith's apartment. She walked in the shadows and off the sidewalk. She could see a car with two people in it – one man, one woman – and smoke rising up out the window. She looked up at the light in the second floor window with several men inside.

Oh harah. Pantera's in trouble.

The fire escape was a bad idea because she would be in clear view of the people in the car. The front entrance was the only other way in, she prayed no tenants would see her. The front door was no challenge and within seconds she was up the stairs and down the hall. She heard commotion from the apartment stopping just at the doorway edge.

Kat placed her gun between her legs to silence it as she cocked the first round. She took a deep breath, walked in, and shot the two men in the back standing over a seated Pantera.

"Head shots silly – they're wearing Kevlar!" Pantera yelled.

Kat shot the two men in the head as they turned around, then shot the third man in the leg. Without stopping, she continued straight up to the third man and placed her suppressor muzzle on his forehead as he was crouched down on one knee wincing in pain. The man was visibly shaken.

"I'm going to assume you want one alive?" She stood pointing her Beretta 70 at the leader's head.

"Sure. That would be nice of you."

"I hope you're well-paid. From here it is really going to hurt?" Kat smiled her Cheshire cat smile and tilted her head.

The leader dropped his weapon with a shaking hand.

"Cut him loose," Kat directed.

Pantera hobbled out of the chair switching positions with the masked leader.

"Hi honey. Sure took your sweet time," Pantera said, smiling at Kat then turned on the man. "Who are you and who do you work for?" He took the mask off and Kat took the masks off the other two dead men.

"These guys are all Shore Patrol. I remember those two guys from the train platform." Pantera's intensity increased. "Tell me who you work for or I will scoop your eyeballs out with a spoon." *Why am I so obsessed with eyeballs tonight?*

"I don't know. We get paid in cash and given instructions. If we refuse, we die." He trembled.

Through the open window they could hear a car start up and drive away.

"Well. There went their boss and my best lead." Pantera shook his head.

"Oh well." Kat shot the man in the head.

"What are you doing?"

"What? You wanted the privilege? You should have said so. We have to clean this place up and get out of here."

"You're right. Let's regroup at the lodge, up for some popcorn and a movie?" Pantera gave her a half smile as he tore up the bed sheet to wrap his leg.

Kat was surprised at how fast Pantera could change his emotional state. "Through and through?" she asked as he wrapped his thigh.

"Yeah."

"Movie? Sure, great idea, but no chick-flicks, I am thinking an action adventure," she returned.

Pantera laughed. "Deal, I have another question for you." Pantera limped over to pick up his spent casing and dig his bullet out of the cabinet across the room.

"Right now? Are you sure it can't wait?" Kat put Pantera in a chair in the dining room and started bandaging his thigh.

"I'd like to get it off my chest. I know we've only been dating about six months and you have only met the guys of the platoon but ..."

What could you be asking that is so serious it had to be in the middle of a trashed apartment surrounded by four dead bodies? Kat's head was spinning. *Oh no ... not yet. I'm not ready for marriage.*

"... would you consider being my date to our company's awards banquet?"

"Huh? What?" She looked up at him in surprise.

"Would you be my date to our awards ceremony?" he repeated. "You don't have to answer right now. You can think on it. It's next weekend."

Kat's mind slowed as she processed the information. "Yes ... of course I will. You were going to take someone else?"

"Ah no, definitely not, I just didn't know if you were, where I am, in this relationship. This ceremony is a sort of a *coming-out* event for relationships. You can't bring a fling to this." He cringed, from the injury.

Whew, she thought. "I'm exactly where you are in this relationship, *Navy boy.* Now, let's finish this place and get to the lodge."

* * *

Kat was waiting for Pantera when he arrived at the lodge with a big hug and kiss. The question on her mind took over her thoughts.

"Well. How did we do?"

"With what?" he said, playing coy.

"Were we successful at staging Ray's apartment, you have had me waiting for over a week."

"I had to make sure they were heading off in the wrong direction, but yes. Napoli police classified it as a robbery homicide, with the perpetrators killed on scene. Obviously with a little help from ISA, but you and I both know they couldn't have the police sniffing around their office. I think the rumor is that Gaston Leroux was a writer, irony I am sure, with a gambling habit that got out of control. Good enough for me." He smiled, returned her kiss and started getting ready for the awards banquet.

"And no one at your unit is curious?"

"These guys are warriors. They do. They don't ask. Nobody liked *Gaston* anyway."

CHAPTER 91

Kat was satisfied. She walked back into the bathroom. Pantera got undressed and started getting ready.

"Kat? Did you see the little bag with the onyx shirt studs in it?" Pantera was half dressed rummaging around his garment bag.

Kat walked out from the bathroom, half-ready and stopped dead in her tracks. "What in the ... are those garters?"

Pantera glanced up. "Oh yeah," he said, blushing, "These are *shirt stays*. By connecting my shirt to my socks they keep my shirt tucked, nice and tight. How do you think those Marines keep their shirts so tightly tucked in their pants?"

"I will admit those guys look hot with those shirts all starched and tucked. If a woman knew this," she said, pointing to Pantera's garters, "all your little Marine buddies would be getting *laid* a lot more often."

Kat snatched the shirt studs from the dresser, handed them to Pantera with one hand, and grabbed his backside full-handed with the other. She whispered in his ear, "You are *NOT* undressing yourself tonight, *Navy boy*. That's now my job, you feel me?"

"Oh girl ... I always feel you," he replied, giving her a kiss on top of her head to avoid messing up her make-up. *My gawd, I just kissed an assassin. What am I supposed to do now?*

"Since we have a few minutes before we have to leave ... Can I ask *you* a question?" She stood with the bathroom light behind her outlining her full form underneath the silk full slip.

"Sure," he answered, pensively.

"Why do you say, *thank you*, to me when you get up in the morning?" she said, crossing her arms with a quizzical look.

"I adopted it from Grit. Something he tells Rose every morning."

"Go on." She tilted her head.

"Grit thanks Rose every morning for everything she has given him – three kids, a safe home, someone who listens and doesn't judge, and, most importantly, someone who *accepts* and doesn't *expect*. In my humble opinion, you provide me the same – minus the kids. After thinking about it, not that I'm any relationship expert, a person who *expects* something from their partner will almost always be disappointed. Someone who *accepts* their partner will never be disappointed." He gave a hesitant smile.

Kat stood staring at Pantera. "For a man with the empathy of a box of carrots, you can really come up with some emotional gems."

"It just makes logical sense." He shrugged.

"Just so I understand. You had no emotional training or practice as a child?"

"Nope, don't get me wrong. My grandmother was a loving person, but most of the time she was half crocked in the bottle. I spent a lot of time with my grandfather in chess parks all across the country." He buttoned up his shirt.

"Where did you grow up?"

"All over. Florida. Texas. Kentucky. New York. Arizona. And last was California."

"How do they know you were a genius?"

"I started beating my grandfather in chess at five and most adults by seven. When I was twelve I earned my Grandmaster status and was accepted to Mensa. Somehow I read pretty fast, too."

"So just raw smarts and no real education?"

"That's me, smart and unsophisticated. Maybe you'd like to change that, professor?"

"Sounds like a major undertaking, but I think I'm up for the job. Ready to go?"

"Yes Ma'am."

It was still light outside as they walked downstairs when Rosina, the owner of their frequented B&B, caught them.

"Si prega di smettere. Ho bisogno di fare una foto nel cortile." [Please stop. I need to take a picture in the courtyard.] Kat and Pantera posed like a prom picture. Then Rosina let them go.

* * *

The Navy Support Activity awards banquet was held at the *Palazzo Delle Arti Di Napoli* – an incredibly old and respected museum. It was the only time each year when the base commander was able to see the United Nations *sponsored* group in dinner dress uniforms, regulation haircuts and clean shaven – if at all. Though not technically under the US Navy's command, they are always invited as a courtesy.

"Why is everyone in your platoon shaven? Aren't you on that *relaxed grooming standards* thing?" Kat didn't see one person in uniform who wasn't clean shaven.

"Yes we are, but it's unbefitting the uniform to be scruffy and scraggly."

* * *

The location was truly a sight – one of the most beautiful locations in Naples with highly decorated men from almost every UN-represented country. Kat was remembering when she and Rose stood on the flight line as these guys got off the plane after six days in the field. How different and how diverse they looked in their rainbow-colored uniforms.

This is like an embassy ball, Kat thought.

"Who are you looking for?" Pantera asked.

"Rose."

"Oh yeah, your new best friend."

"Is there a problem *Mister Grit Doyen*," Kat snapped, with a smile, referring to Pantera's plagiarism of Grit's relationship techniques.

"Absolutely not, no Ma'am," he quickly replied, standing rigid, out of respect.

After getting through cocktails and leaving the receiving line Kat and Pantera found Rose and Grit. Rose was able to swap a couple name plates to get them seats next to her and Grit. The men left to hunt for drinks as the women stood behind their chairs.

"Same rules as an embassy dinner it seems," Kat asked Rose.

"I'm guessing so. Never been to one, but if sitting by status is the etiquette then you know what you're in for." Rose stood in her full length, black shimmering sequin dress with a glass of red wine in her hand.

The voice of the Admiral took their attention from their conversation. "And for our last two medal recipients of the night – the highest awards *and* ... orders for their new ranks."

The room roared with cheers. Kat and Rose looked at their men with surprise and stood up with the rest of the crowd.

"First Sergeant Chris O'Malley and Hospital Corpsman First-Class Marcus Sinclair ... please approach the podium."

Grit and Pantera stood up, nodded at everyone and made their way through the room full of tables to the podium.

"To Gunnery Sergeant Chris O'Malley – I award the Silver Star who distinguished himself by *gallantry in action* in connection with a classified United Nations operation. Unfortunately I can't read the narrative due to the classified nature of the operation. With that ... by his gallantry and devotion to duty Gunnery Sergeant O'Malley has reflected great credit upon himself and the United States Marine Corps ... given under my hand this day. The award will remain in his confidential personnel file and should the operation be declassified the Marine Corps will forward the award to him."

The Admiral pinned the medal on a corner of Grit's left pocket flap next to his gold jump wings and five rows of ribbons.

Grit looked down at his beaming wife and winked.

"To Hospital Corpsman Second-Class Sinclair – I award the Bronze Star who distinguished himself by extraordinary meritorious service in connection with a classified military operation against a hostile force. Unfortunately I can't read the mission narrative on this either."

He read the last paragraph.

"He consistently manifested exemplary professionalism and initiative in obtaining outstanding results. His rapid assessment and solution to numerous problems greatly enhanced the allied effectiveness against a determined and aggressive enemy. Despite many adversities, and under the harshest conditions, he consistently performed his duties in a resolute and efficient manner. Enthusiastically applying his sound judgment and extensive knowledge, he has contributed materially to the successful accomplishment of the United States Navy mission. His loyalty, diligence, and devotion to duty were in keeping with the highest traditions of the military service and reflect great credit upon himself and the United States Navy – given under my hand this day. The award will remain in his confidential personnel file and should this operation be declassified the US Navy will forward the award it to him."

Holy cow! Jack wasn't kidding when he said the director put me in for a medal. What is he going to write when I earn the Distinguished Intelligence Cross. Wish Uncle Bill was here.

The Admiral pinned the medal on his lapel next to his gold jump wings and two rows of ribbons. Pantera looked down at Kat who was glowing with pride and returned a responsive smile.

"It should be noted for those of you who may not know, Sergeant O'Malley's medal is for an operation that took place last year with his current unit and Petty Officer Sinclair's award was for an operation with his last CONUS-based unit which also took place earlier this year. Ladies and gentlemen ... will you please join me in giving *First Sergeant* Chris O'Malley and Hospital Corpsman *First-Class* Marcus Sinclair a round of applause."

Everyone gave them a standing ovation with numerous whistles from Baby-face, Cracker, Bullseye and Harry Franklin.

CHAPTER 92

"That concludes our ceremony. May I suggest we move into the other room for after-dinner cocktails and dancing," the admiral announced.

The crowd knew to wait on the senior officers before moving.

Kat stared up at Pantera giving him a big hug. "So, you are a hero ... and now you are *my hero*," she said, batting her eyes at him.

"Thank you, Princess," he returned. The attention from everyone, except from Kat, was making him uncomfortable.

Grit and Pantera could not have been in a better mental place. They had the two most attractive women at the banquet, were awarded two of the highest awards in the military, and gained rank. For Pantera the rank was merely a cover, but he sat quietly with Grit soaking up the sights and smells when ...

Grit's pager went off. A minute later Pantera's pager joined in. Before long, several other pagers went off as the men looked to Grit.

"Damn." Grit looked at Pantera and the men. "Alright gentlemen, you know what to do ... situation room in one hour."

Pantera turned to Kat. "Honey, I'm so sorry. I know slow dancing was on your agenda tonight. I'll make it up to you, I promise."

Kat smiled her cute little "knowing" smile and looked up into his big blue eyes. "Hey. Look at me. Last weekend I got a movie, popcorn *and* saved my boyfriend's ass," she whispered. "What else could a girl ask for? All this was a bonus. This is who you are. I accept that. *No expectations.* You just better bring that body home in one piece. Besides ..." Kat said, looking over at Rose, "... this just became a girls' night out. Woohoo!"

Rose threw both her arms up in the air. "Yeah, First Sergeant, be safe. I love you. And now ... Kat and I are going to ... *Par-tee!*"

Grit and Pantera looked at each other with the same thought, *Oh shit.*

Pantera knew Kat could take care of herself but in the interest of teammates taking care of their own, he grabbed Baby-face. "Sam, did you get paged?"

"No? Why?" His tone curved up.

"Would you to do me a big favor?" Pantera asked, knowing it was a leading question.

Sam cringed. "Aw dude, that drums up an enormous number of possibilities and most of them were not so good."

"I think you will like this favor. You see these two gorgeous women. You are now their escort for the rest of evening. Keep them safe and out of trouble." He pointed to both Rose and Kat.

Both were looking at each other with a raised eyebrow.

Deciding to play along, they both jumped up and grabbed Sam under each arm.

"He's cute," Kat started.

"He'll do," Rose finished.

Both walked away with their arms tucked under Sam's.

Grit looked at Pantera. Pantera shrugged.

Pantera motioned for Sam to stop and waved Kat closer. Slowly placing his hands around Kat's waist and sliding them up her side, he bent down to give her a soft loving kiss. Kat felt as if she and Pantera were the only people in the room. Opening her eyes she looked up at him inquisitively. He opened his eyes and stared at her – memorizing every millimeter of her face.

" *Thank you.*"

428 · JD WALLACE

He gave her the softest smile she had ever seen. Her eyes filled as she gave him a tight hug and smacked him on the butt. "Go get'em tiger!"

She returned to Sam and Rose as they entered the next room filled with loud music and a sea of flickering lights and colors.

* * *

"Sorry to take you away from the party, but we have a situation in Rwanda that needs your attention." McFarland started the briefing without the usual roll call. This meant only one thing, this was a *drop everything and go* mission.

"This request comes from the French government. On good authority they believe the threatening Rwandan Patriotic Front (RPF) is about to mobilize against the current Rwandan regime and their military force, the Rwandan Armed Forces (FAR). The French could care less about the ensuing civil war, which they are happy to make some money from, but there is a French arms dealer who is selling to the RPF. The French don't want the world to think they're backing both sides for profit, unless they could get away with it. Unfortunately, this is not *that* situation." McFarland clicked a picture of the arms dealer on the board.

Pantera looked up at the photo and then sneered down at the two remaining intelligence officers, Alexandre Dumas and Mary Shelley. *It was nice knowing you freaks. Hope we cross paths again. I wonder where Jack is going to send me next. I'd like to continue with Kat, but how do I tell her the truth?*

"The arms dealer is a wild card. He has to be taken out of the equation. This is a single squad task, plus the interrogator/medic. There is a secondary objective, however. The arms dealer will be meeting with one of the RPF commanders. Interrogation of this person should return good intel as to the RPF attack timeline and their routes. Having this timeline will allow the UN to withdraw non-combatant workers from the area. Shantal is passing their pictures to you. Captain Naquida will provide the operations plan."

McFarland looked up at Grit. "Congratulations Gunny. I guess we can call you, *Top,* now."

"Thank you, sir." Grit's voice echoed back.

"Good evening, gentlemen. I'm Captain Naquida of the South African Air Force and we will be your ride tonight. This is a twenty-eight-thousand-foot HALO authorized jump into a small DZ east of the town of *Nyagatare* in the northern part of Rwanda. According to intel reports the RFP have most of their troops currently working inside the Ugandan National Army and when signaled they will move across the border into Rwanda. The transaction is scheduled to take place at 1800HRS the day after tomorrow in a small village north of the *Nyagatare* Police Station. It is believed most of the police force is part of the RPF. You have forty-five hours to reach the transaction point, take out the arms dealer and interrogate the RPF commander. Your extraction will be through the *Akagara National Park* to the east – on the border of Rwanda and Tanzania. Thank you everyone. Be on the flight line in one hour. Dismissed." He tucked his cap under his arm and left the stage.

CHAPTER 93

The flight engineer bent down to yell into Grit's ear, "Weather report over the DZ is horrific ... high winds, rain, thunderstorms, and numerous lightning strikes. We'll let you out above the storm, but you'll fall right through it. Make sure your altimeters are working properly. Cloud ceiling is about 300 meters."

Grit used hand signals to pass along the message.

The team was asleep spread out all over the plane in comfortable jump seats with their down sleeping bags. It was an eleven-hour flight on a C-130 that could carry up to sixty-four airborne troops. They were seven in number.

"First Sergeant, please wake up your team and start pre-oxygenation. We're about forty-five minutes out from the DZ," the flight engineer yelled, shaking Grit to wake him up.

Grit walked around and gave everyone the signal. Pantera was standing quietly in the corner of the plane – reviewing his checklists, putting on his vest, checking his gear and putting on his parachute harness.

Okay baby. Let's get in the zone, Pantera thought.

The red light started blinking and the flight engineer gave the signal to switch from the oxygen system to their jump oxygen canisters and seal their masks. Once everyone gave the thumbs up, the yellow light started blinking and the back cargo door opened.

Everyone cleared their ears to equalize the pressure.

The cargo door locked in place and the team shuffled to the ramp. The light started blinking green. The whole team galloped off the ramp into the bright light of the day above the vast billowy dark storm clouds below. Within thirty seconds they had hit the storm and the winds were extraordinarily strong – tossing them around like Ping-Pong balls with condensation and raindrops obscuring their vision.

The clouds were so dense the line of sight to their teammates was impossible. They could barely read their own altimeters – a hair-raising experience for even the most fearsome warrior.

Two minutes. Not being able to see the ground gave Pantera motion sickness because there was no horizon.

Man o' man, this is like turning the lights off in a pitch black room and trying to hit a stamp with my nose.

Pantera looked down at his altimeter: 2500, 2000, 1500.

"Damn this thing better work ... not that I would know it if it didn't," he yelled. To be safe he pulled his parachute early.

The ram chute filled with air completely.

Whew. Love it when that happens.

Just as he reached up to grab the toggles, an ear-busting crack of lightning struck the parachute ripping it to pieces and the unmistakable smell of ozone fill his nose. The parachute caused him to spin wildly. At one hundred and twenty-five miles an hour he looked like *Icarus* streaking back to earth. He couldn't find the release to cut away the main. The backpack on his chest was blocking it. Falling and spinning with an enormous amount of angular velocity his right hand found the release. He pulled it and counted to make sure the main was fully gone before deploying the reserve. The main tore away from his body.

Three, two, one ...

With his left hand he pulled the release. The reserve deployed fully.

He looked down at the altimeter: 500, 450, 400. Pantera was still traveling more than seventy miles an hour.

Holy crap, this is going to leave a mark.

He pulled both toggles as hard as he could as the ground came up rapidly to greet him.

The whole team watched as Pantera came shrieking through the clouds, "Grit we've got a streamer," Harry beckoned over the radio.

They saw the cut-away and the reserve chute deploy. A collective "Oh shit", then a, "whew," could be heard. His speed was still too fast. The whole team jumped out of their harnesses and started running to his estimated impact point.

Someone was chanting under their breath. "PLF, PLF, PLF." [Parachute Landing Fall]

Pantera hit the ground and looked as though he crumpled ... *Aghhh. Feet, calves, thighs, butt, lats ... roll.*

He rolled as he hit the hard, rocky ground being dragged through the lowland scrub brush. A rock broke the face piece and seal of the mask. Another rock struck him in the rib cage.

I better not have torn those sutures on my leg.

Grit stared down at the hysterically laughing corpsman. "What the fuck happened to you?"

"Duuude. My chute got hit by lightning. Did you hear that damn thing? Nearly broke my ear drums!"

Pantera was lying flat on his back laughing uncontrollably, more from fear than happiness. He was holding his side as he felt a twinge of pain from his ribs. *Bruised ribs ... great.*

Grit couldn't help but laugh with him, as did the rest of the team.

"Staff Sergeant, let's gather up the gear and tag it so we can get out of here," Grit directed Harry, grinning and shaking his head as he walked away.

* * *

"Two clicks from target site." Brandy's voice came over the radio.

The terrain was primarily lowland scrub with various shades of brown and very little green. There was an unorganized grid pattern with several dirt roads crisscrossing around the area. Not a paved road in sight. There were infrequent small farms growing basic food crops. The compound became clearer as they approached.

"One road into the compound, looks like about a click and a half to the main road," Harry radioed.

The village was a large, north-south, rectangle. On the south end there were ten small homes – two rows of four homes, a second row of two homes. The pattern was repeated on the north end. In the center there were four long buildings in the shape of the letter "C" with the open side facing west. There were two small buildings in the center of the "C" compound. The two buildings looked like the guard shacks.

"We'll approach from the east. Meet up at the house five hundred meters to the east of the compound." Grit's voice was slow and firm.

The team circled the perimeter of the house then entered.

"Damn. Looks like this place was a massacre," Pantera said, looking at the bloody walls and basic wooden furniture.

"The males were probably all killed or dragged off to join one of the militias. If they were Tutsi females they will be raped by Hutu men and forced to have Hutu children in special compounds – their unique version of genocide – to extinguish the Tutsi race." Grit tilted his head in a sign of ambivalence – *Animals, the lot of 'em.*

"Hey Top, we've done everything we can for now. We'll have to wait until dark to continue surveillance," Harry reported to Grit.

"Sounds good, let's set up a watch on the compound and get an idea of who the friendlies and hostiles are. We've got about thirty hours until go-time, hopefully the storm will have passed by then." Grit called to Brandy. "Set-up comms for this area then radio Lion King and give him our SITREP."

CHAPTER 94

The radio woke Pantera. "We have one hour until the meet. Let's get set up." He threw some water on his face and walked into the kitchen as he ate a Baby-Ruth candy bar. *The best pre-raid snack.*

Grit laid out the sketch of the compound on the table. "Gentlemen. We're not going to jerk this one around. Once the second target enters the compound, the clock starts. Harry and Brandy. You take the guard shack. Bullseye. The arms dealer and his guards. If he is second to the compound, take him out as soon as he exits the vehicle and then everyone with him. If he is first, then track him until you hear shooting – then drop him."

Bullseye popped his gum, his special version of "affirmative."

"Charlie-four, you'll support Bullseye from a ground location. Charlie-Five, you have the roving guards. Pantera and I will dust off the commander's support group and take him for interrogation. Questions?"

The men cocked their weapons and filed out of the building.

* * *

"We're thirty minutes past the meet time. Do you think we were blown?" Harry called to Grit.

"No. You know how these puppet pseudo-military types like to play their little power games. Whoever is last is the "power player" – obviously in their own head." Grit laughed.

It was getting dark and the team switched to night-vision starlight goggles.

"We have lights coming up the road. One car and one truck," Brandy radioed.

The guards waved the two vehicles through and they parked in the center of the compound. Four men got out of the car and four men got out of the truck. It was the arms dealer.

Grit looked at Pantera and shook his head. "Looks like beta plan is in effect," Grit radioed.

The arms dealer's men all stayed with their vehicles. About ten minutes later a single set of headlights came up the road. The guards waved the car through. It parked next to the truck in the middle of the compound and four men got out. Grit could see Bullseye make adjustments. One man from each group approached each other. A deathlike stillness descended upon the compound – no insects, no animals, nothing moved. The inhabitants from the compound went inside their buildings – no one lingered outside to watch these men transact their business.

"Bullseye take the shot," Grit snapped, echoing in the team's collective ear.

It was go-time. Within three seconds … Bullseye took out the arms dealer with a melon shot and dropped the arms dealers' three closest guards. Pantera and Grit simultaneously moved out from cover and dropped the three guards standing next to the commander.

Two thuds from Harry and Brandy could be heard at the guard shack.

Charlie-four dropped the truck guards and in the distance three soft thuds from Charlie-five. It was a total of five seconds and fourteen bodies lay dead on the ground. It was still again.

Standing amongst the bodies was the commander. He slowly raised his hands in the air and turned to face Grit and Pantera. Two black masked shadows approached slowly and turned on their lasers so the commander remained frozen in fear.

The commander looked around as more black shadows came out of the darkness. The surreal experience griped his soul and sent a cold shiver down his spine. Seven lasers targeted his chest.

"On your knees, cross your ankles, put your hands on your head, and interlace your fingers," Grit said, in English.

* * *

The man hesitated. His first thought was to try playing the ... *I don't speak English card.* Realizing that this group was far superior to anything he had ever heard about. If they knew the meet time and location – they definitely knew all about him and his European education – including the fact that he just returned from a course at the US Command and General Staff College.

"Okay. Okay. You obviously want me alive for something," the commander said, smiling mischievously.

* * *

Pantera walked up to him, pulled out his razor-sharp stiletto, and cut off the man's ear. The man's screams echoed through the village.

"No. Not really, but if there's something you'd like to tell us, we'll listen." Pantera answered, while zip-tying the man and escorting him to one of the empty long buildings. Grit and Pantera sat him down, tied him to a chair, and sprayed some coagulant on his ear.

"Harry. Setup a perimeter and let's eat," Grit radioed.

The man yelled at Pantera, "You're violating my Geneva Convention rights!"

Pantera smiled. "You mean the rights your army doesn't follow?" He bent down speaking into his good ear. "Those same rights of which you speak are for those who follow the Geneva Convention articles themselves – which you do not. You are not afforded those rights. Hell. The odds of your country ever becoming a UN member are ZERO anyway. Any other topics you wish to discuss, smartass?"

"I'll tell you anything you want. I swear," he replied, sweat streamed down his temples.

Pantera started laughing. "Oh, I'm sure you will talk for days on topics you think, *I want to hear.* Utter garbage. The problem is ... that's not the correct answer." He stabbed the commander with an Epipen. "What I want is everything *you know*, not anything you think I want to hear."

After spending hundreds of hours working with Dr. Merriwhether and her team, Pantera learned, among other things, many subconscious speech-pattern avoidance techniques. This included one of the most obvious – the ... *I will talk and tell you nothing* technique. It's very common in an attempt to avoid torture.

"Now my little friend, I could stand around here and give you the girly interrogation of waterboarding, loud sounds, and parading you naked in front of all those Tutsi women you have locked up here – which you and I know truly does absolutely nothing. You know this. We know this. You see, I'm *not* one of *those* interrogators. I'm the interrogator no one talks about and most have never heard of. You will die in this chair. End of discussion. The only question is – whether you die quickly, by eating a bullet, or slowly over days with your skin dissolved off and every bone in your body broken." Pantera took inventory of the room.

The commander's body shook. "You can kiss my African ass. There is nothing you can do to force me to give up my people," he said, vigilantly.

"You know how many times I've heard that before?" Pantera turned to Grit. "Looks like we're ready. Let's lay him prone on the table." Pantera and Grit lifted the little man on the table, zip-tied his arms and legs to the table legs, and cut off his shirt.

Pantera pulled a rope from his backpack. He interlaced it around the man's shoulders and found a hook in the wall. Each ankle was

438 · JD WALLACE

wrapped and tied to the wall. With all of his and Grit's strength they tightened the rope. The man was stretched out across the table, tight as a drum.

"How many troops does the RPF have?" Grit asked.

The man paused. "Well. That's hard to say, we ..."

"Ding, ding, ding," Pantera interrupted. "Wrong answer, what do we have for him today, Johnny? Listen dumbass. We already know the answer to that question. We were just giving you an opportunity to be straight with us." Pantera pulled out a small T-shaped device which looked as if the handle held two "D" sized batteries and laid it down where the man could see it.

"What's that?" he screeched. "No, no, no, I will answer!"

"This my friend ... is a custom-designed *Zimmer*, battery-powered, *Dermatome*. Skin harvesters all over the world use these for collecting skin from dead bodies. That skin is then sent to burn centers around the world to be graphed onto burn victims – saving tens of thousands of lives each year. In your case you will be a *living* donor. I will use this little baby to cut the top layer of skin off your body. If you remember how sensitive the skin under a blister is ... imagine your whole back feeling that way. You don't even want to know what I do after that. Waahoo!"

CHAPTER 95

Pantera laid out a cloth on an unused portion of the table and started laying instruments on it as he continued talking to the small, thin man. "You'll love this story. I was inserted into a prominent academic institution in the U.S.A. as a *Tissue Technologist* to investigate hospital staff believed to be selling organs and tissues illegally to the international market. That's where I met this little baby. Unfortunately no one makes battery powered dermatomes. I hired a genius engineer friend to rig it up for me. I must say this little gem works beautifully on dead bodies ... haven't had the chance to use it on a live one yet. I'm really excited to see how well it works. Thank you for being my first participant." Pantera grinned at Grit.

"Could you go 'round up a couple more chairs?" Grit waved at Brandy.

Pantera put on his gloves, coated the commander's back with a couple drops of baby oil, picked up the dermatome in his right hand and a pair of Allis tissue forceps in the left. He placed the dermatome on top of the commander's butt on the left side of his body and started slicing down to his lower back and up his back. The fatty tissue jiggled as the black skin was removed revealing a fresh young white moist layer.

The commander screamed so loud Grit thought the guy was going to blow a cerebral blood vessel while trying everything he could to move away from the intense pain. The ropes were too tight.

"Sorry commander. Please, no anal leakage. We're really good at making a human immovable," Pantera said, continuing to move up his back while pulling skin from the dermatome.

Grit winced when he saw Pantera pull one long continuous, six centimeter wide, piece of skin from the dermatome – a length spanning the distance from the top of the man's butt to the top of his shoulder. Just as he finished with the first strip of skin the commander fell unconscious.

"Hot damn! This is more effective than removing the cranial cap or the *Dremel* finger holes. And no burnt bone smell." Pantera nodded at Grit. "We should be home in time for corn flakes." Pantera set the dermatome down and stabbed the man with another Epipen.

The commander woke up again screaming as Pantera leaned in close to his ear. "You thought I was fuckin' kidding, didn't you? Sorry to disappoint. How is that bullet looking now? Oh, and by the way, that was just one little part of your body. Wait until I peel the skin off your penis. Before that though, I've got this really cool salt mixture which will feel like you're being burned alive. Just wait. Shall we continue?"

"If I die you will get nothing," the commander yelled.

"So true, though very painful, this does very little toward killing you ... I can keep you alive for days in this state. Isn't that great? I love modern medicine." Pantera pulled out a bottle from his bag.

"Doc, we have a problem." Harry walked into the room and noticed the commander's back. "Wow! Now that's gotta sting. We've got a pregnant woman about to pop."

Grit turned in his chair raising an eyebrow. "You've got to be kiddin' me. What a cluster fuck."

Pantera poured the salt mixture on the commander's white strip and every muscle in his body started seizing as he passed out, again. "Harry, could you watch ballsack here. In a couple minutes jab him with this. Maybe when I'm done delivering a freakin' baby he'll be ready to talk."

Pantera grabbed his trauma bag and he and Grit left the room headed up to one of the small houses on the north end of the compound. They walked past the dead bodies in the parking lot and noticed something on four of the bodies: a frog, a swan, a dog and a crane. All made of Bazooka bubble gum cartoons.

Grit looked at Pantera and smiled. "I know, huh. That guy is an *Ar-teest.*"

There were over a dozen heavily scarred women milling around outside the hut as they entered. A woman approached speaking broken English.

"No one know how to help. No can get doctor in town. You doctor?"

Grit answered, "Yes, he's *our* doctor."

Pantera nodded and took her hand. "She will be good."

"You think they really have a doctor in *podunkville?*" Grit asked, standing behind him.

"Gawd no, at best they have a midwife, at worst a shaman or some other useless spiritual healer," speaking to Grit over his shoulder as they walked into the next smaller room. They were met by a half a dozen women. Four women were standing and two kneeling down on either side of the young girl. The girl was no older than fourteen years of age, lying on the ground with her legs spread wide.

Grit looked down at the girl. "Oh for Pete's sake, she's no older than Jesse AND I was really hoping to not see *that* ever again."

"Geez, tough it out Mister *I-have-three-kids-and-cut-the-cord,*" Pantera chided, kneeling down between the legs of the young girl. "The good news is she's crowning. We're halfway there." Pantera called to the woman who spoke English, "Please have those four women get bowls of water and towels – hot water if possible."

He gave hand signals the women recognized as the head cleared the birth canal.

"Stop pushing! Man, this day just gets better and better. Grit, I need two locking hemostats, preferably without teeth, and a pair of scissors or scalpel blade. The umbilical cord is wrapped around the neck." He adjusted his position for the procedure.

"Looks like you have one chest-tube clamp, one pair of Kellys and a number fifteen blade."

"Yeah, it's a trauma kit, not an obstetrical kit for crying out loud. Pass'em over. I'm going to need one of those towels. As soon as I cut this cord that baby is going to fly out of there like a football." He turned his focus back to the baby.

Pantera clamped the chest tube clamp on to the umbilical cord and then about one inch away clamped with the Kelly forceps. Placing his two fingers under the cord, he cut between them and through the cord. The cord fell away from around the baby's neck and Pantera directed the two women to let the girl continue pushing.

Within a minute the baby was out and wrapped in a blanket. He then gave the baby to the oldest-looking woman and left.

"Anyone with hemorrhoids? I can go for a trifecta," he said, sarcastically, as they walked back to the commander.

When they entered the room Harry met them. "I think he's ready to talk. He's been crying the whole time since he woke up."

The commander was breathing heavy and there seemed to be no struggle or fight within him.

Grit started with a couple test questions and felt the commander was being honest, so he continued – periodically throwing in another test question for good measure.

"Please kill me. Please. Please," the commander cried, developing a large puddle underneath the table.

Pantera was already cleaned up and sitting in the corner watching Grit and the commander's interaction. "I think Snickers is my favorite post-torture snack. Anyway want one?" He raised the candy bar in the air looking around and smiling.

Grit looked over at Pantera. "I think we're done here."

Pantera gestured. "Please, by all means, my gift for being *Top*."

Grit drew his handgun, tapped the man in the head, and his brains blew out all over the wall.

"We might still make corn flakes." Pantera threw his bag over his shoulder.

"You think I might get some advancement points for delivering a baby for the indigenous population while on mission? Isn't that what those silly fellows in the US Army do?"

CHAPTER 96

Kat picked up the phone.

"Hi shwee-tee." The words tumbled out of Pantera incoherently.

"What is wrong with you? Were you poisoned? Hit by a tranquillizer dart? Where are you?"

After a long pause. "Ahh. Noo-paa. I don't sheenk sho."

"Are you ... drunk?" she asked, reluctantly.

"Yup."

"Where are you?" Kat ran to the dining room table and grabbed her purse.

"Alley off *Via Andrea d'Isneria* and *Via Arco Mirelli* ... happy daisies." The phone went dead.

Kat ran to the car, jumped in and drove off.

* * *

She drove around the neighborhood for thirty minutes when she finally found an unconscious Pantera lying in a dark alley next to a commercial trash dumpster. Next to him a half-empty bottle of *A.H. Hirsch Reserve* bourbon and a pool of vomit. The neighborhood was commercial and desolate.

"Hey," she said, shaking him. "What kind of swill have you been drinking?" She spotted the bottle. "Bourbon? Isn't that for poor people from Kentucky?"

Kat knelt down next to Pantera and slapped him, hard.

"Huh? Her-roo scwoo-pee, sco-be-do-be-do," he gurgled, drooling down his jacket, his eyes blood shot.

"Oh, *harah*. Marcus Lachlann Sinclair, get your ass up right now!" Kat yelled, bending over him.

Pantera stiffened and slowly rose like a fallen Godzilla. His big dark structure continued to increase in size from the crumpled rag-like form it once was. Moving mechanically he stood facing Kat, then fell on her. She tried to hold him upright until she was in position to throw him over her shoulder to carry him back to the car. By her third step he vomited again all down Kat's backside and into her boots.

"Just wait until you get sober. I'm going to kick your ass," she bayed. Kat threw him in the car and drove to Rosina's B&B hoping she had a room available. She found Rosina sitting on the porch with a fine rosé in her hand.

"Rosina, dimmi che hai a disposizione una stanza? Per Favore?" [Rosina, tell me you have a room available? Please?] Kat walked around the car to greet her.

Rosina could see in the car where Pantera was folded up like a cheap suit.

"Yes. Yes. Your apartment open, you need help? I call Alberto," she said, watching Kat pull Pantera from the car and throw him over her shoulder.

"No thank you. I can take it from here," she grunted, carrying him up the stairs.

Kat threw Pantera down in the bathtub. He barely moved.

"What did you do to yourself and why? You hate alcohol," she said under her breath, turning on the cold water.

Kat went to the kitchen and grabbed all the water bottles.

Intelligence officers are taught early in their training how to handle their alcohol consumption. Basic physiology: water. Alcohol replaces water causing the body to malfunction. Blood Alcohol Content (BAC) is a percentage of alcohol in the blood. The fastest way to decrease alcohol in the blood is to increase the water in the blood and let the kidneys do the rest.

After another hour of constant cold water Pantera stirred. He opened his eyes to Kat handling him a bottle of water.

"Drink," she snarled.

"Ugh. No way," he said, belligerently.

"Either start drinking or I turn you over and insert the bottle in your other orifice." She leaned in closer.

"Okay. Okay," he said, taking the bottle from her; "How did I get here?"

"I carried your *ragged-bourdon-smelling* ass. Keep drinking." She stared stonefaced at him.

"S'was I ...?"

"Yes, you were. Mind telling me why? Considering your family history with alcohol and the fact I have to beg you to drink a bottle of wine with me ... and *bourbon* of all choices? I could see a good scotch, but bourbon. Next time try battery acid," she said, wrinkling her nose at him.

"That s'was a funf-hundert-deutstch-mark bottle, sank you bery mulch. And ..." he stopped, his sanguine swollen eyes teared. "I killed an innocent." He turned and rolled up into a fetal position hugging his bottle of water.

"Wait. Start from the beginning. Who was this *innocent* you killed? Was it in Kuwait?"

"No ... it was *Ray Smith*. The guy I tortured and killed." The anguish on Pantera's face was jerking at Kat's heart-strings.

She never believed she would see this reaction out of an unempathetic interrogator who she thought was emotionally bankrupt.

"I'm confused. How do you know Ray Smith was innocent?"

"I called my handler. He told me two more intelligence officers investigating the Federal Reserve traitor case were killed in Luxembourg while I was in Kuwait. Ray couldn't have given out that information. They arrived in Luxembourg after Ray's death." Pantera finished the first bottle of water and grabbed a second. His tears stopped abruptly.

"Oh, umm, well, that's part of doing what we do." Kat shrugged jumping up on the wash basin cabinet. "Innocents occasionally die so many more can live."

"Oh please, don't give me the *so-many-may-live* speech. I've heard it too many times," he said, standing up unsteadily and turning off the water. "That's a load of crap. We're supposed to be better than that. With that logic we should just drop bombs on apartment buildings if there's a *possibility* of killing one high value target. Utter bullshit."

"That's not what I'm saying. If *you* kill five or ten high value targets a year and one innocent goes, then I think *you're* doing good." Kat was very careful to use pronouns directed at him instead of pronouns that would imply she killed people for a living. She knew, even drunk, Pantera would notice.

"I don't kill innocent people. Period," he roared, clenching his jaw.

Kat didn't know how to respond. Pantera had a code. She respected that, but she also knew being inflexible with a code can lead to enormous emotional conflicts.

"I respect the code. I do, but being inflexible is not a good mental state to have in this business. You have to accept, *you didn't kill him.* Someone lead you to him. Someone made you *their* tool. You need to find *that person* and take your anger out on them," she said, nodding and trying to get him to nod along with her.

"How am I gonna do that? Both pieces of evidence I had led to Ray. The trail has gone cold. I've got nothing now." Pantera sat on the edge of the tub with his head in his hands.

"Stop feeling sorry for yourself. You have three dead shore patrol guys, a car with a male and female in it and, whether the mole knows it or not, their human ... and fallible. And why am I doing your job for you?" she asked, crossing her arms staring at him. "I have enough problems of my own."

"You're right. This little *Talpidae* is going down. If I backtrack, I only have two suspects left ... Dumas and Shelley." His red-rimmed eyes narrowed.

"And with that ... I have a theory I want you to consider. I believe it might help us both." Kat didn't know if she was on the right path, but her gut nagged at her.

"Okay. I'm listening," he said, up-ending the water bottle.

"My problem seems to be connected to someone inside Mossad. This Mossad traitor must be providing information to my Katsa huntress. You have an information peddler who is selling intelligence to the highest bidder. What if your peddler is selling to my Katsa Killer?" She leaned back and waited.

"Are you saying what I think you're saying?"

Kat just shrugged.

CHAPTER 97

"A Mossad officer inside *The Activity* is my mole? A person working for Mossad, a traitor to Mossad, working for ISA ... AND ... working for the owners of the Federal Reserve, presumably Rothschild Bank." Pantera rolled his eyes. "You're into conspiracy theories, too?"

"And ..." she hastily replied, pushing him.

"You really think she's that good?" He raised his eyebrows at her.

"Yes," she answered, definitively.

"Fraggle Rock. If I catch her without evidence and I can't get anything out of her ... they will ..."

"NO! No, no, no," she shouted, in a diminuendo tone. "We have to wait until she makes a mistake. She's been at this a long time – patience like a panther, Pantera. We sit in the tree and wait for her to come to us."

"Waiting for her to make a mistake means I have to continue to work with her and you," he said, pointing at her, "have to keep being chased by little miss *wunder-killer*." He pointed out the window.

"I can handle myself. Can you?"

"I can," he said, standing up wobbly in his vomit-soaked clothes drinking from his third liter of water.

"Now that you're in a more amenable mood, I've another request of you." She switched gears. "You're off blue cycle this week, right?"

"Yes ... and," Pantera said, apprehensively.

"You can use your four-day pass this weekend, right?" Her last word lingered, before rolling off her tongue.

"Um, maybe," he said, with a half shake, half nod. "Grit has to sign off on all passes. It's based on manpower requirements and all that stuff. I'm sure other guys already put in their request chit for our first weekend of freedom."

"Would you meet me in Montreux on Friday? I already spoke to Grit about the pass for this weekend and it would mean a lot to me." Kat blinked excessively, playing up the guilt.

"Kat? You already spoke to Grit about *my pass?*" he asked, tone changing, "And when did you do this?"

"At the Shootout, when we made that side bet. If you won you would let me cover the cost of a trip to Switzerland. You can call Grit. He was a witness after all," she said, speaking as flat and serious as she could.

"I remember the bet and for crying out loud, why this first weekend?" Pantera shook his head.

"Well, honey ... dearest ... my very special boyfriend. It's Alona's wedding this weekend." Kat closed her eyes and took a big breath in preparing for the volcano to erupt.

He gave Kat a blank stare, thinking, *More painful ... this or the case of blue balls?*

Pantera learned an important lesson from his grandparents, they never yelled. Conversely, he did spend some time with his biological mother – who yelled every time a snowflake hit the ground. He swore an oath to himself he would never yell in a relationship. Kat did as well, but for different reasons, she found yelling beneath her.

Kat knew there was something special about their relationship. She knew he would pull it together so she waited him out. *Here is my first boyfriend who hates yelling as much as I do.*

Pantera, head still spinning, replied, "Kat, you know I love you ..." With tensed jaw muscles as the lactic acid build up from the alcohol burning inside his body he closed his eyes and started speaking slowly. "Let me make sure I understand the situation. You have *known* about this wedding for months. Last month you *manipulated* me into a bet to guarantee I would have time off. Then you *conspired* with my boss to make sure he would give me that time off. And now ... you're just telling me less than a week from the event. Would I be correct in my summation of this situation?" He opened his eyes and tilted his chin down.

Kat sat still, unable to respond, or breathe, as the voice in her mind was preoccupied. *You said you love me?! Qevdesh harah! I did not see that coming.* Ignoring the rest, she asked, "You love me?"

I said that out loud? Damn. That will teach me to let my subconscious participate in a conversation. What do I say now? If I pause too long she'll probably pull that polycarbonate blade and stab me.

"Yes. Yes I do love you, Alyn Katryna David. From the moment I first met you when I was scared out of my gourd. I've been in love with you every second since then. From kicking my ass on the Parkour course to losing gracefully to me at the Shootout ... and every tumultuous moment in between. That is part of the reason I say, *thank you.* I just can't tell if you feel the same way," He sat down in his wet smelly clothes next to the tub as his last drop of emotion hit the floor.

Kat's mind was a jumble of words, all of them not making any sense. *What do I say to you? I'm not sure? Maybe tomorrow ... want a bagel and lox?* "Yes. Of course I love you. You're a very important person in my life," she said, sitting down next to him on the floor. "I *am* really sorry for all the surprises. I really don't plan them all – most, but not all. Honestly ... your schedule, my schedule, I had no idea if you would've made it back in time for the wedding anyway. Had I told you beforehand and you couldn't have made it, you would have just felt bad for not making it. I would never hold it against you ... *you* would hold it against you. That in turn would make me feel bad. It's a vicious cycle which I never wanted to get into. We'll have a nice big bedroom in Jacques' apartment – that's Alona's fiancé by the way – and we get four days of fun and frolic. There will be a gift if you show up." She kissed his cheek, not believing she said that all at once.

"Alright, fine. You have to promise me you will keep these *manipulations* to a minimum," his said, shoulders drooping as he looked up at the ceiling. "What do you want me to do?"

"Go get your pass signed by Grit. Buy the 6:05 a.m. ticket from Naples to Milan and the 12:25 p.m. ticket from Milan to Montreux. I'll meet you at the Montreux train station at 3:30 p.m. and we will be naked by 4:00 p.m. Oh and by the way, you have to be at the tailor at 6:00 p.m. and the pre-wedding dinner is at 8:00 p.m." She gave him her patented Cheshire cat smile.

"Geez Kat, seriously? Did you schedule me time to take a pee in there anywhere?"

"Of course I did, as long as I'm holding it. I meant that both literally and figuratively."

"What day is this again." He continued to gulp from his water bottle.

"This Friday, I leave on Thursday." Kat sighed, pleased with herself. *It sure started off rough, but we made it out the other end.*

CHAPTER 98

"GET UP!" Rose yelled into Pantera's ear.

"Huh?" Pantera struggled to open his eyes.

"You have to be at the train platform in twenty minutes," she shouted, throwing his backpack on his chest.

It was 0604HRS by the time Pantera ran up the train platform with a blistering headache, red crusty eyes, and a bursting bladder. All compliments of the end of cycle event called, "B-cubed", also known as, "Bye-Bye Blue." B-cubed is a religious event thrown every year by the platoon sergeant for the whole platoon and support units.

Pantera laid across two seats and pulled out the half-gallon sized milk container Rose filled with water for him.

The B-cubed party originally started years before by a platoon sergeant who was just happy that his team made it through blue cycle with no one getting killed – a very rare event. This last cycle they lost two. Delta-three was KIA and Delta-two died two weeks later due to an infection at Ramstein Air Base in Germany. Their deaths were reported to their families as training accidents. Their bodies, shipped back to their hometown via special UN detail.

Pantera fell asleep with Grit's words floating through a sea of dreams.

You lie at rest among the best,
And so you'll understand our pride.
While fighting for a justly cause,
Among the best you died!

You gave your all without restraint,
And now with duty done.
You lie at peace without complaint,
And apologize to none!

For you gave all your tomorrows,
You gave in freedom's name.
Though time will heal and dim all sorrow,
We think of you as we seek no fame.

* * *

Eight hours, a gallon of water, twelve trips to the bathroom, and four energy bars ... he was ready to handle his next adventure.

An unknown town, unknown people, no clothes, and more alcohol – this woman is going to be the death of me.

"Montreux," the voice over the loudspeaker resonated through the train. Kat stood as bright as the sun and lovelier than daylight striking a daisy on a spring day. Pantera had not been off the train ten meters when Kat ran up and jumped on him. Kat wrapped her arms around his neck and lip-locked him for over a minute. She leaned her head back maintaining her position and leg lock.

"What is that smell? Not again. I thought we solved that. And your eyes, what in the ..."

Pantera smiled. "It was the end of the cycle party at Grit's. I had to participate and no, it's not the beginning of something. Nothing has changed," he said, slowing the last sentence.

"Wow. Such honesty, I like it. Okay. You're forgiven. If I'm forgiven for springing this on you last minute? Am I forgiven?" Kat grabbed his shoulders and started shaking him while increasing her tension around his waist.

"Yes! Geez Kat, stop. I need some food and can we stop freakin' out the locals ... again?" Pantera looked around at the people looking at them.

* * *

"Whoa there partner." Pantera said staring down at the tailor measuring his inseam. "Shouldn't you buy me a drink first?"

Kat laughed so hard she fell off the bench. "Honey," she said, using her calming voice, "This is a *bespoke* tailored suit. Look on the bright side – you'll never have to go through this again ... unless of course you get fat." *That sounded better in my head.*

"Ha. So there is an incentive to staying in shape," he said, trying to keep one eye on the tailor and the other on her.

"Sir, which side do you dress?" The tailor stood up looking at him in the eye.

Pantera glanced at Kat. "Which side do I dress?" he asked, with a quizzical look on his face.

"He wants to know which side you hang." Kat blushed, taking her index finger and pointing to the ground, swinging it from her right leg to her left leg.

Pantera's eyes went wide. "Oh! Hmm, the right side?"

He stepped down from the tailor box and walked around the shop. Nothing had a price tag on it. Then he overheard the tailor speaking to Kat.

"Auriez-vous besoin d'un gilet aussi Mademoiselle?" [Would you need a waistcoat also Mademoiselle?]

"Oui, s'il vous plaît," Kat answered.

"Coût total, £3250."

Pantera didn't understand most of the conversation, but he did understand the last words out of the tailor's mouth. He felt suckerpunched as his inner voice yelled at him. *Dude, she just bought you a car. Who is this woman I am in love with?*

Grit's words bellowed in his head and counterbalanced the sticker shock. *No expectations, just acceptance.*

On the way back to the apartment, Pantera asked, "Kat. Can I ask a question about the suit and what all that was back there?"

Kat knew the suit made Pantera uncomfortable, but she was prepared. "Yes. Ask away."

"You already know what I'm going to ask, but I have to ask. You know I'd be happy with a *Brooks Brothers* suit. Not that I've been to a store, you get my meaning. Why spend so much on something I may never wear again?" He put his arm around her.

Kat didn't know whether to be happy at his humility or angry at his naïveté.

"There are several reasons. One: On a financial level. I do well and don't spend much on myself. As you know, I value the intangible over the tangible. Two: On a relationship level. This is an investment in our relationship. The suit represents my commitment to you for the long term. This may not be a *Saville Row bespoke*, but it's a fifteen-ounce *Swiss bespoke* suit and will still last over ten years." She stared up at him to make sure he was still following the conversation. "And three: It is as much a gift for me as you. You're a humble man. I get that. One thing my mother taught me about being involved with a humble man – you must sometimes take charge of his wardrobe. Despite being humble you still represent 'us'. I'm sure you would feel comfortable wearing a burlap bag at a cotillion. However, we dress in public as a reflection of our love and respect for each other. This is a common social mores. And honestly, when we go to a nice restaurant ... you really need to stop borrowing a dinner jacket from Grit," she said, giving him a swat on the butt.

Pantera took several minutes to absorb what he just heard.

"Wow. I figured you'd have an answer. I didn't know you'd put that much thought into it. I heard everything you said and I accept most graciously on one condition. The suit stays at your place. You can tell me to wear it whenever you want." He extended his hand to close the deal.

You have no idea, Navy boy. You have no idea.

CHAPTER 99

Kat and Pantera returned to the apartment. They found a chubby, dapper young man with red spiked hair and freckles unpacking his custom designed *Domenico Vacca* alligator skin travel bag and *Louis Vuitton* suit bag in one of the bedrooms of the specious four bedroom, four and a half bath, apartment. Christophe, Jacques younger brother, heard the two walk in and approached them in the living room.

"Hello Christophe," Kat snapped, giving him a frosty greeting.

"Kat et son goût garçon-jouet du mois," [Kat and her boy-toy flavor of the month] Christophe quipped.

Pantera raised an eyebrow seeing Kat's reaction to Christophe's comment.

"Tout d'abord, vous allez m'appeler Alyn, vous n'avez pas à m'appeler Kat. Deuxièmement, c'est Marcus, mon copain et vous sera respectueux et parler l'anglais en sa présence." [First, you will call me Alyn, you don't get to call me Kat. Second, this is Marcus, my boyfriend and you will be respectful and speak English in his presence.]

Pantera watched as Kat's patience waned.

"Pourquoi devrais-je être respectueux à un monolingue idiot américain? Dites-lui pour apprendre le français!" [Why should I have to be respectful to an idiot-American monoglot? Tell him to learn French!]

Christophe never attempted to shake Pantera's hand. He turned to return to his room when Kat slapped him open-handed knocking him clear across the room into the wall three meters away. She moved toward him to continue his beating when Pantera stuck his arm out and stopped her.

"Please go cool off. I'll finish this." Pantera walked over and knelt down beside the stunned little fat man.

"Hi, I'm Marcus. You must be the *frat-boy* she speaks so highly of. Don't let me get in the middle of that. However, may I make a suggestion? As a man who's been in your position – *so many times I've lost count* – go get a hotel room and stay away from Kat for the rest of the weekend. If she chooses to start kicking your ass again, I highly doubt anyone could pull her off you. Except maybe me, but then again, you probably just insulted me, but didn't have the *balls* to do it in English so ... I won't be coming to your aid anytime soon. *Com ... pren ... do, mo ... fo?*" Pantera gave Christophe a little *urbanized Tex-Mex Spanish* to really piss him off.

Christophe got up holding his face. "Wait until she leaves you for a girl," he snarled, returning to his room he packed his things and left the apartment.

Pantera said nothing and smiled. He found Kat, still fuming and sitting on the edge of the bed. Kat grabbed Pantera's hand, kissed it, and pulled him down to sit next to her on the bed.

"I'm so sorry. I guess I owe you an explanation," she said, holding his hand in her lap.

Pantera gave her an omniscient smile. "You don't owe me anything. I already know. You and Christophe had a thing in the distant past, he treated you like a piece of meat, you got tired of it, and dumped him. He's hated you ever since. How did I do?" A query game he learned from Grit.

Pantera watched as Kat's face lit up.

"How did you ... in like, a couple minutes?"

"Like I said before, being unempathetic doesn't mean I can't read people and their situations. It was on his face like a van Gogh. And as a man, trying to be a good man, I have made bad decisions regarding women, too."

"So there are some angry women in your past?" She smiled.

"Oh yes. Women don't understand that as men, we are single-minded idiots who never get anything right the first time. We spend most of our twenties screwing up, or *practicing*, with girls we hope are not ... *the one*. With enough women and learning, we finally reach our *one-and-done* relationship praying we've developed the tools to go the distance with her," he said, starting off into space.

"Christophe's in his late twenties. What's his problem?"

"Unfortunately for guys like Christophe, he never learned from past relationships. He continues to grow more and more bitter as time marches on – treating all past girlfriends with disdain and all future one's with well ... you know. It's quite sad really. I'm guessing he wasn't always a fatty?"

"No. He wasn't."

"Huge indicator of distain for himself and those around him ... disrespect of the body. Well girlfriend, are we good? Is it chow time?" Pantera laughed, jumping up and moved to the door.

Kat cocked her head to the side as she turned to look up at him. "Ya' know, just when I think I have you figured out, you throw one of those *hit-the-nail-on-the-head* explanations at me." She got up and looked deep into his eyes. "*Thank you.* I think we have a few minutes before dinner." Her eyes twinkled.

* * *

Kat and Pantera arrived to the restaurant late, but happy and in good spirits. The restaurant was about four kilometers from the apartment and was a moderately sized, traditional, Swiss design with one portion of the building having three stories and other parts having two. One part of the building was blue, one was yellow, and the third – the original building – was made of stone masonry. No big sign on top of the building, like most American restaurants, but the name in the small door window read: "Le Pont de Brent."

Kat immediately spotted Pantera's apprehension. "Is it the food or the people? I can protect you from both."

"Both, and I don't doubt that."

Pantera flashed back to when he first arrived in Naples. He and a couple Marines decided to eat in a café just outside the gate. When the café owner returned with the pizza Pantera ordered, he insulted the man by telling him, "*This cracker with tomato juice, funny leaves and ugly cheese wasn't a real pizza and Americans made real pizza.*"

Being a typical untraveled, uneducated American, Pantera's concept of pizza was skewed thanks to his first Italian dining experience at a San Diego restaurant called, *Filippi's Pizza Groto,* as a child. He was hoping to not repeat the offense at Kat's sister's pre-wedding dinner. That was a different day and a different Pantera.

Returning from the beyond, he nodded at Kat.

Kat straightened Pantera's shirt collar. "Here's what you need to know. One: The food is predominately seafood, small portions, high in fat and filling. This is one of the best restaurants in Switzerland. You won't starve. And two: The parents are here. My mom is the typical Jewish mom. She will want a hug, give her one. My dad is cold and standoffish, don't take it personally. You've spoken to Alona over the phone so that is covered. She enjoys your formality. Jacques is sort of like a civilian you. He's quiet until he gets to know you, except he has no ability to fight or run, whatsoever. He's calm and open-minded. And you met Christophe. I've never met Jacques' parents so we'll both have to play that by ear. Briefing over, Navy boy, ready?" She looked up and took a deep breath.

Pantera stopped and grabbed Kat's arm. "You have two older brothers where are they?"

"Not here."

Pantera knew he struck a nerve. "I'm sorry," he said, rubbing her back.

They took a deep breath together, nodded and Pantera opened the door for Kat. Alona came running up to give her sister a big hug and then stared up at Pantera.

"You said he was a tree. I didn't envision he was the *Árbol del Tule*." She stuck her hand out to shake hands formally. "Hi, I'm Alona."

CHAPTER 100

Alona was smaller in frame than her younger sister and much more fragile looking, but still well-proportioned with black hair, flowing straight down to her shoulders, and green eyes. Pantera paused and stretched out both arms in an unspoken request for a hug. Alona quickly fulfilled the request and almost disappeared into his chest.

"Oh yeah, I like this guy. You can keep him," she said, using a phase their mother had said to Alona several times, but never to Kat.

After the hug, Alona turned to Kat. "So, I heard you bitch-slapped Christophe. Man. I wish I was there. He has this *huge* handprint on his face. Way to go, *Achut,*" she said, giving her sister a high-five.

"What did Jacques say?" Kat said, concerned.

"Jacques told him that he probably deserved it and he has to pay for his own hotel room," Alona said, with pride.

Hearing how Jacques handled the Christophe situation Pantera looked forward to meeting him.

"What about *Abba*? Is he going to continue ignoring me? Not that I care." Kat glanced around the restaurant.

"He said he wants to speak with you. After dinner," Alona said, straight-faced.

"You're going to be there, too? I'm not talking to him alone."

"Yes. I'll be there too. Now smile. It's my *Nisu'in!*" She raised her arms in the air and dove back into the crowd.

The farther into the restaurant Pantera walked the more he noticed only people from the wedding.

"Did your parents rent out the whole restaurant?" he asked.

"Yes. Now breathe."

Kat and Alona marched Pantera around the room introducing him to everyone, never leaving his side for too long until dinner started.

"Marcus. This is my *Imah*, Tirzah David, and my *Abba*, Gideon David." Kat didn't look at her father.

"Nice to meet you both," Pantera said, nodding respectfully.

"Do you speak Hebrew? Are you Jew or *gentile?*" Tirzah smiled.

"*Imah?!* Marcus is Jewish. Sheesh," Kat said, shaking her head.

Mister David stood quietly and watched Pantera interact with his wife.

"Let's eat." Jacques' voice could be heard in the background.

The conversation with Kat's parents during dinner continued but never strayed too far from generic topics – mostly about places he's seen in Italy and America – no penetrating background or family history questions, which made Pantera comfortable. After dinner Gideon David stood up and looked at Kat giving her a directional nod.

"Alyn, may I speak with you outside, please," he said in a soft but firm tone.

Alona had a keen eye on her father all through dinner. When he got up, she got up to follow. She knew it was time.

"I'll be outside if you need me," Kat whispered in Pantera's ear.

"He'll be fine, *Baht*," Tirzah said to Kat, patting Pantera's arm.

Alona and Kat reached the door at the same time. They looked at each other. Alona winked at Kat giving her goose bumps.

"Alona, you may go back inside," Gideon directed.

"No. She's not. You want to speak with me? You speak to us both. I don't want any confusion as to what was said right here ... right now." Kat said with force, pointing to the ground.

"Okay. I have taken out a family embarrassment upon you and I apologize, but you have to understand ..."

"What family embarrassment?" Kat trampled over her father. "Your brother or me? No. I don't have to understand. It's very black and white. He was bad and no one would do anything about him, so I did."

"You are wrong. We, the patriarchs of our families, we were going to do something. We needed to wait for the right time," he said, standing rigid with his hands on his hips.

"And when would that *right time* be ... exactly. When the girls he harmed were over thirty and so screwed up they can't see straight," she shouted, spinning her index finger around her ear. "Just so that you, *the patriarchs*, could say it was too long ago and to get over it?! Screw you and your misogynistic patriarchal society."

"You cannot take the law into your own hands, Alyn."

"That's where *you're* wrong. I do it nearly a dozen times a year and would do it a million times over. Men are just *sperm-donors* and should be treated as such." Her eyes narrowed and lips tensed.

Alona stood next to Kat in silent support, nodding in agreement.

"*Abba*, I respect you, but not your *man-laws*. For thousands of years MEN have ruled the earth. And for thousands of years the human race has been at war – suffering under that rule. Your male-controlled societies and male-dominated religions are coming to an end. If I have to remove every man who doesn't see a woman as an equal, then I can guarantee you ... I'm up for the task! Let me tell you, that man I'm with in there ... he respects me and will stand behind me as I do it." She crossed her arms and waited for his rebuttal.

Gideon looked at Alona.

"You know where I stand, *Abba*." Alona put her arm around her sister.

"I love you both, but men will never allow women to lead, ever. They are put on this earth to have children and maintain the home for their master. Females are weak ..." Gideon stopped. He stared at his two grown, fiercely independent daughters. "Until the time when women do take over the world, and stop all the wars and change all the religions, it's still a man's world, today. And will be for the next thousand years, even if all the women on earth wanted change. By retiring your uncle, you were wrong. You forget. If you were not in a Mossad family, your life would have ended up quite differently."

"You're right. I would have spent the rest of my life in jail, both physically and emotionally – all at the hands of men. You should be so proud, *Abba*," she said, turning to look at her sister then stomped back inside.

"*Abba*, I am so sorry," Alona said, shaking her head.

"I know. She will see what I mean someday."

"No. I'm not apologizing for Kat, she is one hundred percent correct. I'm apologizing for you. You are so blind as to not see what she's talking about. Even you see women as nothing more than slaves. Is that what you want for your daughters and granddaughters ... slavery?" Alona turned and followed her sister into the restaurant.

"No, but what can I do about it?" he said, under his breath.

CHAPTER 101

Pantera opened his eyes. Staring straight into Kat's face he whispered, "*Toda Raba.*" [Thank you.] He slipped out of bed. After pouring a glass of orange juice he walked out on the balcony and watched the sun's dark reddish-orange rays of light dance across the water as it rose from behind him. The last day's exhibition of pageantry played in his mind.

After the pre-wedding dinner Kat took off with Alona to the *Mikveh*. The next morning the wedding ceremony was held at the *Grande Synagogue de Lausanne*, built in 1909. It had a beautiful façade with two domes beside a symbolic representation of the Torah. Pantera learned all the parts to a formal Jewish marriage ceremony: *the Kabolas Panim, Badeken, Chuppah,* the reading of the *Rebbe's Letter, Mitzvah Blessings, Rings,* reading of the *Ketubah, Sheva Brochos,* multiple *Mazal-Tovs, Yichud room, Seudat Mitzvah,* and then the *Sheva Brochot.* He was back in Hebrew school all over again.

His mind flashed forward. *Would Kat want all this? She doesn't seem the type.*

Pantera had no problems dealing with work. He told one lie after another but it was all easy to manage. His personal life, however, jettisoned him into the unknown. An expanded realm of new beginnings had invaded his otherwise structured world. There were many events this country boy had to digest and, as he stared out over the crystal blue water of Lake Geneva he ticked them off one-by-one in his analytical mind.

The unbelievable emotional experiences in the most mesmerizing locations melded into a brightly colored collage of firsts. His first *blown-off-your-feet, love-at-first-sight* encounter with the most beautiful woman imaginable topped the list. She goes on to defeat him, of all people, on a Parkour course not only shocking him, but conversely not offending him. She then gifts him a bespoke suit – an outrageously expensive suit tailor-fitted just for him. If that wasn't enough, he had never told a woman he loved her or met the parents of anyone he dated or ever attended a wedding, any wedding. And then to even think, as he had just done moments ago, about whether Kat would want the same type of wedding – a subconscious thought placing him closer to another miraculous first – the concept of marriage.

Pantera couldn't help but think about the events at the wedding and then the dialogue with Jacques crept into his thoughts.

"Marcus. I just wanted to thank you for coming. I know you and Kat work in jobs with very difficult schedules and I feel blessed that you both could be here. I hope this wasn't *too* Jewish for you. It's mostly for our parents, as you can see." Jacques had a kind and soft face, stood about five foot eight and weighed a wiry one hundred and fifty pounds. He spoke in a genuine and elegant manner.

"Thank you Jacques, but it is I who should be thanking you for inviting me. I'm honored you guys even know my name considering Kat and I have only been dating such a short time." Pantera watched Jacques trying to figure out how he could be genetically related to Christophe.

"I'll be honest with you, just as you were with my brother, for which I thank you. Maybe he'll wake up one day. Kat probably never told you this, so here you go. You didn't hear this from me ..."

Pantera braced for some surprising news he was sure Kat would not want him to know, so he listened intently.

"All four of us went to university together. Despite Kat and Alona being four years apart, they entered university together. I was a junior and my brother was a freshman with them. Kat and Christophe dated for three years. Unfortunately my brother chose the rich frat-boy tract and Kat, in senior year, dumped him. It wasn't until a couple years ago that I ran across Alona again. Alona tells me all about Kat's relationship exploits. Kat told Alona she would only introduce her "*Bashert*" or, *soul mate*, the term she used, to her and her parents. Her parents don't know this, but I think they suspected it since not one guy has ever made it to their door ... until now."

Jacques' mannerism changed almost imperceptibly, but Pantera caught it. "She is way out there and she's all yours, my friend. Just treat her well, she's the best and deserves nothing but the best."

Pantera absorbed the whole dialogue as if it were a *Pennsylvania Dutch-style* cheesecake. "Gosh. I don't know what to say. I don't think I'm *the best*, but I'll do my best to make her happy. Thank you, Jacques. What you've told me explains a lot." Pantera reached out to shake Jacques' hand and then the two men embraced in a firm man-hug. Pantera heard the patter of little feet on the marble floor and his mind returned.

"What time is it?" Kat came stumbling out on the patio.

Pantera turned around to see a big mop of black hair encompassing what could only be described as something similar to the iridescent glow of the inside of an abalone shell. "Well Princess, it's morning to most. To you, I'm thinking it's still *Mazal-Tov* time." He had never seen Kat in such disarray and liked it. "You need to start drinking water. By the way, did I look this bad when I got off the train?"

"You're funny. You still looked good when you got off the train and I hate you for it," she said, holding her arm up to block the sun. "I had to drink for my sister so she could function last night. Wouldn't want her passing out on her first night of *you-know-what* with *you-know-who*, she has six more nights to go." Kat did not have the energy to jump up on him, so she just fell into his chest for a hug.

Pantera let out a single laugh. "You mean those two brittle be-ings ... every night for a week. I think my head'll explode with that visual. Good on them. Let's get you hydrated."

"I only have two more days of you. I'll drink your friggin' water, but only if you come back to bed and snuggle with me. Then I'm going to need a big brunch." Without looking up, she staggered back inside as the phone rang.

Kat answered.

"Kat? Can you talk?" Alona sounded serious.

She looked at Pantera standing on the balcony. "Sure."

"I have bad news ... really bad news."

"Speak."

"Pantera doesn't work for the UN-SOG." Alona paused.

"I was there. I know he does. I met his boss and went to that damn *Shootout*."

"He infiltrated the UN-SOG. I don't think anyone at the UN-SOG knows that he actually works for the CIA. He's not only a black site interrogator, *he's a hunter*. My source couldn't find out his assignment because he's part of a *special access program* compart-mentalized by the Director of the CIA."

"What's a *hunter*?"

"My source said that CIA employs a small group who can infil-trate any organization to hunt *and* kill their targets. Whereas Mossad has one group that hunts and another, your group, to kill." Rain could be heard in the background.

"Okay, well, I didn't tell him what I did either. So we're even. Thanks."

"There's one other thing. Pantera works for the same group that killed ... *Adamm* ... and tried to kill you. He could be hunting you," she said, with a soft intensity.

There was silence on the other side of the phone. Kat stared at Pantera through the glass as she looked around the kitchen for a knife. She cut the phone cord.

CHAPTER 102

"Honey, could you come in here, please?" Kat stood behind the island in the kitchen. She knew if she went toe-to-toe with him she would lose, but she would not back down either.

"Yes, Ma'am."

Pantera walked in and immediately read her body position, her location in the kitchen, and the weapon in her hand. "Something sure went south in a hurry."

"Stand very still," Kat said, gritting her teeth.

Pantera stood in the living room with a glass of orange juice in his hand.

"Answer me. Who do you work for?"

The hair on the back of Pantera's neck stood up. *She found out? But how? What ... five people have the clearance? Must have been Alona, how did she find out? Doesn't look like that question is going to get answered anytime soon, should I come clean? What about you, Kat? When are you going to come clean?* "Sure. Right after you tell me who you work for?" he asked, raising his eyebrows.

Kat adjusted her position. *How did you find out? That CIA guy you killed? What about all that 'I killed an innocent' crap? You are setting a trap to get closer to me.*

"Deal, you first," she said, pointing the knife at him.

"I work for the Special Activities Division of the CIA," he said, in a stone-cold response.

"Not good enough. What do you do?"

"I hunt and kill individuals who violate the trust of the United States Government."

"Have you ever hunted a Mossad officer?"

"No. This is my first Middle East assignment. How about you? Miss *Kidon*. Or should I call you, *Hash-sha-sheen*? Did I pronounce it correctly?" He took a sip of his orange juice.

"When did you find out?"

"Ray Smith said Tal Cohen, or Mary Shelley, told him. He tried to give you up in trade." *If I get out of this alive ...*

"Yes, it's true I killed my uncle when I was fourteen because no MAN would do it. That's what my father and I were fighting about outside the restaurant yesterday – after ten-plus years," she said, leaning against the kitchen island.

"Damn. That's some cool shit. I heard the story."

"Yeah, well my father doesn't seem to think so. Look. This," she said, pointing back and forth between them, "isn't going to work out. You need to go." Tears streamed down her face.

"Wait one second. You lied, I lied. You kept from me, I kept from you. I agree with not lying in a personal relationship, but withholding is a different matter entirely. Withholding is not lying. It's a form of protection, not deception. Withholding from someone you're dating is a person's right. They should be able to tell their partner information about themselves only when they're ready, it's not for someone else to decide when that time is." He felt a numbness he never felt before.

"It's not about withholding," she said, her body shaking, "Your CIA division killed my brother, Adamm, and tried to kill me!"

He stood, dazed. "You're penalizing me for the past actions of my agency? Are you serious?"

"How do I, *not know*, I'll wake up one day when your boss, or your boss' boss, decides our relationship isn't in the *best interest of the United States* and sends one of your colleagues to retire me or worse, makes you do it?"

I'm always ten moves ahead, why do I feel I'm ten moves behind?

Pantera shook his head. "I don't have an answer for that. I'll get my stuff, but before I go ... you might want to ask Alona how she got her information. You know who I'm hunting. Think about it." For the first time he was no longer intimidated by Mossad, now it was his own agency.

Pantera left the suit on the bed and closed the door to the apartment behind him. Kat fell fetal to the kitchen floor and cried harder than she did after Nyssa's death. Kat's life was turned upside down.

* * *

With only a couple reports left Kat slowly and methodically reviewed each piece of paper without seeing the words. She was numb and the mindless paperwork gave her other things to think about – both a boon and a bane. The ringing of the phone jolted her.

"Alyn Katryna David. Stop what you're doing right now!" Alona's energy reverbed through the receiver.

"Huh? What is it this time?" she said, monotone and hollow.

"Palermo! I'll be down in a couple hours."

"Oh *harah*! You have been dragging me all over the country for the last month. Please let me have this weekend to crawl into bed and read a good book. Please."

"I'm coming down anyway. Jacques has to go to the States so I need something to do."

There was a knock at Kat's office door.

"Hold on, Alona."

"Come in," Kat responded to the knock.

"High Priority for Alyn David." The diplomatic courier peeked in the door.

"Thanks." Kat took the package.

It was thinner than usual. Maybe she would not have to leave until next week. She prayed to the assignment gods. She opened the envelope. It was an airline ticket, a piece of paper, and a hotel room key. The airline ticket was in the name of one of her aliases. Desti-nation: *Mitiga International Airport* – Tripoli. Leaving tonight. *Fuck me. This sucks.*

"Alona. I'm off to Libya. Call you when I get in and keep your mobile on. You remember how bad Libya is."

"Ciao' *Achut*. Stay safe." Alona hung up.

The slip of paper read:

Byblos Presidential Suite
Radisson Blu Al Mahary Hotel
Tripoli
Contact will meet you at hotel for briefing
Happy Hunting.

CHAPTER 103

The distraught Kat slept curled up on the terrace deck lounge chair of the presidential suite. The moonlit glimmer of the Mediterranean Sea outlined everything in the ferry port. The doorbell aroused her.

"Hello Rashid," she said, looking down at his shoes; "Still wearing those ugly loafers I see."

Rashid Saidenberg, Kat's handler, was a third-generation Libyan Mossad agent and a member of one of the last Jewish families in Libya since Gaddafi took control. His family stopped practicing Judaism openly and feigned Islamism after Gaddafi started confiscating all Jewish assets and cancelling all debts owed to any Jew. Despite being considered by Mossad as one of the bravest Jewish assets, Rashid was in Kat's humble opinion, was one of the worst handlers she had ever worked with – second only to Avner Hershfeld. Kat believed it was far better to have no handler than Rashid.

"Let's sit in the dining room. Can I get you some tea?"

"No thank you, I drink coffee." He smiled.

"Of course you do," she returned, with a condescending smirk. *This better be a simple contract. Libyans are nothing but neik-jerboa-shoes.*

Rashid handed Kat the dossier of the target. "Miss David. I know you don't like me and I apologize for my poor performance on the last assignment. I believe this will go quite smoothly. Your target is *Abu al-Qadhafi*, a Libyan Magistrate and one of Gaddafi's chief judges. For the last year, Mister al-Qadhafi has issued three assignation contracts for an Israeli judge who is holding al-Qadhafi's son at *Maasiyahu Prison* on terrorism charges."

"This is the father of the last remaining Flight 722 terrorist from last year's bombing?"

"Yes. Mossad killed two of the three, but Shin Bet captured the last one."

"I know. I took out one of those two. Now the father needs to go. Fine," she snapped, thinking, *a hit it and forget it contract – the best kind.*

Kat was having a hard time focusing with the emotional scars from the wedding catastrophe still fresh in her mind.

Rashid continued. "Tomorrow, the magistrate will be working in his office as he does almost every Saturday. Security will be low and there will be no regular guards. The building is about three hundred meters from here to the southwest. You have two entry options. One is to covertly enter the facility through this route that I have already mapped. The other you can use these credentials of a single woman with no family who works for one of the other magistrates. Her credentials will allow for direct access bypassing all the security points through this back door here and this stairwell. I took her out yesterday. This badge is good for the weekend. I'll go downstairs and see if your boxes have arrived. Thank you for working with me again." Rashid got up and left.

Kat seemed pleased at the briefing and at Rashid's attitude – a departure from the last time they had worked together. She left all the paperwork on the table and went to bed.

Tomorrow is going to be a long day.

* * *

Kat was having morning tea on the terrace when Rashid arrived. "We have a problem," he said, with dread in his voice.

Kat looked up from reading the newspaper and raised an eyebrow. Something she picked up from Pantera.

"Let me guess. The same thing that happened last time," she retorted.

Rashid lowered his head. "I have no resources, no embassy, and no diplomatic couriers. I have to use native Libyans who often rip open packages and steal from them. I've brought what I can – some weapons and knives – but I have no chemicals or other instrumentation."

Kat shook her head. "This place is the fuckin' armpit of the universe with a perpetual riot mentality. A country run by monkeys would be better to live in. Libya just needs to be blown off the planet. Let's go." She jumped up and headed for the door.

"Where are we going?" he asked, looking inquisitively.

"To the woman's residence you killed. Let's see if she has any clothes and accoutrements I can use. I obviously can't use the covert route into the building, now can I?" Kat said, over her shoulder.

Rashid followed like a sullen child.

* * *

They both walked in and looked around the small, sparse one bedroom flat. The smell of cheap perfume and gunpowder was still in the air. Kat moved quickly to the bedroom. The woman was still under the sheets with a bullet wound to her temple.

Clean hit – must say that for him.

She started rummaging through the closet pulling out one outfit and a bag to carry. She laid the bag on the bed and dumped everything from the jewelry case into it. The woman was slightly taller than Kat which would work just fine. Closing up the bag she headed for the front door.

"Next time you finish someone. Leave a clue as to who and why she was killed so the idiot police will think what you want them to think. Not that these idiots could ever figure it out unless you put it on a bulletin board." Kat was in a foul mood as she returned to the hotel.

The bag flew onto the bed. She changed into the outfit, holstered as many weapons as possible, and threw a few more in her purse for good measure.

"Geez, I look like a train wreck," she grunted, glancing in the mirror.

* * *

"If I'm not back in two hours, Rashid, let me repeat ... *two hours*. Call this number, first. This is my sister Alona then call the office. You know what to do and you better do it ... so help me. And stay out of the damn mini-bar this time." She slammed the suite door and headed for the private elevator.

Once she reached the outside, the warm salty air hit her – giving her flashbacks to her first weekend with Pantera at *'A Fenestella* in *Posillipo*. The emotion welled up tears as her mind wandered.

Stop! Get control of yourself.

She ran the route to the magistrate's office in her mind as she approached the back door, slid the security card down the reader, and heard the door lock click open. The door opened revealing a solid-white, tiled staircase and the smell of harsh tobacco. She reached the fourth floor and started down the hall. The floor was completely deserted. She reached the magistrate's door, inspected it for security issues, but found none. The doorknob was locked with a simple six-pin cylinder lock. *Cake. At least something is going right.*

Kat pulled out two *Kirbys* from her hair and within a minute the door was unlocked. She opened the door slowly since she had no lubricant for the door hinges. The door was rather quiet despite its age. She took off her shoes and put them in her bag. The Beretta M1935's flat black color was faded. She screwed on the suppressor then sniffed it. The lack of smell told her it had not been fired in a while, nor did it smell like it had been ever oiled. *It would be just my luck that this damn thing blows up in my face.*

She heard sounds coming from a room to her left. She slipped up to the doorframe and peeked around the corner. A gray-bearded man in a modern suit with a *Cheche*, a traditional *Tuareg* turban, sat behind an ornate executive style desk. The room was much more elaborate than she would have expected. Modern fixtures adorned the room and the walls were shelved with legal books in numerous languages. She didn't hear anyone else in the room so she walked through the doorway. Taking two steps into the room the man immediately looked up. She fired one shot straight through his left cheek. It did not come out the other side. The magistrate's head bounced off the back of the chair and hit the desk like an empty bowl.

Melon shot! She could hear the boys' favorite phrase in the distance.

Out of nowhere there was a gasp from Kat's left side. She didn't see the woman sitting in the corner as she entered. Kat spun to her left, the women's face covered in fear. Without thinking she shot the woman in the head – one small hole, no exit. *How old are these bullets? Glad they can at least enter the head. Geez.*

CHAPTER 104

Without touching anything Kat put her shoes back on, dropped the gun back into her purse, and headed for the stairwell. She opened the door to the familiar smell of salt air as she calculated her route back to the private entrance of her suite. She looked at her watch. One hour and twenty minutes from the time she left the suite. *That could be a new record despite the obstacles. Let's get out of this god-forsaken city.*

She thought about how glad she was to be done with this country as she turned left from Dahmani Street heading back across a vacant lot with the sight of the hotel in the distance.

SMACK.

Out of nowhere she felt a stinging pain in her left rhomboid muscle. Kat couldn't reach the dart. Finally, she pulled it out. It was too late. The venom was released.

She turned around to see a moderately dark skinned woman approach her as the memories overwhelmed her. *Sorbonne ... Berlin ... Belgrade ... Thailand ... Athens. The Katsa Killer! Son of a ...*

Kat reached for her Beretta but the woman was lightning fast. She grabbed Kat's bag throwing it far behind her. She attempted to hit Kat on the head with her air pistol but Kat blocked it and elbowed her in the face spinning to square off against her opponent.

I'm going to take you down you towel-headed-couscous-eating-titless-goat!

The woman recoiled and came back with a front kick toward Kat's diaphragm. Kat moved to the side and kicked the lateral side of her other knee in a typical *Krav Maga* move – snapping a couple tendons in the killer's knee. The killer shrieked in pain and collapsed to the ground. Very few men could take Kat in a fight – absolutely no women. Kat stepped closer to the woman giving her an open-palm hit to the cheek. She stepped back preparing for another hit when her body went weak. Her muscles failed and her mind wondered as the poison started taking effect. Kat's vision blurred. She could only think of escape.

Kat turned to run. Her sight was gone.

The world went black.

* * *

"Alona?"

"Yes? Who's this?"

"It's Rashid from the Tripoli office."

"You have got to be kiddin' me ... she's in Tripoli of all places. Don't call the office. I'll take of everything. Just stay and have a drink at the mini-bar." She slammed down the phone.

* * *

Luxottica Group, come il mio io dirigo la chiamata?" [Luxottica Group, how my I direct your call?]

"This is Mantis. Operation code four-five in progress," Alona said in a clear, but harried voice.

"Security code please." The voice on the other end was calm and professional.

"Piranha-nine-nine-three-cheetah-five-eight-one-kidon-one-seven-two," Alona said, straining to remember all the requirements to get through to the special operations officer of the day (OOD).

"Please stand by."

Muzak came through the phone.

"OOD Loewenstein, what's the situation?"

Alona recognized Ezekiel Loewenstein's voice. Ezekiel worked in the communications support unit for the Kidon group.

"Ezekiel, it's Alona, I have an agent in a hot zone and she missed her check-in."

"Who's the agent? How long ago was the agent's check-in and was the mission completed?"

Alona could hear the papers shuffling with computer keys being punched.

"Angel two-five-three, one hour, and I don't know." Alona sat on Kat's couch, knees bouncing.

"Who ... angel two-five-three? Where is she? She's not in the system."

"What do you mean?! She was assigned a contract for Tripoli yesterday."

"You know how we operate. If she takes an independent contract we cannot send an exfiltration team and ... if she's in Tripoli ... Alona you know the rules regarding that country."

Alona could not hear any further sounds on the other side of the phone.

"It wasn't a friggin' outside contract! I was on the phone with her when she received the message from the diplomatic courier." Alona's voice became an octave higher.

"I will look into it, but if it's not sanctioned ... my hands are tied. Alona, I'm sorry."

Alona slammed the phone down, again. She had only one option left and no idea if that option would even take her call. She called Pantera's number, reached the answering machine and left a message. Alona paced, a plan came to mind.

* * *

"33rd Logistics Company, Chief Ricketts, how may I help you, sir or ma'am?"

"Chief Ricketts, this is Petty Officer Kissimmee at the JAG office, could you please page Petty Officer First Class Marcus Sinclair to this number? We have some paperwork for him to sign," Alona said in a Southern American accent.

"Sure Petty Officer. I'll do it right now."

Alona was pleased. She rarely interacted with non-intel people and didn't realize how easily it was to manipulate them. Within minutes her phone rang and she answered.

"This is Petty Officer Sinclair. I was paged to this number," Pantera said in a firm professional tone.

"Marcus. It's me ... Alona. Please don't hang up, Kat's in trouble." She rushed to get the words out.

Pantera paused. Not only for Alona calling him, but how she was able to get into their system.

"What audacity! Really? Why would I help you, her or your Israeli *frankenville* country?" Pantera nodded at Grit.

"Because you love her ... and you wouldn't want anything to happen to her," Alona said, her hands shaking. She wanted to blurt out, 'because Kat told you about Tal!', but she knew it would be on Pantera's mind and giving up his cover is a, *thou shalt not do*, rule. Alona and Kat knew this all too well.

"Who is it?" Grit wanted confirmation.

"It's Alona. She says Kat's in trouble." Pantera turned back to Alona, "What do you think I can do about it?"

"You can ask your unit to go get her and I get my father to pay for it." Alona was uncomfortable having Grit participating, but it was too late.

Pantera turned back to Grit. "She says if we go, Shin Bet will pay for it."

Grit slid his glasses down to the end of his nose and looked at Pantera. "Tell her we'll go to Major McFarland and advise him of the situation. Shin Bet or Mossad or whoever will have to call him to handle the back end of the operation."

"Did you hear that?" Pantera asked Alona.

"Yes. You get her and bring her back safe. I'll be down there in two hours." Alona hung up the phone and did a victory dance.

* * *

Pantera and Grit walked down the hall to the Commanding Officer's office. Pantera was a scintillating mess of emotions wound tight as a drum.

"Ready for this? Grit smiled at Pantera.

"No. Ready as I'll ever be," he shot back, his eyes widened.

"Gentlemen, follow me to my office." McFarland manner was relaxed.

"Major. We have a very prickly situation and it seems we are the only ones capable of pulling this off." Grit said, standing behind a chair across from the CO's desk.

"I'm listening." McFarland sat down and motioned for both men to follow.

"There's a Mossad agent in Libya who missed a check-in. Because the mission is in Libya, Mossad cannot send in a team – but they can fund the rescue. One of their people contacted us to do an *off-book* hostage extraction. We were told we'll have whatever resources we need to get in and get out – as long as no Israeli sets foot on Libyan soil," Grit said, crossing his legs and leaning back.

CHAPTER 105

"Oh. Not what I was expecting. A Mossad officer in trouble, you say. Hmm. You're going to lead this expedition, First Sergeant?"

"Yes sir. I will."

A voice over the intercom: "Shin Bet protocol officer on line 3, sir."

"Major McFarland," he answered, motioning for the two men to stay seated.

"I understand. I'll put a team together right away. Let me have you talk to our executive officer and he will give you our DAX information line and account numbers for payment."

He listened as the other man spoke.

"Good. Hold on just one minute," McFarland yelled into the next office, "Abraham, transfer him to the XO, please."

"Okay gentlemen, looks like your mission is a go. Good luck." McFarland nodded to them. "When I get the file set up I will see you both and the squad in the briefing room in ten."

Grit and Pantera stood at attention, nodded to the Major and left. The realization of the mission had just become a reality. Pantera felt sick.

I have to save my ex-girlfriend who I'm still in love with and will probably be cut up into little pieces. This sucks.

Grit saw the look on Pantera's face. "If you're not up for this I can get Cracker. No one would blame you for signing off this mission."

"I'm okay," Pantera said, lying through his teeth.

We will see about that, Grit thought.

* * *

McFarland stood at the podium as Charlie squad walked in.

"Is everyone here, *Top?*"

"Yes sir," Grit responded.

"Gentlemen, we have an unusual situation today. What I am about to brief you on is an *off-book* mission. We are on contract to Mossad who has requested our help through back channels. This is not, and I repeat, NOT an UNSC-sanctioned mission. No one is obligated to participate and can walk out of this room right now." McFarland stopped and looked into every face on the team. No one moved.

"A little over three hours ago a Mossad agent was taken captive in Tripoli. The last signal from the implanted GPS locator was at a warehouse in the *Souq Al Jum'ee* district – between *Mitiga Airport* and the *Metiga Hospital*," he said, flashing his laser pointed at the map behind him. "This mission is unusual because the agent in question is someone you all know, Alyn Katryn David – affectionately known to most of you as 'Kat'." A picture of Kat popped up on the board.

The room grew so quiet a feather could be heard hitting the floor. All eyes were on Pantera sitting motionless in the front row. A voice echoed in the room.

"Then what the fuck are we still doing here ... sir? Let's get moving, Top."

The rest of the squad all roared in agreement. Pantera's head fell in to his hands. Grit stepped up to the podium.

"Here we go. This is the map of the area. Our complete support for this operation will be Mossad funded and all assets will be Israeli assets. Currently there is a Chinook on the tarmac ready to go. We'll helocast and rendezvous with the *INS Tarnin*, a GAL Class submarine. We will take their Juergensen Mark 16 Mod 3, Mark V electronics rebreather units, and the Mark 8-type Submersible Delivery Vehicle (SDV). We will anchor the SDV and egress to the beach. At the beach we will switch to thobes and keffiyehs since this is a daylight operation and proceed to rally point November six-one, here. After performing a S.A.L.U.T.E. (Size, Actions, Locations, Units, Time, and Equipment/Weapons) report we will determine the next phase of the operation. Once the hostage is recovered and stabilized evacuation from the site will be between these two buildings and through this fence. A Chinook that is "under repairs" will be stationed at the north end of the airport. Let's pray they don't move her farther inland. This could turn into another chase like the Iraq-Iran debacle. Grab your gear and be on the flight line in fifteen minutes." Grit closed his briefing packet and walked out from behind the podium towards Pantera.

The squad yelled, "OOORAH!"

"Put your game face on, brother. There's a person out there who's hoping you have your head in the game. Let's show her who we *really* are." Grit slapped Pantera on the back.

Pantera stood up and took in a deep breath and held it. He looked up into the faces of the team – a team he had already gone to hell and back a number of times in the short six months of his assignment. If the roles were reversed, he would do it for them in a heartbeat. They all knew that.

It took all of his strength to keep from falling down and crying like a baby. That was not him and it was definitely not the person Kat fell in love with. Pantera shook off the pain and filled it with anger.

"TODAY GENTLEMEN ... IS A GOOD DAY TO KILL LIBYANS!" Harry yelled.

Grit watched Pantera as he exited the room, he secretly hoped Kat could stay alive long enough.

CHAPTER 106

Kat woke up to a bucket full of icy cold water. She found herself stripped naked and hanging from a meat hook in a squassation position in a large metal walled room. A weathered woman with matted, scraggly, black hair and an extremely pissed-off look on her face stared up her.

"So. I've finally caught you, you ... *aw aleklebh*. Miss Alyn David of the Mossad ... Kidon," the woman snarled.

"Sorry. I haven't had the pleasure. Who are you?" Kat replied.

"I am the wife of a man you murdered last year. I will now take my vengeance out on you for taking him away from me," she snarled, limping over to a chair.

"You'll have to be *a little more* specific. I killed quite a few men last year ... it was a good year." She calculated the amount of energy it would take to jump off the hook.

"My husband was Amar Ahmadi, Libyan agent, and true patriot of the Libyan people ... AND YOU MURDERED HIM IN COLD BLOOD, YOU FUCKING JEW BITCH!" she screamed at Kat.

This fuckball is a tool. There's no way this 'sharmuta' broke into the Aman database.

"YOU BITCH! YOU BITCH! YOU BITCH!" she continued to rant, throwing her fists up and down in the air.

"You're friggin' mental," Kat said. "Yeah, yeah ... your husband was the whack-job who blew up Flight 722, killing what ... a hundred and seventy people at the *N'Djamena Airport* in Chad." *I knew I should have tracked down his whole crazy-socks family.* "I'm just sorry I couldn't get to that third freak sitting in an Israeli prison right now, and put him out his misery, like I'm gonna do to you."

The woman unrolled a pocketed piece of fabric with twelve syringes as her mannerism calmed. "I'm going to kill you, but not quickly. I'm going to make you beg me for your death. You may have heard of the *chemical rollercoaster.* Then, while you're out," she said, showing Kat two pairs of brass knuckles. "I'm going to beat you until every bone in your body is broken."

"You silly *hashish-smoking-camel-humping* bitch, I'd love to see your point of view, but I can't stick my head that far up my own ass. You'd better get on with this because I guarantee you, and your incestuous brothers over there, you all will be dead by sundown." Kat swung her legs up and back.

The woman hobbled over to stop Kat from swinging. Kat immediately wrapped her legs around the woman's neck and locked them in a scissors move, using the woman as leverage to unhook herself. The woman tried to continue standing to shake Kat off, but Kat was able to keep her legs clamped around the woman's head while she peed on her face and in her mouth. The woman fell to the floor coughing uncontrollably as Kat flipped backwards to land on her feet in a crouched position. Orienting herself to the door she stood up. Two prongs hit her in the left breast and every muscle in her body spasmed. She fell to the ground like a vibrating statue. The woman got up and shambled over. She looking down at Kat and spit in her face.

"You didn't think it would be that easy, did you? You fuckin' Jewish whore." She started kicking her in the stomach with her combat boots.

Two men walked over and hung Kat back on the hook. Then they secured her rope shackle to the hook with duct tape. The woman took out a syringe and stabbed Kat in the leg with it. Kat was unconscious within a minute.

She put the brass knuckles on and started using Kat as a punching bag.

Kat woke up after her third round of the deadly concoction. She could feel she had several broken ribs and the searing pain in her shoulders continued to grow.

"Bring her down," the women barked. "Put her in the chair and strap her in tight."

"What? You *flea-ridden* troll," Kat said, breathing heavy, "am I tiring you out?" Kat swore to herself she would be belligerent to the end. She felt the end was not too far away.

"Salma!" A stern voice could be heard in the distance. "Why is she not dead yet?"

Kat raised her head, looking through a fog of drugs, racked with pain, and having a hard time breathing she tried to see who this other woman was, but couldn't.

The Katsa Killer turned to the woman. "You said I can do whatever I want with her."

Kat heard the unmistaken tone of subservience.

"I did, but that doesn't mean you have days to do it. Mossad will eventually ask the UN-SOG Shadow Knights to come get her. You know that." The unknown women's voice commanded.

Kat continued to listen. *That voice sounds so familiar.*

"She will be dead long before that happens. What about the GPS tracer?" Salma asked.

"Leave it in. Kill her and leave the body here. Since this contract has been completed my employers would like you to set up in Lebanon. I've purchased a *Hezbollah* safe house in Beirut." The woman walked up to Kat.

"Hello Kat," the mysterious woman said, crouching down to eye level.

The woman's face slowly came into focus as Kat's vision sharpened through the billowy clouds of pain.

"Tal? TAL?! NO! It can't be." Kat's heart nearly exploded, praying she was wrong, she wasn't. Her gut was right.

"Yes. Very good, my favorite *Puss-in-Boots,* or should a say, *Il gatto con gli stivali.*" Tal Cohen smiled without remorse.

"You *capra stronzo!* Why? Why would you do such harm to your country ... to your fellow Katsa?" Kat cried.

"My country?! Mossad tells me that my husband is expendable in service to *my country.* 'A eugenics experiment gone wrong' they say. Then they put me out to pasture like I was some mid-level, loafer-wearing, unskilled spoon! When I thought I hit rock bottom, a group of fine gentlemen recruited me and told me they value my skills. I must say, they pay extremely well. I was really hoping to recruit you, but with your relationship with Pantera. Well, you know," she said with a shrug, looking at her fingernails.

"Who do you work for? Since I'll be dead and all."

"Let's just say they're a group of very wealthy bankers who can create money out of thin air and like to make sure their interests are protected ... and have figured out how to get governments to do their bidding."

"You ... are ... the mole?" Kat asked, speaking in a raspy hoarse tone, tears flowing down her face.

"Yes. I'm the one Pantera, and the CIA, have been looking for – for over ten years – and MI-6 and GSG-9, and, and, and. I'm the one who framed Ray Smith. I'm the one who broke into Aman and framed Avner Hershfeld. I'm the one who lured you to Tripoli ... AND ... I'll be the last person to see you alive. Hell, I even informed Qusay that Pantera's unit was coming during the Kuwaiti Ambassador kidnapping." Tal laughed, standing up straight. "Don't take it personally, it's just business. Just so you know; Pantera's next on my list. You will see each other very soon." Tal looked over at Salma. "Where's her family ring? I'll send it to the Kidon Director as a gift."

"He will get you." Kat said, through heaving breath. "You *Looney Tunes* bitch! You may kill me ... but he will get you. I hope he cuts you up into little pieces." Kat started coughing up blood.

"I doubt that very much, he's not *that good*. Good-bye ... *Hash-sha-sheen*. You *were* a very special girl." Tal turned to the table, picked up the ring and walked out of the room.

"Now," Salma said, cattle prod in hand, "I'm going to break your arms and legs – one bone at a time." She shocked Kat then howled as her body would tense causing her to bite her tongue. After a dozen shocks Kat's tongue bled down her chest as her head dangled from her neck like ball on a rope. The woman hit Kat with another round of barbiturates and amphetamines.

CHAPTER 107

When Kat aroused for the fourth time Salma took a mallet and struck her left forearm. The snap of the bones could be heard by the two large men, they grinned. Kat screamed through a clenched jaw showing her teeth to her torturer. She gave Kat a fifth round of drugs. Kat's response to the amphetamines diminished. She continued to shock her, laughing each time Kat bit her tongue. The woman then put the brass knuckles back on and hit Kat in the face with enough force to break her jaw and left cheekbone.

Kat's breathing continued to decrease.

The woman hit her with a sixth round of drugs, but the amphetamines didn't revive Kat this time. Kat slumped lifeless in the chair.

Salma shouted to the roof. "Damn it! It's only been six hours of glorious revenge. Praise Allah!" She raised her hands to her ears then touched them to her face. "Guess she was wrong. The sun's going down and we're still here." She turned to her guards. "Let's eat. I'm hungry. If she's dead when we get back, then we're done. After a year of chasing this bitch and killing her Katsa girlfriends ... I was really expecting more ... so much more."

Salma, the Katsa Killer, and her two guards left the room laughing.

* * *

The team was awakened by a high-pitch buzzing sound. Grit looked up to see the yellow warning light blinking. He gave the 'ready' signal to the squad. Everyone put on their fins, adjusted their masks, and grabbed their gear bags. The cast master gave everyone the three-minutes-to-go signal.

The green light turned on.

One-by-one they jumped out the back of the helicopter dropping down ten meters into the warm Mediterranean water. It was a hundred-meter swim to the submarine. The Swimmer Delivery Vehicle (SDV) sat on deck. Pantera and Charlie-four, a former UK SBS member, rigged up the unit while the rest of the team prepared their rebreathers and stored gear bags. Grit gave the signal to the submarine captain to begin submersion. At fifteen meters, the SDV disconnected and started heading straight for the coordinates of Kat's last GPS location. The team exited the water about fifty to seventy-five meters from each other. Pulling throbes out of their waterproof bags, they threw their wetsuit and gear in their wet bags.

The beach was reasonably secluded because the road, *Beach Road*, was elevated above the beach. One at a time they climbed up to the road. Crossing when there was little or no traffic the whole squad disappeared into the abandoned building across the street. Grit was the last to arrive at the November six-one rally point. Once they arrived at the warehouse the GPS locator signal was weak, but traceable. The team changed into black outfits, hooked up their communication units and assembled their weapons.

Brandy's voice came over the radio. "Radio check."

Everyone nodded.

"Alright gentlemen, kill all contacts, speed is of the essence. Kat's signal is coming from a building about one click from here." Grit said, monotone.

The squad approached the single-story building. It looked abandon with an overgrowth of dying desert shrubbery around the outside.

"Harry, you guys are team one. Take your team in through the east doors. We'll go in through the west. The signal's weak, look for a basement. Brandy, place the high-frequency jammer over this place. We don't need these guys calling for reinforcements. Let's go. First team to find her gets a free bottle of whiskey." Grit gave a chin-up to Pantera.

Each man had twice the normal amount of ammunition than usual and Pantera's trauma bag was carrying a small operating room inside.

Charlie-four inspected the doors. They had industrial locks. He pulled out a mini jaws-of-life with a foot pump and slipped it between the doors. Within a couple pumps the door hinges broke. The building was an old compartmentalized industrial warehouse with musty, dusty large wooden crates strewn about. The smell of death wafted. The main floor of the building looked as if it had not been used in years.

Walking down a short set of steps they found a recently used path from the doorway down to a room off to the right. He signaled his team to head in that direction.

"Charlie-two on point." Grit pointed.

Charlie-two was first to the bottom of the steps finding two men half leaning against some crates. He hit one in the neck and the other in the side of the chest, blowing his lung contents all over the crates. They died before ever knowing someone was there. The team followed the path to the room.

Charlie-two signaled to stop.

Grit signaled Charlie-two to scan left to right and he would scan right to left. They turned the corner. From a couple steps behind Pantera heard four double taps. The next room had a decrepit circular iron staircase leading down. The whole team moved single-file as the staircase creaked under all the weight. Before Pantera could see into the next room, he heard another four men go down. They were sitting in chairs talking, no weapons on them.

Grit and Pantera looked down at them.

Grit shrugged, and said, "Wrong place, wrong time."

Pantera stared at them. Kat's words echoed in his mind, *some innocents must die for others to live.*

The team took off down the hall. The rooms were all basically empty or had remnants of squatters. They came to the end of the hallway, the signal got stronger.

Radio: "Grit, it's Harry. We have her. Northeast corner. Need medic A-SAP. She's alive."

With weapons still in the ready position, Grit's team was at Harry's location within minutes. Grit looked at Kat then moved toward Harry.

"Sam and I will stay with Doc. You clear the rest of the building and prepare for evac." Grit's manner slowed.

Pantera came in last and stopped, staring at her mangled body, afraid to touch her.

Kat was unconscious, choking on blood and vomit, shaking on the floor with a thermal blanket draped over her naked form. Pantera could barely move. He saw the hook and the chair, her blood on both. He could feel her pain. *I can feel her pain?* Months of an unbelievable roller-coaster relationship with this woman flashed before his eyes. Then the pain of their final discussion and break-up sent a shiver up his spine and reopened the gaping hole in his heart. Everything slowed as if his feet were in sand.

Grit punched him in the arm. "Snap out of it brother. We gotta go."

The focus in Pantera's eyes returned. *She's just another patient,* remembering their time in Florence.

Grit watched Pantera in amazement.

The *grief-stricken-still-in-love* ex-boyfriend transformed himself into the *medical trauma specialist machine.* Suddenly his emotional connection to Kat was cut.

"Kat, can you hear me?" Pantera knelt down.

He scanned her body. Nobody knew that body like he did. He couldn't believe his eyes. Everywhere he looked had some type of trauma – broken bone swellings, half her face bloated, and blunt force skin avulsions.

"Kat? Can you hear me?!" he yelled.

496 · JD WALLACE

He slowly rolled her over onto her back. There was no grimace of pain.

She opened one eye and saw him. A tear rolled out of her right eye. She tried to speak but coughed blood and pink frothy sputum all over him. He leaned down to her, placing his ear over her mouth. She coughed again coating his ear and side of his face with a wild concoction of fluids. Then whispered with all the air she had left with a jaw that wouldn't move.

"Wo-man ..." she said, then tried to say something else but lost consciousness and stopped breathing.

"Grit, we're looking for a woman!" Pantera yelled, giving her mouth-to-mouth; "I need the intubation tray and suction unit."

Grit was immediately on the radio as he started digging through the trauma bag. "Harry. Find me a woman in this building and if she's not here, I'm sure she'll return, so ambush her ass. I want her head on a friggin' platter. I'm sure Pantera would like to ... *talk with her*," he said.

Harry understood what he meant.

CHAPTER 108

Pantera pulled the stethoscope from his ears. "Laryngoscope with a 110mm Magill blade." He inserted an 8mm endotracheal tube and connected it to the small bag-valve-mask (BVM). "She's tachycardic with no breath sounds on the right side. I need the chest tube tray, 40G catheter and a half-bottle of water."

Grit was back to grabbing and throwing.

"Next up: IV tray, bag of Lactated Ringers, bag of Plasmanate, and get the Pneumatic Anti-Shock Garment ready. We need to get that on her after I get this chest tube in. Then I can get the IV fluids started." He moved with machine-like efficiency.

Grit watched in awe.

"Keep squeezing the BVM until I can get the positive pressure unit hooked up. She better be unconscious. I'm doing this chest tube without *Xylocaine*." Pantera moved the tray closer. "Sam, could you cut a hole in the top of the water bottle and dump out about half?"

Scalpel in hand Pantera made a cut between two of her many broken ribs. He separated the muscle tissue with the clamps until he reached the harder sinewy fibers of the pleura. He poked a small hole through the fibers and a large amount of blood came squirting out all over him and the ground – then a wheeze of air. *There must be over two quarts of blood there.*

Pantera knew Kat just lost a third of her blood volume in an instant. Kat let out a gasp and a cough – more from reflex than consciousness. There were more air bubbles than blood droplets this time, a good sign.

"One problem solved." Pantera shook his head looking over at Grit.

Pantera clamped the chest tube and inserted it into the small hole through the pleura. He gently sutured the tube in place and then taped the area as securely as he could. He inserted the other end into the water bottle.

"Stop the BVM." Pantera asked. Her breathing didn't return. "Continue." He took her blood pressure, it was still too low and her heart was still racing.

"Let's get her in the PASG," he said, pointing to the green trousers. They velcro'd her in the PASG and pumped them up to 50mmHg.

"Two IV trays with a 10G and 14G catheter, please," Pantera charged. He placed an intravenous line in her right external jugular for the plasmanate and the 14G in her right antecubital fossa for the LR. The right arm had less damage than the left. After another couple minutes, he took her blood pressure again, it was rising as her pulse was slowing. He finished by placing air splints on her forearms and taping her cervical collar to the *Kendricks* sled.

Since Kat was stabilizing and the positive pressure machine was operating. Grit stood up and looked around. He walked over to the table where a number of bloody instruments lay – all easily identifiable – a mallet, cattle prod, brass knuckles, and syringes. He packed them up and put them in his bag. He had not seen syringes for torture in years. Grit thought, *only the most monstrous CIA freaks do pharmacological torture.*

"Hey look." He motioned to the table. "Kat survived the *roller-coaster cocktail.* By the looks of it, about six rounds. Man, this is *Project MKULTRA* stuff." Grit rubbed his hands over his face.

Pantera looked over. "Fuckin' great, that rules out a lot of meds I can give her. Almost everything I have interacts with that shit. Let's hope I can keep the lidocaine to a minimum. We need to get her on the pneumatic stretcher and get out of here. I'm guessing it's dark by now."

"Harry, prepare for evac. I need two for litter duty. Brandy, send SITREP to bird's nest," Grit charged, over the radio.

* * *

Brandy was on the satphone within minutes. "Bird's nest this is groundhog, over."

"Go ahead groundhog." McFarland could be heard on the other end.

"Rescue successful, one female recovered and stable – moving to evac location," Brandy reported.

McFarland looked over at Alona as she collapsed in her chair. "Roger. Be advised. Client has changed destination to Tel Aviv," McFarland replied.

"Bird's nest standby," Brandy asked, then yelled to Grit, "They're rerouting us to Tel Aviv, boss."

"What the hell?" Grit stopped what he was doing and matched looks with Pantera. The two men stared at each other for a minute calculating all the reasons to be mad and happy.

"Maybe it's better." Grit rolled his shoulders. "First: Mossad will be able to protect her during recovery because we obviously haven't found whoever did this. Second: She'll be with her family. And third: They're the client and they're paying the bills."

Pantera's harrowed eyes looked back at him. "It's three hours to Naples and nearly eight to Tel Aviv. I'm going to need supplies or she won't survive the trip. We need to raid that hospital before we leave."

"Brandy, advise WILCO," Grit radioed back to Brandy. "Harry to my location," Grit called, forming the next phase of the plan.

"What's up, boss?" Harry walked in.

"Hit the hospital. Pantera will give you the list," Grit tilted his head toward Pantera; "Meet you at the chopper."

Harry looked over at Pantera. "Whatcha need?"

Pantera finished writing the list. "Equipment: I need a Foley catheter kit, another chest tube tray, nasogastric tube, two bags of LR, two bags of D5WNS and a powered suction unit – if you can find one. Drugs: I need Narcan, Thiamine, two D50s, Sodium Bicarb, Nitroglycerin and Lasix. I think I have everything else I need for this long *friggin'* boat ride to China," he said, rolling his eyes.

Pantera grabbed Harry's arm. "Thanks Harry."

Harry paused. "She'll be fine, dude. She's in the best hands I've ever seen. See you at the chopper." Harry waved to Charlie-three and they ran out of the building.

* * *

Harry and Charlie-three were already at the helicopter when the rest of the team arrived. The airport was empty at the north end of the runway.

Pantera secured Kat into the cargo netting jump bench and moved up to speak to the pilots. "Guys, I need to be on the radio to the hospital as soon as you can get a signal."

The pilot nodded. "The flight crew will notify you when we've raised them on the radio."

The twin turbines of the Chinook MH-47D roared to life, performed a high angle ascent, and left a storm of dust and debris in their wake.

CHAPTER 109

It was a long, bumpy flight for medic, patient and passengers. After eight hours, several close calls and touch-and-go events the flight engineer motioned for Pantera to come forward. "Sir, we have *Ichilov Hospital* on the radio. Our call sign is Blackbird four-seven. We're forty minutes out."

Pantera nodded and put on the headset.

"Ichilov Hospital. This is Blackbird four-seven, do you copy?"

The voice over the radio replied, "Yes Blackbird, this is Doctor Kashuk. I'm a trauma surgeon. We've been advised of your arrival."

Pantera pulled a piece of paper from his pocket and took in a slow deep breath, "Prepare for report. Patient is a female in her mid-twenties with multiple blunt-force fractures to the left zygomatic arch and mandible, open fractures of the left ulna and radius, at least five ribs on one side and a flail chest on the other, and the left tibia. Patient has a pneumothorax, possible kidney damage, and possible cardiac contusion. Copy?" Pantera wanted to make sure the information was received.

"Confirm. Received. Please continue Blackbird four-seven," Kashuk acknowledged.

"Patient has no known allergies and her vital signs are: pulse – one hundred, twenty-two and regular with occasional supraventricular contractions on palpation, blood pressure is one hundred over sixty and widening. She is intubated receiving a mixture with three liters of oxygen by positive pressure at a rate of twelve. We have no pulse ox, glucose, or ECG equipment on board. Glasgow Coma Score is currently a THREE, but has been as high as a SIX several times during the trip with two seizure episodes. Eyes are PERRLA. Foley catheter is patent and secure, urine is tea colored. Patient is currently withdrawing from barbiturate and amphetamine overdose, with one unit of Narcan and one unit of D50 delivered. Chest tube is secure and connected to underwater seal. IV fluids delivered includes one unit of plasmanate and two units of LR. Currently she is on one LR at the right EJ and one D5WNS in the right AF, both at TKO. PASG is inflated at 50mmHg. Nothing else is remarkable. End of report. Over." Pantera sat back in his jump seat taking in several heavy breaths. The rest of the team looked on in awe of the herculean amount of work done in the last eight hours to keep Kat alive – something that could only be experienced and never forgotten.

"Roger Blackbird, report received. We'll see you on the helipad."

The doctor turned and picked up the phone. "Get trauma one ready and call plastics and orthopedics STAT. We have a Level-One trauma inbound. ETA: thirty minutes."

* * *

Doctor Kashuk stood looking out over the city of Tel Aviv as he and two nurses stood on the circular helipad on top of the thirteen-story glass façade building. He looked up at the windsock, there was a slight breeze coming from the ocean to the southwest. In the distance, a black tandem-blade helicopter loomed. It continued to get bigger as it steadily advanced. It crossed the line of his comprehension when a thought entered the doctor's mind as to whether the flying black behemoth would even fit on what seemed, by comparison, a little chalk circle drawn by children.

"Wow." The three medical personnel gasped as the helicopter stopped and pivoted in mid-air above them. The rotor wash nearly blew them back through the doors of the hospital. The helicopter rotated to line up for a landing as the cargo door lowered and a man in a green jump suit stood on the rear ramp as it locked in place – a scene right out of *Star Wars*. The cargo door and the landing wheels hit the ground simultaneously – shaking the building and rattling the doors behind them.

The flight crewman jumped off the cargo door and motioned for the doctor and his team to approach. Six hulking masked men dressed all in black and fully armed slowly walked down the ramp giving the three white lab coats pause. Evenly spaced they took up an armed protection path between the helicopter and the entrance.

The three white lab coats stood at the bottom of the ramp staring up into the black belly of the mechanical beast afraid of what would happen if they continued. Another green jumpsuit emerged from the shadow and motioned for them to proceed. They did, reluctantly.

The doctor had no idea who this patient was but they definitely had a more menacing security detail than the Prime Minister of Israel. They were escorted up into the helicopter by the two green crewmen when they were met by another huge man in all black.

"Doctor Kashuk, I'm the medical officer." Pantera took off his mask and one of his gloves extending his hand in greeting. "Sorry about the lack of equipment, sometimes we can't carry an ICU with us. Do you have any questions for me?"

"No sir. Your report was quite thorough, anything new in the last forty minutes?" Kashuk stood in awe of the grandeur of everything inside the aircraft – despite it not being an ICU.

Pantera shook his head and turned to the two nurses standing over Kat. They were familiarizing themselves with all the lines and equipment, when they stopped. Pantera smiled when he noticed that they couldn't figure out how to get Kat out of the jump bench and onto the gurney. He grabbed the four cargo loops, two in each hand and lifted the pneumatic stretcher gently placing Kat on the gurney.

Pantera made eye contact with the doctor one last time. "Take care of her doc. She's very special. We'll be back to check on her," he said, giving the doctor a reassuring smile – knowing a civilian could misconstrue his comment as a threat, given the circumstances.

Kashuk nodded.

The three medical professionals rushed Kat into the building. Pantera walked down the ramp as if he had just finished an ultramarathon. He met and shook the hand of every team member as they re-boarded the helicopter. Grit stopped him as he was about to walk back up the ramp.

"Sorry brother, you're staying here. Until Mossad or Shin Bet assigns a unit to guard her, you're all she has. Get your ass by her side and don't you leave her until you've been properly relieved. Sorry man, but that's an order. Her protection is still on our watch. We have a safe-house thanks to whoever paid for all this. We'll bring you back some clothes and grub." He slapped Pantera on the shoulder.

Pantera stared at Grit and despite the pain in his heart, he knew what he had to do.

"Aye, aye, skipper. Do you want to clear my weapons?"

Grit shook his head. "No. You're on protection detail. I'm sure the hospital staff knows."

Pantera and Grit shook hands.

"See you in a couple of hours, boss."

CHAPTER 110

Pantera adjusted his tactical vest, swung his MP5 around from back to front, and watched the cargo door rise as the helicopter lifted off. This was the first time Pantera had ever been in a hospital wearing a black combat uniform and fully armed tactical gear – louder and more visible than wearing a florescent clown outfit. He walked down the hallway, gaining curious looks of everyone he passed, to the trauma surgical suites. Because of years of medical training with a significant amount of time in hospitals, he learned no matter where in the world he was, every hospital was designed basically the same way. He had a good idea where the operating suites were and where Kat was being put back together.

He looked up and saw the "Trauma" sign, hit the door pad, and entered the OR suite. He could see the doors to the individual OR rooms. He spotted OR Room One and headed in that direction. From behind him, he could hear a familiar female voice calling out to him.

"Marcus? Marcus!" Alona yelled, nearly tackling him.

"Alona? What are you doing here?" he said, confused. She emerged from a room he just passed. Surprised at his military guise and his sheer mass, he had an almost *Robocop* look about him. Compared to the last time they saw each other, he was wearing a bespoke tailored suit.

"You remember? *I called you?* We're all here." Alona grabbed his arm and turned him around. "Can we talk for minute?"

"Sure," he said, giving her a quizzical look. "I have guard duty but if you want to talk while I stand guard." His mannerism turned cold.

"I'm sorry. You know, in finding out about you. I was so scared that you were after Kat I didn't wait and ... I could have handled it better. I'm really sorry." Alona's eyes filled with tears.

"Kat was right. We can't have *that* hanging over our heads for the rest of our lives," he said with a thawing tone.

"I've had over a month to think about this. What if no one finds out?"

"Finds out what?"

"Finds out that you're ... *dating*. And if you both choose to take the next step, I have an idea on how to handle that, too." Alona's eyes lit up.

"You have an idea? If we choose to take it to the next step. What exactly does that mean?"

"Think about it and when you're ready, find me, and I'll explain. For now, I have a favor."

"Aren't you full of ..." His mouth left open.

"Yes I am," Alona interrupted, "haven't you figured that out by now? She said you were so smart. I'm not so sure." She smiled. "Kat and I decided not to tell anyone the two of you broke up." She blurted out as fast as she could.

"You what?!" he asked, dumbfounded. "What the ..."

"Stay with me. I need you to go to the waiting room and be the big hero *boyfriend* and give an *Oscar-winning* performance that Kat and I know you can. It will work itself out ... trust me." Alona smiled, gave him a big hug and kiss, and walked back down the hallway.

Pantera was truly afraid. *Oscar-winning performance ... who do you think I am?*

In the waiting room Kat's parents and Jacques stood up as he walked in. Kat's mother was the first to give him a *Jewish-mother* hug. Jacques followed with a handshake and man-hug combo. Even

Kat's father, who had red rimmed eyes, embraced him – with no ability to speak. Despite being overly tired and emotionally wiped out, Pantera was holding it together as best he could.

"What of my precious daughter? Can you tell us anything?" Tirzah said in English, with a soft Hebrew accent.

Pantera saw the pain in her eyes, but felt little. He stiffened to be the military medical officer he portrayed himself to be. The best actor, or intelligence officer, the CIA had to offer.

Pantera sat on the table. "It was a long trip. She's the strongest patient I've ever cared for, woman or man. Alona, please close the door. She has fractures over half her body. One of the ribs punctured her lung. She has kidney damage, probably a bruised heart, and I think her cheekbone and jaw were broken. She's coming off a barbiturate *and* amphetamine overdose. I was able to keep her stable for over eight hours. It's up to Doctor Kashuk and his team now. In addition, we never found the person who did this," he said, then stood up. "Sorry, but I have to go and keep watch. I'm her only security until someone relieves me." His mannerisms were cold and professional.

Everyone sat in shock as Pantera listed her injuries.

Alona became emotional upon hearing the news and hugged her mother.

"Is she going to live?" Kat's mother looked up at him.

"Yes. She doesn't have my permission to die," he answered, trying to give a reassuring smile. Pantera wanted to say something else but instead chose something more politically correct.

Alona grabbed him again with both arms wrapped around his neck pulling him down to her level to whisper in his ear, "You know she thinks you're her *Beshert.*"

"I know." He looked at her. "Jacques told me. Unfortunately, that is long ... well, you know."

"Don't worry. Go stand your post. We'll talk later," she said, giving me a wink.

Pantera went to stand next to the OR door as a nurse approached.

"I'm sorry sir, but you can't be here. This is a restricted area," she barked.

Without stopping, he replied, "I'm security for the woman who just came in." He laid his hand on his weapon and stood in a pose that unspokenly dared anyone to move him.

"I'm calling security." The nurse was undeterred.

Before the nurse could reach the phone Alona and Gideon were standing next to her. Gideon flashed his credentials, and said, "He's one of ours."

The nurse stopped and went on about her business. The two men gave each other a nod. Alona and Gideon walked back to the waiting room.

A mountain at the door, Pantera stood on alert.

* * *

Grit and the team showed up at the hospital four hours later. Pantera noticed Tal Cohen was with them. The team walked down the hallway toward Pantera. When they came into view he let out a single burst of laughter catching the nursing staff completely off guard. The team looked like they were attacked by a 1970s fashionista from an Israeli Salvation Army.

Pantera was still giggling to himself as Grit approached. "Damn Grit. Please tell me *you didn't* bring me any of *those* clothes."

Grit laughed. "Of course we did – one for all and all for one. And what delectable morsels we brought you, too." He peeked in the small door window. "She still in ..."

Pantera nodded.

Sam stepped up to Pantera in a formal military manner. "You are relieved," Sam said, firmly.

Pantera stiffened up. "I am relieved."

Pantera handed his weapons and tactical vest over to Sam.

Grit greeted Pantera with a man-hug after he came off duty and they walked back down the hallway toward the waiting room.

CHAPTER 111

Gideon and Tal were speaking in the hallway when they both witnessed the transfer of duty.

Gideon said, under his breath, "They truly are the best."

Tal heard him and nodded. "They are ... nobody better." She knew she was in the eye of a storm, but finding out *who-knows-what* is what her employers pay her for.

Grit, Pantera, Gideon and Tal stood in the hall speaking soft enough so no one in the waiting room could hear them. Tal was reading Pantera. Pantera was reading Tal. It was a Mexican stand-off. Pantera had nothing and Tal knew it, unless Kat was able to talk. Tal's reading of Pantera gave her the feeling Kat didn't, or wasn't able to, out her as the mole or the Katsa Killer's employer. Tal still had time to fix the situation. Pantera knew there was something off about Tal, but he felt that the first day they met. He needed more than he had and he had been empty-handed for over a month.

"Were you able to find anything to assist our search for this *Katsa Killer*?" Gideon's voice was sharp and assured, unlike when Pantera first came into the waiting room.

"Well sir. A lot of old style instruments and a rollercoaster cocktail," Grit answered.

"Rollercoaster cocktail? You mean ... old school CIA techniques?" he replied, rubbing his forehead.

"Yes. She is a current or former intelligence officer who works for a country that was a United States ally many years ago. That would be my guess."

"Like Libya," Gideon snorted, and nodded.

Grit nodded with a half grin in return.

* * *

Pantera, Grit, and the team walked into the waiting room with Gideon and Tal. The family stood up as the imposing men, despite the outfits, entered the room.

Pantera gave a general introduction. "Gideon, Tirzah, Alona, Jacques ... this is the team who volunteered to rescue Kat." Kat's mother and sister openly cried as they hugged each man. The men had never met the family of a person they rescued. They were genuinely touched and they themselves were fighting to keep their composure.

It had been nine hours since Kat entered surgery and not one person left the waiting room – other than for supplies or micturition. Doctor Kashuk entered the waiting room covered in sweat. He was caught off guard by how many people there were.

"Hello. Mister and Mrs. David," Kashuk said, in Hebrew, looking around the room. Then in English, he said, "I would like to speak to the family privately please."

The men got up to leave.

Gideon said, "Doctor Kashuk, this *is* her family. You tell all of us." He waved everyone down.

Kashuk gave an understanding nod as he recognized Pantera. "You're the medical officer who brought her in, excellent work."

Pantera nodded tightening his lips.

Gideon wanted the doctor to know the other side of Pantera's responsibilities so he added in Hebrew. "He's also her boyfriend." Gideon chose his words carefully. He used the Hebrew term for "life-long partner" than something less meaningful.

Pantera raised an eyebrow at Alona as she met his gaze.

"Miss David is strong and in critical, but stable condition. We had no complications during the multiple surgeries. We found she had a small concussion and a temporal bone fracture which we will be watching closely. Plastics came in and assisted with a small plate for her cheekbone. It was an oral procedure, so she'll have no scars on her face. The jaw was only cracked and the socket was intact so they didn't wire her mouth shut, but the soft tissue was severely damaged. It will be several weeks of pureed food and talking will have to be kept to a minimum. We also found several ligament and tendon tears in her shoulders. Looks like she was hanging for some time, we don't usually see *that type* of injury around here and ..." Kashuk realized what he was about to say and decided against it.

"She doesn't talk much anyway," Alona said, slipping in for levity.

"Orthopedics placed an internal fixation device on the left radius, but no device was needed for the ulna because it was a clean break and should heal perfectly. Her chest tube location and placement was perfect so I decided to leave it in place for a couple more days."

Kashuk looked over at Pantera and nodded.

"There is nothing I can do about the rib fractures, they will heal just fine and should not cause any more damage to the lung. Her kidneys and heart look to be only bruised and should heal without any trouble. The tibia was quite damaged and an external device was placed there. We'll keep her in a controlled comatose state for another couple days because of the concussion mixed with the barbiturate and amphetamine overdose. I would prefer that she remain sedated as she detoxes. She should be transferred to intensive care in a couple hours, but please keep the numbers to a minimum when visiting. Are there any questions I can answer?"

"Any permanent damage and what's her prognosis?" Pantera asked.

Kashuk stood up and faced Pantera. "I don't think so. It's going to be a long, hard road to full recovery. The shoulders will take longer to heal than the bones. She'll have a few scars, not anywhere noticeable, except to her husband." He winked. "You guys did a hell of a good job," he said, patting Pantera on the shoulder. "She has quite the group of guardian angels on her side."

After Kashuk left a man came in and whispered something to Gideon. Gideon stood up, "Gentlemen, my daughter and my family owe you a debt we will *never* be able to repay. Know this ... if ever you need my help, it is yours without hesitation. I've just been informed that our Shin Bet team has arrived and you're now officially relieved of your security duty. Your team leader has an envelope which I'd like you to use to get some good food and rest, and please, by all means, enjoy the night life here in Tel Aviv. Tal and I will be by the house for brunch on Monday and will review the plan for getting you home to your families. Shalom."

Grit nodded to the team.

Pantera walked out with Grit. "I'm gonna need ..."

"I know," Grit interrupted, "How much leave do you have on the books?"

Pantera glanced off into the distance. "At least a month ... since before Panama."

Grit placed his hand on Pantera's shoulder. "I'll put you in for two weeks medical leave. We can talk about your formal leave request chit later. Deal?"

Pantera grinned. "Deal. Top."

* * *

Pantera sat down on the table in front of Kat's Mom and Alona as they were holding each other. Jacques and Gideon were sitting next to them on either side.

"I'm going to the safe house with the guys, get cleaned up and take a nap. I'll be here for the next two weeks, or more. I'm not going anywhere." He took Tirzah's hand. "I want you to know Kat is more important to me than anyone or anything else."

Alona smiled at Pantera. "Marcus. Mom knows. Kat told her everything at the wedding ... about your relationship." Alona made a facial expression making sure Pantera knew Kat did not tell her mother about the break-up.

Pantera gave a – *this better work* – look back at her.

Kat's mother's eyes swelled as tears poured out. "I know who you are ... Kat's *Beshert* ... her *Nefesh Te'oma*. I know who you are," she said, putting the back of Pantera's hand to her forehead.

Oh crap. A little too over the top, ya think? Oh well. In for a penny, in for a pound, is what grandfather used to say. Let the two chicks clean up the mess. I have a mole to get back to. "Then you know I *will* make her whole, as soon as she is able." He gave her a soft smile.

"Yes. Please do. Would you please consider staying with us during your time here?" Gideon placed his hand on Pantera's shoulder.

Pantera nodded. "Thank you." Before leaving he gave Alona a two-cheek kiss, then shook hands and hugged Jacques on his way out.

CHAPTER 112

Pantera woke to the vibrating pager bouncing across the night-stand. The gift from Gideon felt more like a leash, but a good leash. He called the number.

"Come to the hospital café right now. They're going to wake Kat in a couple hours." Alona said, hopped up on caffeine. "Let's finish our talk before she wakes."

"Okay. Okay. And lay off the coffee for cryin' out loud, your heart is going to blow up." He crawled out of bed. A bed he had just crawled into after a long evening of Tel Aviv night life.

"You're so funny. Now hurry up!"

Pantera performed his SSS and was out the door as the rest of the team slept sprawled out all over the two-bedroom house like college students after a drunken frat party. He looked at his watch as he entered the hospital café. It was 0634HRS. He spotted Alona sitting in the corner by herself.

"I'm here. I'm here," Pantera said, sliding into the plastic unfor-giving chair. "Tell me your grand plan for keeping Kat and I to-gether." He was outwardly skeptical and inwardly hopeful.

"It's simple. If you want to marry Kat then don't tell either of your employers." Alona leaned back with a big smile.

"That's it. That's your grand plan? That won't work. What are we going to do, hire cut-outs for social events, etcetera, etcetera? You and I both know we can trip on the smallest detail." He shook his head then dropped it onto his forearm.

"Then don't trip. You both will be each other's cut-out. It's brilliant! If I do say so myself."

"Hold on. We'll be cut-outs for each other's social events?"

"Yes exactly. We'll create a full backstory, documents, the works, for you both. Not like *that* will be a problem. Example: You're married to, insert name here, who is a fashion model and UN translator. Kat is married to you, insert name here, who is an import/export businessman ... or whatever. Mossad thinks you're a civilian and CIA thinks Kat's a civilian. Voilà! Problem solved ... you live happily ever after," she said, slapping her hands together as if trying to remove pizza flour from them.

"Okay genius. What about geography?" he asked, raising an eyebrow.

"Oh please. I can't solve all your problems. That's for the two of you to figure out. However, I'll monitor both systems and make sure your aliases hold."

"You really think we can pull this off?" Pantera sat back tilting his head in disbelief.

"Absolutely." Alona nodded emphatically.

"Now you have to sell it to Kat." He gave her a half-smile.

"We already spoke about it. She didn't think you'd go for it. I was on my way down to pick her up and take her to Naples to see you, when she got called to Tripoli. I lied and told her we were going to Palermo." She smiled, giving herself an ethereal pat on the back.

"Now who's the actor?"

Alona looked at her watch. "It's time. Let's go up."

Pantera and Alona continued to talk as they walked to the ICU. The doors swung open after they announced their names into the intercom. "Good Morning, Miss David and Mister Sinclair, welcome back."

"Good Morning." Pantera returned. *Being the daughter of the Director of Shin Bet has its perks.*

After they turned the corner to walk down the hall Pantera spotted a small commotion outside of Kat's room.

"Alona go straight into Kat's room and make sure you know everyone who walks in or yell as loud as you can."

Alona did what she was told.

The Shin Bet guard was not allowing a nurse access to the room. The hair on the back of Pantera's neck stood up as he walked up and stood behind the woman.

"Rafa, is there a problem?"

The woman seemed startled when Pantera spoke from behind her.

"She claims she's the charge nurse and is helping Kat's nurse, but she's not on the list."

Shin Bet officers are the best in the world when it comes to protection. Guarding the daughter of the Director of Shin Bet is the second highest honor given, behind the prime minster.

Pantera immediately pulled his suppressed Walther PPK-L, a gift from Gideon. Touching it to the back of the woman's neck, Pantera directed, "Rafa, take her badge, go to the board, and read the name of the charge nurse." He whispered, into the woman's ear, "Get on your knees, cross your ankles, put your hands on your head, and interlace your fingers."

The woman tried to explain.

"Don't make me say it again," Pantera growled.

Rafa walked over to the board. Regaining eye contact with Pantera he shook his head, and pulled out *his* Beretta 70 as Pantera searched her – finding a small vial and syringe. Rafa radioed downstairs to his team.

Suddenly the door to Kat's room swung open with a frightened little nurse's aide standing in the doorway.

Pantera immediately grabbed the women's interlaced fingers and dropped his knee down on top of her calves. She tried to move, but her struggle was in vain.

"Don't even think about it. Be happy you were caught *here*. If my team caught you ... I would've scalped and skinned you alive.

You must be getting paid extremely well to attempt something as stupid as this in front of Shin Bet, but then again, I'm sure you knew that all her nurses are also Shin Bet." Pantera felt confident Kat's torturer was captured.

"Rafa, give me your cuffs. Let's hold her here until Kat wakes up." He traded the cuffs for the vial. "And could you get this vial analyzed?" Rafa sat the woman down in a chair outside the room as two more Shin Bet ran up. Pantera put his weapon away just as Doctor Kashuk and a nurse walked over from the nursing station.

"Good Morning Mister Sinclair. Are we ready to see how Kat has fared?" He stood proud in his freshly pressed lab coat with a cup of coffee in his hand.

Pantera nodded and followed them in. He looked around and noticed that Gideon wasn't in the room. He looked over at Alona with a question mark on his face.

"Work, he'll be here later." She mouthed back to him.

The nurse prepared a syringe and handed it to the doctor. The doctor stuck it in the intravenous line access port and squeezed. "It should take a few minutes," he said, grabbing the medical chart, sat down and started writing.

The room was as quiet as a soft breeze coming off a butterfly's wing as each minute ticked away like the months on a calendar.

Kat stirred. A grimace of pain could be seen on her face.

"We can't keep all the pain away, she is still going to feel some," Kashuk reassured everyone.

Pantera moved to her right side – softly touching her functional hand. Kat blinked her right eye. The left eye was swollen and covered. Each part of Kat's body slowly rebooted itself testing its own capabilities and parameters of pain. Her left arm moved then stopped. Her left leg moved then stopped. Her eye opened and tried to focus on the ceiling, blinking as if using it for the first time.

"Miss David. Can you hear me?" he said, in Hebrew, getting up and moving to the left side of the bed. He leaned over her placing his face in her field of vision.

CHAPTER 113

Kat's focus turned to the doctor. Afraid to nod, she blinked twice.

"You're in the hospital in Tel Aviv. Your neck is fine. The left side of your face and jaw, chest, left arm and left leg have sustained a significant amount of damage. Do you understand what I'm saying?" he said slowly.

Kat hesitated then nodded. Her one good eye peered out like a small azure puddle surrounded by a sea of white bandages as it searched the room. She paused at each person. The doctor. The nurse. Alona. Jacques. Her mother. Then she looked up at Pantera. Her eye spontaneously filled with fluid as waves of water flowed onto the pillow, blinking incessantly to keep her vision of Pantera. Realizing she had no pain in her right hand she grabbed Pantera's hand with all her might. Her eye widened with a fearful stare. Pantera knew what she wanted.

"Relax. Breathe. It's okay," Pantera said, remembering her words back from the pre-wedding dinner. Pantera reached over to the nightstand and grabbed a piece of paper and pen. He placed it under her hand.

"Write," he whispered.

She clumsily felt for the pen with her right hand, being left handed. Without looking at the pen and paper she drew a large heart. Inside the heart she placed the letter "P". Pantera looked down and immediately couldn't see through the blur of tears. Blinking like window shutters in a wind storm, he fought through the pain of his heart being sewn back together. He tore the paper from the pad and handed it to Alona.

Alona started crying. "I knew it!" she said under her breath.

"Kat listen. We don't have a lot of time," he said, struggling on choked breath, "Do you have a name? A description? Anything? We need to let you rest." Pantera asked the doctor and nurse to leave.

Kat nodded. Her hand moved slow and steady. The first letter was ... "T." Pantera knew.

"TAL?! You saw her ... she was there with you?" he whispered, with force.

She nodded while blinking her eye.

Pantera knew Tal Cohen was not a person to perform in the field. She was a commander – a *sit-on-my-ass-get-everyone-else-killed* type of commander. Pantera immediately walked outside the room and grabbed the fake nurse. With one hand he clutched a head full of hair and his other her arm, yanking her up out of her chair in the hallway. The Shin Bet men followed. Forcefully he shoved the woman's face next to Kat's.

"Is this your *Katsa Killer*?" he asked, leaning down next to the woman and Kat's ear.

Kat shook her head.

Before anyone else responded to Kat's answer, Pantera pulled the woman back and was marching her out of the room. He threw her down the hallway bouncing her off the opposite wall and turned to the three Shin Bet men.

"You two. Take her for interrogation. She's mine. Rafa, radio downstairs. Tal Cohen has to be somewhere close by. She needs Kat dead," he said, slow and methodical, directly from Grit's playbook. "Alona. Call your office and put a capture order out for Tal Cohen."

"You ... are ... kidding!" Alona pulled her mobile phone from her purse.

* * *

Pantera and Rafa ran out of the ICU, down the nine flights of stairs to the lobby and out to the parking lot. Scanning the parking lot he spotted a red Ferrari Testarossa F512 sitting in the last row with a clear view of the entrance to the hospital.

Are you serious? A Ferrari? How cliché.

He walked toward the car as he pulled his weapon from its sheath, not knowing if she was in it. However, it stuck out like a sore thumb in a sea of humble vehicles and in his professional opinion, her ego called for a car like that. The car turned on and revved up as he approached. He trained his gun at the windshield and marched toward her. The car shifted into gear, tires burning, and roared to life; galloping toward Pantera.

This bitch is coo coo for Coco Puffs.

Pantera fired in rapid succession at the windshield. Because of the deep angle the bullets ricocheted off with barely a scratch. The car screeched toward him. He dove out of the way and in one smooth Parkour motion was up and shooting again, but the little .32 calibre was no match for the hardened steel of an armored Ferrari body and engine. Tal Cohen, Mary Shelley, the mole, the information peddler, the Katsa Killer's employer, the link to the owners of the US Federal Reserve, and God knows what, or who, else ... was in the wind.

So this is what failure feels like. Wow this sucks! I have a name and a face, Jack can't be all that pissed.

* * *

Gideon and Alona arrived at the safe house. It had been a couple days since Kat's historic revival. Pantera thought it best to not show his face around the hospital for a time. Not because of the relationship where he felt secure and was in no rush. He was waiting on Gideon who had to clean up his mess – bodies being thrown around the hospital and gun shots in the parking lot had the Israeli authorities in an uproar. He also wanted to spend time with his team before they got shipped back to Naples. When Gideon and

Alona entered, the house was immaculate. The men's gear packed with military precision and stored in a corner near the door ready for departure. Several men that were sitting stood up as they entered. Alona, unaccustomed to such military respect smiled in return.

"Gentlemen, I'll make this brief. Please accept what I'm about to give you. You earned no more and no less than what Shin Bet or Mossad would have paid an outside contractor to perform this same operation – with a smaller chance of success. I've worked out a concession with your commanding officer regarding the paperwork of the mission. It will be charged in the paperwork as a training mission in a foreign country," Gideon said, in a soft, but firm tone.

All the men nodded.

"With that, I have an envelope for each of you as recompense for a job well done and services rendered to both Shin Bet and Mossad. What you did was above and beyond the call of duty. Unfortunately there will be nothing in your personnel file nor can any medals be given. If I could, I would. In this envelope you will find a small amount of cash, a bank debit card, and a pre-paid first-class airline ticket. The cash is self-explanatory. The bank debit card is to a non-traceable numbered account for the remainder of payment. The PIN is on the back. The pre-paid first-class airline ticket is to pay for a round trip to anywhere in the world to be taken at any time. Let me reiterate. Your services are valued and the country of Israel is very appreciative. You will fly back on our G-5. Shalom."

Gideon gave each man their envelope, shook their hand, and thanked them personally – then left.

CHAPTER 114

Grit turned to Pantera. "Hey, spoke to Rose last night. She wanted me to give you and Kat her blessings. We also decided it was time to take one of my four-day passes ... to Tel Aviv."

Pantera stood firm, but smiled. "... And the kids?"

"Yup, they're coming. We won't bring them to the hospital, but in all the time we've been in Europe we haven't seen Israel. Now, would be a good time. If that's okay?"

"Of course it is. Thank you." He placed his hand on Grit's shoulder. "I'll ask Gideon for a safe house you guys can use. Oh, talk to Alona about taking the kids around the city when you guys are at the hospital. I think she'll like that."

Grit smiled. "We'll be back on Saturday. I'll get McFarland to write my liberty pass for Monday through Thursday ... *Top Shirt* privilege."

They gave each other a handshake and a man-hug.

* * *

Pantera opened one eye staring at the phone as it rang. Recovering from a week of night shifts with Kat, his mind wound up. *Today is Grit and Rose's last day in Israel ... let's make it memorable.*

"Shalom Alona."

"How'd you know it was me?"

"Who else wakes me up after only leaving the hospital a couple hours ago?"

"Aren't you the pleasant-cranky pants? Kat wants to speak to you before Grit and Rose show up for brunch."

"Okay. Let me get some tea and jump-start my brain. See you shortly."

For the last week, Pantera sat and watched Kat relive her torture in her nightmares. The stress was too much for Kat's parents, Jacques or Alona – so he volunteered to sit with her every night. Kat and Pantera have not spoken since that first day. He prayed she was getting better. Last night was the first time Kat slept straight through. He was hoping the mental pain of the torture was beginning to wane and they could start discussing where they were going ... as a couple.

* * *

Pantera walked into Kat's room. "Hello." He looked at her food tray. "Eww, yum, strained carrots and pureed peas."

"Mom. Alona. Can you give us a minute?" Kat said, just above a whisper. After a week of pen and paper, her voice reverberated through the room.

Pantera closed the door behind them. "Yes Ma'am. How are you feeling?"

"We need to catch up and get on the same page, mister." She looked at him with a good eye and a black eye, nearly healed thanks to the Arnica gel he left for her.

Pantera sat down on the side of Kat's bed looking at her swollen multi-colored face, the metal rods sticking out of her leg, and her once-beautiful black hair now cut short and placed in a tied Israeli *Tichel*. At this moment none of that mattered to him. She was, and would always be, the most beautiful woman he had ever seen – because it was her heart and strength of will, that captured his heart.

"Let's go, hit me." He winked.

"Where's Tal and her little gal pal?"

"Don't know. Nobody knows. We do know the name of your Katsa Killer: Nazneen 'Salma' Ahmadi. Add that to Tal Cohen and Lebanon, and it looks like *we* have some leads."

"What about *we*? Are *we* okay?"

"Yes. We're good. How are you? I'm guessing Alona told you her plan?" He crossed his arms on the bed, placing his chin on top.

"Yes. We spoke before I got into this mess. I want you to know, my feelings for you have never changed, Marcus. I didn't think you'd felt the same."

"No. I'm stronger than I was before," he said, taking her hand softly.

"Good, because Alona already started working on our files," she said, giving him her Cheshire-cat smile.

"She's fast." He laughed.

"So that I know we're on the same page. You and I are going after these bitches? Right?"

"Oh yes. Deez bitches are goin' down!" He jumped up pretending to spike a football.

There was a knock on the door and Grit's head poked through. "Is it all clear?"

"Wait!" Pantera yelled, turning to Kat he whispered, "What do we tell them about Tal? They're our best friends."

"Nothing. Let's meet with Alona first. You know the rule – the less said, not dead."

Pantera turned toward the door, and said, "Come on in." He got up from the bed and hugged them both.

"We brought grub." Grit laughed. "And bite-size food for the Israeli rabbit."

"Aren't you funny?" Kat smirked.

The two happy couples sat, ate and joked as Alona, Jacques, Gideon and Tirzah came in to join the festivities.

* * *

"Excuse me, everyone. I'd like to make an announcement." Pantera stood up.

The room became quiet. Even Kat was curious as to Pantera's intentions.

"As you all know it has been a tumultuous year for Kat and I, but we've come through it and I think we're stronger for it. So with that ..." he said, getting down on one knee beside the bed.

He took her enlarged left forearm and softly placed her swollen, purple and blue chaffed hand in his. He withdrew a small light blue box from his pocket. He opened the small box – a box holding a glimmering princess-cut engagement ring totaling over three flawless carats. The electricity in the room crackled as everyone drew in a huge breath. The sound of air rushing in from under the door could be heard filling the vacuum.

"... and thanks to Jacques' help over this last week." He winked at Jacques. "I guess it's time to make us whole as is Jewish custom. Alyn Katryna David, you are my *Beshert*, my *Nefesh Te'oma*. I knew it the moment I first laid eyes on you, despite how scared you made me feel. Would you make me the happiest man on earth ... and do me the greatest honor ...

Will you marry me?"

SILENT CATS will return.

EPILOGUE

Pantera shivered. He remembered every moment of every day of his life with Kat. Although he ached to hear her voice, to see her smile, to have her jump into his arms – those would only be a memory, but a memory that would never fade. Not ever. He knew their souls were linked and she would always be a part of him.

Pantera moved to his eldest daughter, bent down and caressed her cold cheek, kissed her on the forehead and whispered, "I love you, Electra."

He moved to his youngest daughter, bent down and stroked her hair, kissed her on the forehead and whispered, "I love you, Jade."

He inched closer to Kat, he could see beyond the stillness of death into her soul. He leaned down and fully embraced her, kissing her cheeks, and a last kiss on her cold lips.

"Thank you, my darling. *Thank you*," he softly uttered, knowing she heard him, wherever she was.

Time had no place now. He wasn't sure how long he had been standing next to the bodies of his wife and daughters, but he was sure of one thing. He would avenge their deaths.

Pantera stiffened. The tears were gone and a steely resolve took their place. If anyone would have looked into his eyes at that moment, they would have trembled.

In his mind a voice said to him, *"Go get'em, Navy boy."*

"AB-SO-FUCKIN-LUTE-LY."

ABOUT THE AUTHOR

After spending the first ten years of his career with a US-based intelligence agency, Mr. Wallace went on to work for foreign intelligence agencies, law firms, political figures, royals, sovereigns and private corporations for the next twenty years. He is considered one of the top corporate infiltrators in the world. Mr. Wallace holds Bachelors' degrees in Mammalian Physiology and Environmental Chemistry and a Master's degree in Physiology/Nutrition and an MBA in Finance. Currently the widower resides in San Diego, California, with his Welsh Border Collie — "Kelly." This is his first novel.

Facebook Author Page: facebook.com/marcus.sinclair.826

Twitter: twitter.com/thesilentcats